D1230495

The Workhouse Children

Lindsey Hutchinson was born and raised in Wednesbury, West Midlands. She now lives in the Shropshire countryside with her husband and Labrador, loves to read and has recently discovered photography. She is the daughter of million-copy bestselling author Meg Hutchinson.

Also by Lindsey Hutchinson

The Wives' Revenge

Lindsey Hutchinson

The Workhouse Children

First published as an ebook in 2016 by Aria,
an imprint of Head of Zeus Ltd

First published in print in the UK in 2017 by Aria

Copyright © Lindsey Hutchinson, 2016

The moral right of Lindsey Hutchinson to be identified as the author of this work has been asserted in accordance with the Copyright, Designs and Patents Act of 1988.

All rights reserved. No part of this publication may be reproduced, stored in a retrieval system, or transmitted, in any form or by any means, electronic, mechanical, photocopying, recording, or otherwise, without the prior permission of both the copyright owner and the above publisher of this book.

This is a work of fiction. All characters, organizations, and events portrayed in this novel are either products of the author's imagination or are used fictitiously.

9 7 5 3 1 2 4 6 8

A CIP catalogue record for this book is available from the British Library.

ISBN (HB): 9781786696700
ISBN (E): 9781786692511

Typeset by Divaddict Publishing Solutions Ltd

Printed and bound by CPI Group (UK) Ltd, Croydon, CR0 4YY

Head of Zeus Ltd
5–8 Hardwick Street
London EC1R 4RG

WWW.HEADOFZEUS.COM

For my husband, Paul Salomon, who has supported me in my every endeavour.

One

Elizabeth Flowers was exhausted. She had been doing someone else's washing all day and she had just sat down. She was sick to the back teeth of taking in washing while her husband, John, was away on his cart. Just then she heard the cart wheels grind to a halt. Her heart skipped a beat – he was home.

A loud thump told her he was drunk again and a giggle confirmed it. He had fallen from the driving seat of the cart. Jumping up, Elizabeth ushered her two young children upstairs.

'Stay up there until I call you down, do you understand?' she said hastily.

Charlie and Daisy nodded as they scrambled up the bare wooden staircase which led off the living room.

The back door of their ramshackle cottage flew open and John stood swaying in the doorway. Elizabeth paled at the sight of him. He was very drunk which meant there would be no housekeeping money – again.

'Hello my little dove,' he said as he tottered into the kitchen. 'You got a kissssh for your old man?'

Elizabeth backed away from him. She could feel her heart hammering in her chest as she glanced at the stairs checking the children were safe. Looking back to John, she saw him advance and the all too familiar fear gripped her.

Silently Elizabeth threw up a prayer, 'Please God, let him finish it this time – or die trying.'

As she skirted round the table, John made a lunge for her. Grabbing her blonde hair, he dragged his wife towards him. A whimper escaped Elizabeth's lips as he tugged her hair sharply. Planting a kiss on her cheek, John slurred, 'What'sshh for my dinner?'

'There's nothing in the house, John,' Elizabeth answered, wincing as he yanked her hair again.

'Chrisht, woman! What you done with the money I gave you?' John continued to shake her by the hair.

'That was two weeks ago! How far do you think it will stretch?' Elizabeth's frightened eyes closed tight as John threw her away from him.

'Bloody hell!' he yelled. 'You besht get my supper or else!'

Elizabeth moved slowly to the other side of the table. If she could keep the table between them she might stand a chance. 'I can't give you what we don't have,' she said as they circled the table like prize fighters.

John's toe caught the leg of a kitchen chair and he picked it up and flung it against the wall. The resounding crash sent an echo around the tiny kitchen and splinters of wood flew everywhere.

'I want my supper… NOW!' His voice boomed out.

'John…' Elizabeth began then sidestepped quickly as he rounded the table.

Grabbing her long skirt, he yanked her back towards him. Elizabeth tried to pull away from him and she heard the stitching of her skirt give way. Whirling her round to face him, John slapped her cheek hard and Elizabeth stumbled against the table.

Steeling herself for what was to come, she drew in a breath. Suddenly John was on her, raining blows down on the helpless woman. Elizabeth's screams rang out as fists landed on her face, arms and torso. She tried desperately to scrabble away from the world of hurt she found herself in yet again, but John pinned her to the kitchen floor. It felt like he was pounding the life out of her frail body as he continued to punch her.

Tiptoeing downstairs and watching from the doorway, their two children cried silently at the spectacle in front of them. Daisy stood slightly behind her big brother, her fingers in her mouth as she sobbed. The drool from her nose and mouth dribbled down her hands. Seven-year-old Charlie had his arm extended protectively to keep Daisy back. Tears rolled down the boy's face as he watched his mother take yet another beating. Anger boiled in him as he wished he was big enough to take on his bullying father.

Elizabeth had not seen her children as her screams turned to whimpers. John finally tired and ignoring his quietly sobbing children, he staggered out of the door and lurched across the heathland in search of the nearest public house.

The children ran to their mother who was dragging herself to her feet groaning at the pain which had been inflicted on her. Placing an arm around each of them, she said quietly, 'Shush, my darlings, it's all over now.'

Elizabeth carefully sat down on the last remaining kitchen chair with her children in front of her. Touching her mouth, she winced, he had split her lip… yet again. Sad eyes looked at her children and she felt the right one begin to swell. That would be swollen shut before morning.

'Mummy,' Daisy sobbed, trying to climb on Elizabeth's lap. Elizabeth settled her five-year-old on her knee and wrapped her arm around her young son who stood by her. She tried desperately to hide the aches and pains, knowing the following day it would feel far worse.

'Mum,' Charlie said as he wiped away his tears on his shirtsleeve.

'I know, son, I know. Your dad's drunk again.' Elizabeth winced once more at the pain in her lip.

'But mum, he hurt you!' Charlie's anger was building again.

Shaking her head and wishing she hadn't, Elizabeth said, 'Sweetheart, I'm not making excuses for him, I'm telling it as it is.'

'Mummy, I don't like Daddy,' Daisy said between sobs.

'I don't like him much either when he's like this,' Elizabeth answered. 'He'll be back later, so I want you two in bed by then.'

'But mum…' Charlie began.

'No, Charlie, please son, don't make this any harder than it already is. I can take this. What I couldn't take is him starting on you two. So please do as I say and stay in your beds when he gets home.'

The children nodded, but neither was happy about it.

*

Later that night two men carried John Flowers into the living room of his cottage and laid him on the sofa. He was out cold. Muttering their apologies to Elizabeth, they left.

Elizabeth dragged herself upstairs, every bone in her body aching. Peeping in on her children who shared a bedroom, she saw they were sleeping, and closing the door quietly, she crossed the tiny landing to her own room. Carefully undressing, she inspected her bruised and battered body. It was a miracle nothing was broken. Slowly pulling on her nightgown, she tentatively lay down on the bed.

Warm tears rolled down her cheeks as she lay there. This couldn't go on, she knew, for one day he would surely kill her. Thoughts swirled in her mind. She couldn't leave him – she had two young children to think about. Where would they go? How would they survive? Besides, she knew he would find them if they left. The battering she'd just taken would be nothing compared to what she'd get then.

Up to now, John had never laid a finger on their children, but who was to say he wouldn't in the future. Elizabeth began to sob as she realized, short of death, there was no way out for her and her children. She had married him and now she was stuck with him.

Closing her eyes, Elizabeth silently prayed. 'Dear God, please find me a way out of this – please!'

The following morning Elizabeth could barely move. Slowly and carefully, she dressed herself, her face screwing up in pain at every movement she made.

One step at a time she made her way down the stairs and into the kitchen. She could hear John outside whistling a merry tune. Elizabeth wondered at the man. From a drunken stupor to bright and breezy; he never even suffered a hangover!

She heard the children running down the stairs and saw through her unswollen eye as they tumbled into the kitchen. Sad eyes looked up at her. She realized then how bad she must look to them.

The back door opened and John marched in. 'I want you two out scavenging in the market.' He looked over at the children who shrank back. 'NOW!'

Charlie and Daisy ran through the living room and out of the front door.

'Right,' John went on, 'I got the cart ready. Today, you're coming with me.'

Elizabeth's glance shot to the living room door where her children had dashed out.

'Oh don't worry about them, they can look after themselves. Now come on, let's get on the road, I ain't got all day!' John grabbed Elizabeth's arm and she winced. Dragging her through the door, she struggled, trying to free herself.

'John, I can't leave the children, they're only babies!' she sobbed.

'I said... you're coming with me!' John swung an arm round the back of Elizabeth's legs and lifted her off the ground. He virtually threw her onto the cart and she yelped in pain.

Climbing into the driving seat, he clucked to the horse to walk on. He ignored his wife as she swivelled round to stare back at their cottage. Her one good eye scanned the heathland for sight of her children. They were gone. Elizabeth cried quietly as the cart rumbled away. Misery wrapped itself around her as John began to whistle once more.

'Why couldn't I stay home with the children, John?' Elizabeth asked quietly.

'Because I need you to fulfil your wifely duties. I miss it when I'm away from home. I can't *not* be away from home can I? So... you can come along with me from now on. The kids can look after themselves.'

Elizabeth sobbed quietly into the hem of her dress as she

thought about her poor babies having to scavenge to survive.

John slapped her soundly across the side of the head as he shouted, 'For God's sake woman, shut that wailing up! You have to think about me now, not those snot nosed kids!'

Elizabeth held her breath for a moment to quell her tears, but she knew she would shed far more in the future not knowing how her children would survive.

*

Later that day the children arrived back at the cottage with scraps of food kindly given to them by the women on the market. Charlie knew, even at his young age, that their parents had gone. What he didn't know was whether they were coming back.

'Where's Mummy?' Daisy asked.

'I think *he* took her with him,' Charlie answered scathingly.

'When will she be back?' the little girl whimpered.

Shaking his head, Charlie said gently, 'I don't know, kiddo.' Placing his arms around his sobbing sister, he went on, 'Don't cry, I'll look after you until they do come back. Now, come on let's have something to eat.'

Daisy nodded and ran her nose along her cardigan sleeve.

Charlie gazed out of the kitchen window as a heavy feeling settled on him. He had not known his mother to go off with his father before. She always stayed at home with Daisy and himself, and he was worried about her. Would *he* hurt her? Charlie prayed he wouldn't. He feared at that moment it was very unlikely they would see either of their parents again.

Two

The old Queen, Victoria, had passed away and her son Edward VII had ascended the throne. The year was now 1901 and would be known as the Edwardian era. The newspapers were full of the news about the new king and speculation of a date when he would be crowned. History would show this to be in August of the following year.

The people of Bilston town which was situated midway between Wolverhampton and Birmingham, in the heart of the industrial West Midlands, known as the Black Country, would be talking about their new king during the time until his coronation. The nickname given to the area was coined due to the smoke from factories and domestic chimneys that belched out night and day, leaving a pall hanging over the area. Men working in the collieries suffered with terrible breathing problems from the fine coal dust hanging in the air; often this bad health preceded their premature death.

The poverty all over the Black Country was appalling and it was hoped the new king might be able to help rectify the situation, but nobody really believed it would happen.

In a house in Proud's Lane, Bilston, Cara Flowers sat at the bedside of her aged grandmother with tears streaming down her face. 'Grandma, please don't leave me!' She sobbed.

'Now, child,' Henrietta whispered with a gentle smile, 'it's time. I need to go and be with your grandfather again.'

'Nooo... please, please... I need you!' Cara wailed.

Dr Bart placed a hand on the sobbing girl's shoulder, but Cara ignored him. She only had watery eyes for her beloved grandmother; the woman who had raised her from infancy.

'Cara,' the whisper came again, 'I love you, child, God knows I do, but I have to leave you now to live your life. We all have to die, and now it's my time.' Henrietta squeezed the hand of her granddaughter before continuing. 'You know that Martin Lander has my affairs in order, go and see him. Cara... I love you so very much.' Henrietta closed her eyes for the last time and with a smile still on her lips, released her last breath.

'Grandma!' Cara pleaded. 'Grandma, wake up!'

Pushing the frantic girl aside, Dr Bart felt for a pulse. Finding none, he gently pulled the sheet over Henrietta's face. Leading a sobbing Cara from the bedroom, he seated her in the parlour. Tugging on the bell pull at the side of the fireplace, he summoned the maid to bring tea.

Cara stared into her teacup; she felt so lost and alone. Tears were coming and going and she knew it was her body going into shock despite having been warned that her grandmother would not be in this world much longer.

Giving instruction to the maid to fetch the undertaker, Dr Bart sat with Cara and watched her as she endeavoured to come to terms with her great loss. He saw her body shake with great sobs. He knew it would take time for her to truly understand that she was, now, alone. 'There will be things to organize girl,' he said kindly, 'the funeral and the reading of the will.'

Cara nodded and with a sob said, 'Thank you Dr Bart... for everything.'

The elderly doctor nodded once. 'I'll wait until...' Cara burst into tears once more. Folding her in his arms, he said gently, 'Cry it out, you'll feel better for it.'

*

A week later and the snow was still falling steadily and silently as the maid entered the parlour. 'It's time, Miss Cara,' she said quietly.

Cara looked out onto the extensive lawns of The Laburnums. This was the house she had shared with her grandmother in the small town of Bilston; the place she grew up in.

'Thank you Molly.' Cara sighed as she stood to put on her black coat and hat. It was the day of her grandmother's funeral and the girl was dreading it. Tucking her blonde curls beneath her cartwheel hat, Cara buttoned up her long black woollen coat. A fur stole draped her shoulders, and for her hands a matching fur muff which hung around her neck on a plaited silk string.

She was ready, or as ready as she would ever be.

Climbing into the horse-drawn carriage that would take her down Proud's Lane and along Fletcher Street to St. Leonard's Church, Cara shivered, but not just from the cold.

The small church was filled to capacity when Cara arrived, and the service began. Normally the service would have been conducted at the graveside but the vicar had decided it was far too cold to be standing outside and called everyone into the church. His voice droned on but Cara heard no words. Silent tears spilled from cornflower blue eyes as she watched the coffin carried out to the graveside where it was lowered reverently into its final resting place.

Cara led the procession of mourners in the age-old practice of throwing a handful of dirt onto the coffin before moving away. Her tears were falling still as she shook hands with people she didn't know before they alighted their carriages once more to travel home. Cara stood a long time at the graveside staring down into the hole. Snowflakes floated down to settle on her hat and coat, but Cara was oblivious to the weather. Her mind was reliving the years she had spent with her grandmother, until, eventually, a polite cough brought her back to the present. The gravedigger had stood by, shovel in hand, eager to complete his work and be out of the cold. Cara nodded to him and turned away.

Sitting in the black carriage as it rumbled over the cobblestone street, Cara sat silently wishing it was all a dream. Now it was over, her grandmother was finally gone from her and she realized it was no dream. It was real and her heart ached from the void left there that she knew would never be filled.

Sitting at home in the parlour once more Cara watched the snow fall. Questions crowded into her mind as the crackle of the fire drew her to its warmth. Would this house be hers now? Or would she have to leave? Martin Lander, the solicitor, would know. He would tell her at the reading of Henrietta's will. How would she pay the bills? Cara had no money of her own. She was eighteen years old. She had been well-schooled but had never considered the prospect she might have to find work. What could she do? Again tears rolled silently down her cheeks.

Molly brought in the tea tray and asked if Cara was all

right. Cara nodded and Molly left the room quietly. The tick of the clock and the rustle of Molly's long black skirt on her boots the only sounds.

*

Molly Barton had been the maid at The Laburnums for five years and as she sat in the kitchen she spoke to the cook, 'Mrs Cox, I feel so sorry for Miss Cara, she can't stop crying.'

Gracie Cox nodded as she settled her ample weight onto a kitchen chair. 'Ar wench, I know. What I'm wondering now is... what will happen to us two?'

Molly looked at the older woman, 'Crikey! I never thought of that!'

Gracie drew her lips into a tight line and nodded her head as Molly went on, 'We could be out on the streets! Oh Lordy Lord!

'Now, now, don't let's go worrying too much, we have to wait and see what happens,' Gracie said in an effort to console Molly.

Silence descended on the kitchen as cook and maid drank their tea each lost in their own private thoughts.

*

Two weeks after Henrietta Selby had been laid to rest, her granddaughter received the solicitor's letter asking that she attend his office.

Cara wrapped up warmly against the cold wind and as she walked down Proud's Lane she was glad the snow had begun to melt, albeit leaving behind a filthy slush. Her side-buttoned boots tapped out a steady rhythm on the cobbled street and she deftly stepped over puddles as she hitched up her long dress and coat. Her breath left a stream of mist in the cold air as she hurried on, eager to be out of the freezing winds.

Branching off, Cara made her way down Dover Street before crossing over the Wolverhampton & Dudley Branch of the Great Western Railway via Arthur Street. Looking along the tracks, she knew the steam train was not due for another hour. On into Cambridge Street she searched for the nameplate of the offices of Lander, Holmes & Durwood, Solicitors at Law. Cambridge Street was where the landscape changed. All around her were offices, shops and houses. Buildings shoved one against the next; all covered with a layer of grime. The trains puffed out clouds of steam as they traversed the railway tracks that connected the small town with larger ones such as Wolverhampton and Birmingham. The steam mixed with fine particles of coal dust which the wind laid on the buildings before drying to a thin dirty paste.

Greeted by a secretary as she walked into the office, Cara was asked to take a seat while she waited for Mr Lander who would be with her shortly. A trilling sound made Cara jump and the secretary smiled at her. The office had one of those new-fangled telephones! Cara watched as the secretary finished speaking and hung the earpiece on the side of the telephone stand. Cara marvelled at the brilliant invention and determined to have one installed at home, it would make life so much easier.

A door opened and a young man spoke as he extended his hand. 'Miss Flowers, please do come in, my name is Martin Lander.'

Looking at the man opposite her, she was surprised to see he was not what she had expected. She had envisaged a much older man, not one in his early thirties. Very young to be a qualified solicitor, she thought. Martin Lander had dark hair and deep brown eyes which held a constant twinkle.

Cara entered his office and sat by his desk.

'Firstly, Miss Flowers, I am very sorry for your loss. How are you getting on?' Lander asked.

'Fine, thank you.' Cara answered meekly, her eyes dropping to her gloves lying in her lap.

'Right then, perhaps we should read your grandmother's will if you are prepared?' Cara nodded and Martin unrolled a parchment. Seeing her puzzled look, he said, 'Henrietta was an old-fashioned sort, as you know. This is how she wanted it done.' Martin held up the scroll and waved it in the air.

Cara gave a thin smile and watched him closely as he read out the words on the document.

When he reached the end, Martin rolled it up again and passed it over to her.

'If there is anything more I can do for you, Miss Flowers, please feel free to call on me.'

Thanking him, Cara walked out of the office in a daze, the parchment safely in her drawstring bag. Head down against the wind, Cara stepped smartly down the street and once again came to the railway. She heard the clickety-clack of the train's wheels on the track and smelled the steam as it chugged its way to its destination. She had been in the solicitor's office for an hour and as she hurried on, she heard his voice again in her mind as he read out Henrietta's last will and testament.

Three

Sitting in the parlour once more, Cara read over the will left by her grandmother to herself. Molly popped her head round the door and a tearful Cara asked, 'Molly, would you and Gracie be kind enough to join me? I have things to discuss with you.' The maid bobbed a quick curtsy and shot down to the kitchen all of a fluster.

'Miss Cara wants to see us in the parlour,' she announced as the cook's eyes met hers.

A moment later Molly returned with Gracie in tow, both looking a little worried. Was this it? Was this the day they would find themselves out of work and home?

'Please sit down,' drying her eyes on her handkerchief, Cara motioned to the settee drawn up to the fire. 'Now,' she sniffed, 'it seems Grandma left everything to me. I would be very pleased if you would both stay on here and... I wish we could be less formal in our relationships. What I mean is, can we be friends rather than employer and staff? I certainly would be glad of it.'

The cook and maid smiled in unison, allowing held breath to be released. They had felt sure they would find themselves out of a job now the old lady had passed, and relief flooded them both.

'Also,' Cara went on, 'I propose to give you both a raise in earnings.' Another beam crossed the women's faces. 'I only ask one thing in return.' The women shared a glance as Cara resumed. 'I ask that you would both help me with a task set down by Grandma... a challenge you might say. I have been tasked to find and take care of any living blood relatives.'

Molly and Gracie exchanged another look before returning their eyes to their new mistress.

Molly piped up, 'I thought you was an only child!'

Gracie dug the maid in the ribs with her elbow at the girl's outburst, but Cara gave a wan smile as she said, 'So did I, Molly!'

'Beggin' your pardon Miss Cara, but what makes you think you might have other family? We've certainly never heard Mrs Selby talk about it.' Gracie Cox looked at the maid sat alongside her, who nodded her agreement, before returning her eyes to the young woman sat opposite.

Cara held up the scroll and said simply, 'Grandma must have thought so!'

'Why did Mrs Selby think there might be others in the family?' Gracie asked.

'I have no idea,' Cara answered.

'Surely she would have said something as you were growing up, wouldn't she?' Molly asked.

'She never said a thing,' Cara answered again. 'I used to ask her about my parents, who they were and where they were. Grandma would get upset with me and tell me not to ask such questions. It was the only thing she ever got cross with me about.' Her glance moved from one face to the other as she spoke.

'That's very strange,' Gracie mused, 'something terrible must have happened to cause such a rift.'

'As I got older I thought the same, Gracie. I couldn't fathom it out at all.' Cara's eyes became dreamy as she pondered the past.

'Well, obviously your parents and your grandma fell out over something!' Molly chimed in. She gave a scowl as Gracie dug her in the ribs again. 'What? I was only saying!'

Cara gave a little grin, saying, 'You're right, Molly, but what was it they disagreed about? It must have been something important.'

'Important enough for you to grow up here with your grandma and not with your parents,' Gracie added.

'Indeed,' Cara nodded, 'I wonder if I will ever find out? It's awful not knowing anything about one's parents.'

'There was times I wished I didn't know about mine!' Molly said, which caused smiles to break out. 'Lord, could them two fight! Then they was all lovey-dovey. I didn't know if I was coming or going!'

Cara tittered behind her hand as the tension was broken. Gracie gave out a belly laugh. Molly spoke again, 'So, how you going to go about finding any lost relatives?'

Cara sighed heavily. 'I haven't a clue,' she said simply.

As the discussions went on, Cara found herself fighting a losing battle with her tears. Her emotions constantly burst their banks and she fought desperately to keep control of herself. Regaining her composure, Cara responded to Gracie's suggestion that any siblings be called Flowers.

'I would have thought so,' she said, 'and probably younger than myself.'

'Why do you say that?' Molly asked.

'Well, I would have thought any siblings older than me

would have grown up here too.' Cara held out her hands.

'Oh yes! I never thought of that,' Molly screwed up her mouth and pushed her chin forward. 'Tch! Silly me, I should have known that!'

Going to the bureau, Cara took out a pencil and paper and, retaking her seat, said, 'If you're willing to help me, perhaps we should start by making a note of things we know, and also any questions we have.'

'Good idea,' Gracie said as she settled herself more comfortably on the sofa.

Cara began the list; they needed to find anyone with the surname of Flowers and investigate further. How would they go about this? Who could they ask?

In the beginning the cook and maid were wary about getting involved in the family mystery, but eventually their excitement grew as did the list of things to do. The challenge was becoming infectious.

Mrs Cox sent Molly to the kitchen for more tea, then said, 'Miss Cara, what exactly did the will say?'

Cara picked up the scroll once more and scanned the words. Locating the relevant passage, she read aloud as Molly trundled in with the tea tray. *'Cara Flowers is hereby tasked with finding any living blood relative: her mother Elizabeth Flowers; her father John Flowers; and any other children they may have had. It is my wish that Cara takes care of any other children discovered, for the term of their or her natural life.'*

Gracie and Molly exchanged a look. Then opening a personal letter left by her grandmother, Cara read on. *'Cara, Elizabeth Selby, my daughter, married John Flowers against my wishes. John was a drunken waster and Elizabeth became pregnant before the wedding. I heard later that John died, but*

I cannot be sure of this. If you should discover I have other grandchildren, please Cara, take care of them on my behalf. Also, if you find my daughter, please tell her I rue the day I ignored her plea. I'm sorry you have to find out this way, sweetheart, but it's time you knew. I know I should have told you this long ago… please forgive me.'

'Bloody hell!' Gracie Cox gasped. 'She's set you a fine task there and no mistake!'

Cara tried to hide the smile Gracie's language induced and went on, 'I know, Gracie, that's why I'm asking you to help me. I feel so lonely and I really don't want to do this alone.' Cara looked from one to the other as her tears came once again. Steeling herself, she went on, 'Martin Lander is aware of my grandmother's last wish… but not this personal letter. Grandma left it for me on her bedside table, only to be opened after…'

'Well,' Gracie cut her off, afraid she would burst into tears again, 'we could ask Mr Lander's help an' all.'

'I was thinking I might ask him, Gracie, he could perhaps suggest things we haven't thought of.' A tiny spark shone in Cara's blue eyes as she added his name to the list.

'What's he like, Miss Cara? Is he nice? Do you think he might help?' Molly asked with a cheeky smile.

Cara nodded, a blush flowing into her cheeks.

'Oh-oh,' Gracie said and all three burst out laughing. Tears had been avoided and they had managed to coax a laugh from the young girl they both had come to love to distraction in the time they had lived and worked at the house.

*

Cara lay in bed sniffing away her tears and listening to the icy wind blasting through the laburnum trees surrounding the house. *Her* house. 'The Laburnums' now belonged to her, along with an unbelievably large amount of money which Cara knew was passed down from the family buying and selling property. There were no other sounds, save the wind. The large house stood in its own grounds backing onto the Allotment Gardens. It was well away from the factories and shops of the town and so remained relatively quiet and grime-free. With eight bedrooms and servants' quarters, it also had been fitted with an indoor lavatory; a luxury not many houses sported.

Wondering if she did, in fact, have any brothers and sisters, a thought suddenly struck her. 'You crafty madam!' Cara muttered into the darkness. She suspected her grandmother had set her this task in an effort to beat off the girl's grieving. More to the point, it was working. With a thin smile, Cara Flowers snuggled beneath the covers and finally slipped into a dreamless sleep.

After breakfast the following morning, Cara said, 'I had a thought last night, what say we visit the Registrar of Births, Deaths and Marriages? Maybe he could find something in his records.'

'Right then, get your coats on, you two, let's go and see old Colley!' Gracie said as she bustled from the kitchen. Molly shook her head at Gracie's bossiness. Cara smiled, it gave her a warm feeling; Gracie being bossy felt, to her, a bit like being mothered.

Josiah Colley had his office in Wellington Road, an upmarket part of the town. As the three women walked along the street, Cara said, 'It might be that you ladies are the closest thing to family I have after all is said and done.'

'Well hopefully Mr Colley should be able to shed some light on that,' Gracie said as she beamed her pleasure at being considered family.

Wrapped up warmly, they chatted quietly as they walked briskly down Wellington Road.

Once in the office Cara introduced herself and her two companions. Holding tight to her emotions, Cara explained: 'Mr Colley, I was hoping you may be able to aid me in a quest set down by my grandmother.'

'Ah, Mrs Selby, God rest her soul. My condolences, Miss Flowers.' Josiah tipped his head in respect.

'Thank you,' Cara said. Feeling a crack in her emotions, she rushed on. 'We are searching for any family with the surname of Flowers. Grandma tasked me to find and take care of them.'

Colley's eyebrows shot up and he scratched the back of his head. 'Quite an undertaking, Miss Flowers. Do you have any dates that might help? Birthdays or the like?'

Cara shook her head, 'I don't even know if I have any family.'

'I'm afraid without dates to go on, it might prove immensely difficult and would take some considerable time to search the listings.' Colley swung his arm around the room. 'Do you have any idea of how many records are kept here?' Seeing the young woman's shoulders slump, he added quickly, 'I will do my best, Miss Flowers, but don't expect any news for quite a while.'

Cara's heart sank as she felt the weight of her loss and the huge burden she'd been given settle on her. Gracie urged her on, saying next to visit was the telephone company to have one of the new gadgets fitted in the house.

'You said you wanted one, to make things easier than going out on errands, as well as to telephone Mr Colley for any further news.' Gracie said.

Cara said she would see to it later; they really needed to speak with the solicitor first.

The three women then walked on to Martin Lander's office. Ushering them in, he pulled up chairs for each.

Cara introduced Gracie and Molly before saying, 'Mr Lander, I would ask you to read this passage from a personal letter left to me by Grandma. Then I would ask for any advice you may be able to give.' Handing him the letter, the women watched as Lander read the relevant words. Handing the letter back, Martin nodded.

Cara went on, 'Mr Colley, the Registrar, agreed to go through his records for anyone with the Flowers surname, but there may be too many to actually help us narrow down the search.'

Martin Lander thought for a moment before saying, 'Well, you do have a challenge on your hands! May I suggest… you might visit… the workhouse?' He looked pained.

'Oh yes!' Cara said suddenly. 'We didn't think of that!'

Despite Cara's excitement, Gracie's spirits dropped at the very thought of visiting the most dreaded building in the town. She'd heard the stories of the terrible life people had in there; of having little food, of working their fingers to the bone for no pay, and of the possibility of never having a life outside the place again.

'Of course,' Martin went on, 'any relatives could well have moved away. Maybe they travelled looking for work, which would make things far more difficult for you.'

'I'm really looking for any siblings, so they would probably be younger than me. However, if my parents did move away, then the children would have gone with them.' Cara felt a twinge of disappointment as she thought out loud.

'Forgive my asking, Miss Flowers, but how is it you came to be raised by Mrs Selby in the first place?' Martin Lander enquired.

'Oh! To be honest, Mr Lander, I don't really know.' Cara frowned. 'Grandma would never speak of it.' She bit her lower lip in an effort to beat off tears threatening to fall yet again.

'If you can discover the reason, it might shed light on other things you may need to know,' he said helpfully. 'Your parents' wedding certificate should list their occupations... it's a place to start.'

Cara's spirits lifted slightly when Martin spoke again. He asked tentatively, 'Would you like me to make an appointment at the workhouse on your behalf?' Cara nodded and Martin pulled the telephone towards him. Gracie and Molly exchanged a look of abject horror.

Thanking him, the women left his office and made for home, struggling against the icy wind that blew around their long skirts and coats. By the time they arrived, their noses were red and cold and their fingers and toes were tingling.

Cara elected to eat her meal in the warmth of the kitchen with Gracie and Molly so they could discuss the day's events.

'So how did you feel about finding out that you were on the way before your mum and dad was married?' Molly asked innocently.

Cara stared open-mouthed. Molly shrank back into her chair frightened she'd upset the girl with her forthright question. Gracie slapped the back of the maid's head and Molly cursed.

'Molly, you are a genius!' Cara gasped. The cook and maid

shared a quick glance. 'Don't you see? If I was "on the way", as you so delicately put it, before they married, that gives us an idea of a wedding date! We should be able to find their wedding certificate... which might tell us their occupations!'

'Damn my eyes!' Gracie said, slapping a hand on the table, making the others jump.

Staying in the warmth of the kitchen, they made plans for the next day. They would again visit Josiah Colley; this time he would probably have more of an idea where to look for information on Cara's parents and/or siblings.

*

Martin Lander sat in his small living room in his house in Alice Street which ran behind the ironworks. It was a comfortable two-up, two-down dwelling and it belonged to him. Working hard, he was now a junior partner in the business; he had his own home and now all he needed was a wife. He was in no hurry to be married, but as his thoughts roamed, he could not prevent the picture of Cara Flowers forming in his mind. She was a rare beauty. Hair like sunshine, eyes the colour of cornflowers. She had an innocence about her that added to her attraction. His mind moved to the challenge she'd been set by her wily old grandmother. It was a formidable task, one she apparently was undertaking with gusto despite being in mourning. Martin felt if there *were* any of Cara's relations out there, she would most definitely find them. She had an air of sophistication about her too and he guessed she would not suffer fools gladly.

He whiled away the evening hours thinking about ways he might be able to further help the beautiful Miss Cara Flowers. This was a lady he would like to get to know better.

Besides her English rose beauty, she had an inordinate amount of money, which certainly added to the attraction!

In his office the following day, Martin thought about his own ambition. He wanted to have his own suite of offices... his own business. If he could be instrumental in Cara having a desirable outcome to her search, this would add to his kudos. Once word was out about his successful case, more business would come his way. People would begin to request to see *him* by name. Then he could think about breaking free from the partnership and opening his own law practice. Happy to work towards his ultimate goal, he sighed contentedly and settled down to his work.

*

Cara was excited as she visited the Registrar for the second time. Once given an approximate date, Josiah Colley quickly found the marriage certificate of Elizabeth Selby and John Flowers. Cara saw her mother was listed as a housewife and her father was a carter. A carter... a profession where a man could travel many miles, visit many towns; her father could be anywhere. Elizabeth, a housewife – where? In Bilston? Or had she moved further afield with her husband? Where could Cara look next?

Cara looked at the kindly old man who shook his head, then said, 'I promise I will keep looking through my records now I have a better idea of what to look for.'

Cara's emotions fought with themselves as she walked home. Gracie and Molly had questioned her visiting the Registrar alone, but she had assured them she would be fine, she just needed to get out of the house for a while. One question had been answered regarding her parents' professions, but that in turn had led to other questions. It was like being in a maze, unsure of where to go next.

Much like any other town in the Black Country, Bilston had its shops and businesses. These were surrounded by great expanses of open heathland dotted with old coal shafts and disused collieries. The Great Western Railway sliced straight through the centre of the town and on either side of the tracks warehouses and factories had sprung up. To the east lay the semicircular Birmingham Canal with its many wharfs and basins. Connected to other towns by a series of smaller inland waterways, it was an essential means of transporting cargo... and gossip. The 'cut-rats', or canal people, would carry messages to and from their destinations for those unable to travel. Narrowboats and barges could be seen lining the wharfs or moored up in the basins night and day.

Bilston sported galvanizing works, ironworks, brass foundries and a massive area given over to the stone quarries. The disused collieries remained a blot on the landscape, unchanged since the last man had left their employ.

Bilston also had its pretty areas; the allotment gardens in spring and summer boasted flowers that could rival Kew Gardens. Lunt Gardens also provided benches where people sat to enjoy its beauty. Picnics were often taken by families and it was made into a day out for their children.

Despite the many businesses trading, however, poverty and unemployment was at an all-time high. With collieries closing down, the miners found themselves out of work and standing in the bread line every day in the hope of someone giving them a job. Many people were starving, some finding admittance to the dreaded workhouse preferable to death; while others took their chances away from that hellhole.

Cara noticed nothing of the town she lived in as she

walked back to The Laburnums, her mind preoccupied with questions that gave her no answers. *However*, she thought, *maybe the workhouse will provide some information.* Her eyes on the ground as she walked, Cara didn't really hold out much hope of that.

Four

The workhouse had been built at the end of Green Lanes, not too far from the Infectious Diseases Hospital. Situated on the edge of the town, everyone knew where these buildings were, and with the amount of poverty, unemployment and illness, people considered themselves very fortunate not to be in either one.

Very few had the money to pay for a doctor's visit when illness struck and so home remedies were heavily relied upon. A mustard and goose fat poultice bound on the chest for ailments such as pneumonia or chest infections was often used, but it rarely helped with the illness it was believed it would cure. The winter months took old and young alike to meet their maker; it was the undertaker's busiest time.

Cara shivered, she couldn't wait for springtime to finally arrive, when new life would begin in nature. However, it would mean more babies would be born. Most households had six to eight children, and with both parents working, it was often up to the eldest to see to the younger ones. With only two bedrooms, the houses were overcrowded, but still the birth rate rose ever higher.

Cara, with Molly and Gracie flanking her, walked through the cobbled streets, dodging wagons and carriages on their way to Green Lanes.

'I don't fancy this one bit!' Molly fretted.

'Nor do I,' Cara answered, 'but I have to see. If you prefer, you can both wait outside for me.'

'Not a chance, wench!' Gracie was adamant they would go inside with Cara. It was bad enough having to visit the place, but for the girl to go in alone? No, she wouldn't even entertain the idea.

Passing the allotment gardens, they trudged over the scrubland that separated the workhouse from the town. At the end of Green Lanes, they saw the imposing building which stood behind two massive wrought-iron gates and was surrounded by a high brick wall.

Through the gates they could see the workhouse itself. Built in a single-storey cross shape, there were exercise yards between each arm of the structure. At its centre was a two-storey dwelling – the Master's quarters. This had windows on all sides so the Master could look down on each part of the workhouse at any one time. A huge oak door dominated the front wall of the building, with arched windows either side. What couldn't be seen from the front were the outbuildings at the back. These were the bakery, the laundry and the mortuary. Further back still were the bone and stone crushing grounds, which provided work for the adult males. Chimneys sprouted from the buildings but were rarely used; coal was too expensive to be wasted on inmates. Just inside the wrought-iron gates was the small porter's lodge. The building seemed out of place amid the poverty strangling the town. The whole had the grandeur of a stately home, but its reputation preceded it and people had been known to take their own lives before being forced in there. Some people would starve to death rather than accept the 'ticket' offered by the Relieving Officer which allowed them admittance.

Drawing in a breath, she cast a glance at the women by her side. This was Cara's first visit to the awful place and her mouth dried out at the thought of entering. She, as many others, had avoided it all of her life. She looked around her then seeing the handle on the gate she took hold of it and pulled. A moment later a porter appeared from somewhere behind the wall. A short man wrapped in an overcoat that reached almost to his boots, he wore a flat cap and muffler round his neck. His hands were shoved deep into his coat pockets.

The man looked at the three women standing at the other side of the gate. Dressed in their finest clothes, he determined they had come to buy a servant or two.

Cara waited and the porter waited. Each watching the other, neither spoke. Exasperated, Cara eventually said, 'I'm here to see the Master.'

Doffing his cap, the porter pulled a ring of keys from his thick leather belt wrapped around his overcoat. Shuffling through attempting to locate the correct key, he grinned at the women, showing his tobacco-stained teeth.

'Please be quick, it's rather cold out here,' Cara said, feigning impatience.

'Tell me about it. I'm doing my best lady,' the man answered indignantly.

'How long have you worked here?' Cara asked as the gate opened.

'Fifteen years, man and boy,' the porter said proudly, hoping it would impress the women.

'Well, after fifteen years you should know which key is the

correct one!' Cara sniffed as she walked through the now open gate. Gracie stifled a laugh and Molly sniggered. The porter slammed the gate shut with a bang, muttering as he watched the women walk away from him.

Giving the knocker on the door three sharp raps, they waited. Just being on the inside of the grounds gave them a shiver, and Cara wondered how long the doom and gloom she felt wrapping itself around her would last. The door slowly slid open to reveal a thin, pasty-looking woman. Standing aside to allow them entry, she then shoved the door closed. Hooking a finger, she beckoned them to follow her. They walked through the long cold corridor to a small room where the woman knocked on the door and promptly fled. The three exchanged a glance at the woman's strange behaviour.

'Come!' A man's voice boomed out.

Cara opened the door and they trooped into the office.

A burly man sat behind a desk with a pair of spectacles perched on the end of his nose. A mass of unruly salt and pepper hair surrounded a fat face. Grey eyes looked over the spectacles at the women who stood in his office. Seeing their attire, he immediately softened his demeanour.

'Ladies,' he said with an affected charm, 'what can I do for you?'

Looking around her, Cara saw no chairs – obviously no one was invited to sit whilst in this room. 'I am Cara Flowers and I have an appointment,' she said as she looked back to the man slouching in his chair.

As her eyes had roamed the room, she had noticed a glass-fronted cupboard which held an array of canes. Stifling the shudder she had felt beginning to rise, she continued, 'I have come to enquire after anyone with the surname of Flowers that may *reside* here.'

'Have you now?' The man slouched further into his chair, his thumb and index finger rubbing his chin. 'For what reason?'

'I don't have to explain myself to you Mr…?' Cara huffed, anger now replacing the nervousness she had felt on entering the office.

'Tulley,' the man said with a grin, 'and you do have to explain yourself to me as you'm in my place!'

'Mr Tulley, I am looking for anyone who might be connected to my family.' It stung that he had won that round, but she maintained her confidence and bit back her anger.

'There now, that wasn't so bad, was it?' Tulley grinned again. 'I don't think we have anyone of that name here.'

Cara changed tack and smiled sweetly. 'How many people are housed here, Mr Tulley?' She asked, all innocence now.

'Oh a couple of hundred, I would think.' The man was enjoying seeing the shrinking violet in front of him.

Cara nodded and his eyes widened as she leaned both hands on his desk and said, 'You think! You don't know… exactly?' She leaned in closer, 'And you know all of these people by name, do you?'

Tulley blustered, 'Well… no, of course not!'

'Then I suggest you check the records… now!' Cara let loose her anger before straightening her posture. Gracie's nod added the full stop to her sentence.

Snatching a large ledger from a drawer, the man dropped it on the desk top with a bang. He then ran his eyes and a finger down the columns. After what felt like hours he finally said, 'We do have a Charlie Flowers here… boy aged twelve years.' Tulley looked up. 'No others.'

Using his words of earlier, Cara said, 'There now, that wasn't so bad, was it? I'd like to see him.'

Drawing an irate breath, Tulley looked like he might refuse her request, but Cara cut him off. 'Now, Mr Tulley, unless of course you'd prefer I make a complaint to the Board of Guardians?'

Throwing the ledger back in the drawer, he slammed it shut. 'Follow me,' he muttered.

Cara's excitement grew as they walked through the cold dark corridors once more to the back of the building. They entered a work shed which stood at the end of the exercise yard. There was little light and the boys inside were oakum picking – unpicking old rope with a metal spike. With fingers sore and bleeding, the children sat on the floor with nothing between the cold slabs and their trousers.

'Flowers! Charlie Flowers!' Tulley bellowed.

A small voice called from the back of the room. 'Yes sir?'

'Here to me, at once!' Tulley yelled.

The young boy stepped forward and Cara sucked in a shocked breath. Rail-thin, pasty skin and dressed in rags, the boy stood before her, his eyes downcast. His mind was searching for a way out of whatever it was that awaited him.

Turning to the burly man, Cara gathered her courage and said, 'I'd like to speak to the boy in private.'

Shaking his head so his fat jowls jiggled, Tulley spoke. 'I'm afraid that's not possible.'

'Then I request you move back, this conversation is not for your ears!' Cara snapped.

Tulley harrumphed and stepped back a few paces bumping into Gracie who stood behind Cara. Gracie pushed him away from her. Molly scowled at the man as he leaned forward in a desperate effort to overhear what was being said. With a grumble he moved back further still.

Bending down in front of the boy, Cara whispered,

'Charlie, I have a few questions for you, and it's really important you answer them truthfully.' Charlie's blue eyes looked into hers and she went on. 'What is your mother's name?'

'Elizabeth Flowers, Miss,' the boy whispered back.

Cara drew in a breath with a shudder and felt rather than saw Gracie and Molly exchange a glance. 'Good boy, and your father's name?'

'John Flowers, Miss.'

'Do you know where your parents are, Charlie?' Cara's excitement grew but she held it in check as she pressed gently. Charlie shook his head and lowered his eyes. Placing a finger beneath his chin, Cara lifted his head. 'It's all right, Charlie, you are doing very well.' A thought flitted through her mind just then, was it possible her parents were in this dreadful place too? Cara sighed with disappointment as the thought left as quickly as it had come. She remembered Tulley's words... '*We do have a Charlie Flowers here... boy aged twelve years... no others.*'

Gently she asked, 'Now, do you have any brothers or sisters?'

Nodding, the boy rasped, 'A sister, Daisy, but *he* sold her!' Charlie indicated with a tip of his head the man still straining to listen in to the conversation. Gracie and Molly turned to face Tulley and both scowled at him. Cara's jaws clamped together. She was horrified and fought to keep it hidden for the sake of the child.

'Good boy. Here, this is for you.' Cara gave the child a toffee wrapped in pretty gold paper. The sweet was in his mouth before she could wink, a grin by way of thanks.

Standing once more, Cara turned to the man watching her.

'Mr Tulley, I want this boy released into my custody... today!'

Stepping towards her, his piggy eyes screamed greed as he rubbed his whiskers. 'Well now...'

Cara held up her hand, forestalling his words. 'Mr Tulley, please don't play games with me! I'm not sure how this works, so I suggest we all retire to your office where we can sort this out.' Turning to Charlie once more, she added, 'Charlie, please come with me.'

The boy nodded and moved closer to the young woman who had given him the toffee.

In Tulley's office, Cara watched as he produced the necessary paper for Charlie's release, which he waved in the air, and eyed her expectantly. Guessing what he was about, she rummaged in her bag and produced five pounds which she placed on his desk and watched his eyes light up.

'Now then,' Cara said, 'I wish to know the address for Daisy Flowers.'

'I couldn't possibly divulge...' Tulley began.

Cara sighed audibly as she cast a glance at Gracie; the cook nodded once. 'Look Mr Tulley,' Cara said, 'I need to find Daisy and I am willing to pay for the information. Now, think on this... once she is in my custody, the people who bought her will need another to replace her. Where will they go? Why, to you of course. So you will have made another sale.'

Watching her words sink in, Cara then gave Charlie a sly wink. An imperceptible nod from the boy told her he understood what she was about.

Tulley retrieved another large ledger from a drawer and ran his fat finger down the column. Turning the book in her direction, she saw what she'd been looking for. Gracie and Molly leaned forward to view the address.

Cara passed over another five pound note and turned to leave. Taking Charlie's hand, she moved to lead the little group from the building.

'This paperwork needs to be completed before I can release the boy and have his own clothing returned to him. Three hours' notice has to be given for release,' Tulley said with a spiteful grin. 'You can wait *outside* the gate.' He waved the paper in his hand towards the door.

Cara inwardly fumed but held her tongue at being dismissed in such a manner. Turning to the boy, she said, 'I'll see you outside, Charlie. I'll wait for you *outside* the gate.' Charlie gave a grin and nodded. Cara strode from the office with her head high.

The porter saw them coming and held open the huge gate for them to pass through. Marching past him, Cara lifted her chin pushing her nose in the air.

The porter relocked the gate and disappeared back to his tiny lodge behind the wall.

Cara looked at Gracie and Molly then gave out a whoop of delight.

'Bloody hell!' Gracie said in astonishment. 'You've got a brother and sister!'

Cara stopped the little jig she was dancing and stared at Gracie. 'Oh my goodness, I have!'

'How do you feel about that then?' Molly asked.

Gracie butted in with, 'I think that little dance just now said it all, don't you?'

'Oh Molly!' Cara said, wrapping an arm around the shoulder of her friends. 'This is a wonderful day! How marvellous to know I have other family besides you two lovely ladies!'

After three and a half hours of stamping around outside

the gate in an effort to keep warm, Cara saw Charlie emerge from the building alone.

As he approached, he shivered as the chill cut through the rags he wore. 'Miss, where we going?'

Cara slipped off her coat and wrapped it around the boy as she said, 'Home, Charlie. We're going home.'

Five

Fred Tulley grinned as he pocketed the money from Cara Flowers. Making his way through the corridors to the dining hall, he knew his wife, Ada, would be thrilled with the extra money. The large room had two rows of refectory tables stretching from end to end with benches either side of each table. The boys were crammed together on the benches as they slurped the thin broth made from overripe vegetables. Glad of something to fill their bellies, they didn't complain. Not one child looked up as Tulley strode the length of the room towards his wife.

'Mrs Tulley,' he greeted her.

'Mr Tulley,' she greeted him back.

It was their custom to speak to each other in such a manner in an effort to reinforce respect to the children in their care.

Fred whispered his news and his wife beamed her joy at having a few extra pounds in their savings.

Ringing the large handbell, they watched as bowls were tipped to lips in an effort to swallow the last dregs of the thin soup. With hardly a sound, the bowls were replaced on the tables and the boys filed out of the room in an orderly fashion to return to their work of oakum picking.

Tulley nodded to his wife in praise of how well she had trained the youngsters. A moment later a few thin dirty women entered and began to collect the bowls for washing. No one looked at the Tulleys as they worked. Other women brought in more bowls of broth and set them out before leaving the dining hall. The young girls then quietly entered the room and sat on the benches vacated by the boys moments earlier.

Tulley smiled; the whole place ran like clockwork while he and his wife raked in the money.

Fred considered himself fortunate as he patrolled the workhouse which was divided up into sections: one for the men, one for the women, one for the boys and the other for the female children. There were rules, which he often ignored, but no one dared to complain.

Tulley ran over the rulings in his mind as he continued his patrol. No corporal punishment was allowed on any girl. None on any boy, except by the schoolmaster a rule which Fred always ignored. This was to be given by rod, and only then if approved by the Board of Guardians or Visiting Committee. Another rule Fred often flouted, as he thrashed the boys into submission. This caning could only be administered after two hours had elapsed from the time an offence had been committed. Many other rules were listed, but there were few he adhered to.

Three hours a day should be given over to the teaching of reading, writing and arithmetic; the rest of the day the children spent working. The boys worked oakum picking and the girls worked in the laundry or bakery. Fred didn't consider the learning of letters and numbers to be important to these children. They would never need to use them anyway.

Fred knew each dormitory could hold at least twenty five children and more often than not there were two to a bed. The beds were wooden structures with a thin flock mattress. There were no pillows and each child was allocated two blankets. Lost or torn blankets were not replaced. Fred thought they should consider themselves lucky to have what they did.

Children coming into the workhouse had their hair cropped short in an endeavour to keep head lice to a minimum, before their thin bodies were given a scrub down. Girls were given a long dress, a shift, a poke bonnet and knee-length stockings, plus a pair of hobnailed boots. Boys were given shirts, trousers, under drawers and boots. Such was the uniform of the workhouse, which was worn until it fell apart. Their own clothes were put into storage until such time as the inmate left the workhouse. Tulley smiled to himself; very few left this place, unless by way of a box, or he managed to sell them on as servants.

The women worked the bake house, cleaned the workrooms and washrooms and did the laundry for the whole building. The men worked in the mortuary or outside breaking stones and crushing bones which were to be used in fertilizer.

The sadness in the eyes of the people who first came into the workhouse soon turned to a glassy inevitability. Most knew they would die in that place, the only question left to them was… when?

Fred Tulley congratulated himself as he sat in his office and counted the money again. Yet another job well done. His mind turned to the young woman who had bought out Charlie Flowers. Who was she? Where did she come from?

How come she had family in the workhouse? Why had she not come for them sooner? Didn't she know she didn't have to pay for their release? Tulley dismissed the silly girl from his thoughts. He didn't have time to waste on her, he had people coming in later with a view to purchasing a couple of boys as stable lads. Fred rubbed his hands together as he thought of yet more money finding its way into his pocket.

*

The three women and the scruffy boy wrapped in a coat which dragged on the floor walked over the patch of scrubland. Charlie asked, 'Miss... how come you brought me out of the Spike?'

Cara said gently, 'It is my belief we are family, Charlie. I think I am your big sister.'

'What?' Charlie stopped walking, an astonished look on his face.

'I'll explain everything to you when we get home. Come on, it's not too far now.' Cara gave him a reassuring smile.

They walked on past the allotment gardens and over more heathland until they reached Proud's Lane. At the end of the street, Cara stopped. Digging into her drawstring bag, she pulled out her purse.

'Molly, would you be good enough to go into town and buy Charlie some new clothes?' She handed over some money.

'You're twelve, right Charlie?' Molly asked. At his nod she went on. 'Right, it's young man's clothes for you then, none of this kiddie tat, eh?'

Charlie beamed and Cara and Gracie shared a knowing smile.

Molly gave the boy a wink then walked quickly down the street. Cara, Charlie and Gracie carried on into the driveway of 'The Laburnums.'

Charlie whistled through his teeth as he walked up the gravel driveway and looked up at the large house. 'Blimey! Do you live here, Miss?'

'Yes, Charlie, we all do… and now you do too.' Cara smiled down at the boy, who stared with his mouth hanging open.

Gracie went directly to the kitchen to set the kettle to boil. Lifting down a tin bath hung on the scullery wall, she then set large pans of water to heat on the range. The lad was to have a bath, whether he liked it or not! Going to the cupboard in the hall, she took out two large fluffy towels and set them on a chair by the tin bath. A chunk of soap was placed on the top.

Setting the tea tray, Gracie went to the larder for bread, butter, cheese and cake. Charlie Flowers needed feeding up but slowly and carefully. He'd probably only eaten slop in a long while, so Gracie took it upon herself to give the boy good nourishing food, but this would do as a start.

Meanwhile in the parlour, Cara was dismayed when she looked into the grate. 'Oh no, the fire has gone out,' she said.

'It's all right,' Charlie said, 'I'll do it.' The coat lent to him was removed and draped over a chair. He snatched up the poker and raked it over the fire bed. Loose ash fell through the grating and he grabbed a sheet of newspaper from the table, screwing it up loosely. Taking the kindling sticks kept in the grate, he laid them in a flat wigwam over the paper. Rifling through the coal scuttle, he found some small nuggets of coal which he sat carefully on the sticks. Looking around, he found matches on the mantelshelf and another sheet of newspaper on the table.

Cara watched as he held the struck match to one side of the paper then once it had caught he moved it to the other side. Satisfied, he then held the sheet of newspaper across the front of the fireplace. Hearing the air pull the flames up the chimney, he nodded and removed the newspaper which had begun to turn brown. The coal chips were glowing red now and Charlie carefully added more coal nuggets. Then, wiping his hands on his trousers, he stood back to admire his handiwork.

'Well done!' Cara said.

'Oh it weren't nothing,' the boy answered, 'but give it a minute and you'll have a blaze fit to rival a furnace.'

They smiled at each other as Gracie brought in the tea tray and a dish towel which she laid on a chair for Charlie to sit on. The boy's eyes widened and his mouth watered as he watched bread being thickly smothered in butter and a chunk of cheese placed beside it. Taking the plate offered to him, he said, 'Oooh ta!'

Gracie replied, 'You're welcome. Now... don't bolt it, else you'll be bad.'

Nodding, Charlie bit into the bread and butter and closed his eyes savouring the flavour. He'd never tasted butter before, he had only ever had a thin coating of margarine on day-old hard bread.

Cara and Gracie smiled at each other as Molly came in loaded down with parcels. 'Oh tea! Just what I need. Right, I got trousers, shirts, underwear, socks, jumpers, cap and a jacket. Boots will have to wait, he'll need to try them on for a good fit. Oh and I got pyjamas too.'

Charlie looked from one to another as he quietly ate his bread and butter and cheese before his eyes rested on the cake.

After tea, Gracie said, 'Right, my lad, you come to the scullery with me.' Seeing his eyes lower, she went on, 'Oh lad, you ain't going in there to work… you'm to have a bath.'

'I ain't!' Charlie rounded on the cook. 'Last time I had a bath I nearly drowned in the cold water!'

The three women shared a smile and Gracie said, 'You can't drown in a tin bath, it ain't big enough! Besides, I've warmed the water for you, so you stir your stumps right now!'

Still unsure, Charlie reluctantly followed the cook to the scullery. He watched as she filled the tub halfway with water.

Testing the temperature with an elbow, she nodded. 'Right. Get them rags off and put yer arse in that water.' Gracie pointed to the bath. Seeing his horrified look, she rolled her eyes and turned her back while he stripped down and climbed into the water. 'There's soap there, use it well… otherwise I will,' she said over her shoulder.

Gracie scooped up his old clothes and shoved them into the fire in the range. Leaving the scullery door open a little way, she set about the task of preparing their evening meal.

Molly and Cara tiptoed into the kitchen and heard Charlie splashing about in the bath. When the noise of the water abated they heard him humming a little tune.

The three women smiled as they listened. They had found and rescued Cara's brother.

Sitting at the kitchen table, Cara thought the first part of her challenge had been completed. She was pleased with her accomplishment, then Cara realized she had made herself responsible for the young brother she never knew existed until that day. It felt very strange to have a brother and she thought the boy must be feeling the same. She had never imagined having siblings but a loving warmth filled her as the joy of it overcame her. Still a teenager herself, she had not considered having to take care of a child until she was married and had a family of her own. Nevertheless, she had found Charlie and would do her utmost to make him feel part of the family. She felt again the ache in her heart as she thought how proud her grandmother would have been. Now though, she had to find Daisy. Would that complete their family or could there be others? Then of course there was the possible discovery of her parents. Cara's mind reeled with unanswered questions as she listened to her brother singing softly as he splashed about again in the tin bath.

Six

After their evening meal of faggots, grey peas and potatoes, Cara began to explain the events of the last few months. Charlie listened as Cara said, 'Our grandmother, Henrietta Selby, wanted me to find any remaining family and take care of them. Gracie and Molly, are helping me.'

Charlie nodded to each before returning his eyes to Cara.

'It was Martin Lander, the solicitor, who suggested we look in the workhouse in the first instance,' Cara added.

'So how come we didn't know about you?' Charlie asked.

'I don't know,' Cara answered truthfully, 'but until today, I didn't know about you and Daisy either. That's why I asked you about your parents' names, I needed to be sure they were the same as mine. That proves we are family, don't you think?' Cara's mounting excitement was infectious.

Charlie nodded with a big grin on his face. 'Our Daisy will be over the moon when she hears we have a big sister!' Then a forlorn look crossed his face as he thought about his younger sibling and where she might be.

'Charlie, may I ask you some more questions?' At his nod,

Cara went on, 'How did you and Daisy come to be in the workhouse?'

A sadness began to cloud his eyes as he spoke. 'Me dad was a carter an' he travelled all over the place. He never brought me mum any money – he spent it on beer before he got home.' A disgusted look crossed his face. 'Mum struggled to feed us, so I used to scavenge in the market. Daisy would have to coal pick on the slag heaps. Then one day me father came home drunk as a lord. Oh God, he battered our mum senseless! I couldn't stop him! I was only seven at the time. Our Daisy was five and scared witless.' Tears streamed from his eyes at the memory. 'Mum… mum had told us to stay upstairs, but we didn't.' He wiped his nose on the back of his hand before taking a deep breath to continue. 'We crept down to the kitchen and stood in the doorway. Daisy was bawling her eyes out as…' His speech stalled as he tried desperately to keep his sobs in check. '…dad kept hitting our mum! Sometimes I can still hear her screams!' Charlie's shoulders heaved as he finally gave way to his tears. After a moment he finally dragged his emotions in check and said, 'The next day dad sent us kids scavenging like nothing had happened!'

'Oh lad!' Gracie said, wiping away her tears.

Charlie had more to say. 'Well, when we got back from the market, the house was empty – they'd gone, both of them.'

'Oh my God!' Gracie said. 'They up and left you kids on your own?'

Cara's heart tightened at the thought of the children being abandoned so easily. This poor child had been left to take care of his younger sister and Cara felt a sob in her throat. How could parents do such things? How could *her* parents have done this terrible thing? More to the point, why had they done it?

Charlie nodded, shaking loose yet more tears from his eyes, then said, 'I don't think mum would have left us, but I suspect she had no choice.'

'Why is that, sweetheart?' Cara asked.

The endearment brought a quick smile to the boy's lips. 'Cos our dad was a bully! He probably would have killed her if she had refused him!' Tears welled up in his blue eyes.

'Don't distress yourself, mate,' Molly put in, 'I'm sure you would have pasted him good and proper had you been able.'

'I would an' all!' Charlie spat. 'It's our Daisy I worry about, she's ten… she's just a kid!'

Cara smiled inwardly. At only twelve himself he was hardly a man yet. 'Well don't you worry, we'll find Daisy.'

'How, Miss?' Charlie choked on his tears, desperately trying to hold them back.

'Cara, my name is Cara. You don't have to call me "Miss" because I'm your sister. I know it might feel awkward, but we have to get used to the idea we are family. As for Daisy… well, we have the address she went to, so I think we should visit.'

'But what if she ain't there anymore?' Charlie became increasingly agitated.

'It's a start, isn't it? Besides, we found you. What were the odds of that? Now then, I think it's time you got some sleep. Come on and I'll show you your bedroom.' Cara walked from the kitchen and up the stairs. Behind her Charlie said his goodnights and thanked Gracie for his 'lovely dinner'.

Cara led Charlie up the stairs and opening a door leading off the landing said, 'This will be your room, Charlie.' Cara watched the boy look around him. 'Molly will give it a clean for you once a week, other than that no one will enter. If you need quiet time, this is the place.'

The young boy rushed up to her, throwing his arms around her waist. 'Thank you Cara, thank you, thank you, thank you!' He sobbed like his heart would break. He had tried so hard to pretend he was a grown-up, but he now gave way to being a child once more. Tears of relief flowed freely as he pushed his life in the workhouse behind him.

Cara felt his small frame shudder as she wrapped her arms around him. 'It's all right, little brother, you're safe now. No one will ever hurt you again, I promise.'

As his sobs subsided she held him tightly and kissed his forehead. 'Tomorrow,' she whispered, 'we'll set out on another adventure. Tomorrow we're going to look for Daisy.'

Molly and Gracie had been discussing the fate of the Flowers children while Cara settled her new found brother in his bedroom.

As she returned to the kitchen wiping away her own tears, the discussion began again.

'Well we now know the children were abandoned. I wonder how they ended up in the workhouse,' Cara said as she sat at the table once more.

'Buggered if I know,' Gracie muttered as she poured more tea.

'Do you think Charlie took them there in utter desperation?' Cara asked. 'Or do you think they were forced in by someone else?'

Molly asked, 'Who? Who would force a couple of kids into that dreadful place?'

Cara shook her head. 'This challenge is leading us along an unknown path. However, I'm certainly learning quickly.

Money opens doors and provides confidential information. I know there's poverty here in Bilston, but it seems nothing compared to the lives of those poor people in the workhouse.' Breathing in through her nose, she went on, anger lacing her words. 'Lives is entirely the wrong word – existence! Those people are merely existing in that place, waiting for the day they will die and be free of their misery!'

Molly and Gracie exchanged a look as Cara spat, 'Something must be done about that place!'

'If only...' Gracie muttered.

'Gracie, the Tulleys are getting fat off the backs of people who can't defend themselves!' Cara was getting herself in a state about the whole thing.

'I know that, wench, but what can we do?' Gracie held out her hands.

Cara sighed through her nose, her lips set in a tight line. Then she said, 'I don't know... as yet.'

The cook and the maid exchanged another look which said, *'Look out! Cara's got a bee in her bonnet now!'*

'I think maybe it's time to have another word with Martin Lander,' Cara said as if to herself.

*

Charlie woke early out of habit but was afraid to open his eyes in case it had all been a beautiful dream. The sound of the birds' dawn chorus made him snap open his eyes and, sitting up, he gazed around. It had not been a dream, it was true. He *had* been rescued! He had been found and saved by an older sister he never knew he had. He sat in his bed for a moment and pondered. He liked Cara, she was gentle and caring and he was glad she was his sister. Then his mind turned to Daisy and the joy he was feeling was tempered. But then again, if Cara had found him, maybe she would find their little sister. His excitement grew again at the prospect.

Jumping out of bed, his toe caught against something cold which emitted a resounding ring. Looking beneath the bedstead, he found a chamber pot.

'Bloody hell!' he muttered. 'I've even got me own guzunder!' Laughing to himself, he dressed in the new clothes Molly had bought for him. The luxury of woollen socks meant his boots would no longer rub his feet raw.

Dashing down to the kitchen, he fed the range with coal and set the kettle to boil. Looking in the pantry, he gasped. There was enough food here to feed the whole workhouse!

Grabbing eggs and bacon, he scraped lard into a frying pan and dropping in the bacon he heard it sizzle.

The aroma of cooking bacon drifted upstairs and before long Gracie was rushing into the kitchen in her dressing gown.

Looking around, she gasped. The table was set and breakfast was almost ready. Plopping into a chair, she accepted the cup of tea offered by Charlie.

Moments later, Molly and Cara appeared, also in their dressing gowns, and laughed when Charlie said, 'Breakfast is up.' Sitting at the table, they all tucked in to bacon, eggs and fried bread washed down with hot tea.

When the women returned to the kitchen having dressed, delight showed on their faces. Not only had Charlie cooked breakfast, but he had also washed the dishes!

*

Charlie Flowers looked down at his new boots and grinned.

Never having had new footwear before, he felt like a king. 'These ain't half posh, I feel like a real toff now,' he laughed as he danced a little jig.

Walking from the shoe shop in Princes Street, the group sauntered down Duke Street. Charlie pulled his cap tight against his head, very much aware of his 'workhouse haircut.' Coming to the office of Lander, Holmes & Durwood, they all trooped inside requesting to see Mr Lander. Being led directly into his office, he greeted them all warmly. Once seated, Cara introduced her brother to Martin. The boy and man shook hands before Lander asked, 'How can I help you today, Miss Flowers?'

'Charlie's sister... *our* sister...' Cara corrected herself, 'was sold from the workhouse to this address.' She pushed a slip of paper across the desk. Martin read the address then nodded as he looked back at Cara. 'What we'd like to know is... can we get her back – legally?'

Mr Lander smiled then said, 'Is she definitely part of your family would be my first question?'

'Yes,' Cara answered without hesitation.

'Then yes, you can. The people who bought her may want proof, but legally they cannot refuse your request to return her to your care.' Martin gave the slip of paper back to Cara.

Charlie beamed. 'Can we go and get her now, Cara? Pleeease?'

'Shortly, but first I need to speak with Mr Lander in private.' Cara looked at Gracie.

Nodding, Gracie said, 'Come on, little man, Molly and me know where there's a bostin' suck shop.' Charlie's face lit up at the prospect of having some sweets.

Cara smiled at Gracie's use of the old Black Country term as the three filed out of the room.

'Mr Lander,' Cara launched in when the door was closed, 'Mr and Mrs Tulley who run the workhouse are making a great deal of money selling off the children. These children are kept in squalid conditions and fed slop! They are worked half to death and I fear the adults fare no better. What I want to know is... what can be done about this?'

Martin Lander drew in a deep breath and leaned back in his chair. 'Sadly, Miss Flowers, nothing can be done about it. The Board of Guardians are the ones who oversee the workhouse, and it's my guess they're probably unaware of the true goings-on in that place.'

'But...' Cara began.

Lander held up his hands, saying, 'I'm on your side regarding this, Miss Flowers. I don't like it any more than you do, but I don't see any way around it.'

'I want that place closed down!' Cara snapped.

'I can't see that happening in the foreseeable future,' Martin said with an apologetic smile. 'You see, proof... written proof... would be needed of Tulley's misdeeds. Or witnesses who would testify in court about cruelty or starvation suffered at the hands of that man.'

'There are over two hundred souls in that place, Mr Lander, any one of whom would stand up in court to testify, I'm sure.' Cara was not about to concede; her blood was up.

'All right, put it this way. Supposing Tulley was thrown in jail for his offences, would the Board of Guardians appoint another to take his place? Inarguably yes. So then we're back to square one. If, by some miracle, the place *was* closed down, what would happen to those two hundred souls you spoke of?' Martin dropped his hands on the arms of his chair indicating he had finished speaking.

This was something she hadn't considered. She felt the

anger rise in her and tears of pure frustration lined her lashes as she shook his hand. She was determined she would not cry in front of this man, but it took all her strength not to do so. Leaving his office, she thought, *Damn Tulley and his workhouse!*

Seven

Cara was still seething as they set out to look for Daisy, so Gracie suggested a calming cup of tea. Marching down the street, the others trailing in her wake, they eventually bustled into a small building squashed between two others.

Sitting at the back of the almost empty tea shop, Cara fought to quell the emotions she was feeling, then once she felt a little calmer, she quietly directed her words to Charlie. 'I need to know an awful lot more about that workhouse, Charlie. It needs shutting down, but I have to know how things work before I can even think about campaigning for its closure!'

'I don't know much about the workings of it, but I can tell you about what happened to me,' the boy said as he eyed the cream cake in his hand.

'That would be a good start. Maybe when we get home you could tell me what you know.' Cara smiled as Charlie nodded, his mouth full of cake. Then looking at her friends, she said, 'I'm on a mission, ladies, and it's your choice whether you join me or not.'

'I'm with you!' Gracie said.

'Me an' all,' Molly added.

'Good, but first we have to get our sister back, right Charlie?'

The boy nodded with a big smile but, truth be told, his attention was more on his cake at that precise moment. He'd never had a cream cake before and he was savouring its delicious flavour, his eyes closing to enjoy the full experience.

*

Passing the railway station, Cara stopped and gazed at the wealthier members of the town as they came and went. Ladies in their large feathered hats, parasols clutched in gloved hands. Gentlemen in their great coats and bowler or top hats holding onto silver-topped canes.

Moving on into Railway Street, Cara saw a distinct change in the clothing of the people. Here the women wore long dark skirts over worn-out boots. No hats adorned these heads, only patched shawls draped over hair that looked none too clean. The men walked with a weariness that cut to the soul, their moleskin trousers ending just short of hob nailed boots. They wore collarless shirts and waistcoats, with mufflers tied about the throat; their jackets were threadbare. No top hats here, only flat caps pulled low over tired eyes.

Walking down the street that ran parallel to the railway line, Cara studied the buildings around her and the people she passed. Even in the weak sunshine, everyone walked with lowered heads. Poverty was beating them down; ambitions once felt in their youth had left them. The only thing left to them was where their next meal would come from, old age and death.

No one spoke as Cara, Charlie, Molly and Gracie trudged

up Queen Street. The buildings were more scattered, in fact only a handful were still standing along with the Prince of Wales public house. The house they were to visit sat directly opposite the pub and Cara, the others in tow, marched up the garden path. Her anger had not completely abated and she hammered on the front door. A woman in a dirty apron answered, her hair escaping the confines of a make-shift turban.

'What?' The woman was obviously unhappy about being disturbed.

Cara's anger bubbled up once more at being spoken to in such a way. Manners cost nothing.

'I'm looking for a child called Daisy Flowers.'

'Well, her ain't here,' the woman said, wiping her hands on the apron.

'Can you tell me where she is?' Cara heard Charlie gasp then asked.

'No.' The woman's hands now rested on her hips.

'May I ask why not?' Cara sighed. This was the usual way Black Country people communicated – short answers but 'going around the houses' to get to the point.

'You can ask,' the woman said.

'Why can't you tell me where she is?' Cara only just held on to her temper.

'Cos I don't know where her is!' the woman retorted.

'And why would that be?' Cara's patience was fast running out.

'Her run off a few weeks back... I ain't seen her since.'

Charlie, who stood by Cara's side, gasped at the woman's words.

'Thank you!' Cara snapped. Turning on her heel, she marched between Molly and Gracie, and grabbing Charlie's hand walked swiftly away from the house, hearing the sound of the door slamming behind her.

Retracing their steps, again no one spoke. They had reached a dead end. Cara's anger at the woman receded as she considered where they could next search for Daisy. The child could be anywhere. She felt a coldness in her bones as she wondered if her sister was still alive. She could have starved to death; she could have died at the hands of another...

Pushing away the thoughts that left her shivering, she picked up her pace. She wanted to have everyone safely home.

*

Martin Lander leaned back in his chair and propped his feet on the desk in his office, contemplating the conversation he'd had with Cara Flowers. He did not know the lady well but her determination to find her siblings was evident. She had found young Charlie and was now in pursuit of a sister called Daisy. Once the child was safely in her care, Martin felt sure Cara would find a way to take on the institution known as the workhouse. How she would go about this he didn't know, but he was certain she would give her all in an attempt to, at the very least, upset the regime.

Martin knew little about that place other than sharing the dread of it with every person in the town. He had heard the stories of the cruelty and starvation which were told by people who had been 'bought out' as servants. The majority of inmates, however, were resigned to their fate of never being free from institutional life again.

His heart sank as he considered this: how would he feel about being locked away for the rest of his life? Of having very little food? Of having to break rocks for no pay? Of spending all his time with other men and not seeing another female form? Of never being married or having children of his own? As he considered these questions he felt the anger of it all rise within him. The people in that place were prisoners, held fast by their own unfortunate circumstances. It was certainly a gross injustice.

Moving to the little fire on the other side of his office, he stabbed it with the poker then threw on more coal. As the flames licked the nuggets, he wondered how cold the workhouse was in winter. Again his anger bubbled up. As he retook his seat, a realization struck him which made him smile. Now he knew how Cara Flowers felt! He understood what fuelled her anger and frustration, it was that no one was helping the poor ensconced in the Workhouse, and he set his mind to helping the pretty young woman in any way he could.

*

Back at The Laburnums, Charlie, Gracie and Molly sat around the kitchen table, as Cara's frustration mounted. She paced back and forth, her hands clenching and unclenching. She drew breath in through her nose and puffed it out of her mouth. 'Why couldn't the woman answer my question in the first place?'

'Cos that aint the Black Country way, wench,' Gracie said.

'Now we have no idea where Daisy might be.'

'She could be anywhere,' Charlie agreed sadly.

'Well at least we know she's not in the dreadful workhouse or with that termagant of a woman!' Cara said.

Cara felt Charlie's eyes on her and as she looked back her heart went out to him. He was relying on her to find

Daisy. The onus was squarely on her shoulders to discover the whereabouts of the child.

'Charlie,' she said gently, 'I know it must be painful for you, but I have to know everything you can tell me, so I might know where to look for Daisy.'

The boy's head dropped as he relived old memories. Then, taking a deep breath, he began. 'We lived in a little cottage out on the heath by the railway. It was a dump, but it was our dump!' His chest puffed out slightly, showing he was immensely proud of their 'dump'. 'I aint sure who it belonged to, but mum never had the rent money, cos that.... Cos dad had drunk it all up the wall! So when the rent man came calling, we had to hide. Mum turned it into a game for us so Daisy wouldn't get scared.' He tried to give a little smile at the memory, but it only lifted the corners of his mouth.

Cara gave him a small smile of encouragement.

'When Daisy and me came back and found them gone, mum and dad I mean, we d'aint know what to do at first. Daisy cried and cried, and I tell you I felt like it an' all, but I knew I had to be strong for her. So we went scavenging, and I turned it into a game like our mum would have done.' A sob escaped his lips and the tears showed themselves once more. 'Then we waited, hoping they'd come home, but they didn't. Well, one day we didn't hide fast enough when the rent man came. When he found out our parents had done a flit, he reported us and we was chucked in the workhouse.' His eyes moved to Gracie on her sharp intake of breath. 'When we was took in there, our Daisy was put in with the other girls and she screamed the place down. I couldn't get to her, they held me back and she was crying and screaming out my name as the women dragged her away.' Charlie began to cry out loud, unable to hold back any longer. 'I ain't never felt so bad in all my life!' He said at last, 'Then I was dragged away as well and told I'd be in with the boys. The matron had my hair shaved off and then I was scrubbed down with carbolic soap. My own clothes were taken away, and I was given them rotten old clothes you burnt, Mrs Cox. My own clothes d'aint fit any more anyway.' Charlie wiped his nose on a handkerchief handed to him by Gracie, but his sobs continued.

'What was the food like, Charlie?' Gracie asked.

'Thin soup mostly, made outta rotting vegetables. God, it was horrible, tasted like horse…' His sentence trailed off as he cast a glance at Cara. 'At least when I scavenged, the bits I got were fresh!' Charlie swelled a little with pride at the memory.

'Go on, Charlie, you're doing so well,' Cara whispered.

'Ar well,' he sniffed, 'we was supposed to go to school in the workhouse… and some did for three hours a day, but old Tulley kept me oakum picking. That's unpicking old rope with a metal spike. It don't half hurt your hands, makes 'em bleed if you don't do it right. It d'aint matter about the school though, cos our mum had taught us our letters and numbers.' Again, tears formed at the memory and Charlie lowered his head to hide his misery.

Gracie listened as she bustled about the kitchen making tea. Molly grabbed the cake and sliced it, her eyes constantly darting to the young boy.

'Now, Charlie, when I was in Tulley's office I saw a cupboard full of canes.' Cara saw him nod. 'Were you ever caned?'

He shook his head and Cara sighed with relief.

Gracie spoke up, 'Thank the Lord for that!'

With tea and cake before him, Charlie nodded his thanks

before he continued. 'No, I wasn't caned but there was plenty who were.'

'Whatever for?' Molly asked in disbelief.

'Some of the older lads got cocky and answered Tulley back, for which they got a thrashing. The schoolmaster caned some for being unable to learn their letters. It weren't their fault, they was just slow.' Charlie bit into his cake as he watched the women exchange a glance. 'One little kid got so scared he wet his pants and we found him in a drawstring bag hanging from the rafters crying his heart out. A couple of the big boys got him down and Tulley thrashed them for interfering.' Charlie finished his cake and sipped his hot tea.

'Jesus Christ!' Gracie gasped, her hand flying to her chest. 'You hear such terrible stories about this sort of thing, but I always hoped it weren't true.'

'It still goes on, Mrs Cox, and it will until someone puts a stop to it.' Charlie's eyes moved back to his big sister and Cara felt the weight of obligation settle on her.

'The Matron used to thrash us with a stick as well sometimes,' Charlie muttered.

'Christ A'mighty!' Gracie rasped through clenched teeth. 'What I'd like to do to that woman!'

'Me an' all,' Molly added.

'Charlie, a very important question now. Was anyone killed while you were there?' Cara had to ask, she needed ammunition if she were to fight this battle.

'Not killed as far as I know. If somebody got ill they was put in the hospital part and the doctor would come. I couldn't be sure about anyone dying, cos it were the men who worked the mortuary.' Charlie sighed as if in resignation. 'I suppose that's life... or in this case... death.'

Cara was amazed at the adult way Charlie was relating his experiences of the workhouse.

'I think that's enough for now.' Cara said, 'Charlie you've done well.'

'What about our Daisy?' he asked.

'We will find her, but at the moment I'm not sure where to look. One thing I am sure of though, I won't give up looking for her.' Cara steeled her resolve once more.

The boy said quietly, 'Neither will I.'

Eight

Cara sat on the bench in the garden enjoying the sunshine. A warm breeze blew and the birds were singing and squabbling in the laburnum trees. She shaded her eyes to watch them a moment then her mind drifted back to the missing child – her sister. Where was Daisy Flowers? Where would she have gone when she ran away from the house in Queen Street? Did she know the area?

Suddenly jumping up, Cara ran into the house yelling for Charlie. The boy came running immediately at the urgency of her call.

'Charlie, does Daisy know the area?' Cara asked quickly as she held onto the boy's shoulders.

'Ar, I suppose. Her used to come scavenging with me, so her knows the market and her knows the cottage we lived in.'

'Get your coat,' Cara said, 'we're going out.'

Charlie grabbed his jacket from the coat stand in the hall while Cara dashed to the kitchen to inform Gracie and Molly where they were going.

Brother and sister walked briskly down Proud's Lane.

'Where we going?' Charlie asked.

'We are going to the market first. We'll ask around, maybe someone has seen Daisy,' Cara said as they crossed the bridge over the railway line.

'I never thought of that!' Charlie laughed.

'Well let's not get too excited, but at least it's another avenue to explore,' Cara said. However, unable to contain their excitement, they both walked a little faster.

Eventually coming to the market in Vine Street, Cara stopped. 'I need you to take me everywhere you went to scavenge. Do people here know you?'

Charlie's head bobbed up and down, saying, 'Ar, me and Daisy was well known by the stallholders. They helped us a lot; they gave us stuff, you know, like an old frock for Daisy once, but more important was they gave us bits of food. At least we could have a bit of dinner then, otherwise we'd have gone hungry, which we did often enough. I may be a bit older now, but I'm sure they'll still remember me.'

'Right, let's go.' Cara followed behind the boy as he walked through the outdoor market. Threading his way between the stalls, he passed the time of day with the women. Cara smiled at the ease with which Charlie laughed and joked with the stallholders. He was comfortable with them because he trusted them.

Going to a woman who had once saved him from being caught by the market inspector by hiding him beneath her long outer skirt, he asked, 'Hiya Mrs, remember me?' He pasted a grin on his face.

'Who could forget you, you young rascal!' The woman returned.

'Here, have you seen our Daisy lately?' he asked.

'Ar Charlie, her was here yesterday… why? You ain't gone and lost her have you?' The woman grinned.

Charlie said, 'You know our Daisy, always going missing. Thanks Mrs.' Turning to Cara, he said joyfully. 'Well, at least she's still alive!' Then his smile turned down, 'Where is Daisy now though?'

'Where is your old cottage?' Cara asked, feeling her heart beat faster as hope began to rise within her.

'My God! You think her's gone back there?' Charlie was beside himself and began to shuffle from foot to foot as his excitement rose.

'Let's go and have a look!' Cara said as she tugged on the boy's sleeve.

Setting off, they ran through the streets so fast it made people stare. On past the iron and brass foundry and out onto the small heath that separated the dilapidated building from the town, they ran.

Stopping short, Charlie gasped. 'Look!'

Cara followed the direction his finger pointed and saw the faintest wisp of smoke escape the broken chimney. As they ran, she saw the true state of the cottage. She was sure it could fall down at any minute. Clearly it had been deserted and had stood empty for some time. She struggled to keep up with her brother as he sped across the uneven ground.

Bursting in through the door, he yelled, 'Daisy? Daisy, you here? Daisy, it's me... Charlie!'

Boots sounded on the wooden stairs and a small dirty girl shot through the doorway straight into Charlie's arms.

'Charlie...!' The girl sobbed. 'Oh Charlie! I d'aint never think to see you again!'

Charlie held onto his sister's thin body as she cried. 'Awww, come on it ain't that bad,' he said, trying to quell Daisy's tears as well as his own. However, she was having none of it and cried all the harder. She held him so tight he thought his ribs would crack.

'It's all right now, kiddo, I'm back!' he said, holding her tight. 'Look here, this is Cara.'

The girl peeped shyly at Cara before her tears began to fall again.

Charlie kept his arms tight around her thin frame as he talked quietly to her. 'Daisy... stop crying and listen to me,' he urged, but no amount of coaxing would encourage Daisy to stop. 'All right half pint, you cry it out.' Kissing the top of her head, he waited while his younger sibling wept.

Cara stood by and watched, her brows drawn together in angst. She placed her hand over her mouth to silence the sobs she felt pulling at her chest. She didn't feel she could intervene; this was something they needed to do together, for all she wanted to gather them both in her arms. Her heart was close to breaking as she saw Charlie's shoulders heaving up and down as he held Daisy close to him. He was silently sobbing his heart out too.

Cara felt her own tears sting then roll down her cheeks as she watched her family, until at last sniffs took the place of sobs.

Then Charlie spoke again. 'Where have you been, Daisy? You been in this place since you ran away from Queen Street?'

The child nodded, 'How did you know I ran away?'

'Well... first of all, this lady is Cara Flowers...' Charlie began.

Daisy glanced over and cut in with, 'You got the same name as us!' Then she sniffed loudly before wiping her nose with her sleeve.

Cara stepped forward, handing her a clean handkerchief. 'That's because we are family. I'm your big sister, Daisy.'

'Well Charlie is my brother!' Daisy stated.

'I know, he's my brother too,' Cara smiled down at the dirty face watching her.

'It's right, kiddo, Cara found me and got me out of the Spike and took me to her house. Then we set out to look for you!'

Daisy eyed the young woman Charlie called Cara suspiciously before turning her attention back to her brother. 'I ain't half glad you found me, Charlie. I was ever so worried. I thought you was killed. Have I got to go to her house as well? I want to stay here, I want to stay at home. Why can't we both stay here, Charlie, just you and me like it was before?' Daisy still clung on tightly to her big brother.

Cara felt she had her work cut out with this young lady. Charlie looked at Cara for help and she answered gently, 'It's cold here, Daisy, and there's no food. When you get to my house, you'll have a nice hot dinner and... a room of your own!'

The young girl was still not convinced. She cowered behind Charlie's legs. Cara knew she was afraid. After all she'd been through, now a stranger had come to take her away from her home again. As she thought about the best way to coax the child into coming with her, Cara was surprised by a question.

'Did you find our mum and dad?' Daisy suddenly asked.

Cara scooched down so her eyes were at the same level as Daisy's. 'No, Daisy, not yet, but I will search for them.'

'Can I help?' the child asked.

'Yes of course you can, but first let's get home and get you fed, shall we?'

Reluctantly Daisy took a step to the side of her big brother and grasped his hand tightly. Her other hand went to her mouth as she dipped her head shyly.

Cara walked from the cottage; Charlie and Daisy behind her, chatting quietly together.

Relief had flooded Charlie when they had found Daisy. He had been unable to hold back his tears of joy, and had vowed to himself he would forever watch over her, no matter how old she was. He thought he would dearly like to find his mum too… but he prayed he never met up with his dad this side of the grave, so great was his anger at the man.

On their walk back to The Laburnums, Daisy clung to Charlie's hand. She began to speak and talked the whole way there.

'Mrs Tulley told me I was going to live with a nice lady who would look after me,' she said, 'well, the lady wasn't nice at all! I had to do all the chores and I didn't get much to eat. What you scavenged from the market was better, our Charlie.'

Cara and the boy exchanged a smile as Daisy's voice droned on. 'Then I got smacked a lot cos she said I back-chatted her. I suppose I did, a bit, but not enough to be clouted for it, and then…'

Cara grinned at Charlie as he shrugged his shoulders. Obviously he was au fait with Daisy's incessant chatter. For Cara it would take some getting used to.

Cara could hear Charlie reassuring his sister all would be well and there was nothing to be afraid of. She smiled to herself when she heard Daisy chuckle at something Charlie had whispered. She hoped this meant the young girl was warming to the idea of having a sister as well as a brother, and that they would all be living together. She knew it would take time to adjust, but she prayed Daisy would be happy once she'd settled in.

Arriving at the house, Cara led them straight to the kitchen.

'Daisy, this is Gracie Cox, my friend and she's a fantastic cook. This is Molly Barton, who is also my friend and the maid here,' Cara said, 'Ladies, this is our sister, Daisy Flowers!'

The two women welcomed the young girl with hot tea and a plate of sausage and mash with thick onion gravy. All sat around the table to enjoy their meal. Daisy continued to talk between mouthfuls of food. Sly grins passed across the table as they all listened.

Later, Molly prepared the tin bath and set water to heat. Cara found one of her nightgowns for Daisy to use until new clothes could be purchased later in the day.

Daisy watched the flurry of activity whilst staying close to her brother.

'Daisy,' Molly said tenderly, 'when you've finished your dinner you can have a nice warm bath.'

The child's eyes opened in horror at the thought, but Charlie held his nose between his thumb and index finger and said, 'Our Daisy, you do stink a bit.'

'That's not a nice thing to say to a lady!' Daisy retorted and everyone fell about laughing.

'I'm so sorry, your Highness,' Charlie said, giving a little bow, 'but just so you know, I had a bath too when I came here.'

Daisy cocked an eyebrow and looked at him as though she didn't believe a word of it.

Molly whispered in Daisy's ear, just loud enough for everyone to hear. 'I know where Cara keeps her fancy soap.' With a wink from the maid and a nod from Daisy, the bargain was struck. She would relent and have a bath on the proviso she could use Cara's special soap. Cara was delighted that Daisy appeared to be settling in quite well, and pretended not to have overheard the whispered conversation.

Gracie filled the bath and again ensured the temperature was correct. Everyone left the kitchen while Gracie bathed the young girl, singing softly to her all the time.

Dressed now in a voluminous white cotton nightgown which belonged to Cara, Daisy followed Cara upstairs and into her bedroom, which was next door to Charlie's room.

'Charlie's room is right there in case you need him,' Cara said as she watched Daisy gaze around in awe. For once the girl was speechless. 'Molly said she'll go to town for some new clothes for you later, then tomorrow we'll go shopping and you can fill your wardrobe and drawers. We'll get you some new shoes and a bonnet until your hair grows back properly.' She smiled as Daisy rubbed a hand over her short hair.

Daisy felt like she was in a dream, her only fear was she would wake and find herself back in the workhouse. She had never seen such luxury. A bed of her own, which meant she didn't have to share a pallet with Charlie. She walked over and touched the pretty curtains and peered through the window at the garden. Her small hand stroked the dresser gently as she walked around the room. *Her* room. She twirled around with her arms outstretched and began to sing a little ditty. Her excitement became contagious and Cara joined her. Dizzy, they both fell on the bed laughing heartily.

Later, Daisy sat by the fire in the parlour with the others and listened as Cara explained about the challenge set down by their grandmother before she died. She heard about Charlie being bought out of the workhouse, and how Molly and Gracie helped find her brother. The next step of the challenge was to discover if their parents were still alive, and if so, where they were.

A talkative Daisy asked many questions which were answered by a patient Cara. The youngster related her experience of the workhouse to the others; how Ada Tulley had smacked her often for being outspoken.

Charlie fumed as he listened. He said, 'The matron informed me herself that Daisy had been sold and laughed spitefully as she did so.'

Daisy added, 'I sometimes had to work in the kitchen but it weren't so bad, cos the inmates gave me little treats. I once had a bendy carrot. Another time I had a whole apple all to myself! I liked the cook, she was a nice lady.' Daisy prattled on and before long she began to yawn.

'Come on young lady I think it's time for you to be heading up the wooden hills to Bedfordshire,' Cara said with a smile.

Daisy nodded and said her goodnights following her big sister up the stairs. Cara settled a very tired Daisy into bed, leaving the door open in case the child became frightened in the night. Then she returned to the parlour.

Charlie had also retired to bed and for a while they could hear the children talking and laughing. Then all went quiet… asleep at last.

'She's sound asleep now by the sound of it.' Cara whispered.

Tiptoeing up the stairs and peeping into Daisy's room, she saw her sister snuggled up in the bedclothes and big brother lying on top of the bed close to her, both fast asleep. Despite having their own rooms, they were obviously overjoyed to be together again and Cara smiled at the scene before her. With both hands covering her mouth, Cara stood and watched them for a while. A tear of joy seeped from the corner of her eye as she whispered, 'Goodnight, my darlings, sleep well.'

Quietly making her way downstairs, Cara sat again in the kitchen and the three women began to discuss the day's events.

'Thank God the little mite was found safe and well,' Gracie said. 'So, what's next?'

'I suppose I should try to find my parents,' Cara muttered, 'though I have no idea how to go about it. I have to say too that I'm a bit scared of finding my father after what Charlie told us about him. Maybe I should visit Josiah Colley again; it might be he's discovered something in his records. After all, deaths as well as marriages are recorded. If they are dead, then our search ends right there.'

'What if he's not found anything?' Molly asked.

Cara shrugged her tired shoulders. 'We could ask questions of the carters, one of them may have known my father. For now, however, I'm just glad we saved those two upstairs.' She raised her eyes to the ceiling indicating the two sleeping children.

The women clinked teacups in congratulations.

'Now they are safe at last,' Cara said. Looking up, she saw Molly stifle a sob. 'Oh Molly, don't get upset.'

'I'm not upset, I'm just so… happy!' Molly answered, her tears flowing now.

Gracie lifted her apron to her eyes to dry her own eyes and before long all three were crying tears of happiness.

Lying in bed later that evening, tired but unable to sleep, Cara's mind went over the events of the day. Thrilled at finding Daisy alive, she knew she now had two children to take care of. It was a big responsibility for someone so young, but she was determined she would do her best.

Besides, she had Gracie and Molly to help. Her friends were proving to be invaluable assets and she felt blessed.

Cara whispered into the darkness, 'I've found your other granddaughter now too, Grandma. I wish you were here to see her. You would love her dearly.' Cara wept quietly as she felt again the pain of her loss. 'Oh Grandma, I miss you so much!' Burying her face in her pillow, she finally gave way to great heaving sobs.

*

The fortnightly meeting of the Board of Guardians of the workhouse was in full swing. The Board was constructed entirely of prominent businessmen who were elected into office by the parishioners. Under the Poor Law Regulations, the parishioners were required to pay rates which were collected by the Parish Overseer. These monies were used to run the workhouse. The overall organization of the place and management of the inmates was undertaken by the Master. Being a Master meant a job for life, unless he was dismissed for some proven indiscretion. It was the Board's decision whether a Master should be forgiven or summarily dismissed. The Matron, usually wife or sister to the Master, but not always, had the responsibility for management of the women and children. She was considered a deputy to the Master.

There was also a visiting committee made up of members of the Board of Guardians. It was a very tight-knit community which was involved with the day-to-day running of the institution. Each of the Board members were friends and would often meet socially as well as for business.

The visiting committee visited weekly to check that the

workhouse was being run properly and the inmates were treated fairly. They were also there to listen to any complaints, which would be recorded in the visitor's book. Tulley's book had no complaints listed, which gave the Board the impression no one ever grumbled about the food or dire conditions in which they lived. In truth, the dread of punishment kept all inmates' mouths firmly closed.

There were fourteen questions the Board were required to ask of workhouse staff, and so it went...

Is the workhouse clean and well ventilated and are the beds in proper order?

Mrs Tulley nodded as she said, 'Yes, indeed they are.'

Are the inmates clean and orderly in their behaviour, and are their clothes changed regularly?

Another nod from the Matron, another 'Yes.' In point of fact the inmates were rarely given access to the bathing facilities, and their clothes were changed when Ada felt the need, which was once a week, usually on the days the Board convened.

Are the inmates kept in work and is that work unobjectionable?

Fred Tulley assured the Board that work was being undertaken. The bone and stone crushing was most definitely objectionable to the inmates, but not to Tulley. After all, he didn't have to do it.

Are the infirm properly attended to?

'We have no infirm inmates at the present time,' the Master said keeping his mouth shut about the two women who his wife had told him complained of having bad backs.

Are the children properly instructed in school and their industrial training properly attended to?

'Three hours a day, as laid down in the rules,' Mrs Tulley

answered knowing full well the rules would be ignored and the children put to work instead.

Are the younger children properly nursed and has every child been vaccinated?

'Yes indeed sirs!' Ada beamed. It was the doctor attached to the workhouse who insisted he be called out to undertake the vaccinations of all new children admitted.

Is there regular attendance by a medical officer; are inmates in proper sick wards; are there any infectious diseases in the workhouse?

Fred assured the Board all was well on that score. The doctor came as soon as he was called, the sick ward was empty and there were no infectious diseases in *his* workhouse!

Were there any dangerous lunatics or idiots in the workhouse?

Tulley shook his head in answer, accompanied by a firm, 'No. We would inform the lunatic asylum should we feel the need.'

Are prayers regularly read?

The Master nodded, saying they were. A lie, but lies slipped too easily from Tulley's tongue. He was not prepared to pay out good money to the vicar to perform Sunday service. If the inmates wished to pray, they could do it at their work or in their beds.

Is the customary established diet duly observed and are mealtimes adhered to?

'Most definitely!' Ada confirmed. What Ada considered to be the customary diet was not at all in agreement with the rulings; it was, however, served at regular times.

Are provisions and other supplies of the qualities contracted for?

Another nod from Tulley, 'Indeed sirs.'

Is the classification properly observed?

'It is, each inmate in their own wing of the house, sirs,' Tulley said.

Have there been any complaints by the paupers against an officer or about the accommodation?

'Most definitely not!' Ada said, smoothing her long apron and drawing her head back on her neck revealing a saggy double chin. She was aware the inmates knew better than to complain.

Does the number of inmates exceed that fixed by the Poor Law Commissioners?

'No, sirs. In fact we have plenty of room for more,' Tulley grinned. The more coming in, the more could be sold on, the more money in his pocket. To Tulley, this made good business sense.

Every two weeks the same questions, the same answers. It was a necessary business procedure that needed to be adhered to before the serious business of eating could begin.

As the Board members cleared away their papers and headed for the dining hall, thin women brought out platters of cheese, cold beef and ham, pickles, fresh baked bread still warm from the oven, butter and an array of fruit. Wine was poured into glasses which stood by china plates flanked by metal cutlery. Condiments graced the centre of the table. Napkins were folded neatly on the plates.

The serving women kept their eyes on the floor as they laid the food on the table before quietly leaving the room. Conversation began as food was piled onto plates. The wine flowed freely and the afternoon passed with business being conducted which had absolutely nothing whatsoever to do with the management of the workhouse.

The Master's laughter boomed out as his wife ensured all

the wine glasses were kept topped up. Tulley was a happy man, his wealth from selling inmates was growing, he was well fed and he had a job for life. He had no way of knowing that at some time in the not too distant future his world would be turned upside down… by the young woman he had so recently met for the first time. He had underestimated her, but only time would confirm this.

Nine

Cara was dressed to impress in a bottle-green suit. The long velvet skirt brushed against her leather boots as she walked. Her jacket nipped in at the waist and the deep reveres lay over a white high-neck lace blouse. Stepping into the office of Lander, Holmes & Durwood, she nodded at the secretary. Moments later she sat opposite Martin Lander.

'I'm glad to see you again, Miss Flowers,' Martin's eyes twinkled as he smiled at her.

'And I, you, Mr Lander.' Cara returned the smile. 'I have come to tell you that we have found Daisy Flowers and she is safe at home with her... *my* brother.'

'That is very good news!' Lander said as he clasped his hands together. 'So what can I do for you today?'

'Mr Lander... I need to be appointed to the Board of Guardians at the workhouse.' Cara kept her voice calm.

The smile on Martin's face instantly disappeared and shock replaced it as he shot forward in his chair. He saw no smile on Cara's face which told him she was not joking. 'Miss Flowers! That, I'm afraid, is quite impossible!' *My God!* he thought, *this girl is perfectly serious!* 'Miss Flowers... Cara...'

Martin said in a placating manner, 'the Board of Guardians are all well-respected gentlemen of the town. Businessmen who were elected to office by the parishioners. If you will forgive my saying, you are not well known in the town, you are not in business and… you are a woman.'

Cara guessed he might cite these reasons and she readied herself. 'Mr Lander, the Master is selling off the *inmates*!' Her voice showed her disgust at the term used for the people forced into the workhouse through no fault of their own. 'He is selling them as slaves to the wealthy!'

'Do you have proof of your accusations, Miss Flowers?' Martin was shocked at the outburst from who he saw as a delicate young woman.

'Yes I do!' Cara confirmed. 'I have the paperwork I received in exchange for Charlie!' She was becoming angry that she was making no inroads with this man.

'May I see it please?' Martin asked.

Cara rummaged in her bag and produced the paper. She watched as the solicitor read it.

Looking up, he sighed and said, 'How much did you pay for Charlie's release?'

'Five pounds!' Cara suddenly felt her stomach lurch, her anger suddenly turning to despair. 'The amount is written on the paper… isn't it?'

Passing the paper back to her, Cara's eyes scanned every word. There was no mention of any money exchanged. Tear-filled eyes looked at the man sat at the other side of the huge desk, his mouth set in a tight line. Cara wondered how she could have been so stupid.

'Tulley is a sly one, Cara. I'm afraid you've been duped.' Martin felt sorry for the beautiful girl sat in his office.

'However, the saving grace is you did rescue Charlie and now you have found Daisy too.'

Nodding, Cara put the paper back in her bag. 'Thank you Mr Lander,' she said as she rose to leave.

'I'm sorry I couldn't help you, Miss Flowers, but don't be disheartened.' Martin rounded the desk to show her out.

Giving a single nod, Cara walked through the open doorway, leaving the office without a backward glance. Her anger rose as she made her way home, by which time it was replaced by frustrated tears.

Back home, Gracie patted Cara's back gently as she cried, 'Lander is right, Cara, the Board of Guardians… them's dead men's shoes.' Seeing the puzzled look, Gracie explained: 'You'd have to wait for one of them to die before applying for the position. Besides which, you being a woman… they'd never allow it.'

'Oh Gracie, we have to do something… those poor children!' Cara was adamant but at a loss as to what to do next.

'Maybe we should concentrate on trying to find your parents first,' Molly interjected.

'Perhaps you're right,' Cara muttered, feeling utterly dejected.

The cook and the maid exchanged a glance; they knew full well Cara was not about to let this go. Molly raised her eyebrows and Gracie gave an imperceptible shake of her head. They knew she was determined enough to find a way of trying to help the families living in Bilston workhouse.

Lying in bed that night, Cara went over in her mind what she knew of the workhouse. The Relieving Officer would visit poor families in the parish and offer them a 'ticket' to the place, if it were deemed they could not provide for themselves adequately. She knew about the Local Government Board and the Board of Guardians. Other than what Charlie had told her she knew very little else and set her mind to finding out more. If she were to take on the might of these two prestigious boards, she had to be very sure of herself. As everyone had told her it was one thing to challenge the workhouse, it was quite another to do so as a woman!

*

Martin Lander had also set himself a task – for the past couple of days since Cara had announced her intentions of joining the Board of Guardians, he had been brushing up on his knowledge of the New Poor Law of 1834 and any revisions made in recent years. Searching out the necessary books, he began to read up on the law and he noted the main provisions were to discourage vagrancy; also, any relief given to the poor of the parish in their own homes was stopped.

A grin came over his face as he noted that in 1875 in Kensington the first woman was appointed to the Board of Guardians. To apply for the position women had to meet the property requirement. This was good news and he felt Cara would be delighted. However, she would have to be voted in by the parishioners at the next elections. Scouring his books, he discovered the next round of elections was the following year. Cara had twelve months to make herself and her intentions known to the general populace. Leaning back in his chair, Martin wondered how the girl would go about it.

Later that day, Lander telephoned Cara. She had called in the previous day and given him the number of the newly installed telephone system, 'Miss Flowers, I have good news for you!' he said excitedly.

On the other end of the line, Cara listened carefully. This was the first time she had used the telephone and it was proving very useful indeed. She'd spent the last couple of days, in between settling the children in, trying to come up with a plan for the workhouse, but all of her ideas had been fruitless, until now. Thanking Martin, Cara placed the handset down and returned to the others in the kitchen. Explaining what Martin had told her, she grinned when Molly asked, 'You ain't thinking of becoming a member of the Board of Guardians, surely?'

'I think that's exactly what she has in mind!' Gracie said.

'According to Martin, I have one year to prepare for it. Now what I need are ideas on how to go about getting myself known in the town. I need to let people know I'm out to improve things for their benefit.'

Charlie had stood quietly in the doorway listening to the conversation, then he said, 'Start in the market.'

Cara whipped round at his voice. 'Oh Charlie, you startled me, I didn't know you were there. Come on in and join us.'

Charlie, closely followed by Daisy, moved into the kitchen. 'The women in the market work long and hard and have a mortal fear of that workhouse.'

'So you think I should get the women onside to further my cause?' Cara asked.

The boy nodded. 'No woman wants to have to take her kids in that awful place. Unless someone steps in, it won't ever get any better.'

'The lad has a point there,' Gracie said as she brought out some biscuits for the children.

'Looks like I will have to campaign. I'm going to need a good strategy because the men on the current Board will not take kindly to a woman standing for election.' Cara sat resting her elbows on the table, her chin on her hands. Daisy climbed onto a chair and mimicked her big sister's actions, much to the amusement of them all. Quiet titters ran round the room as Cara sighed; Daisy did the same. Cara slapped her hands on the table; Daisy copied her. Cara's hand went to her forehead, as did Daisy's. Cara poked out her tongue and Daisy squealed with delight. Everyone fell about laughing.

*

After trawling the market and engaging in lengthy discussions with the women who stood behind the stalls, Cara was left feeling despondent to say the least. They all gave the same answers to her questions. Yes, they wanted something done about the workhouse. Yes, they thought it was a good idea to have a woman on the Board of Guardians. Yes, given the chance they would elect her onto that Board. However, it was only the men who were allowed to vote in those elections. Cara knew now she would have to find another way to achieve her goal.

Dragging herself home to The Laburnums, she found herself walking along Wellington Street. Her eyes followed the dirt track that led up to Green Lanes where the workhouse was situated. On one side of the dirt road stood some empty buildings. These were mostly small cottages falling into ruin. She noticed they were in three blocks of three... nine empty dilapidated cottages, surrounded by heathland. Cara wondered who they belonged to and why they were being left to eventually fall down.

Walking up the dirt track, she stepped towards the first short row of buildings as a thought formulated in her mind. What if she could discover who they belonged to? What if she could buy them? Having a good look around each cottage, she saw they were not as bad as she first thought. Her excitement grew at the prospect she had in mind.

Cara worked on her plan as she strode purposefully back into the town. There was someone she needed to see.

Ten

Fred Tulley had been informed that there were five more families coming into the workhouse... the 'Spike' as it was colloquially known. It was believed the name had derived from inmates using a large metal spike in their work of oakum picking. Tulley walked from his office through the dark corridor to the boys' exercise yard, which was a patch of ground surrounded by buildings. It was empty; the boys would be hard at work at this time of the day.

Along the corridor again, he crossed through a small room and out onto the girls' exercise yard, which was precisely the same layout. The girls were all dressed in identical dresses. Some ambled around the dirt patch lethargically, while others sat holding their stomachs and groaning.

Striding towards his wife, sat on a chair in the shade, he nodded towards the shuffling female children, raising his eyebrows in question.

'They've got the bellyache,' Ada Tulley said in answer as she mopped her brow with a handkerchief.

'What, all of them?' Tulley boomed.

'Ar, seems that bit of meat in the broth weren't exactly fresh.' Ada shook her head.

'Does the doctor need to be called?' Tulley asked immediately, thinking of the expense.

Ada Tulley shook her head again, her mob cap wobbling precariously. 'I don't think it's necessary. It will work its way through on its own.'

Tulley nodded once, screwing up his nose at the thought. 'The Board have informed me that five more families will be coming in this week. See to the arrangements, will you?'

'Certainly,' Ada grinned, showing teeth beginning to blacken with decay.

Tulley grimaced as he walked away.

*

The five families all entered the workhouse on the same day and were immediately separated out. The screaming children were dragged away from their sobbing mothers. The fathers, with hearts silently breaking, were led away to the men's quarters. All were bathed, had their hair shorn and given the 'uniform' to wear. Their own clothes they were told would be put into storage and returned on their release.

The boys were shown to the dormitories where they would share a straw-filled mattress on a wooden frame with another child. Then they were taken to the oakum shed to learn to unpick old rope.

The women shared a similar fate in their quarters, albeit having their own bed. Some were taken to the kitchen to work, others to the laundry. Here they would scrub the clothes for the whole workhouse in boiling water, by hand.

After rinsing in cold water, the garments would be put through the mangle and hung out to dry. Only the Master and Matron's clothes would be ironed.

The men also had a bed of their own or a straw pallet on the floor. At the back of the workhouse itself were huge piles of stone to be smashed into rubble. Further along, other men were crushing bones for use in fertilizer. Some men walked endlessly round the treadmill working two giant stones which ground the corn.

These families, like so many of the others of the town who had lost hope, were now firmly in the clutches of workhouse life. They thought only a miracle would set them free now.

*

'Christ, girl, where you been? I was that worried!' Gracie said as Cara stepped into the kitchen. Daisy had been helping the cook to bake and Charlie had been reading in the parlour with Molly's aid. All now sat round the kitchen table listening as Cara spoke.

'The women on the market said only the men get to elect the Board of Guardians.' Cara paused as snorts of disgust sounded. 'So that means I have to attack this problem from another angle. Between Wellington Street and Green Lanes are nine old empty cottages and I wondered who owned them? So I went to the estate agent in Cambridge Street. Mr Harris, the man in charge, said they had once belonged to the owner of the Millfields Colliery. The colliery is no longer in use and the owner upped and left to work in Wolverhampton. The paperwork for the cottages was left with Mr Harris and they now belong to me!'

'You've bought nine cottages? Whatever for?' Gracie was aghast.

'They were virtually given to me, Gracie! Mr Harris had leave to sell them straight away and I got them for a song.' Cara was bubbling with excitement. 'I could hardly believe it when I went in there earlier... then I came out with nine cottages!'

'What are you going to do with nine cottages, Cara?' Charlie asked innocently.

'I'm going to find a way to get nine families out of the workhouse, although I'm not sure yet how to do it. Of course I'll have to persuade them to work on the buildings to make them habitable whilst they live in them, perhaps pay them a small wage, but in the end they will have a home outside of that dreadful workhouse.' Cara said.

'Then what?' Molly asked.

'Then I'll look round for more and do the same again!'

'What about the families? Once the work is finished, what will those families do... go back to the workhouse?' Gracie said sharply.

'Nooo!' Cara said. 'I'll find them work of some sort. I want them to stay on living in those cottages. I don't want them to have to return to that awful place! I want to give them a chance at life once more!'

Gracie stood with her hands on her hips, feeling her patience slip away, and said, 'Cara, whilst I like your ideas, I don't think you've thought this through properly.' Holding up her hands, she went on, 'Now, you have the properties, you can get the families out to work on them. They have to be fed in the meantime and there will be tools and such to buy. Then... when the cottages are finished, how will the people living in them get by? And… are you expecting rent?' Gracie sat down and laid her hands flat on the table waiting for answers.

'I… I… Oh Gracie! I don't know! I just thought it was a good idea to get people out of that dreadful place!' Cara mewled, she felt like she'd had the wind knocked out of her sails. It seemed every which way she turned, she was blocked. All she wanted to do was help. She began to pace the floor in sheer exasperation.

Daisy who had sat quietly during the conversation looking from one face to another suddenly piped up, 'Our mum used to take in washing while our dad was away working, you could do that, Cara.' Twinkling blue eyes again scanned the faces as they all laughed out across the table. Gracie could not imagine Cara washing other people's clothes. The young woman had never had to do mundane chores and wouldn't know where to start.

'Good thought, Daisy,' Cara praised. 'Washing, baking… the women could do that. As for the men, they could work on any other properties we acquire!'

'You'll have to pay them,' Charlie said ruefully.

'I can do that,' Cara added, 'then we can see how things go. Just think… eventually we could empty the workhouse… we could put it out of business!' Cara's excitement bubbled over at the prospect.

Molly laid her arms on the table, dropping her head on them with a loud sigh at the thought of what Cara would come up with next.

Laughter filled the kitchen once more as Daisy copied her.

*

Cara and her small entourage walked down Proud's Lane into Dover Street. Each on the lookout for any empty property that might be of use. Turning into Wellington Street, they ambled along, passing familiar houses that had stood for many years but were only now really seeing properly for the first time. Following the dirt track Cara had taken the day before, they came to the nine cottages.

'Bloody hellfire!' Gracie exclaimed, making Daisy giggle. 'They're going to take a hell of a lot of work, girl!'

'I know, Gracie, but just think, this might help to get me on the Board of Guardians yet!'

The little group roamed around and inspected each property in turn, and Cara, taking out a pencil and paper from her bag, made a note of the things they needed to make them habitable.

That done, they walked home past the allotment gardens chatting about the work needing to be done. They parted company and as Cara made her way to Cambridge Street, the others trundled home. Cara had a favour to ask of Martin Lander.

At The Laburnums Gracie set out the tea things on the table and muttered, 'I ain't sure what Cara's up to, but one thing I do know, Molly, is... you and me are going to be very busy, very soon!'

Eleven

The sick children in the Spike were too ill to work and Tulley became concerned.

'What if it's more than just a bad belly?' he muttered to his wife as they watched the children groaning in their beds. 'What if it's infectious?'

'Pah!' Ada spat. 'It ain't! These kids are trying to pull the wool over your eyes, Mr Tulley! But… if you'm that worried, call the doctor in; just remember you have to pay him!' Ada Tulley strode off, her mob cap wobbling with each step she took.

Fred Tulley scuttled down the dark corridor to his office, where he telephoned for the doctor. He was taking no chances. The medical officer was attached to the workhouse on a part-time basis, as was the schoolmaster; the doctor said he would come at once.

An hour later, the medical officer pronounced each child very definitely unfit for work. Joshua Cooper had been a doctor for many years and knew exactly what ailed these children. He was also not afraid to speak his mind.

'Whatever slop you've been feeding them has made them very poorly indeed!' Dr Cooper said.

'I don't care for your attitude or your words, Dr Cooper!' Ada Tulley snapped.

'And I don't care a bugger!' the doctor snapped back. 'This...' he spread his arms, 'is an utter disgrace! Bad meat, Mrs Tulley, that's what has caused this. You could have poisoned every last one of them!'

'I don't have to listen to this!' Ada bristled as she wiped her hands on her long white apron.

'Shut up, woman!' Fred snapped at his wife, his eyes burning with anger. In his mind, Fred saw the loss of work as well as the cost for calling out the doctor, and his fury mounted even higher.

'But he's saying...' Ada protested.

Fred growled quietly, 'Just be quiet, Ada, for once in your life shut that yap of yours!'

Ada Tulley stormed away to the laundry in a foul mood, leaving her husband and the doctor behind.

'Anyone else sick?' Dr Cooper asked.

Tulley shook his head.

The doctor went on, 'Right, I'll deal with these and then I'll write up my report for the Board.' Seeing Tulley snap his head round, the doctor screwed his mouth up before saying, 'Your wife has finally blotted your copybook, Tulley!'

The inmates could hear the yelling coming from the Master's two-storey residence later that day. Muttering to each other, they wondered what had happened to make the Master and Matron have such severe words. Certain of these words rang louder than the rest, *'...doctor... children... sick...'* Panic began to rise in mothers and fathers alike as they feared for the lives of their children.

Tulley addressed the women as they sat for their evening meal.

'The kids have a bad belly, nothing to worry about. I've called in the doctor and he is administering medicine. He assures me all will be well by the morning.'

He then went to speak with the men in their dormitories; he gave them the same speech.

Worried looks passed among the inmates before they began their meal of stale bread and thin broth. Eyeing the broth first, each waited for the next to start. Was it the food that had caused the children to be sick? It *was* disgusting food, but it was better than starving. Resignedly they began to eat. It was all there was so they didn't have much choice.

Dr Cooper stayed in the dormitories with the children all night. He chose not to move them to the medical ward, which wouldn't have been big enough anyway, but he moved between the boys' and girls' quarters regularly. He had instructed Tulley to send for a nurse to help with the children as they continued to dry-heave and sweat. There was nothing left in their small stomachs to bring up. Tulley ignored the doctor's instruction regarding the nurse, he felt he'd paid out enough as it was, and he wouldn't lay out more expense on a nurse.

By morning, most of the children were feeling better but exhausted. Only one little girl lost her battle to survive. Carrying her tiny body to the medical ward, the doctor washed her gently and dressed her in the clothes she had worn on entering the Spike. As he worked, Joshua Cooper whispered, 'There you go, little wench, all nice and tidy now for your mum. You look just like you're sleeping.' Looking down at the child on the bed, he shook his head, unable to prevent the lone tear rolling down his face. 'Poor little bugger, you didn't ask for this and it was so unnecessary! Rest well until the Lord holds you in his arms.'

Dr Cooper then dispatched Mrs Tulley to fetch the child's mother.

Liza Townsend's screams and wails could be heard resonating all over the workhouse when the doctor explained what had occurred.

'I'm so sorry, Mrs Townsend,' Dr Cooper said as he held up the woman's sagging body. 'I did all I could for your little girl.'

Liza let out another howl and the doctor sat her in a chair in the sick ward. 'When you're ready, I'll take you to her.'

Liza's eyes found his and he saw the pleading in them. Helping her to her feet, he led her through to the bed where her daughter lay.

Picking up the lifeless child, Liza walked round and round the room, holding her tightly. She sang quietly as she paced the floor, never taking her eyes from her little girl's face. Then she whispered, 'I have missed you, my sweetheart. I didn't think they'd ever let me see you again, you know. That doctor is a nice man, bringing me to see you.' Liza began to sing quietly again as she paced. Her arms ached but she ignored the pain. She had her daughter back and she wasn't about to let her go again. An hour later the doctor entered the room with the Tulleys close behind.

Liza's screams came again as the child was prised from her arms. She kicked and fought like a wild animal and eventually she was dragged from the ward.

The undertaker had arrived with a small wooden coffin in which the child's body was to be placed. He'd stood outside the medical ward whilst the Tulleys tried to calm Liza enough to take her out and back to the dormitory.

The woman's screams almost burst his eardrums as she was dragged past him, and his heart went out to her. Very gently the undertaker lifted the child and laid her in the wooden box. 'Goodnight, my little wench,' he muttered before placing the lid on the box. The little girl would be buried in a pauper's grave with nothing to mark the spot. He knew there would be no mourners at least not at the child's funeral.

Liza Townsend was pushed into the room she shared with a number of others and left there. After the door closed the women gathered around Liza and held her as she sobbed her heart out. Each woman shed a tear for Liza's daughter; saying a silent prayer for the child.

No one in the workhouse slept that night. Liza's wails for her lost daughter bounced off the stone walls and carried on the still night air.

Fred and Ada lay awake listening to the mournful cries of Liza Townsend. The repercussions of this debacle did not bear thinking about, but all the Tulleys *could* think about was... what would happen to them now?

The women stayed close to Liza all night and watched as her grief appeared to turn her mind. Liza mumbled nonsense into the darkness of the room. She cackled loudly before screaming and crying once more. The loss of her daughter had, in their opinions, sent Liza Townsend quite mad.

The men lay abed each with their own thoughts of the woman who had screamed her anguish. They knew they were the cries of a distraught mother; one who had lost her child. These wails had a sound unlike any other; they were the cries of utter futility. The woman had finally lost all hope.

Those children who had recovered shivered at the sounds that echoed through their rooms. They knew what the woman was going through and why. The girls were one child short in their dormitory.

The following day, the Tulleys stood in the boardroom where the Board of Guardians sat around the table. The emergency meeting had been called regarding the death of the Townsend child. Dr Cooper was also in attendance.

The local Magistrate, who was also the Chairman of the Board, spoke first.

'Mr Tulley, we have all read Dr Cooper's report regarding the child, Miss Townsend, and now we would wish to hear what you have to say on the matter.'

Fred sent a withering look at the doctor before saying, 'The kiddie was poorly.... Children die all the time, sir, I don't know what else I can say.'

Checking the report again, the Chairman said, 'According to the good doctor here...' he pointed to Dr Cooper who nodded in answer, '...the child was six years old. She had the body of a two-year-old due, in his opinion, to malnutrition.' The Chairman looked up at the Master before his eyes went back to the report. 'The child was so undernourished she could not regain enough strength to fight off her ailment and as a result she expired at 8.05 last evening. The cause of the ailment that claimed the child's life was due to being fed bad meat resulting in food poisoning.' Again the Chairman looked up.

'Sir,' Ada Tulley put in quickly, 'I would never feed any of the inmates bad meat!'

Fred squeezed his eyes shut, wishing his wife would keep her mouth firmly closed.

The Chairman nodded slowly as if accepting her answer. Then he whispered to his colleagues, before excusing himself and leaving the room.

The Tulleys watched him go, wondering where he was off to. Neither dared ask, for fear of reprisals. They were in enough trouble as it was.

During the ten minutes the Chairman was out of the room, the Tulleys stood feeling the Board members' eyes burning into them. Ada shuffled her feet and Fred shot her a look that told her in no uncertain terms to keep still. By the time the Chairman returned and retook his seat, nervous sweat was pouring down Fred's face.

'It appears,' he began, 'that the cook agrees with you, Mrs Tulley.'

Ada sighed heavily with relief, as did Fred.

'Now, we would wish to speak with Mrs Townsend...' Seeing Ada prepare to turn to fetch Liza, the Chairman went on quickly, 'We will go to her, Mrs Tulley, if you don't mind.'

Ada sniffed her annoyance at being told what to do by this man. It was bad enough having to listen to Fred giving out his orders, now the Chairman was at it as well!

Threading their way through the corridors, they passed the empty women's quarters. Liza Townsend had been assigned to the laundry, so the group cut across the exercise yard to the building where steam escaped an open door. Liza was found wandering up and down the washing lines outside, clutching a handful of dolly pegs to her chest. She was singing softly to herself.

'Townsend!' Ada Tulley yelled. Liza ignored the call and continued to pace. Mrs Tulley began to walk towards the singing woman as Liza turned to pace back the way she had come.

Wild eyes settled on Ada as the woman stepped forward. With a howl like a banshee, Liza launched herself at the Matron. Dropping the pegs, Liza's hands grabbed the woman's hair as they both fell to the ground, her teeth seeking anything to latch onto. Liza screeched as she fought like a wild cat, 'You killed my babby! You evil, spiteful witch! You made the cook use that bad food! You killed my babby!'

Ada Tulley tried desperately to free herself from the raving woman and received a bite to her hand for her efforts.

Fred Tulley ran across to where the women struggled on the floor, and wrapping his arms around Liza's waist he hauled her off his wife. Liza continued to kick out and scream abuse at the woman who was now scrambling to her feet in a most undignified manner.

The Chairman and other Board members turned quickly and scrambled around each other in an effort to get out of the laundry. Never had they experienced such a debacle and they wanted to be away from the screaming woman as quickly as possible. Tulley pushed Liza Townsend hard. She stumbled and Dr Cooper rushed towards her to prevent her falling. 'Come on,' he said as he gently led her to the other inmates who quickly gathered round her to comfort her.

Once more in the Boardroom, the Chairman drew in a deep breath. 'It would seem that Mrs Townsend would be more appropriately housed in the lunatic asylum.' Nods all around showed agreement, all except the doctor. 'Now, Mrs Tulley, this is a warning to you. All foods served to the inmates in the future must be fresh, do you understand?' Mrs Tulley nodded. Fred Tulley sighed with relief that his wife had wisely chosen to keep her mouth shut this time. The Chairman continued, 'This incident will be noted down in the record book and I will arrange for Mrs Townsend to be moved as soon as possible.'

'Thank you, sir,' Tulley said quietly.

Dr Cooper snorted in disgust. 'This is an utter disgrace!'

he snapped. 'Never in all my born days have I seen such a mishandling of a situation as this! You are not fit to be a Board of Guardians, any of you! These two should be punished for what they've done, and you know it. But no, it would upset the regime, wouldn't it? I am disgusted with the lot of you!' He marched from the room, his temper at boiling point. They were under no illusion as to how riled he was that the matter had not been better dealt with.

Twelve

Sitting once more in his office, Cara explained her ideas to an intrigued Martin Lander. When she finished speaking, he said, 'I see. May I ask how you propose to get nine families out of the workhouse?' Cara again told him her plan and Martin grinned like a little boy. 'I hope it works for you,' he said, 'but how can I help?'

'Is it possible you could telephone to make an appointment on behalf of a "client"?' Cara asked.

Nodding, Martin pulled the telephone towards him and made the call.

'Tomorrow morning at 10 o'clock,' he said with another smile. 'Cara, would you like me to come with you?'

'Oh yes! That would help enormously, thank you. I have to admit I was rather dreading going alone. It's so kind of you to put yourself out, I really can't thank you enough.' They agreed he would collect her at a quarter to ten in a cab and they would drive there.

Cara could barely contain her excitement as she walked home to tell the others her plan was underway. It had begun to rain and the scrubland underfoot soon turned to mud, but Cara's spirits soared. Even the rain could not dampen her mood.

*

Arriving at the workhouse exactly on time the next morning, the porter opened the gate, giving Cara a snide look as she passed through, followed by Martin Lander. Cara nodded once and walked on.

Mrs Tulley met them at the door and ushered them straight to the office, bowing and scraping as they went. Ada opened the office door without knocking and heard Fred sigh loudly. She grinned at him nastily before leaving the room.

'We meet again,' Tulley said as he saw Cara. 'Mr Lander, nice to see you.'

'Mr Tulley,' Martin answered. 'We are here at the request of my client here, Miss Flowers.'

Tulley's head slowly rocked back and forth on his neck as he slouched in his chair.

'Mr Tulley,' Cara took up, 'I am still searching for family and hoped you might be in a position to help.' Her quiet speech and gentle manner somewhat disarmed the man.

'I see, and what name are we looking for this time?' the Master asked sarcastically.

Taking a deep breath and sending up a silent prayer, and an apology for her little white lie, Cara said, 'Johnson.'

The Master slid the ledger over his desk, his eyes still on the young woman stood before him. Then, scanning the columns, he said, 'We have five Johnsons… men, here at the moment.'

Martin interjected, 'Would it be possible to meet with them?'

Sighing loudly, the Master rose and led them out of the

office and down the dark corridors before reaching the bone crushing area outside.

'Johnsons! To me!' Tulley yelled. Five men stepped forward, brushing dust from their clothing.

'In private if you don't mind, Mr Tulley, this is a legal matter,' Lander said confidently.

Rolling his eyes, Fred moved back into the doorway of the building and watched carefully.

Cara leaned forward and whispered to the men, 'Do you wish to get out of here?' They all nodded. 'Then we will have to say you are my cousins. Do you have family here?' Again nods. 'Good. My name is Cara Flowers and I have jobs for each of you. I will ensure you all get a new life outside of this place.' Grins spread on the faces of the men as Lander called Fred Tulley over to them.

'These men appear to be cousins to Miss Flowers and they, along with their families, wish to be released today.'

Sighing loudly again, Tulley turned on his heel and walked back to the office. Cara and Martin, along with the Johnsons, followed behind.

The other inmates had stopped work, wondering what was going on. They watched in bewilderment as the group left the bone crushing area.

'You can go while I fill out the paperwork.' Tulley said to Cara and Martin as if dismissing naughty school children. 'You lot wait in the corridor.' He nodded to the Johnsons.

As he filled in the appropriate forms, Tulley was glad no mention was made of payment with Martin Lander in attendance.

Waiting outside the gate, Cara was elated saying, 'I can't believe our little ruse worked!'

'Well, if you can't beat them, join them.' Martin laughed.

'Tulley is a sly old Devil, but you outwitted him this time.'

'It worked this time, but I'm not sure it would again. We may have to think up a new strategy next time.' Cara beamed her joy.

Eventually five husbands and wives, along with thirteen children stepped through the gate, and as relief flooded her, Cara greeted them all. Husbands shook her hand, wives gave her a hug and the children found new energy to run around laughing at their freedom. As they walked away from the Spike, Cara related her intentions briefly.

'I have some cottages down the track there. They are in sore need of renovation I'm afraid, but at least you will have a roof of your own over your heads.'

The men muttered their thanks and the women, after hugging their children, bawled their eyes out.

'First of all though, we need to get you all a decent meal and a good cup of tea, so we'll go along to my house. You'll pass the cottages on the way, so you can have a quick look before we eat.'

As they marched down the track, they came upon the old buildings and stopped briefly to look them over.

'I know they're not up to much now, but I'm sure they can be greatly improved.' Cara watched as the families appeared to decide which cottage would be theirs. She saw no disappointment from the people she had rescued as they excitedly rushed into the dwelling of their choice.

The two-up two-down cottages were brick built, covered in coal dust on the outside. Some had front doors hanging by one hinge threatening to come off completely if they were touched. The windows, which had been left intact by marauding kids, were covered in grime. Inside smelled mouldy and it was dark and dingy. There was no furniture and cupboard doors were missing altogether. The upstairs was no better, with the two tiny bedrooms empty other than rubbish left behind by children playing inside. The whitewash on the walls had turned to a sickly yellow over time. The toilet blocks at the back were in an even worse state. However, with a bit of elbow grease these broken-down properties could be made habitable.

Having had a quick look around, the families joined Cara and Martin on the track once more and Cara's worries were set at ease as she listened to the quiet chatter. The men were discussing replacing roof tiles and chimney pointing; the women which colour to have regarding curtains.

Grateful thanks were given and Cara began to relax in the knowledge these people were happy to have a battered old cottage because – it would be theirs.

Resuming their walk to her home, Cara looked at the people she had helped. The men were dressed in trousers that had seen better days; their boots full of holes. Some had no jackets and were in shirtsleeves and waistcoats which were threadbare. The women were stick-thin, their clothes hanging off them. They were dirty, and their short hair gave her the shivers as she considered what could be living there. They all carried a bad odour which Cara tried to ignore. The children too were filthy dirty and Cara wondered how they managed to walk on their skinny legs.

Gracie and Molly, having been pre-warned, had the kitchen table laden with food as the group had trooped in and introduced themselves.

After hot tea and a bowl of thick lamb stew packed with fresh vegetables and a chunk of soft fresh bread, Cara addressed the Johnsons.

'You are going to need some coal for fires to help air out the cottages.'

Faces turned to each other and quiet mutterings began. Cara held up her hands and silence descended.

'Also, food and bedding...' She watched the faces take on a look of despair. She knew what the people were thinking: they had no way of acquiring those things. 'You have all met Gracie and Molly,' all eyes turned to the two women then back to Cara, 'who have kindly agreed to sort this out on your behalf.'

Applause rang out in the tiny kitchen as cook and maid nodded their appreciation.

'So,' Cara resumed, 'if you are ready, we shall take you up to your new homes.' Again the applause saw Cara beam her happiness.

Armed with a long list and lots of money, Molly and Gracie set out to accomplish the shopping. Cara had decided any major items should be delivered and the invoices sent to her, that way she could keep a better check on her spending. Gracie said she could pay for the food and bring it along in cabs; mattresses would need to be delivered.

Martin and Cara walked with the adults and Daisy and Charlie ran on in front with the Johnson children.

Cara's heart hammered in her chest as her eyes rested again on the stone buildings; had she really not realized how bad they were? She panicked as she thought she couldn't let these people live in these ruins. Cara was relieved when she saw the families rush into the cottages of their choice. She heard the mothers yelling for their children to hunt the heathland for kindling sticks. She watched as men shoved windows open on rusty hinges. Again she heard their discussions. The men's thanks for a promised wage in exchange for work undertaken on their own and any other property Cara bought. The women excitedly agreed to take in washing for a small fee, or sell their baking. The children's squeals of delight when their parents agreed to their requests of starting small gardens to grow vegetables. And the families' joy at not having to pay rent until all the cottages they were living in were renovated.

Cara saw the first wisps of smoke from the chimneys as the women started fires in the hearths and the children ran off again in search of more sticks. The sound of happy voices and laughter filled her ears and Cara revelled in it.

Just then a couple of cabs arrived full to the brim with bedding and food for all. Cara assured the mothers they would have mattresses for the old bedsteads still *in situ* that same day. She saw the bottoms of petticoats torn off and made into dusters. Men got the standpipe for water working again. Old curtains were torn down. Work was well underway when Cara and her own little family prepared to leave. Hugs of gratitude were given and they left everyone to their allotted tasks.

As they walked home, Cara felt a warm glow of happiness at what she had achieved so far. Her eyes twinkled as Martin congratulated her on her success, bringing a blush to her cheeks. Five families saved in one day! Now all she had to do was save another four to fill her cottages. Cara needed a way to get more people released from the dreaded workhouse.

*

Martin Lander researched the Poor Law yet again as he sat in his office in Cambridge Street. He also read through everything he could find on the rulings of the workhouse. He was extremely surprised to find that people could, in fact, come and go more or less as they wished! All they had to do was give three hours' notice of their intention to leave. If a man left, then his whole family was dismissed with him. How had he missed this on his previous research? Had his mind been elsewhere maybe? Had he been thinking of Cara at the time and completely overlooked this important information? So there had been no need for the 'family' ruse to release the Johnsons, but no matter, it had worked and they were free now. Now he had this new information, Martin knew the next time it would be easier to get people out of the workhouse.

Martin was glad of the excuse to speak to Cara again and immediately telephoned her with his findings. Hearing her tinkling laugh was music to his ears. He jumped at the chance to once again accompany her to the Spike to offer a home and job to four more families. Martin agreed to her request to make the appointment for the following day, eager to please her in any way he could.

Tulley's voice filtered into his ear as Martin asked for an appointment. 'What for this time? Has the lady yet more family in here?' A sarcastic chuckle followed his words.

'Mr Tulley, I wish to make an appointment for Miss Flowers to offer four men some work. Now, having perused the rules, the men wishing to take her up on her offer are required to give three hours' notice whilst their paperwork is completed. Then they are free to leave accompanied by their families. We will be there at ten o'clock sharp tomorrow morning and expect to speak with any man willing to sign himself out.' Martin's voice said he would brook no arguments. Tulley harrumphed his reply and the conversation ended there.

Pleased with himself, Martin leaned back in his chair and

began to daydream about Cara Flowers. A knock on his office door brought him sharply out of his reverie.

A head popped round the open doorway and his business partner said, 'Meeting… five minutes.'

The meeting in five minutes took precisely the same amount of time. Martin, they said, was not pulling his weight. The Flowers account was bringing in quite a lot of revenue, agreed, but he was neglecting his other cases, and they had received complaints to that effect. They had carried him long enough and felt they could no longer do so. The time had come to make changes. The ultimatum given was for Martin to either sell his share of the business to them or be dismissed from the firm. He could not afford the scandal that would surround his dismissal, so he was left with only one alternative. He had to sell, and suddenly Martin Lander found himself devoid of a career and an income!

Thirteen

Fred Tulley was more than a little relieved that he and his wife had not been dismissed from their employment. He knew they had come dangerously close to being out on the streets themselves. They had scraped through the poisoning incident by the skin of their teeth which had pleased him. Mulling over the visit from Lander and that young woman, Flowers, his anger began to mount. She had done him out of good workers and he felt there was something more going on there, something he needed to keep an eye on. Just then the office door flew open, breaking his train of thought, and Ada bustled in.

'Can't you bloody knock, woman?' Tulley growled.

'Well excuse me!' his wife said, placing her hands on her bony hips. 'The men from the lunatic asylum are here for Liza Townsend.'

'Right.' Tulley grabbed the papers from his desk and strode past his wife who scuttled along behind him.

As they reached the laundry, the asylum attendants in tow, Liza again espied Ada Tulley. Springing forward, Liza barged into the unsuspecting Matron, sending her sprawling on the floor. Screams of abuse spat from Liza's lips as she fought like a demon. 'Tulley, I warned you! You nasty piece of work! You're for it now!' Ada had not thought the woman would attack her again and had paid for her mistake. Liza had her pinned to the floor and was hitting the woman as hard as she could.

Ada covered her head with her arms in order to shield herself from the blows. The two asylum attendants rushed to untangle the women. A length of rope was slipped from the pocket of one of the men and in a heartbeat Liza's wrists were tied together behind her back.

'You bitch!' Liza screeched venomously at the Matron, who was now back on her feet and trying to secure her mob cap once more. 'You are a born liar! You know what you did! You got away with killing my babby, but just you remember, Ada Tulley… God sees all! God sees aaaallllll!'

The struggling woman was dragged away by the two attendants, still attempting to kick out at the woman she hated beyond measure. Her screams and shouting could be heard echoing through the corridors as she was hauled away to what was to be her new home; one she would almost certainly never leave alive. Liza continued to kick and scream, bellowing over and over, 'Why are you doing this to me? I know where we're going! You're taking me to the lunatic asylum! Why can't you understand, I'm not insane – I am bloody angry!'

The women working in the laundry watched as Liza was being hauled away. Silent nods said they knew what she faced and their sorrow weighed heavily as they returned to the washing. There was always a chance of leaving the workhouse, but there was no chance of leaving the place where Liza Townsend was now being taken to.

Mr and Mrs Tulley ambled back to the office and Ada said, 'I'm glad to see the back of that one!'

'You stupid woman!' Fred rasped. His anger was at its peak as he rounded on her. 'This is all your fault! You pinch a penny and the kids get sick. One of them dies and I have to pay that bloody doctor. Then we almost get chucked out by the Board… and now we've lost a worker to the asylum!'

Ada stared at her husband whose face was blood red with temper. 'She attacked me… twice!' Ada screamed back. 'She could have killed me!'

'You know what… she should have tried harder!' Fred glared at his wife; he was at boiling point and a vein in his neck began to pulse. 'Now, to top it all, we've got Lander and that bloody girl coming to offer work to four more men!'

'I didn't know about that!' Ada Tulley snapped.

'You don't have to know everything, you're only second in command here… something you'd do well to remember!' Fred's voice bounced off the office walls. 'Now, go and do something useful… welcome our *guests*.'

Ada harrumphed as she spun around; leaving the office, she banged the door shut behind her.

Tulley sighed heavily as he slumped into his chair. His thoughts began to swirl in his brain. That wife of his was becoming a nuisance, as was the woman about to visit with her solicitor friend. His job was hard enough without all this nonsense, and that blasted Miss Flowers wasn't helping any by taking his inmate workers. Maybe it was time to leave the workhouse, find employment elsewhere. If he did move he could leave that termagant of a wife behind – it might be worth doing for that reason alone. As he sat thinking about his wife, he realized just how much things had changed between them. They had married more for companionship than for love, and over the years even that had slowly died. This latest incident had just about killed any feeling he had for Ada.

A sharp rap on the door shattered his thoughts. 'Come!' he yelled.

Cara and Martin walked in each sporting a smile, which Tulley returned with a grimace. This was the last thing he needed.

*

The families had called their new homes by a nickname, 'Cara's Cottages', and they gathered in the sunshine to share a mid-morning cup of tea. Their conversation centred on the young woman who had cared enough to offer them a home and a job. Who was she? Why had she done what she did? Clearly her cottages were in sore need of renovation, but why not hire men from the 'bread line' to restore them?

The bread line constituted a line of men who gathered at strategic points in the town every day in the hope of finding work. These men needed to 'earn a crust', which was what was thought to have given rise to the name. The businessmen knew where to find workers if they were needed, but more often than not, the men returned home with no work. So it came as a surprise to the families that Cara had selected them as opposed to employing men from the breadline.

The children of the families were busy running over the scrubland collecting sticks for the fires as their parents continued their conversation. The mothers didn't care why Cara had chosen the path she had, they were just grateful she had done so.

It was then that Gracie and Molly arrived with Charlie and Daisy, who immediately dashed off to join the other kids. The cook and maid were loaded down with mop heads and stales, buckets, old linen to be torn into cleaning rags, soap, pots and pans, tools for the men... as much as they were able to drag on a handcart. Cara had also sent a little money for each family to buy items such as wind-up clocks, scraps of material to be made into curtains, and some second-hand clothes for the children.

Over a welcome cup of tea, Gracie explained in more detail Cara's plan to help as many people as she could, to get out, and stay out, of the workhouse.

Gathered around, the Johnsons listened as Gracie spoke quietly. 'Cara's grandmother, on her deathbed, set Cara a challenge to find any family belonging to her, and she asked Molly and me to help.' Molly nodded and Gracie went on. 'Well, she found young Charlie in the workhouse and got him out. Old Tulley had sold Daisy on and so we went looking for her. Daisy had run away, but Cara found her in the end. Then our Cara had the idea to join the Board of Guardians and, as you can imagine, that didn't work out, what with her being a woman an' all. So her other idea was to buy up these cottages to use to house families from the workhouse. That way she could get whole families out, rather than just the odd person here and there. Cara won't rest until she sees that place shut down.'

Now her new tenants had a better idea of the young woman and the reasons she worked so hard with the poor, their admiration for her grew tenfold. They felt they had their very own guardian angel.

*

Fred Tulley called for quiet from the men who were working the stone and bone crushing. Looking at Martin Lander, he stepped back without being asked and he returned the curt nod given by Martin Lander.

'Good morning, gentlemen. I am looking for four men with families, to work on some old cottages I have bought,' Cara said. She watched as the unmarried men moved back, a look of sadness crossing each face. She thought that although she hadn't got around to these men as yet, she would before too long. That still left a lot of men standing before them. 'I will take the four who have the most children with me today, but I *will* be back, gentlemen, be assured of that.'

Cara turned to Fred Tulley in time to see him roll his eyes. She flashed a satisfied smile his way and straightened her back. Tulley gave an audible disgruntled sniff, screwing up his nose in answer. Cara was proud that in a matter of days she had already reduced the number of people suffering workhouse life and she hoped in the not too distant future she would reduce the number entirely.

Again Martin and Cara awaited their new charges outside the gate and after the obligatory three hours the excited group were trudging down the dirt track to their new homes.

The families already ensconced in their cottages came out to greet the new members of their little hamlet, and tea and food was shared. It was a Black Country tradition to offer tea immediately as a visitor arrived and Cara and Martin enjoyed theirs as introductions took place. Squeals of delight echoed across the patch of heathland as all the children began to play together; they were thoroughly enjoying running around freely. Cara knew that these children, as gaunt as they looked now, would be fighting fit in a few days' time.

Lander watched Cara as she observed the people getting reacquainted. She was beaming with the joy of it and he felt an overwhelming desire to hold her in his arms. Then as he thought of his own predicament he knew he had nothing to offer her. Although still a lawyer, he now had no office to work from and no work to do. He would have to tell Cara, but as he watched her laugh and talk with the people around her, he couldn't bring himself to spoil her happiness.

*

The Board of Guardians were informed that the numbers in the workhouse were reducing and people were finding work, but Fred Tulley was clearly disgruntled. He was afraid if this went on he might find himself out of work.

Sitting in their living room that evening as the inmates settled for the night, an eerie silence crept over the building. Most nights he could hear children crying or women sobbing, but this night there was nothing.

'It's quiet tonight,' he muttered to his wife as she drank her beer. 'I wonder why?'

'Don't know, don't care,' Ada said, wiping the beer froth from her mouth with the back of her hand. She ignored her husband's look of distaste.

'Think it has anything to do with that Flowers woman giving out jobs willy-nilly?' Fred asked.

'Maybe. P'raps they hope she'll come back for them.' Ada cackled then poured herself another beer from the jug on the table.

Fred screwed up his face in disgust. His wife was a drunkard and with each passing day he disliked her more and more. 'Well, I ain't having that!' he snapped as he heaped coal on the fire.

'Oh no? And what, may I arshk har you going to do about it?' Ada's words slurred as she spoke.

'I don't rightly know as yet, but I'll think of something.' Ada cackled again and Fred's temper flared. 'Get yourself to bed, you drunken baggage!'

Draining her glass, Ada rose unsteadily to her feet and wove her way to the bedroom, giggling drunkenly as she went. Fred heard her crashing about and sniggering as she attempted to ready herself for sleep.

Whatever happened with Lander and Flowers, Fred felt it was definitely time to be rid of his crapulous wife one way or another!

*

Ada woke in the night with a dreadful thirst. Moving quietly into the living room so as not to wake Fred, she poured herself another beer... and another. She continued to drink until she was quite drunk again.

With a cackle, she grabbed an oil lamp and lit it with a wobbly hand. Snatching her walking stick from the umbrella stand, she slipped through the door and hobbled down the dark and deserted corridor. Quietly she made her way to the boys' dormitory.

'Time for some more fun with the basket treatment,' she muttered. Placing the lamp on the floor, she readied herself. All the boys were sleeping peacefully... for now. With a yell, she strode the length of the room banging her stick on the wooden bed frames. Groans came from the sleeping boys; they all knew what was coming.

'Come on, you lazy little buggersh... get up and get them kecks off!' Ada slurred with a drunken grin.

Taking off their under drawers, the boys stood in a line as naked as the day they were born. One young lad went to a cupboard and retrieved a pile of wicker baskets. Each boy was given a basket which they sat on their head and the line began to slowly walk forward. Ada wobbled alongside the line with the stick in her hand.

The youngest lad's basket began to slip and before he could catch it, it fell to the floor. Ada struck out at the child's bare bottom sharply with her stick and the child screamed out at the pain she inflicted. Ada cackled again.

Time after time, the boys walked the length of the dormitory. Throughout the following hour, almost every boy received a sharp whack with the stick. Ada, tired at last, sat on the one chair that stood by the door. The boys continued to walk as they watched the Matron fall sound asleep.

As the baskets were put back in the cupboard, the children crept silently back to bed rubbing their sore rumps. One basket had been left out.

*

Fred arose the following morning and wondering where Ada was, he began his search of the building. Stomping down the corridors, his temper mounting, he eventually found Ada sitting in the chair in the boys' empty dormitory, snoring loudly in a drunken stupor. His anger dissipated as he could not restrain the grin that crept to his face. Ada was wearing a basket on her head which reminded him of the straw hats the donkeys wore in the summer.

Knocking the basket to the floor, Fred yelled, 'Ada! This has to stop!'

Ada leapt out of the chair, instantly wishing she hadn't. Holding her head, she groaned.

'Ada!' Fred yelled again.

'Don't shout! I ain't deaf... and I've got a headache.' Swaying on her feet, she decided it would be safer to sit down once more. Dropping into the chair, she groaned her discomfort.

'Ada,' Fred said quieter now, 'get a grip, woman! You can't keep doing this, you'll have us thrown out!'

'I was only having a bit of fun, God knows I don't get any with you!' Ada cradled her aching head once more.

Turning to walk away, Fred shouted loudly, 'Ada Tulley you are a bloody disgrace!'

Ada winced before gingerly standing to totter back to their quarters. With a mouth like sandpaper and a brass band playing in her head, Ada felt only another beer would help.

Draining her second glass, Ada began to feel a little better when the living room door flew open and her husband marched in.

Standing in front of her, legs astride and knuckles on hips, Fred said sharply, 'Ada, it's time you quit your drinking!'

Ada raised an eyebrow in a confrontational gesture. 'Fred, it's time you buggered off!'

Fred raged, 'I am the Master here! What I say, goes! Now I say you must stop this behaviour. I cannot allow it to go on any longer!'

Ada came back with, 'I say, if bullshit was music, you'd have your own jazz band!'

Fred shook his head and stormed from the room.

Ada cackled as she poured yet more beer. 'Jazz band... that weren't bad, Ada... not bad at all.' Taking a long drink of her ale, she smacked her lips and propped her feet up on the table.

Fourteen

Sitting by the fireside at home, Martin Lander reflected on his current predicament. He no longer had an office or a business, just one single case remained on his books. Fortunately Cara paid his fees on time, plus he had some savings, and with the money from the sale of his share of the business, he was nowhere near destitute. However, his money would not last forever, so he needed to acquire new business.

Martin had not argued in his own defence; the partners had been correct. Yes he *had* been neglecting his other work in favour of the Flowers case, and yes he'd intended to strike out on his own but he hadn't thought it to be quite so soon.

His thoughts were interrupted by the trill of the telephone. 'Martin, I'm so glad you're home. I wondered if you would care to come to dinner this evening.' Cara's voice filled him with desire once more.

Having readily accepted her invitation, he immediately went to wash and change his clothes. He couldn't wait to see her again.

Martin decided to walk to The Laburnums rather than

take a cab ride. He thought, as he went, it would help conserve his money, albeit by only a few pennies, and the exercise would be good for him. It was a pleasant stroll from his house in Alice Street and along Duke Street. Passing the office he had so recently vacated, he turned into Arthur Street which crossed over the railway lines. The sun began to shine as the first days of spring had taken hold and he ambled along into Dover Street. It was all he could do not to rush up to Proud's Lane, but he didn't want to arrive hot and breathless.

He stopped at the sound of the steam train's whistle as it thundered past. He watched the clouds of steam puff up into the air and dissipate slowly. The smell of burning coal in the steam reached his nose and he breathed it in. Martin Lander loved the progress the small town was making, what with the steam trains and new telephone exchange, but some things lingered in the past; the workhouse being one of them. It clung desperately to old tradition and refused to be brought into these exciting new times.

Martin considered this as he resumed his walk. He could understand how Cara was so passionate about helping to improve life for the poor. How was it, in this modern life and times, there could still be such a huge divide between the rich and the poor? Would that situation ever change in the years to come? Sadly, he felt it would not.

*

'Daisy!' Charlie scolded. 'Use your knife and fork!'

'Fingers came before cutlery, that's what our mum used to say!' Daisy answered with her nose in the air in an act of defiance. She sniffed and continued to use her hands to eat, daring her brother to challenge her again. Seeing him concede by shaking his head, Daisy gave a curt nod feeling pleased she'd won that round.

Laughter sounded around the room as Martin glanced at Cara. The candles on the table flickered and cast a glow on her blonde hair and as she looked back at him, the reflected light danced in her cornflower blue eyes. Martin's heart skipped a beat as he stared unashamedly at his hostess.

Molly and Gracie exchanged a knowing smile as they saw Martin's gaze.

Martin sucked in a breath, this seemed as good a time as any to explain about his having left the office. 'Cara,' he began tentatively, 'I have to tell you I am no longer a partner at the office… the others have bought me out.'

Cara was shocked at the news and everyone listened as he explained the circumstances that now saw him attempting to work from home. Not wanting to admit he'd been spending too much time on Cara's case, Martin gave them a potted version of the facts.

'I am grateful though that I remain your solicitor,' he said finally.

'Oh Martin! I'm so sorry… this is all my fault!' Cara wailed.

'No!' Martin snapped. 'This is most definitely *not* your fault. Besides, it was time I struck out on my own.'

Gracie asked, 'How can we help?'

'Well, I will need an office, something small… you could help me look for one.' Martin was grateful these people, who had come together as a family, had welcomed him into their circle. 'I don't want to spend all my savings on a building to work from in case the work doesn't come in. After all, I certainly don't want to end up residing with Mr Tulley in the workhouse!' He gave an involuntary shudder at the mere thought of ending up in that dreadful place.

'Martin,' Cara said, 'Mr Harris has been most helpful to me regarding property. I feel sure he would have an appropriate building on his books where you could set up an office.'

'It's worth a try,' he said, his mood lifting. 'Then I will need to bring in some work – I'll need clients.'

'That's easy,' Cara laughed. 'Place an advertisement in the newspapers. Businessmen will always need a good lawyer, and your excellent reputation precedes you! Once people know you now have your own office, they will assume you are doing extremely well. This in turn will tell them you are the best, therefore they will come straight to you.'

'But I'm not doing extremely well!' The despondency in his voice was evident to everyone.

'No, not yet, but the people don't know that! No one needs to know the circumstances surrounding your leaving the partnership! Once they see your advertisement, I guarantee the work will pour in!' Cara's excitement shone in her eyes.

'All right, I'll do it! Certainly nothing is lost in trying!' Martin's mood brightened.

*

The whisper had travelled the workhouse like wildfire. Although segregated, snippets of conversations were overheard and surreptitiously passed on by women working in the dining room. It appeared there was a young woman called Cara Flowers who was offering work to the inmates and their families. It was discussed in the dormitories at night... nine families had been given a home with the men being paid a small wage whilst they worked on their properties. Would this Miss Flowers come back for more? How could she afford it? She must be very rich. When would she return to help again? These questions, albeit having no answers, sparked hope. Maybe they would be lucky enough to be chosen next time. Life in the Spike suddenly held new meaning for everyone. Now they had something to look forward to, something to stay alive for.

Fred Tulley noticed the difference in the increased amount of stone and bone being crushed. He also saw the odd glint in the normally glassy eyes of the inmates; a little smile not too well hidden; the sudden energy in the children's play in the exercise yards. He wondered what the hell was going on until it finally hit him like a thunderbolt.

Flowers! She was the cause of this. If he wasn't too careful he could find himself with a revolt on his hands. Either that or they would all sign themselves out and turn up on her doorstep looking for a handout. He grinned as that picture formed in his head.

Snapping his mind back, Tulley remembered, as the Master, he was in charge. It was he who laid down the rules of this house; the Board of Guardians be damned! Smiling to himself, he puffed out his chest. He could make his own decisions, within reason of course. However, the decision he was about to make was anything but within reason. He was about to reiterate exactly who was boss in this place.

Seeking out his wife, Tulley whispered to her exactly what he had in mind and said it was to be implemented the following day. He would enjoy seeing the inmates' faces when they saw what he had planned for them.

*

Cara was dressed in a white dress. Tight around the waist, it rounded close to the hips. The skirt, with a large frill wrapped around the hemline, fell to meet her matching shoes. The bodice fit her figure well and with a high neck the dress sported long sleeves. A straw boater on her head and a parasol and drawstring bag in her hand, she was ready.

The sun beamed down as she stepped out of the house. It was yet another beautiful day and the birds chirruped in the trees. Martin was there to greet her. Dressed in a white linen suit he also wore a straw boater. His brown and white brogues clicked together as he bowed from the waist, a reminder of bygone days, and Cara laughed.

Together they strolled down Proud's Lane side by side, Martin chatted quietly. They were off to see Mr Harris at the estate agents office in Cambridge Street, hoping to find a property suitable for Martin's new office. Cara listened intently as he described what kind of office he wanted, giving her little opportunity to join in the conversation in his excitement.

'Miss Flowers, Mr Lander, how nice to see you both.' Harris said when they arrived. 'After our telephone conversation yesterday, Miss Flowers...'

'Cara, please call me Cara... all my friends do.' She gave him a little smile.

Nodding, the man went on, 'Cara... I searched my books thoroughly. I have a property over in Green Croft, Mr Lander. It's right next to the railway line and though the windows rattle a bit as the trains pass by, I'm sure you can cope with that.'

Cara saw the mischievous twinkle in Harris's eye before looking at Martin. His mouth was open and he looked aghast at the prospect. Cara burst out laughing. 'I think Mr Harris is joking with you, Martin.'

The young man nodded with an '*I knew that*' look on his face.

Harris apologized for his little joke and, serious once more, said, 'I don't have too many places that are appropriate for you, I'm afraid. I have properties down in Gozzard Street at the other end of town, but they are extremely run-down – ramshackle in fact. I am not entirely sure any of them are at all suitable.'

However, the couple agreed to take a look nevertheless.

Before they left, Cara requested, 'Mr Harris, would you be good enough to search your books for old or abandoned houses and cottages? Anything you think might interest me.' He agreed to look for her. He had already heard about 'Cara's Cottages'... in fact the whole town was now talking about it. That woman was an angel, people said. He smiled to himself; she certainly was doing a good job, there was no doubt about that and... he liked her very much.

It was quite a step to Gozzard Street, so Martin hailed a cab and the couple set off on their little adventure. Cara kept her eye on the streets as they passed, looking out for anything she could invest in herself.

Arriving at the building they were there to see in respect of Martin's new office, Cara could barely contain her feelings. The whole street of about twenty buildings on one side and three blocks of six on the other looked shabby and dirty. On the one side were all houses each joined to the next. The blocks on the other side were run-down shops Cara felt sure were no longer trading. A blacksmith's shop, which remained open, stood at the end of the block.

Shouting to the cabbie to take them back to Harris's office, Cara said to Martin, 'No, no, no! Most definitely not! Nowhere good enough for a solicitor. However...'

Martin was disappointed at not having found a property to be used as an office, but he couldn't help but grin when Cara threw back her head and laughed. He knew these old properties wouldn't stand empty for much longer. Despite their dilapidated condition Cara would have families from the workhouse in them in no time.

Fifteen

Their thin porridge and chunk of bread eaten, the male inmates trooped from the dining hall to the large courtyard outside to begin their daily work. Groans sounded as they saw the large cartloads of stone and bone which had been delivered for crushing. Their breakfast ration had been cut and their workload increased.

'Best get cracking if you want to eat again today!' the Master yelled before disappearing inside the building, chuckling at the pun. He considered himself a very witty man.

Walking down the corridor and out to the laundry, he wanted to check his wife had complied with his instructions. Seeing every blanket from the beds on the laundry floor, he saw Ada had indeed carried out his orders. Maybe she was still useful, for now at least. Two blankets per inmate to be washed meant the women would be hard at it all day. Tulley and his wife exchanged a nod then he turned and walked away.

Ada had instructed the children to sweep out the dormitories before mopping the floors, even the little ones were given dusters to clean down the wooden bed frames.

Mattresses, such as they were, had to be turned.

Fred Tulley smiled to himself as he walked the length of the corridor. His workhouse was back on track, and everyone knew he was the Master, he had made sure of that. He ran a tight ship which was once again floating beautifully on the crest of the inmates' hard work. He decided now was a good time to take a look at these 'Cara's Cottages' he'd heard so much about.

Striding out of the front door, he saw the porter jump to attention before unlocking the gate. With a single nod Tulley marched away from the Spike.

Not having far to go, Tulley walked down the dirt track which took him to the place he sought. Nine cottages stood off to one side of the track, each a flurry of activity.

It was the children who first noticed the Master's imposing form swaggering towards them and a shrill whistle informed their parents a visitor approached. Nine women nervously came out to stand in front of their homes. Even though they no longer lived in the workhouse, fear of its Master still ran deep. Nine men ceased banging and hammering to listen.

Tulley strode to the middle of the row and cast a glance both ways.

The woman who stood nearest him folded her arms across her chest and said loudly, 'What you want here?'

'I've come to see where you're living,' Tulley replied, his arms stretched wide.

The other women and children moved swiftly to stand with their friend providing a united front.

The woman spoke again, 'Now you've seen, you can bugger off!'

'Is that any way to speak to the man who took care of you when your husband couldn't?' Fred grinned. The grin drained away as each husband appeared, hammers in hands.

The woman's husband spoke quietly, an underlying menace lacing his words. 'You heard what the lady said – bugger off! If we catch you round here again...' He held up the hammer for Tulley to see.

Fred feigned bravado as he turned and walked back the way he had come, a loud cheer from the cottagers ringing in his ears. *Bastards!* he thought. *But they'll be back with me before long and when they are...!*

*

Ada Tulley had followed Fred quietly along the corridor and watched through the window as her husband strolled through the workhouse gate, wondering where he'd gone. Her eyes never leaving the swaggering man, Ada considered whether he was off to see another woman. The thought provoked her temper, which was rapidly rising. No, she thought, what woman would take him on? Well wherever it was he was going, and she determined to find out on his return, he'd left her to do all the work... again! She couldn't just go out for a walk in the sunshine when the fancy took her. *It hardly takes any effort to sit on your arse and watch the bone and stone crushing now does it?* She thought spitefully.

Watching the women in the laundry feeding blankets between the rollers of the mangle one after another, her thoughts returned to 'Mad' Liza Townsend. The damned woman had tried to kill her! The job of Matron was becoming dangerous and was she paid any more? Was she hell as like!

Thoroughly disgruntled, she stomped away to the kitchen.

Seeing the cook peeling carrots thinly, Ada screeched her disgust across the room. 'What are you doing?'

The cook's eyes found hers as she retorted, 'Diggin' the garden… what does it look like?'

'Don't peel them, it's wasteful! Chop them, and very small at that!'

Shaking her head, Ada wandered over to the large pan on the range. Lifting the lid, she peeped inside and nodded, the awful smell making her nose wrinkle. 'This soup is to last two days… Master's orders!' With that, Ada walked out.

The cook looked at the inmate helpers and slammed the knife down she had been using on the carrots. 'That's it!' Taking off her apron and cap and throwing them on the floor, she said, 'I've had enough of this! Let her cook her own bloody slop, I quit!' Grabbing her bag, the woman stormed from the room, leaving the inmates with smiles on their faces. The women working in the kitchen took the opportunity, while they were no longer supervised, to fill their bellies with anything they could find. Apron pockets were stuffed with apples and carrots to be passed slyly to the children at dinner time.

Returning to the kitchen later, Ada Tulley was furious when she discovered the cook had left her position without as much as a by-your-leave.

Questioning the inmates, Ada shouted, 'Well what did she say? What reason did she give for just walking out?'

The inmates lowered their heads and said nothing.

'Christ, this is a mess!' Ada railed on. 'Right, you lot will have to do the cooking, that's all there is to it because I ain't doing it!' Ada stamped from the kitchen, her anger evident.

After a moment the inmates burst out laughing. It wasn't long before every inmate knew about the cook's departure. Ada marvelled at how the messages managed to be passed, after all, segregation was in effect. She was also totally unaware of the treats being passed as well.

Marching back to the laundry, Ada thought, *No doubt this is something else Fred will blame me for.* She decided to say nothing about the incident until they were in their quarters that evening. With enough beer inside her she wouldn't care when he would inevitably rant and rave.

It wasn't until her first jug of beer had been consumed that evening that Ada broached the subject of the cook.

'The cook left today,' she said, beer glass in hand, feet up on the table.

'What do you mean, left?' Tulley asked gruffly without taking his eyes from the newspaper held in front of his face.

Ada sighed audibly showing her frustration at her husband's stupidity. 'Her's gone! Her's left! Her's done a flit and… her ain't coming back!'

'Why?' Fred boomed, slamming the newspaper onto his knees.

Ada shrugged her shoulders and drained her glass.

'What did you do to her this time?' Fred growled.

'Oh I knew it would have to be my fault!' Ada said as she poured more beer. 'I'll have you know, Fred Tulley, I was carrying out your orders to cut the food ration!'

'Bugger it! Now what will we do?' Fred was now pacing the room.

'I don't know, but I'll tell you this… I ain't doing the cooking and that's final!' Ada yelled before she took a long drink of her ale.

'Bugger it! Bugger it!' Tulley shouted. 'We'll have to get another cook and bloody quick!'

'Good luck with that,' Ada chuckled, wiping her mouth on her sleeve.

'Ada, you are worse than bloody useless!' Tulley yelled, knowing full well his voice would carry on the night air and reach the ears of the inmates. 'Just get me my supper!'

'Supper you say... get your own bloody supper!' Ada screamed back.

In a flash, Fred was before his drunken wife and slapped her face soundly.

Ada dropped her beer glass, spilling its contents over her apron. Just as quickly she jumped up and snatched up a letter opener which had been lying on the table.

Squaring up to him, she yelled, 'That's the first and last time you will strike me, Fred Tulley, you mark my words!' With a snarl she rushed at him and the sharp point of the weapon jabbed into his arm which he raised in defence of the oncoming attack.

Fred screamed out in pain, then he saw the blood oozing from his wound. Looking at his wife who stood with the letter opener held high like a dagger, he saw she was ready to strike again – he had to disarm her.

Fury and hate built up to boiling point now, Fred jumped at his wife, snatching the weapon from her hand. Being so drunk she was unable to keep her balance; she fell to the floor. Fred stood over her, his eyes wild and full of hateful disgust. Unable to contain himself a moment longer, he yelled at the top of his voice, 'Ada, tonight you die!' Lurching forward, he brought down the weapon towards the cowering woman. As she tried to scramble away from him, the letter opener embedded itself in her shoulder. Ada screamed out her pain as Fred stood back, suddenly realizing what he'd done.

Sixteen

Joseph Purcell stepped from his carriage outside the row of dwellings now known as 'Cara's Cottages'. He had been the Magistrate for Bilston town for the last ten years and Chairman of the Board of Guardians for five of those ten. He had heard about the young Miss Cara Flowers and wanted to see for himself how the former inmates of the Spike were faring in their new environment.

A shrill whistle bounced off the cottages, an alert to the mothers from the children that a stranger had arrived. As one, a line of women moved to the front of their houses, arms crossed over chests. Seeing the stranger, their body posture remained rigid. The husbands came forward too and, after introducing himself, Joseph Purcell shook the hand of each man.

'I see the work is coming on,' he said as he looked at the buildings. He gave a thin smile as a chair was dragged outside for him; he noted he was not about to be invited inside.

After tea and cake, he spoke again: 'I have heard a great deal about Cara Flowers and her work, and I wished to see for myself how you good people are faring in your new homes.'

Joseph asked questions of the new residents: were they paying rent? How could they afford that as they had no jobs? Would their children be attending school? Did the men anticipate finding work? How did they feel about Cara being their landlady?

All very forthright questions, and it was one of the women who gave him a forthright answer. 'Now you look here, Mr Purcell, you can ask as many questions as you like but we ain't giving you no answers.' Rumbles of assertive agreement sounded.

'I was just enquiring...' Purcell began, but the woman cut him off.

'Cara Flowers has been bloody good to us,' she spread her arms to encompass the little group, 'so what makes you think we would betray her trust by telling you her business? What goes on between us and her is our business and no one else's. I don't know what it is you want here, but whatever it is, you won't get it from us. I, for one, won't have anything said against that young wench!'

When the applause died down, Purcell said, 'Obviously I have not made myself clear, which has raised suspicion of my visit. I came only to congratulate you all, and praise Miss Flowers for the marvellous work she has undertaken.'

As Purcell said his goodbye and climbed into his carriage to leave, the mutterings began once more.

The men and women remained sceptical at his unannounced visit. They didn't trust the man, for all he was a magistrate. He was fishing in their pool for information... why? What was he up to? They later agreed it would be wise to let Cara know the next time she called.

Joseph leaned back in the carriage seat and pondered what he saw as a wasted half an hour. The residents had told him nothing more than he'd already heard on the town grapevine. That Cara had been tasked by her dying grandmother to find and care for any living relatives. She had found two members of her family and was indeed looking after them. She was on a mission – that much was evident – to help the poor of the town and had set her sights on the workhouse. What was she up to? Why the workhouse? There were more than enough poor folk in the town she could aid. Joseph couldn't help but admire the woman's tenacity and ingenuity. Then he chided himself for such a thought, women should really stay at home and attend to their children, they should not be poking their noses in men's business.

Miss Flowers had become great friends with Martin Lander, too, Purcell had heard. The brilliant young lawyer had been in his courthouse many times and Joseph felt he was a man to reckon with.

As for Cara, Joseph thought he would like to meet her. He wanted to know precisely why she had such a keen interest in the workhouse. As the carriage rumbled over the cobbled streets he made his decision. He would write to this young woman and ask if he may call on her sometime… in his official capacity of course!

*

Martin Lander had eventually found a property in Earle Street, just two streets away from where he lived, and was busy setting up his business there. Mr Harris had been most helpful in suggesting the new location for the solicitor's office.

He thought about Cara and how she had now bought the

twenty houses and the shops in Gozzard Street which had stood empty in a part of town which appeared to be dying. She fully intended to revitalize the area by moving families in who would renovate the buildings and maybe open small businesses eventually. He smiled as he manoeuvred furniture into place in his new premises. He knew she would snap up those empty buildings and, sure enough, she had. His smile turned to a grin when he remembered her driving a hard bargain with Harris regarding the price. Cara was turning out to be a shrewd businesswoman.

*

In the meantime, Cara decided to telephone the workhouse. 'Good morning Mr Tulley,' Cara said into the telephone.

'Miss Flowers,' Fred's voice was followed by a huge sigh, causing Cara to smile.

'I would like to make an appointment to visit please,' she said.

'I'm afraid there's been an incident so you will have to wait a while.' Tulley's voice sounded tired.

'I see. Then I will wait until after the weekend. Thank you, Mr Tulley.' Cara heard a grunt before the connection went dead.

Wondering what the incident could have been, she was startled by a knock on her front door as she walked past it from the hall to the kitchen. Opening the door wide, she was faced with a stout woman wearing a hat with an enormous feather sticking out at an odd angle. The woman nodded and the feather bobbed.

'Miss Flowers?' the woman asked in a no-nonsense manner.

'Yes,' Cara answered, unable to draw her eyes from the

bobbing feather. The woman was not well off, as could be seen by her old high-neck blouse and long skirt with a patch on the side.

'My name is Bertha Jenkins, and until yesterday I was the cook at the workhouse.' Bertha's hands were crossed and lay on her ample stomach.

'Please Mrs Jenkins, won't you come in and have some tea?' Cara urged. As she led the way to the kitchen, Cara wondered if the incident at the workhouse had involved this woman in some way. With Daisy and Charlie playing in the garden, Cara introduced the woman to Gracie Cox and Molly Barton.

'I've been hearing a lot about you and your good deeds, Miss Flowers,' the woman said.

'Cara, please call me Cara... and thank you.'

'Bertha.' The nod of the head confirmed they should use her given name. 'I know about you trying to get them poor buggers out of that place... beggin' your pardon.' Bertha apologized for what she felt may be inappropriate language. Cara nodded that no slight had been taken and Bertha continued. 'I have things to tell you that will make your hair curl!'

Gracie and Molly leaned forward in their seats in their eagerness to hear what Bertha Jenkins was about to divulge.

*

Fred Tulley had called in the doctor, who was now wrapping a bandage around the arm with the stab wound. Folding a sling, he tied it at the back of Tulley's neck before gently placing the arm to rest inside.

'There, that should hold it nicely. Now I think you should

inform Purcell of what has occurred.' Seeing Fred's horror-stricken face, he added, 'Either you do… or I will.'

Leaving it at that, the doctor turned to Ada who was moaning in pain. 'Right, Ada, let's have a look at that shoulder.'

'Ooooh…!' Ada groaned as the doctor cut the sleeve from her dress in order to assess the damage. 'That bastard stabbed me!' she howled.

'I believe it was in retaliation, Mrs Tulley, according to your husband anyway. Now hold still while I take a look at your wound.' The doctor's patience was wearing thin with all that was going on. His mind wandered as he worked, maybe it was time for he, himself, to quit his post at the workhouse.

As he worked, he listened as Fred informed the Chairman of the Board of Guardians, over the telephone, that there had been a terrible accident. Dr Cooper smiled to himself. The Tulleys were in a pickle now and he wondered how they would talk themselves out of this one.

With no cook to instruct in the kitchen, the inmates, unsure of what to do, had argued about whether to make breakfast themselves. Eventually, hunger won out and they began to settle, each to their own job. No thin porridge made with water this morning, but thick creamy oatmeal with sugar sprinkled on top! A large chunk of fresh bread accompanied each bowl served to every person in the building. The Matron was nowhere to be seen, so gossip was passed without hesitation about all the yelling and screaming they'd heard take place. Mothers sobbed their joy at seeing their children again and hugged them freely and fiercely. Husbands and wives spent a few tender moments together before the next sitting was due in. They knew whatever was keeping Ada Tulley occupied, it wouldn't be too long before she was back, so they relished the time they had.

Joseph Purcell arrived disgruntled at having been woken so early. Dropping into a chair in the boardroom, he snapped, 'Right Tulley, explain!' Joseph's eyes remained on the Master standing before him, his arm in a sling. He ignored the Matron, who also wore a sling, and the doctor who stood behind Tulley.

'Well sir, it's like this... Mrs Tulley... that is to say, my wife...' Fred was at a loss as to how to explain.

Stepping forward, Dr Cooper saved him the bother saying quickly, 'Mrs Tulley was drunk... again! She stabbed Mr Tulley who then stabbed her in return. Oh... and the cook has resigned!' Screwing up his mouth, he dropped his chin, his body language screamed... *'Ha!'*

Joseph Purcell stared in disbelief. After a moment he stood, and as he walked out he called over his shoulder, 'I will convene an emergency meeting at two o'clock this afternoon! Everybody be there!'

Dr Cooper shook his head as they filed out of the room; the Tulleys had begun to bicker again as they followed behind him.

'You started it...'

'It was your fault...'

'If you weren't drunk...'

'Oh, put a sock in it...'

Dr Cooper whirled on the argumentative pair. 'Will you both... shut the hell up!' Then he stamped away, leaving the open-mouthed Tulleys in his wake.

*

The Board members had discussed the incident at great length before the doctor and the Tulleys had been invited into the boardroom to join them.

'Mr Tulley,' Joseph spoke confidently, 'this is the second time we have had to call an emergency meeting. This sort of thing simply cannot go on! I must warn you, if anything like this should happen again, the Board will have no option but to see you dismissed!'

Dr Cooper fumed, Tulley was going to get away with it again! He muttered sarcastically, 'Naughty boy, don't do it again.'

Joseph's eyes moved to the doctor. 'Dr Cooper, do you have something to say?'

'Actually I do.' The doctor stepped forward. 'This man and his drunkard of a wife are not fit to run this institution!'

'Dr Cooper, please confine your comments to medical matters only as that is your profession.' Purcell kept his voice calm.

Dr Cooper did not however, and his voice boomed out. 'I did that once before if you remember, regarding the death of the Townsend child, but nothing was done about that!'

'This is an entirely different matter,' Joseph said.

'I was called in on both occasions, which means both incidents were medically related… a connection there I think?' The doctor's voice dripped sarcasm.

'We digress,' Joseph said, trying to regain control of the situation. 'What we have to decide upon now is how to handle this matter quietly.'

Again Dr Cooper jumped in. 'Quietly! Mr Purcell the "matter" of the cook leaving is the talk of the town! Everyone is aware your cook has walked out and her reason for doing so. It won't be long before word is out that the Master and Matron have tried to kill each other!'

'That cannot be allowed to happen, Dr Cooper!' Purcell began to lose his cool demeanour.

'Mr Purcell, word will get out... like it or not. Then will follow how these two...' The doctor tilted his head towards the Tulleys, '... have been treating the inmates. They have overworked and underfed them. They have beaten the children...'

Purcell held up his hands for silence, but the doctor was in full swing.

'Oh no Mr Purcell! I will not be silenced again! The Townsend child died of food poisoning which, as you know, was noted on her death certificate. In effect, she was murdered, albeit inadvertently!'

Gasps sounded around the room as the doctor continued. 'Mrs Tulley is known to be drunk every night. Yes, I am the medical officer for this facility but only because no other bloody doctor would take on the job! Mr Purcell, members of the Board, Mr and Mrs Tulley...' He looked at each in turn then resumed speaking. 'I resign my post as medical officer to the workhouse as of this moment!' Dr Cooper smiled, turned on the spot military style and walked out.

'Now what the hell do we do?' Joseph Purcell asked his esteemed colleagues who were shaking their heads in disbelief at the turn of events. 'Well something has to be done otherwise you'll lose your jobs on the Board... more to the point, I will lose mine as Chairman! No job, no money, and no perks, you best think about that, and soon!'

Seventeen

Martin Lander had arrived at The Laburnums just as Bertha Jenkins was about to reveal all. With tea poured and cake served, Martin listened with the others as Bertha began.

'I was cook at the Spike for years, but yesterday I walked out! I'd had enough and that Tulley woman refusing to allow me to peel carrots was the last straw!'

Gracie, as a cook herself, nodded her approval. Bertha directed her comments to her. 'You know how hard it is to make a meal outta nothing.' Gracie nodded again. 'Well I never had anything but rubbish to work with. Rotting vegetables, meat that was always just turned, potatoes with eyes as big as saucers…' Bertha lowered her eyes, 'and that poor little wench.'

'What wench?' Molly asked, unable to contain herself.

'The Townsend girl… all the kids took sick and the doctor was called in. I told the Matron that meat was too far gone, but her insisted it be used. That's what made the kids poorly and the Townsend girl… died because of it!' Tears rolled down Bertha's face. 'I had to lie to the Board, saying it weren't the meat... I needed that job! But that kiddie haunts me, it turned her mother mad and they carted her off to the lunatic asylum! Now I ain't got a job...'

Cara was shocked to her core. A child had died in the workhouse! 'Was anything done about it Bertha?'

'No, not that I know of. I expect the Tulley's got away with it!' The woman wailed.

'But surely someone would have been told?' Gracie asked.

'The doctor would have come, he would have seen to the kiddie. But... I don't know if it were reported to the powers that be.' Bertha sniffed. 'Oh dear God save me from going in that place as an inmate!'

'You won't, Bertha,' Cara still reeling from the shock, assured the sobbing woman. 'I heard the school at the end of Bow Street, over by the police station, is looking for a cook. Now, don't fret anymore; you did the right thing... Gracie, more tea please?'

A while later, after Bertha had left, Cara joined the others saying, 'Well what do you make of all that?'

'What I make of it is this... the Tulleys should be sacked!' Molly said indignantly.

'I can think of far worse things to do to them!' Gracie mumbled as she cleared the tea things away. 'Fancy a little child dying like that and the Tulley's obviously ain't suffered none by it!'

Cara shook her head in dismay, 'Poor little mite, I hope she didn't suffer too badly.'

'She would have,' Gracie said, 'Food poisoning gives you the bellyache something chronic! The Tulleys should be jailed for what they've done!'

*

The sun shone down on Cara's pale blue dress of fine damask. Her matching parasol shaded her head on which sat her straw boater. The day for her visit to the workhouse had arrived and as she walked briskly across the waste ground opposite her house towards Green Lanes, she was more desperate than ever now to see the inmates out as soon as possible. The information gleaned from Bertha had fuelled her anger and she was adamant she would see the workhouse closed down. Wild flowers were in full bloom and insects buzzed busily between them. Even amid such poverty there was beauty if one knew where to look. Coming to the Allotment Gardens, Cara stopped to admire the flowers, everywhere a host of vibrant colours. She turned her head as the steam train whistle blew and she heard the engine rumble along the tracks.

Arriving at the end of the dirt track, she stopped again to pass the time of day with the people in her cottages. She was amazed to see how much improved the buildings were in such a short time and pleased to discover the women had formed a baking co-operative. They had secured a stall in the marketplace and were now in a position to begin paying rent. These people had been motivated by her helping hand and their progress had been swift.

To the men, Cara said, 'I have more properties over in Gozzard Street if you are in a position to help the new families living there take on the repairs.'

A chorus of 'ayes' went up as she passed out small bags of sweets to their children.

'Cara,' one of the women said, 'we had an unannounced visit from Joseph Purcell the other day.'

'Oh really? What did he want?' Cara asked.

'He wanted to know all about you. The cheeky bugger

asked if we was paying rent! I said we wouldn't answer his questions then I told him to sling his hook!' The woman folded her arms with a flourish.

'Well done! Thank you for that.' Cara smiled.

'We all had a bad feeling, Cara, so you just be on your guard with that man.' The woman's head bobbed up and down.

'I will, thank you all.'

Saying her goodbyes, Cara thought about what she'd been told about Purcell as she made her way up the dirt track. Why was he asking so many questions about her? Was he up to something and, if so, what? She felt an uneasy feeling settle on her as she continued to walk.

Cara approached the gates of the workhouse once more, and the porter opened the gate with a doff of his cap. Cara nodded in response, wondering at his sudden change in demeanour.

The huge oak front door was opened by a painfully thin woman who escorted Cara to the Master's office. The woman scuttled away as Cara knocked on his door. Standing again in Tulley's office, she noticed the sling holding his arm, but made no mention of it.

With hardly a word between them, they walked the dark corridor to the bone and stone yard. Cara was surprised at Tulley's seeming acquiescence but said nothing. Work stopped immediately as the men saw her, and Tulley wandered away leaving her to it. He had more pressing matters on his mind. Leaning his back against the doorway, Tulley nursed his injured arm, still cursing his wife under his breath.

Cara spoke quietly as the men gathered around her. 'I'm sure you are aware it is my wish to eventually get everyone out of his hateful place,' she said, 'but I can only do this a little at a time. That is why I'm asking for families first, but be assured... I won't forget the rest of you. I have nine families in their own homes and in work and I now have twenty houses plus some shops badly in need of renovation down in Gozzard Street. So, I need to know who of you still have family in here.'

Ten hands went up. 'Right, please stand over there, you'll be out in three hours.' The men brushed themselves down and moved to wait in the appointed place, grins on their faces. 'Now, men with wives?' Another ten hands shot up and at her nod they joined the others. To the men left behind, she said, 'I'm sorry, today is not your day, but it will come as soon as I can manage it. Don't lose heart, I *will* be back for you.' A round of applause saw her flush to the roots of her hair.

Cara waited outside the gates while the inmates were signed out. Pacing back and forth, she wondered how many inmates were left inside. She grinned widely when she suddenly realized all the children were free. At least now there would not be another episode like that of the Townsend child. Cara felt badly that she had been unable to help the little girl, but then she hadn't known what was going on at that time. Now all the families were out and now some husbands and wives. She knew, however, that the Relieving Officer was still offering workhouse 'tickets' to the destitute. The places her charges had vacated would be filled by others soon enough. Although she was helping some of the poor of Bilston, she was treating the symptoms rather than the cause. She needed to prevent people going into the workhouse in the first place, and somehow she was determined to find a way.

*

Fred Tulley had lingered just inside the doorway listening to Cara's words to the workers. So, it was her intention to clear the workhouse of its inmates! Tulley grinned to himself. That would never happen, never in a month of Sundays. There were far too many out of work and starving. He could not prevent inmates signing themselves out, but he knew others would be filling those empty places before too long. Cara Flowers was on a road to nowhere. She was, however, becoming a thorn in his side disrupting the smooth running of the place. With his wife getting drunk and trying to kill him, Fred was growing very tired of the two meddling women. He felt no remorse about what he'd done to his wife, in fact he began to wish he'd followed through with it. He smiled when he remembered the last meeting of the Board and the doctor resigning his post. At least that had taken the heat off him and his wife. Now they would live to fight another day in the workhouse and he didn't want to attract the attention of the Board again.

Fred took his time as he completed the paperwork for the release of the men, women and children, knowing full well this would aggravate Cara Flowers to boiling point. Then he watched from the front door as they trooped out of the gate. He saw the hugs and handshakes as they greeted the woman who they saw as their saviour, the High and Mighty Miss Cara Flowers.

Snorting his disgust, he slammed the front door shut and with a sigh he rolled his eyes at the sound of his wife's screeching voice. Now what?

'Mr Tulley!' Ada yelled. 'The children's quarters are empty! We have no kids left!' Her voice assaulted his ears from behind as she followed along behind him. They walked back to his office and he slumped into his chair behind his desk.

'That's correct, Mrs Tulley, I'm glad to see you are your usual observant self.' His sarcasm was lost on her, however, as she continued to rail.

'Whatever shall we say when the Board meets again?'

With another huge sigh, Fred said, 'We will explain to them how Cara Flowers is finding the inmates work and housing and that we now have plenty of room for more to enter this humble abode.' Seeing her grin showing her blackened teeth, he shook his head and screwed up his mouth in disgust.

*

Leading her group away from the Spike, Cara began to explain about the houses in Gozzard Street.

'I'm afraid they are in a terrible state. They need a lot of work doing on them, but if you can live in them while the work is undertaken, then at least you have a home of your own. The workers from my other cottages have agreed to come over and help so it will speed up the repairs.'

Traipsing through the streets, the group looked like a band of raggle-taggle gypsies. Thin frames were almost hidden by the rags they wore. Dirt and grime was ingrained in their skin, and the odour they gave off was appalling. Their short hair was testament to where they had been living. Cara saw the children's shoes with the toes cut away to allow for growth. She noticed one man's boot, the sole flapping loose and slapping in time with his tread. The long skirts of the women had great gaping holes in; they had nothing to patch them with. But, for all that, they were giving their grateful thanks at being given this opportunity to have a life outside of the workhouse.

Arriving in the vicinity of the houses she had bought, Cara saw the men's faces fall and said quickly, 'I did warn you they were in disrepair…' Looking at the buildings, she added, 'I'm so sorry, I think it's more than that… they're dilapidated! I was so eager to get you all released I don't think I realized how bad they are!' Cara felt wretched.

One of the women slapped her child soundly for calling the houses 'shitholes' before she said to him, 'You, young man, can always go back to the Spike, you ungrateful little bugger!' Turning to Cara, she said, 'I ain't half sorry, Miss, but you watch we'll have this lot looking like mansions in no time! We're just grateful for what you're doing for us.'

Cara's spirits lifted slightly at the woman's words.

Her son muttered his apology to Cara and she smiled down at him. 'If your dad and the other men will go to the market for food and other things, maybe they'll bring some sweets back for all you children.' The lad grinned widely.

The women and children immediately went about selecting a house to live in and Cara handed out a few pounds to each of the men. She knew with a few 'bob' in their pockets, the men could hold up their heads with dignity. She smiled as windows were flung wide and the delighted squeals of the children filled her ears. Her spirits lifted even more as she watched work begin, the women shouting orders to their men and children.

Cara walked back into the town with the men. She enjoyed their banter, each promising to pay her rent once they were on their feet.

'I live at The Laburnums in Proud's Lane, so if you have any problems you can find me there,' Cara said. 'Now go and fill your larders and please... don't forget the sweets for the children.'

'More than our life's worth,' one of the men said then added, 'thank you Miss Flowers, thank you from the bottom of every heart here.'

Blushing, Cara said jauntily, 'Be off with you otherwise your wives will be playing hell with you.'

Waving goodbye in the market, she watched the men walk away. Her thoughts turned swiftly to those left behind in the workhouse. She needed to find other properties now. She had to make good on her promise. The warm feeling she'd experienced earlier was replaced by worry now as she thought about how to fulfil that promise.

Walking up Proud's Lane, Cara's thoughts turned back to the people and properties she had just left. Had she made an error in judgement with those particular buildings? Could they be made habitable... or were they too ramshackle? Yes, the people were grateful, but would they have been better off left where they were in the workhouse? No. She could not believe that. She determined to ensure those houses would be made comfortable quickly for the families living in them.

She also remembered approaching the estate agent some while back about the land abutting Cara's Cottages. She had plans for that piece of waste ground and had asked him to discover who it belonged to.

Daisy met her at the door, shouting, 'Cara, a letter's come for you!'

Hugging her younger sister, the young woman took the letter to the kitchen and sat at the table.

'Now then Miss Daisy Flowers, how was school today?' Cara asked.

'Alright,' Daisy answered with a beaming face, 'the teacher said I was good at reading cos I already knew my letters.'

'Good girl. I'm very proud of you.' Cara said then turned to Charlie. 'And you, young man, how was your day?'

'It was okay, I did some sketching and the teacher liked it. She said I had a talent for it.'

'That's marvellous. Oh I have such a clever family.' Cara said clapping her hands together.

As her siblings helped Gracie set the table for tea and cake, she couldn't believe how well they had settled in with their new family, and she was grateful for it.

Opening the letter Daisy had passed to her, she scanned the words. 'Now there's a turn-up for the books,' she said to Gracie and Molly who looked on with puzzled expressions. 'It seems the Chairman of the Board of Guardians wishes to come here and meet with me!'

'Really?' Gracie asked. 'I wonder what he wants.'

'I have no idea,' Cara answered, 'but I'm sure we'll find out soon enough. You know he visited the residents in Cara's Cottages?'

'Why?' Molly asked.

'Apparently he was asking questions… about me. He wanted to know everything, but the cottagers told him to… go away!'

Molly giggled. 'Damn cheek of the man!'

Cara continued, 'Do you think he's out to try and stop me getting people out of the workhouse?'

'I don't rightly see as how he can,' Gracie muttered. 'You ain't breaking the law as far as I know, so it's anyone's guess.'

'I don't like it, Gracie! He's snooping around asking questions of other people about me. Why doesn't he come and ask me those questions rather than bother my tenants?' Cara felt anger rising in her.

'Now then wench, don't get all riled up about it,' Gracie soothed, 'besides, maybe that's why he wants to come over and meet with you.'

Cara nodded but the frustration and anger remained within her.

Whatever the reason, she couldn't shake the feeling of foreboding that began to weigh her down. She had the dreadful feeling this meeting was a ploy… but to what end? Sighing heavily, she knew she would just have to wait and see.

Eighteen

The massive expanse of waste ground behind Cara's Cottages belonged to no one that he could discern and Mr Harris, the estate agent, wondered why Cara Flowers had enquired about it. Over the months of their dealings with other properties, he had promised to direct his clients to use Martin Lander as their solicitor as Cara had promised to continue to use his agency. Mr Harris knew of the actions Cara had taken with regard to the workhouse and he admired her for it. He was also aware that for her to pursue her chosen task she would be on the lookout for any old buildings – and that's where he came in.

Harris scanned his map of Bilston which lay on his desk. The patch of land Cara had indicated was shaped like the side of a house; floor, two sides and a pointed roof. It backed directly onto her cottages. One side was edged by Regent Street and the part which looked like a roof ran along the end of the Allotment Gardens. Behind this area was a larger patch still which abutted half the length of Proud's Lane.

He thought whatever Cara Flowers intended for this scrubland would certainly be an improvement, and Harris had encouraged the young woman to stake her claim to this land with the local council before someone else did.

Folding the map, he dropped it into the drawer of his desk. He would be very interested to see how Cara's next undertaking would pan out.

*

Martin Lander and Cara took a cab to the council offices. The local council, it seemed, owned the land she was interested in.

'Well, Miss Flowers, that land does indeed belong to the council,' the man sitting opposite her said, 'and as far as I can tell there are no plans for its use. Therefore I can see no reason why it should not be sold to you.'

'That's marvellous!' Cara gushed her thanks.

Telling her the asking price, the man was taken aback when Martin intervened. 'That's a great deal of money! Rather too much, I would say!'

Cara glanced at Martin, saying, 'I do need that land, Martin, but as you say, it is rather a lot of money.' Turning to face the council officer again, she said, 'That land is turning into scrubland and, as you point out, there are no further intentions for its use. Therefore, I will offer you half the amount you have asked.' Holding up a hand to prevent the man's counterargument, she went on, 'Consider... empty waste space which no one else wants and you can't be rid of or... money in the bank and the millstone shifted from around your neck.'

Lander smiled as he watched her bargain for the land.

'You have a very valid point there, Miss Flowers. I have to agree, hanging on to the land would not benefit the council in any way.' Looking down at the paperwork then back to the girl, he added, 'Therefore I concede. You may buy the land for your proposed amount.' The council officer smiled as he stood to shake hands with the young woman who had stood her ground, so to speak. He had heard of this girl and was very pleased to see her wanting to help.

Cara beamed her happiness. 'I will arrange for a banker's draft immediately. You will have your money this very afternoon.'

'Miss Flowers, may I ask your intentions for the land you have just purchased?' The man asked as he signed the relevant documentation before passing it to Martin to witness.

Cara told him what she had in mind.

The man nodded then said, 'Everyone in the town is talking of your good work, you are well known for your achievements.' He saw Cara smile shyly and the blush rise to her cheeks. 'You and I have agreed a deal here today and although your money is not yet in the council coffers, I am entrusting the deeds to the land to you right now.' Standing up, he extended his hand. 'Good luck with the land, Miss Flowers, I hope all works out well for you.'

Cara clutched the deeds tightly as they left the building and she chatted excitedly to Martin about her new acquisition on their journey home.

As they travelled, Cara told him of the meeting with the Chairman of the Board of Guardians later in the week and asked if he would be present. He assured her he would be delighted. She told him she was nervous about the upcoming meeting, not being at all sure how to handle herself, but his attendance and support would ease her worry somewhat.

Once more at home, Cara pondered her next move. She knew she now needed workers. She intended to turn the waste land into allotment plots for growing fruit and vegetables, thus providing work for more men to whom she would pay a small wage whilst they were being set up. But unfortunately she was unable to get the other men in the workhouse released as she had no more accommodation available. She had gone over her bank account figures and she had enough to invest in buying more housing for the workers. Knowing her family's buying and selling of property over the years had ensured that Cara was now very wealthy, however she still needed to keep a wary eye on those figures. The last thing she needed was to run out of money before completing her task. She smiled as she realized the buying up of property appeared to run in the family.

The following day Cara hailed a cab and told the driver she would hire him for the day provided he didn't mind waiting for her at times. The driver was more than happy to oblige the pretty young woman who was working so hard for those in need of her help.

Cara's first port of call the following morning was with Mr Harris to collect the list of available properties he'd drawn up. He had told her it would be waiting for her at his office. And indeed it was.

Showing the paper to the cabbie, she asked his advice on the best way to visit all the properties on the list. Scanning the names, the cabbie pointed to each street in turn, and Cara climbed aboard to begin their journey.

The carriage rumbled through the streets slowly, every now and then manoeuvring around carts and people shuffling along. Cara was on her way to Brook Street which lay just around the corner from Gozzard Street. There were five houses vacant and she was eager to see them. These buildings stood on the corner where Brook Street met

Temple Street. Climbing out of the carriage, Cara cast an eye over each. They were locally known as two-up two-down, having a kitchen and living room downstairs and two bedrooms upstairs. Each house was joined to the next and had a front and back door. One entry which led to the back of each house stood at the end of the row. The houses were in a sorry state; roof tiles missing and window frames rotting away. Was it possible they would be habitable whilst renovations were underway? She needed every property she could lay her hands on so she would just have to find a way to make it work.

Cara climbed back into the cab, and it rolled along to its next destination. Chapel Street crossed the bottom of Temple Street so the journey was short. Out of the eight houses on one side of the street, four lay empty. Again, badly in need of repair, they were very much like the others she had viewed. Nine possibilities so far, all of which would need a lot of work doing to them.

The carriage left Chapel Street, crossing the busy main thoroughfare which was Oxford Street then came to a halt in Hare Street. Here four houses and what looked to have once been a warehouse or small factory stood in the shadows. She wondered why so many properties were standing empty? Maybe Mr Harris would know. She made a mental reminder to ask him.

Cara looked over each building. The yards were full of rubbish and the smell emanating caused her nose to wrinkle in disgust. She began to worry that the buildings were too far gone to be of use. Some had the remnants of what were once chimneys. Others had doors missing completely and their windows were smashed. The quarry floor tiles were lifting and would need to be replaced. The whitewash was peeling from the walls and mildew grew in abundance. The brickwork was black with the fine coal dust that seemed to coat everything. They were dark inside and Cara seriously wondered if they could be turned around and made into comfortable homes. But then, even the state they were in was preferable to the workhouse... wasn't it?

Shaking her head in dismay, Cara asked the cabbie to move on to the next street. Here she climbed out to look at the buildings. These were in a dire condition, there was nothing left in the gaps where window frames had once stood. Standing back she noted half of the roof tiles were missing. Some had walls which were crumbling to the ground, they were complete ruins. They were very unsafe and she sighed as she discounted them completely. Climbing back into the cab, she asked to be returned to Harris's office. Thirteen houses and a small factory – how much was Mr Harris willing to sell them for? Certainly they were in worse condition than the others she had purchased and she was determined to remind Mr Harris of that fact.

Once more in the estate agent's office, Cara asked, 'Mr Harris, why are there so many empty properties down in that particular area?'

Pulling out the street map, the man spread it on the desk before her. Coming round to stand next to where she sat, he traced a finger over the area she had just visited. 'As you can see, Gozzard Street is here and Brook Street here. Chapel Street and Hare Street are further down here. Now about ten years ago, scarlet fever broke out in that district and the council cordoned it all off. They didn't know what else to do, so the whole area was put into quarantine as advised by the doctors.' He pointed his finger and ran it around the square of streets, showing its enforced perimeter.

Returning to his own seat, he continued. 'It was a dreadful time, no one was allowed in or out of that area for fear of the illness spreading to the rest of the town. The police patrolled and the council had to leave food by the fence they erected. Only one doctor volunteered to treat the sick.' He shook his head sadly at the memory. 'The fever ravaged the area and whole families succumbed. By the end, very few had survived, fortunately the doctor was one of them.'

'Good grief!' Cara said her hand on her chest. 'That's awful, those poor people!' After a moment of scanning the map again, she realized just how many people must have died of the disease. Then she asked, 'Why did the properties remain empty?'

'Folk were afraid, Cara. Even though the doctor assured everyone the fever had died out, and the fence was removed, people stayed away from the area. They had seen whole streets of families taken to meet their maker, and they didn't wish to join them.' Mr Harris's voice held a sadness as he spoke. 'Eventually, people came to Bilston from other towns and, not knowing the terrible history of the area, some took up residence, but a lot of the houses remained empty. I'm not sure the areas will ever be revived.'

'Look Mr Harris, if I can buy these properties, I assure you I will fill them with people. I will give the area a new lease of life!' Cara's excitement began to rise.

'I can only wish you good luck, but you may well be buying a pig-in-a-poke.' Mr Harris saw her frown, not understanding what he meant. 'Let me explain. Even if you buy these buildings, people, even those from the workhouse, may not wish to live in them. Then you'll have the same problem as me... empty houses no one will move into.'

'We'll see about that, Mr Harris, you let me have these

properties and then watch what I do with them.' Cara was determined not to back down on this.

Eventually Mr Harris conceded. Her contention was – money in his pocket was preferable to having empty buildings on his books. Houses that no one else was interested in. Properties, although almost derelict, she could put to good use and... Mr Harris would be helping in her quest to aid the poor of the town. She left the office as the new owner of properties in the three streets she had visited.

*

Cara had devilment in her and decided not to make an appointment at the Spike, she would just arrive and hope the 'delightful' Mr Tulley would grant her an interview with the inmates. Her confidence was increasing day by day and with each property bought it meant more folk released from the soul-destroying drudgery of the workhouse.

The cab rolled up to the large gate and Cara climbed out. Paying the cabbie, she turned to see the porter had opened the gate to allow her entry. He was unaware she was not expected by the workhouse Master. By now he was used to her comings and goings.

Hammering on the oak door inside, Cara waited. It was opened by the same rail-thin woman, who gave her a wan smile before leading her to the office.

Tulley inwardly fumed at the audacity of the young woman now standing before him.

'Miss Flowers,' he growled, 'it is customary to make an appointment, as well you know!' Cara nodded and placed ten pounds on the desk. She watched his greedy eyes covet the money. 'However,' Tulley looked up at her, 'as we have conducted business on previous occasions, I see no reason why we should not do so again. I am incapacitated as you see…' he indicated his sling, '… so perhaps you might see yourself to the yard. I'm sure you know the way by now.' In reality Tulley, even having given his injury as an excuse, couldn't be bothered to act as this woman's guide.

'I do, sir, but I feel it would be highly inappropriate to wander around your workhouse alone. You are the Master here after all…' Cara smiled sweetly.

Getting to his feet reluctantly, Tulley left the money untouched on the desk and led the way to the bone and stone yard, where Cara's appearance stopped work immediately. They all knew who this lady was and if stopping work irked the Master, they didn't care. Cara Flowers was far more important to them at the moment. It was she who could get them out of this place, and they were desperate to be the next to be taken out. The men gathered around her, taking care not to dirty her clothes.

Tulley retreated into the doorway once more, his mind on the money on his desk.

'Gentlemen,' Cara said as she looked around her. Each man nodded a response. 'You are all aware of my ultimate goal…' More nods. 'All those with children are now out of this place. Therefore if you have a wife in here please wait by the door.' She knew there were no children left in the workhouse, so it would be husbands and wives and possibly single men and women.

Five men shuffled over to where Tulley stood shaking his head.

'Good. Five houses allocated. Now the rest of you I take it are single men?' She watched as the nods came again. 'I have eight more houses very badly in need of repair…' The men looked around, making a mental head count. 'I can take eight of you out with me today or, if you are prepared to share a house, we can double that figure.'

Shuffling feet pushed closer to her as she scanned the faces. She noted there were more than double that number remaining. Every pair of eyes were watching her as she faced the dilemma of who to choose. The younger men, whilst rake thin, still had some colour in their faces, there was some strength left in their bodies, but the older men were hunched over at the shoulders. Their skin was pallid and drawn and she knew these would have to be the first to come out with her.

'I have decided to take the older members of your group first, but rest easy in the knowledge I will come back for those of you remaining.' Her heart ached at the disappointed faces of the men left behind, but she would get them out as soon as she could.

Tulley led Cara and the men back to his office and whilst he put each through the signing out procedure, Cara was dismissed to wait outside the gate.

Pacing back and forth, her frustration began to mount at having to wait, but she knew it would be worth it in the end.

Three hours later, twenty one men and five women walked through the wrought-iron gate to greet her. The joy of their being released eased Cara's tension and she smiled a returned greeting. Explaining her intentions, Cara led the happy group towards their new homes and their new lives.

As the group neared the area they were heading for, quiet mutterings began and the pace slowed. Cara stopped when a woman spoke up. 'Miss Flowers, am we going to the black area?'

Cara asked in return, 'The *black area*?'

'Ar,' the woman went on, 'the place the scarlet fever raged.'

Cara sighed heavily, she had hoped these people would be so glad to be out of the Spike they might not question where they were headed. Now she was faced with having to answer the woman's question and convince them all it was perfectly safe.

Taking a deep breath, she said, 'Yes, but please understand, the properties are perfectly safe now.'

'I ain't so sure,' the woman said, 'don't misunderstand me, Miss Flowers, we'm all very grateful for what you're trying to do, but...'

Cara's eye roamed the twenty six people stood around her, looking on anxiously. Now what would she do? Mr. Harris's prediction was coming true. These people were afraid.

Looking around her, Cara said, 'Right, come with me.' She led them a short way down Queen Street and out onto a patch of scrubland. 'Now, I need you to wait here for me. I need to do a quick errand and I won't be long. I will be back in half an hour.' Taking some money from her bag, she gave it to one of the men. 'Go along to the Prince of Wales pub and get a few jugs of beer to share. I'll be back before you've drunk it.'

The women sat on the wasteland as the men made for the pub. Cara walked briskly back along the street. Hailing a cab sat waiting for a fare, she gave the driver the address she needed to go to.

True to her word, Cara arrived back half an hour later with Dr Cooper at her side. She smiled to see the people chatting and laughing, the beer obviously having gone straight to their heads. It was no wonder, drinking beer on an empty stomach was not a good idea. She should have suggested food, but it was all she could think of at the time and at least the people didn't look so worried.

As she and the doctor had travelled in the cab, she had explained her predicament and had asked the doctor to have a word with the frightened people.

Standing before them now, while Cara asked the cabbie to wait to return the doctor to his home, Dr Cooper began to speak. 'Right then, Miss Flowers has told me what's going on here, so I've come along to explain to you. The scarlet fever can be caught by breathing in bacteria from an infected person, by touching the rash on their skin or from sharing their clothes and bed linen. The symptoms are sore throat, headache, a swollen tongue in some cases and a rash on the chest which spreads over the rest of the body. Infection lasts for a couple of weeks after these symptoms appear.' Dr Cooper watched as the people looked at each other then resumed. 'When this occurred in the black area, it was not diagnosed quickly enough unfortunately, and many people died before the illness ran its course. However, I'm here to tell you... you cannot catch scarlet fever from a building!'

As applause sounded out, Cara thanked the doctor as he climbed into the cab. As she turned back to the people sitting on the scrubland, she was relieved when the woman who had spoken before said, 'Right, you men, get those jugs back to the pub and hurry it up. Miss Flowers ain't got all day!' As the men scrambled to their feet, the woman turned to Cara with a big smile. 'Thanks for that,' she said, 'We all feel better about it now.'

Cara returned the woman's smile while they waited for the men to return from the pub. Maybe Mr Harris would be proven wrong after all.

*

Fred Tulley stared at the ten pounds Cara Flowers had left on his desk. He knew for certain now what she was up to. It *was* her intention to close the Spike and she was attempting to accomplish this by emptying the place.

Fred pondered the twenty six people he had just released and wondered how far the young woman's money would stretch. If Miss Flowers managed to get the majority of inmates released, housed and in work – would the Local Government Board close the place down? Surely they would not keep it open for a handful of residents? Indeed not. Fred Tulley considered the prospect. Maybe it *was* time to move on, to find employment elsewhere. He didn't want to wake up one morning and find himself out of a job, or worse... an inmate in his own workhouse!

The more he thought on the matter, the more the idea appealed to him. He could just take off. He could take the money he and Ada had saved and do a 'moonlight flit'. Best of all, he could leave his wife behind. Freedom from Ada and the Spike beckoned and Fred felt the stirrings of excitement begin to grow.

In the meantime, Ada Tulley had been thinking much the same thing as she sat in her living room, beer in hand. Her husband had tried to murder her and she knew it was just a matter of time before he succeeded. However, life was a great deal harder for a woman alone. Where would she go? What would she do? How would she live? Ada was also aware that at the rate the workhouse was emptying, her position as Matron was under threat. Yes, folk were still trickling into the place, but they were leaving at a faster rate!

Supping on her beer, Ada considered her options. She could up and leave Fred to it or she could stay and see what the future brought. The decision was a difficult one and she pondered it long and hard. Eventually the only conclusion she came to was to have another beer!

Nineteen

Joseph Purcell stepped from his carriage and whistled through his teeth as his eyes rolled over The Laburnums. Cara Flowers certainly lived in style, he thought as he drank in the grandeur of the house and gardens. His own house was not nearly so grand, and he felt jealousy rear in him.

Molly answered the knock on the front door and with a sniff she asked the Chairman to come in. She led him through the hall towards the parlour where Cara and Martin Lander were sitting by the fire. As he followed the maid, Purcell took in the beauty of the inside of the house. Obviously no expense had been spared on this place. Again jealousy seethed in him.

Molly brought in fresh tea before slipping quietly back to the kitchen.

'Miss Flowers, Martin,' Purcell said as he sat on an easy chair. 'Thank you for agreeing to meet with me on such short notice.' Damn! He hadn't expected Lander to be here too.

'You are very welcome, Mr Purcell,' Cara answered. 'What is it I can do for you?' She curled her hands in her lap to quell their nervous shaking.

Joseph smiled inwardly. Straight to business – he liked that, no messing around. 'I wanted to meet the young woman I've heard so much about. People are singing your praises all over the town, Miss Flowers.'

'Please call me Cara,' the girl blushed at the compliment as she brushed a stray blonde curl behind her ear.

Joseph nodded and turned to Martin Lander. 'Martin, I hear also you have set up your own law practice... a wise move in my opinion.'

Martin nodded his thanks. 'One that has benefited me already.' Indeed work was pouring into his office and was keeping him very busy. He wisely chose to say nothing about his partners forcing him into the move.

Cara eyed her visitor, wondering at the true reason for his calling at her home. She remembered what she'd been told by the residents of Cara's Cottages regarding this man's visit to them previously and to remain on her guard.

As if reading her thoughts, Joseph moved his eyes back to hers. 'Miss... Cara,' he corrected himself, 'it is widely known of your good deeds regarding rehousing workhouse inmates...' Cara gave him a beautiful smile and Purcell found himself beguiled. 'I was wondering why you chose inmates over the poor of the town living outside of the Spike gates?'

'Mr Purcell, the *inmates*, as you call them, do not have the luxury of living outside of the workhouse gates. However, it is my intention to remedy that problem. In time I hope to see that awful place empty of its residents. It is my fervent hope that it will be closed down... for good!' Cara's voice held a quiet determination.

'I see.' Joseph was surprised at her words. 'May I ask why you think it should be closed down?'

Cara felt the look of disbelief cross her face as she watched the man she knew little about who sat across from her. 'Why it should...! Mr Purcell, you are the Chairman of the Board of Guardians there and yet you seem oblivious as to what goes on in that dreadful building!' Cara's blood was now up and her anger was already beginning to show.

'In that case, please enlighten me,' he said.

Cara looked at the man aghast. Was he toying with her? Was he mocking her? Or was it that he really was unaware of the goings-on in the place he oversaw? Taking a deep breath, Cara launched into her explanation from the beginning, telling him of her grandmother's challenge.

'It was Martin's suggestion to search the workhouse for my family members and it was there I found my brother Charlie. I was duped out of money in exchange for my brother's release, and my little sister had been sold on only to run away. People in that workhouse are being starved, abused and neglected. The cook left because of it, and has since admitted to the fact she was forced to use rotten food on pain of losing her job. That same rotten food caused the death of an innocent young child. The blame for that lies squarely at the feet of the Tulleys.

'I am using the money left to me by my grandmother to buy up old properties, which are being renovated and lived in by the former workhouse residents. These people have been given back their dignity, the proof of which can be seen in the hard work they are doing on their houses.' Cara's frustration and temper was building and she fought hard to control herself. She had hurried on, barely taking time to draw breath, and so incensed was she, she was totally unaware her guard was well and truly down.

Joseph Purcell listened quietly throughout, nodding every

now and then. He was extremely interested in what this young woman was telling him, so much so he had not taken his eyes from her face. She was up to something and he wanted to know what it was and if it affected him directly.

Martin Lander quietly watched the man watching Cara and he wondered at the other man's motives. He also wondered if Purcell was interested in more than what Cara was telling him. Was he interested in Cara herself? Martin needed to put some distance between Purcell and Cara and to put a stop to what was going on in his mind.

Cara's words came to a halt as Martin got to his feet. 'Perhaps Mr Purcell might like to meet Charlie and hear his account of his experience in the workhouse,' he said.

'I think you could be right, Martin,' Cara said with a smile as she stood to pull the bell pull at the side of the fireplace to summon the maid. Both Martin and Cara were pleased for the distraction, however Purcell was not.

*

The men from Cara's Cottages were lending a hand with the properties in Brook Street, Chapel Street and Hare Street and the work was coming on well, and quickly. So much so in fact that there were whispers about what they would do once that work was at an end. Wally Webb, one of the first to be released from the workhouse by Cara, had been made foreman and spokesman for their little community. He oversaw the work now being done in the three streets across town, and he too realized it was almost at an end.

The women's bakery stall on the market was doing a brisk trade, keeping them very busy, so the women in the newer houses had joined the co-operative. Pies, cakes and pastries were being turned out and carried to the market, where they sold almost immediately. Profits were being made and in turn rent was being paid to Cara each week. It wasn't that important to Cara that rent was coming in on time, but she knew the restored pride of the people she had rescued would not have it any other way. They would want to pay their way to the woman who had turned their lives around.

The derelict shops in Gozzard Street had also been renovated, along with the living quarters above. The small businesses which had been set up by the former workhouse residents were thriving. One became a tailors, another a cobblers, yet another was a sweet shop selling home-made toffees and chocolates.

Wally Webb pondered these developments as he and the other men stood around on their tea break. He knew Cara Flowers had also purchased the old factory building at the end of Hare Street, and he called for the other men's attention. 'I suggest we start work at the old factory next,' he proposed.

'We ain't been instructed to do that as yet,' someone piped up.

Wally replied, 'It's only a matter of time, mate. Besides, it will be a wonderful surprise for Cara and another way of showing our gratitude.'

So it was agreed, and one fellow went off to make a new lock as the others smashed the old one to gain entry.

The men threw open the shutters and the light spilled in and lit up the dust motes floating lazily in the stale air. Doors were propped open and the workers wandered around as Wally tried to decide where they should begin.

'I thought this was an old factory,' Wally said, 'but now I think it may have been a shop.' He heard mutters of agreement as he too wandered from room to room.

The main room was massive and a door led into a huge kitchen and scullery. A water standpipe stood in the yard at the back. Further back still was the privy in its own brick building. Another door led from the shop area onto living quarters, from which a staircase led to three bedrooms.

Wally Webb smiled as he meandered around the place; this would keep them busy for a while. One thing for certain was Cara Flowers wouldn't recognize the place once they'd finished with it.

Taking out a small notebook and pencil, Wally licked the lead and proceeded to make notes of the jobs which the men called out needed to be done.

'Chimneys need pointing and sweeping', shouted one.

'A couple of window frames need replacing,' yelled another.

'Shutter hinges could do with oiling,' from a third.

'New curtains for the bedrooms... Hopefully some of the women can help out on that score...'

'The whole place could do with sweeping, cleaning and painting...'

Wally's little notebook filled rapidly with tasks to be accomplished and he nodded as he saw the finished building in his mind's eye.

One man was set to fix the range in the kitchen, another worked the standpipe to get clean water flowing. Yet another was sent for supplies for their midday meal and to make a good strong cup of tea. The work had begun and Wally took measurements for bedroom curtains in the hope one of the wives would oblige in the making of them. He thought the older kids would tidy the yard and help with window washing, in exchange for a bag of boiled sweets from Teddy Grey's Confectionery Shop. Wally settled to his work comfortably and his excitement grew as he imagined Cara's face on her first visit to the newly renovated building. He prayed silently she would be pleased, and although his heart told him she would be delighted, a prayer sent upstairs would most certainly help, he thought. What Cara would do then with the property was anyone's guess.

Twenty

Charlie Flowers sat next to Cara and eyed the official-looking man sat in the chair opposite.

Cara said, 'This is Mr Purcell, from the Board of Guardians.'

'What's he want?' Charlie asked, trying to be brave. He was suspicious about what was expected of him and he felt most uncomfortable under the man's gaze. He knew the man was associated with the workhouse, and the dread of waking from what he thought might have been a dream and being hauled back there haunted him still.

'I'd like you to tell him about your time in the workhouse and your treatment at the hands of Fred and Ada Tulley.' She urged him to be honest and omit nothing, assuring him he would never again be taken into anyone else's care. 'You are my brother, Charlie and I love you dearly, so please don't be afraid.' She watched as the boy drew in a deep breath. She felt nervous enough for both of them.

Doing as he was bid, Charlie's eyes locked with those of the Chairman as he shared the truth of life in the workhouse.

Purcell listened with surprise, which he kept carefully hidden. He knew the workhouse was no paradise, nor could it be, but he hadn't realized it was as bad as the boy was saying. Was this boy telling the truth? Or was he lying to please his sister? Had they hatched this between them to put the workhouse in a bad light? Were the Tulleys really as bad as the boy was making out? He put these questions to the back of his mind as he listened, he could think about them at a later time.

When Charlie had finished, Cara praised him. 'Well done, Charlie, thank you. Now, you can return to the kitchen and ask Gracie for some cake and milk.' Charlie didn't need to be told twice.

Joseph Purcell drew in a long breath and let it out again slowly.

'So, Mr Purcell, you now see why I have to accomplish what I set out to do,' Cara said with confidence.

Joseph's eyebrows furrowed as he said, 'I'm sure you realize that the problem stretches further than the workhouse. There is poverty all over the town and whilst there is such poverty there will be a need for a workhouse.'

'My initial aim was to get those people away from the dire conditions they were existing in…' Joseph noted she had not said 'living in'. Cara went on, 'I wanted to give them back their dignity, a home, a purpose in life once more! I know there will be others who will be forced to enter that place out of sheer desperation and… and…' Her words trailed off as her eyes filled with frustrated tears she had willed not to come.

'Cara, please don't distress yourself,' Joseph said as he reached out and touched her hand which lay on her knee. It was distasteful to him to be touching this young woman in such a tender fashion, but he felt it was necessary to a point. He needed to glean as much information as he could about her future plans, and whether they would affect him in his capacity of Chairman of the Board of Guardians. Above all, he intended to watch his own back. Therefore if holding her hand helped, then he would do it. She was plotting something and he wanted to know what it was.

Martin Lander saw the movement and a lance of pain shot through him. Was this man making a move on his girl? But then Cara Flowers was not *his girl*, she was his *client*. Nonetheless, Martin's dislike of the Chairman grew in an instant.

'Mr Purcell,' Cara began, 'I can't do it all! I can't do anything about the town's poverty, at least not quickly enough! The best I can do is help those most in need. I cannot find a cure, I can only treat the symptoms.' Cara could hear her own desperation in the words. She knew she was becoming agitated and battled her emotions threatening to spill out.

Purcell nodded, saying, 'Martin has given his help to your cause, I believe. What else can be done?'

Cara's demeanour changed in an instant. She gave him the most beautiful smile as she won control of the tears she had felt so close to falling and said firmly, 'The workhouse can be closed down!'

*

Martin Lander fumed as he made his way home to Alice Street. He thought Joseph Purcell had wormed his way into Cara's affections… and in one day! How could this be? He, Martin, had spent the better part of his time aiding Cara with her quests and had lost his job into the bargain! In a mere few hours, Purcell had managed to get onside. Blast the man! Scowling, Martin stomped through the streets taking his anger out on the cobbles.

The summer was drawing to a close and as he sat by his fire in the tiny living room, Martin determined to watch Purcell closely, he had no intentions of allowing the man to get close to Cara. He knew he had to be very careful, however, for Joseph Purcell was still the Magistrate of the town, which meant they could cross paths frequently in court. If Purcell took a dislike to him, he could lose his cases, as well as the clients who employed him. Nevertheless, his main aim was to protect Cara and her interests.

Magistrate or not, Martin would not allow the man to sweeten his way into courtship with Cara. She must be warned of what Martin saw as Purcell's romantic intentions, and he must be the one to inform her. Gazing into the fire, he turned the situation over in his mind. The last thing he wanted to do was to upset the girl. He didn't want her to think he was out to cause trouble. So how should he go about this? Sometimes he felt Cara was too innocent for her own good and one day it would come back on her. Would this be that one time? Not if he had anything to do with it, it wouldn't!

Martin heard again the words discussed in the parlour at The Laburnums; he saw again Purcell's hand touch Cara's and he suddenly realized she had not pulled away from that touch. Surely she couldn't have feelings for the man after one brief meeting? Besides, Purcell must be at least twenty years her senior. The thought disgusted Martin as he slammed his cup onto its saucer. Was Purcell looking to coax the innocent young woman into his bed? What if he accomplished that? Would he then just leave her to her own devices having got what he wanted? What if she should become pregnant? Would he cast her aside like an old rag?

Martin paced his living room, drawing his hands through his hair. It didn't bear thinking about. What he *did* have to consider was whether he should warn Cara Flowers precisely what Purcell had on his mind!

*

All now gathered in the kitchen, Cara related the discussions to Molly and Gracie.

'Christ Cara!' Gracie said. 'You have to be sensible! You don't really think that man is going to allow himself to be put out of the job of Chairman, do you?' The cook shook her head at Cara's innocence.

'Well…' Suddenly it dawned on her. She hadn't stopped to consider that fact, so incensed had she been earlier at the injustice of it all.

'He won't, you know…' Molly added. 'And he won't put the other Board members out of work either.'

'Oh my God! What have I done?' Cara wailed dropping into a chair. 'He's fully aware of my plans now!' Panic gripped her as she realized her folly.

'The saving grace…' Gracie said sympathetically, '…is that he can't stop you getting folk out of that place, as far as I can tell. He might refuse you visiting, but people can still sign themselves out.'

'So we would need to get a message in to say how many we need to come out… but first we need more housing! Oh Gracie, this is madness… there has to be another way!' Cara was in a state; she stood and paced the floor.

'Well, when you want a message taking, I can do it,' Charlie said simply.

'No Charlie, it would be far too dangerous,' Cara replied.

'It ain't, I can climb up the wall and tell the men, then they could be ready for your call.' The boy grinned.

'We'll see,' Cara smiled at her courageous brother.

'Oooh our mum used to say that when she meant yes, didn't she, Charlie?' Daisy said, not taking her eyes from the doll she was playing with on the table. The boy nodded, his eyes clouded at being reminded of their mother. Daisy's words had been said in all innocence, but Charlie couldn't shake the sadness that he was feeling of still not knowing where his mother was, or even whether she was still alive.

He wondered what was happening about Cara finding their parents, so he said,

'Cara, I was wondering about our mum... about how we can find her.'

'Oh sweetheart, I'm not sure yet. Mr Colley the Registrar telephoned to say he was still searching his records. There must be an awful lot to look through as it seems to be taking a long time. As soon as I hear anything I'll let you know right away.' Cara's heart went out to him as he nodded sadly.

'All right,' Cara went on, 'but first we need to sort out housing for these men. The work won't be a problem, I have some ideas about that.'

'Right,' Gracie chimed in, setting the kettle to boil, 'tea has always been good brain food!'

*

Joseph Purcell made a detour on his way home from The

Laburnums. His carriage rumbled down Brook Street, where he chatted a while with the new residents. Then he did the same in Chapel Street and Hare Street. Asking about the large building the men were working on, he was not surprised when they politely told him to mind his own business.

The men and women adored the young woman who had saved them and their families from a life of hardship and drudgery in the Spike. They would not tolerate her being talked about.

Purcell smiled as he rode home in his big black carriage. Bilston, it seemed, had its very own Florence Nightingale!

Stepping from the carriage, Joseph looked up at his own house. Not nearly as grand as The Laburnums, but he felt it more than adequate for a man living alone save for his servants. Brueton House sat in its own gardens and was situated between James Street and Lewis Street; a rather select area. The house was large with three bedrooms and servants quarters. A living room, parlour, kitchen and scullery made up the ground floor. It would soon sport an indoor lavatory.

The maid opened the front door, saying she would bring his tea immediately. Purcell nodded his thanks and walked to the parlour. Sitting before the fire, he let his thoughts roam.

Cara Flowers was intent on seeing the workhouse closed and she was making progress, albeit slow. He knew as fast as people were leaving the workhouse, others were taking their places. However, considerably more people were leaving than entering. He could not, in all honesty, see her succeeding in this quest she had set herself, but he had to admire her tenacity. She was like a terrier worrying at a bone.

His position of Chairman of the Board of Guardians would not be a great loss to him if it were taken away; he would still be the Magistrate for the town. Having said that, he enjoyed the perks of the job like the meals and wine that Mrs Tulley provided, as well as the extra money paid by way of salary. Then again, the time taken up by that position was proving to be a drain, especially with the emergency meetings having to be called. Damn Tulley and his wife!

Joseph returned his thoughts to the delightful Miss Flowers and her eyes which sparkled like blue diamonds. He had to admit he was rather taken with her as far as her spirit was concerned. Never having found anyone he cared to take as a wife, Purcell suddenly realized that could well change. Cara would make excellent marriage material if he could tame her wild side, and… she had money – lots of it!

The young woman had not spurned him when he laid his hand on hers, he noted, which said she might be willing to consider a courtship, possibly a proposal of marriage – all in good time of course. The more pressing matter, however, was her fight against the workhouse remaining in use. As he mulled this over in his mind he came to the conclusion that if he did not manage to get his hands on her money through marriage, then he fully intended to keep his position as Chairman of the Board and the prestige and perks that went along with it. Therefore, his problem now was finding ways of, at the very least, stalling Cara Flowers' efforts.

*

Autumn began to spread her wondrous cloak over the land, turning everything to shades of golden brown and red. Crows cawed constantly in the trees as they fought for the best position within the branches. The sun still shone down but there was a slight chill in the air as Cara walked across the town to Martin Lander's office. She realized that she had not spoken to him in almost a week, which was unusual, and so she had packed a lunch basket in the hope of sharing a picnic with him. All too soon the winter would set in and eating alfresco would be out of the question.

Cara thought Martin appeared a little offhand as she entered his office. He had merely looked up, and had not greeted her with the smile she had expected. He seemed very flustered and was shuffling papers around on his desk.

'I thought we might eat a picnic together,' she said.

'I am extremely busy, I'm not sure if I can take the time,' he answered, but then felt wretched as he saw her disappointed face. Relenting, he grabbed his jacket and, carrying the basket for her, they left Earle Street and walked up Broad Street and onto The Crescent.

Finding a spot on the heathland that bordered the street, they sat down to enjoy their food.

'Martin, I feel I have been such a fool,' Cara said out of the blue. 'I gave away all my intentions to Joseph Purcell in the hope he may be able to help me. I am so sorry!' Tiny tears lined her lashes as she looked at the man who had been such a help to her.

So, Cara had seen sense, but was it too late?

Martin grasped her hand in his and squeezed it gently. Her fingers returned the gesture and Martin's heart skipped a beat.

'Cara,' he said softly, 'Joseph Purcell does not appear to be as helpful as he seemed, but we can beat him and the workhouse, we just have to continue to work together. You have to be aware though, he has set his sights on you.'

'Oh Martin, thank you! I knew you would understand.' Cara beamed at the man still holding her hand. She was so relieved he had forgiven her stupidity, she completely ignored the rest of his sentence. However her mouth dropped open at his next words.

'Cara Flowers, would you consent to step out with me? Will you be my sweetheart?'

Cara considered his words carefully before giving him her answer. Did she want to be Martin's sweetheart? Did she want to walk out with him? Did she want the world knowing they were an item? Did she love him? She wasn't sure she did but felt she could in time. Certainly Martin Lander could be seen as the catch of the century.

Drawing in a deep breath, she whispered, 'Yes Martin, I will step out with you.'

Martin was delighted, his grin stretching from ear to ear. As she watched him pack away the remains of the picnic, she hoped she had made the right decision.

He chatted on about his work as they returned to his office, but Cara's mind was on other things. She had just consented to become this man's sweetheart. Part of her had wanted to say yes to him, and part of her had cautioned her against it. Why was that? Did that tell her she was definitely not in love with him? She realized she had not really missed him when they had not spoken to each other in the week. Was this another warning sign? Well, she had accepted now, and after all was said and done, Martin was a good man. He worked hard and she knew he would take care of her. Cara snapped her mind back in an effort to listen to what he was saying.

Twenty-One

Cara saw the men standing in the bread line near the market in the hope of work. Although the autumn sun beamed down, she knew they would still gather when the cold snow of winter fell, should they not find work in the meantime. Martin Lander walked by her side. She had decided to attempt to attack the problem of Bilston's poverty at its heart – unemployment, so this is what had brought her here. Cara was unsure at first, remembering she had promised the men still in the workhouse that she would do her utmost to get them released and rehoused; that she would find them work. And she would, but she also realized that if she didn't solve the root cause of the problem, the workhouse would remain open.

Arriving where the men stood in a group, Cara and Martin stopped and the men doffed their caps. They all knew who this young woman was.

At Cara's nod, Martin spoke up loudly.

'Gentlemen.' Out of work they may be, but their dignity was still intact. 'This lady is Miss Cara Flowers.' All eyes turned to her and she nodded in response. 'Miss Flowers is looking for men to work a plot of land she has purchased.' The clamour of men pushing and shoving almost took Cara off her feet. 'Gentlemen please!' Martin shouted and the men settled once more. Standing aside, Martin gave Cara the floor.

'Good morning gentlemen,' she called.

As one they chorused their reply almost like children in a classroom. 'Good morning Miss Flowers'.

Cara joined in their laughter as they nudged each other before she went on, 'As Mr Lander said, I need land workers. I have a large section of waste ground which I feel could be put to good use. It will need to be cleared first then it is my intention to section it off into allotments for growing vegetables. There is sufficient land there for around fifty small plots.' Cara watched as the men scanned the group, each making a quick head count. 'Now my proposal is this… I will pay each man a small wage to clear and work the land. When the plots are up and running and the produce can be harvested and sold, each man will then pay me a small rent for their plot.'

'Miss Flowers,' a man yelled, 'the winter ain't far away, not much is gonna grow then!'

'Gentlemen, once you are allocated your plots it will be up to you what you do with them. I will pay you a small wage whilst you get them up and working, but I hope to be paid rent by next summer.' She smiled.

Cara watched the men laugh and mutter as her words sunk in.

'Miss Flowers,' the man who had spoken previously pushed to stand in front of her and took off his flat cap. 'We all know who you are and of the good work you've been doing regarding the workhouse…' Cara smiled and nodded. 'I, for one, would be glad to take up your offer. Sam Yale at your service, ma'am.' Giving a small bow, he laughed as the other men jostled him.

'Thank you Sam, then you are hereby the foreman of any who wish to take up my offer and work the allotments.' A cheer rang out. 'Now gentlemen please give your names to Sam, so I am able to sort out your first wages which you will receive today.' Another cheer went up as Cara passed a notebook and pencil to her new foreman. She watched as Sam noted down all the names including his own. Her mind was in turmoil, was she doing the right thing? *Well, it's too late now, it's done,* she thought.

'Miss Flowers,' Sam Yale said eventually, 'we have fifty names on the list, but there's two men left standing.'

'Sign them up, Sam, we'll sort something out,' Cara said with a smile. 'Then get them, with any tools they have, over to Proud's Lane. The quicker they start, the better. Oh and Sam, my house is The Laburnums and I will give you the wages to hand out each week if you would be good enough to collect them.'

'Thank you, Miss Flowers, on behalf of us all, thank you!' Sam shoved his cap back on and yelled his orders to the rest. Men shot off in all directions to collect their tools, grateful thanks flung over their shoulders as they went.

Cara and Martin chatted excitedly as they returned to her home to sort out the men's wages.

'I know this is a huge risk I am taking, Martin, I'm not even sure the land will be suitable for growing produce. Only time will tell. However, at least I have put some of the unemployed to work.'

Looking at Martin, she added, 'That's one in the eye for the esteemed Mr Joseph Purcell!'

*

Martin Lander was settling down to his tea in his small house and considered himself an extremely lucky man. Cara Flowers had consented to walk out with him. She was, at last, his sweetheart and he loved her. He was on top of the world and his face was fixed in a constant smile.

Throwing more coal on the fire, Martin was startled by a knock on his front door. Answering, Martin was surprised to see who stood on his doorstep.

'Dr Cooper! Please, come in.' Martin stood aside to allow the man entry.

'Forgive my visit to your home, Mr Lander, but I felt the need to come.' The older man dropped into the chair offered.

Over tea, the doctor explained the reason for his unannounced visit and Martin listened carefully.

'The cook has left the workhouse. The Townsend child died of food poisoning and her mother was shut away in the lunatic asylum.'

Martin realized this echoed what Bertha Jenkins had divulged.

'The inmates are suffering cruelty and starvation. I have now resigned my post there too!'

Martin's eyebrows shot up in surprise. 'Why are you telling this to me, Dr Cooper?'

'People need to know, Mr Lander. I'm not sure what can be done, but the regime at the Spike needs changing, if nothing else. It needs changing soon before there are more deaths! I wondered, with you being a lawyer, whether you could help... legally?'

Martin shook his head, 'I'm not sure how I can help. However, as you probably already know, Cara Flowers is hell-bent on getting as many people out of the workhouse as she can. She's buying up property and land to house the workers and find them employment. I think she would be most interested to hear news of your resignation and also your views on the workhouse.'

After the doctor left, Martin considered what he'd been told. The doctor's words regarding cruelty and starvation had not been new to his ears. He was surprised, however, that the doctor had resigned his post as medical officer to the workhouse. The institution no longer had a doctor to call on and the ramifications of that fact alone were a great concern.

And there was of course the matter of the cook's resignation. So who was cooking the inmates' meals? Were they even getting cooked food? Who would take care of any who fell ill? What was Tulley doing about getting replacement staff? Or did that fall to the Board of Guardians?

Martin pondered the situation for the rest of the evening. He needed to consult with Cara, this could be the loophole they were looking for!

*

'They *must* have a doctor, cook and school master on their books, it's the ruling set down by the Parish Union,' Dr Cooper said to Cara as they sat by the fire in her parlour.

Dr Joshua Cooper had arrived unannounced and had explained to the young woman about the Townsend girl dying of food poisoning, the inmates being overworked and underfed, and his resignation as medical officer for the workhouse.

Cara glanced at Martin, who nodded his agreement with the doctor's words.

'So what will happen now? I'm not sure why you have come to me with this, Dr Cooper.' Cara was puzzled.

'Maybe this could be taken to the Local Government Board... if they were informed of how the place is falling apart, half the staff missing and hardly any inmates left in there...' The doctor's words poured out.

'Oh! Would it be possible? Would they close it down?' Cara's excitement grew as she looked at Martin.

Shaking his head, Martin answered, 'There's only one way to find out!'

Cara was elated that she might finally have a chance to bring the Spike to closure. Dashing into the hall, she picked up the telephone, requesting the operator connect her with the Local Government Board office.

Concluding her conversation, Cara replaced the telephone on the hall table. She threw her arms in the air and danced a little jig on the hall tiles. She had just made an appointment with Mr Isaac Ballard, the Chairman of the Local Government Board for one week hence.

*

Cara sat in the parlour going over the figures the way Gracie had taught her to do. Keeping a check on the 'downstairs' household accounts was one of the jobs the cook undertook in the absence of a butler, and night after night she had drilled it into Cara, for which the girl had been grateful. Now she could manage her own accounts regarding the workhouse project. She realized she still had more going out than was coming in, but it was hardly a drain on the resources she had inherited. The rent from Cara's Cottages was paid on time and she now had rent trickling in from

Gozzard Street, Chapel Street, Brook Street and Hare Street but she saw she was still not profiting. Then again, she thought, this was not about making a profit, it was about aiding the poor people of the town. Their smiling faces more than made up for the financial shortfall. Nevertheless, to make this a worthwhile venture and to enable it to continue, Cara needed to make a profit at some point. Happy with the state of play for the moment she returned her books to the bureau.

Gathering her 'family', Cara said, 'I fancy a trip out to visit our tenants.'

Daisy and Charlie giggled as they pushed Gracie's rump into a cab, making her splutter with indignation. Molly and Cara sniggered quietly.

The day was spent visiting each house to see how the people were faring before they finally arrived in Hare Street. Cara was astounded at how quickly the men and women had licked the buildings into shape. Small gardens of wild flowers had sprung up around the dwellings which the children tended lovingly. The grime had been scrubbed off the outside of the houses and the windows gleamed. Roof tiles had been replaced. How on earth had they managed it? It appeared the men had bartered their services in exchange for tiles, paint... anything that was needed to make their houses habitable. The tradesmen eager to help when they knew these men were Cara's new tenants.

Wally Webb, her foreman overseeing the work, came to greet her as they arrived.

'Cara,' he said eagerly, 'we have something to show you.' Leading the small party to the end of the street to the old factory, Wally spread his arms. The whole building had been transformed. Cara gasped at the sight of it. The clean brickwork and shiny windows were just the beginning. Walking inside, Cara gasped again. Whitewashed walls, tiled floors, folded back shutters allowing the light to flood the rooms, everything was sparkling clean.

'Oh my…!' These were the only words she could manage as she walked from one room to the next. The upstairs rooms had been cleaned and painted and Cara beamed her delight as she wandered around the building.

Wally spoke quietly, 'All you have to do now is decide what to do with the place!'

'Thank you Wally, thank you all.' Cara laughed as she stepped out onto the street once more. 'What a wonderful surprise, I had no idea you were working on this place too!'

The applause and whistles from the men filled her ears and she returned their applause before spreading her arms wide to encompass them all.

Twenty-Two

Joseph Purcell was worried as he travelled to the workhouse. He had a nagging at the back of his brain that told him his position as Chairman of the Board of Guardians was in jeopardy. He had tried to shake the feeling off, but it persisted. His prestige and reputation would be in tatters if Cara did manage to succeed in her quest. He watched the people of Bilston as the cab drove down the cobbled streets and narrow lanes. Was it his imagination or were heads held higher as folk ambled about? The bread line of a few weeks ago had disappeared in one fell swoop, Cara Flowers having set all the men to work. He realized she was now attacking from both ends – she was treating cause and symptom! If this carried on, she might well achieve her goal and see the workhouse closed down. Then he would lose his position as Chairman of the Board. Not only that, but he would not have had a chance to woo Cara and settle his fortune.

The horse trotted up Mount Pleasant before turning onto Wellington Street. This was the wealthier side of town, the street where the doctors and businessmen set up their offices.

Purcell noted with pleasure the nameplates on the buildings; Hipwood Accountants; Josiah Colley, Registrar of Births, Deaths & Marriages; Bowen's Solicitors; Robinson, MRCS Eng. Surgeon. This was the part of town Purcell was happy to be in; where he felt he belonged.

The carriage veered off onto the dirt track and as it passed Cara's Cottages, Purcell's journey was all but at an end. The children waved as the carriage trundled past and he gave a quick wave in return before leaning back on the seat. That would keep them happy and onside, but he did not want the cab driver to see him associate with the families living there.

Marching through the gate held open by the porter, Joseph strode into the workhouse, down the corridor and into the boardroom, taking his usual seat at the head of the large table. Before long the other members arrived for their fortnightly meeting, followed by Tulley and his wife, who were still wearing their arm slings.

As Tulley beamed a greeting which was returned with a scowl, he realized this meeting was not going to be a pleasant one.

Joseph Purcell began with, 'What the hell is going on, Tulley?'

Fred looked from the Chairman to his wife who shook her head. He could see she would be no help at all.

'I don't know what you mean sir,' Tulley mumbled.

Purcell's head rocked back and forth slowly as he said, 'Let me spell it out for you, shall I?' Tulley nodded, wisely saying nothing. 'This damned woman, Flowers, has all but emptied this place and no one is taking up the tickets offered by the Relieving Officer! She has set over fifty men from the bread line to work! She is buying land and property all over the town! This institution has no cook and no medical officer… and now I hear on the grapevine that the schoolmaster has quit also!'

Fred Tulley spluttered, 'Ar well, I was going to tell you about that, sir.'

Ada's snort at not being told this information either was loud in the quiet of the room. Fred shot her a nasty look, which she returned with an even nastier one.

'Were you? As it happens, the whole bloody town is aware of it… before I was myself!' Purcell was livid.

Tulley shuffled from foot to foot clearly uncomfortable. Ada sniggered at his discomfort.

Purcell set his eyes on the woman, 'Then we come to you, Mrs Tulley.' Ada snapped to attention at his words. 'You, I believe, have refused to cook for the inmates.'

'Well, I can't rightly do it, sir… not with this.' Ada lifted her arm held in the sling and winced as she cradled it with the other.

'I see. So, are you telling me these people are not receiving hot food?' Purcell asked.

Ada shook her head, saying, 'The inmates are cooking, sir.'

Purcell nodded once, seemingly satisfied with her answer. Ada relaxed a little and aimed a sly grin at her husband.

'We have been unable to find anyone willing to undertake the vacant posts here; no doctor, cook or schoolmaster, so what do you propose we do about that?' Purcell had put the onus squarely on the shoulders of the Tulleys.

Unable to find an answer Fred shuffled his feet again as he looked down at the floor.

The Chairman's eyes bored into the burly Master. 'You do realize this could lead to closure and you two will be out on your ear?' He jabbed an index finger at husband and wife.

'It ain't that bad,' Tulley spoke up, 'it just needs that lazy

Relieving Officer to work a bit harder!' He certainly had no intention of taking the blame.

'It's nothing to do with the Relieving Officer, Tulley!' Purcell's voice rose an octave. 'This is to do with Cara bloody Flowers!'

Fred looked at Ada, who shrugged her shoulders and winced in pain. Closing his eyes tight, he then returned his attention to the Board members who were whispering quietly.

Purcell glared at the Master again, saying, 'We are in agreement that the Flowers woman is not breaking any law, therefore our hands are tied. The best we can do is allow her no more visits to the inmates. You, Tulley, will ensure she never enters this workhouse again!'

'How?' Fred asked. 'What will I say if she telephones for another appointment?'

'You refuse her, man! I'm sure you pair of conniving...' A dig in the ribs from his colleague halted Purcell's words. Nodding at the man, he resumed. 'I'm sure you two can get your heads together and come up with plenty of reasons as to why Miss Flowers should be kept outside the gates of this institution!'

With that, the Board rose as one and filed out of the room, leaving Tulley staring open-mouthed at his wife.

*

Wally Webb watched in awe as six sets of bunk beds were delivered to the old 'factory' in Hare Street, two for each of the three bedrooms. It was a tight squeeze, but after much pushing and shoving, the beds were finally in place. Another huge range arrived for the kitchen and planks of wood were dropped in the yard. The wives set about making up the beds with the linen delivered at the same time. Wally instructed a couple of men to manoeuvre the range but quickly realized it would need more to get the massive thing into place. Yet others were already working with the delivered wood. He was told there were cupboards, tables and chairs to be made as well as a large counter. Cara informed him she was turning the factory into a bakery!

*

'Yes, good morning, I'd like to place an order please,' Cara said into the telephone. 'I will need this order on a regular basis and invoices to be sent to me. Oh, my name is Cara Flowers.'

'Certainly, Miss Flowers, what is it you will need and in what quantities?' the voice filtered into her ear.

'I am opening a bakery at the end of Hare Street, so I would be glad if you could deliver flour there. I'm hoping it will be a success naturally, so I need to ensure we have plenty in stock.' Cara went on to give her quantity order.

'Of course, I take it there will be breads, pastries, cakes…?'

'Yes,' Cara said quickly, 'my bakers will be doing the ordering once we're up and running so they will be in a better position to know what is needed from week to week. This call is to set up an account initially and order the first supplies.'

Replacing the telephone on the hall table, Cara blew a stray curl from her eyes. This was proving more difficult than she had imagined. She'd had no idea herself of the quantities needed and had asked advice from the women of the baking co-op. They had given her all the answers and she had made careful notes.

Picking up the telephone again, she drew in a breath. Now

she needed to go through the whole thing again with the grocer, before ordering tin pots, pans, patty tins, cake tins and utensils.

Sitting at last in the kitchen after the final telephone call, Cara said, 'Thank goodness that's done! All we need now are bakers. I would have asked the baking co-operative but I think they might be working flat out already.'

Gracie handed her a cup of tea with a smile. 'Did you order the sign for the frontage?'

Cara nodded, 'Yes, I'm calling the bakery 'Cara's Cakes', what do you think to it?'

'Oh that'll do very nicely!' The women laughed together.

Then Cara said, 'Gracie, I know I dismissed the idea of Charlie taking a message to the men still crushing stone in the workhouse, and I still don't like the idea but I can see no other way. Mr Tulley won't let me in again!'

Gracie was shocked and stared with an open mouth. 'How do you know?'

'I telephoned for an appointment and he told me I would not be allowed in anymore.' Cara was getting upset.

'It certainly looks like you've riled old Tulley now!' Changing the subject to calm Cara's upset, Gracie said, 'Here, you ain't thinking of asking these men to do the baking, are you?' She saw Cara's nod.

'That was my plan,' Cara said.

'Oh blimey! I can't wait to see their reaction!' Gracie's laughter rang around the kitchen at Cara's innocent face.

*

'Charlie, you must promise me you will be careful,' Cara said to her brother, who was stood in front of her.

'I will, don't worry,' he grinned, 'I won't be long.'

Cara watched as the young rogue sped from the front door of the house. She prayed he would stay safe on his errand on her behalf.

Charlie ran along the edge of the allocated allotments shouting a quick 'hello' to the men working there. He noticed the land was being mapped out ready for short dividers to be put in place. Yelling a quick greeting to those in Cara's Cottages, he was hailed by one of the women.

'Where you off to in such a hurry then, Charlie Flowers?' The woman asked.

'I'm on an errand for our Cara. I have to deliver a message over the wall to the bone crushers at the Spike. Cara wants twelve of them to sign out, she's got work for them.'

Turning, the woman yelled out. 'Joe!' A tall boy came running. 'Go with Charlie and give him a leg up that workhouse wall,' she said.

The two boys ran excitedly on up the dirt track towards Green Lanes and Charlie explained again what they were about. Circling around to the back of the Spike, they kept close to the wall in an attempt not to be seen. Hearing the sounds of stone being smashed, Charlie stopped. He pointed a finger at the wall. The older boy nodded and cupped his hands and Charlie stepped onto them. Hoisting the younger boy high, Joe tottered a little under the sudden weight pulling on his arms. Charlie grabbed the top of the wall and peeped over the top. Glancing around, he saw Fred Tulley disappear back into the building. Now was his chance.

Giving a whistle, he saw a few heads turn in his direction. Beckoning with his head, he watched a man approach, both keeping a keen eye out for the Master.

'Cara Flowers wants twelve men out in three hours, they need to go to the end of Hare Street.'

The man nodded and grinned as Charlie disappeared back behind the wall. The two boys ran hell for leather back to the cottages. After thanking Joe, and his mother, Charlie raced off home.

Cara was relieved as she saw her brother run up the drive. She had been watching through the parlour window and she dashed to open the front door. She grinned widely as he puffed, 'Joe Johnson came with me, the lad from Cara's Cottages. He gave me a leg up the wall and when I saw Tulley go back in the workhouse I gave a whistle. A chap came over and I delivered your message. Job done!'

'Well done, Charlie!' Cara beamed. 'I'm so proud of you.' She gave him a hug as he laughed along with her.

Cara had asked Wally Webb to look out for the arrival of twelve men from the workhouse and settle them into the bedrooms at the new bakery. Three and a half hours later, he saw them striding purposefully towards him. Wally showed them to the bedrooms, saying Cara would be along the following day to meet them and explain what she had in mind. Thoughtfully he had brought along bread and cheese to at least ensure they had something to eat.

*

Fred Tulley fumed. Another twelve gone from the yard. Why? How? What had prompted their sudden request to sign themselves out? Where would they go? What would they live on? He knew the Flowers woman was behind this, but he couldn't quite work out how she'd done it.

Pacing his office, he cradled his injured arm. 'Bloody

woman!' he snarled nastily. He continued to pace, muttering under his breath. 'First the damned Board and now this!'

The office door flew open and Ada marched in.

'What have I told you about bloody knocking?' Fred yelled.

Ignoring him, Ada Tulley, with a look that would sour milk, let forth a barrage of abuse. 'You idiot! Another twelve gone! Whatever are you playing at? For God's sake... the Board will have another blue fit when they find out!'

Fred shut his eyes tight as her voice made his ears ache. Dropping into his chair, he felt his will to live draining away.

Ada kept up her tirade, 'What caused twelve men to up and leave just like that?' She snapped her fingers. 'What did they say? Did they tell you why they were signing out...? Did they say where they were going? Fred Tulley, are you listening to me?'

'The whole bloody workhouse is listening to you, woman!' Fred yelled back.

'Fred, what are we going to do?' Ada actually had tears in her eyes, something her husband never thought to see, and if Cara Flowers kept this up his wife wouldn't be the only one fighting back the tears.

*

Those wives not part of the baking co-operative were asked by Cara to instruct the twelve new residents in the art of bread and cake making. These well-muscled men weren't at all sure, in the beginning, if they liked the idea of becoming bakers. However, being told by Evie Webb, Wally's wife, they could always return to the stone and bone crushing, the men settled down to learn what they could with no further argument.

A couple of the wives volunteered to work in the bakery

shop once it opened; Cara planned the opening for the following month, in time for Christmas. Time was of the essence and the men knuckled down to learn their new trade. Cara knew she would have to draw in custom from the richer parts of town too, such as the people from Willenhall Road, Bride's Row and Beckett Street, all of which lay on the edge of the town. The custom of the wealthy residents in Pearcroft Lane and Mountford Lane would also be well worth having. The houses there were in their own grounds and the owners usually employed a large staff. She wondered how she could go about spreading the word. In a flash the answer came to her. She would advertise in the newspapers. The higher echelon of society always had a newspaper placed on their breakfast plate which, when finished with, was sent downstairs to the staff. So news of the opening of the bakery would reach the rich and the not-so-well-off in one fell swoop.

She also remembered the town crier. The tallest man in the town who also had the loudest voice. He would walk the streets calling out the news to those who could not read. She made a mental reminder to place the advertisement at the newspaper office the next time she was in town, and also seek out the town crier.

With Cara's Cakes in the capable hands of Evie Webb, the women's co-operative market stall doing well, and the allotment land divided off, Cara pored over her ledgers once more. Rent was coming in. However, the winter would see very little grown in the allotments. Cara had foreseen this and knew spring and summer would bring their own rewards.

Sam Yale was ushered into the parlour by a blushing Molly to collect wages and bring his report on the men working the allotments. Over tea, Cara was updated, then Sam said awkwardly, 'Cara... the bread line is growing again. I just thought you might want to know.' Screwing his mouth up, the young man watched the sadness creep over her face.

'Thank you Sam, I'll see what I can do to help.'

Sam Yale tipped his cap before leaving.

Cara set her mind to try and solve this new challenge placed before her. Her promise to the remaining men in the workhouse was in the forefront of her mind and she knew she had to somehow fulfil that promise first. It upset her that she was unable to help those standing in the bread line at present, but she would do her best to do so in the future. She would find a way. She just hoped they could manage until that time.

As she sat alone in the parlour, she racked her brains as to what she could do to relieve the misery of these men and prevent them going into the workhouse. However, ideas eluded her and her mood turned sombre. Her heart weighed heavy as she desperately tried to find a solution to these problems. She spent the afternoon alone, brooding, turning the situation over and over in her mind. But try as she might, she could not fathom how to solve the predicament she was now faced with.

Twenty-Three

Josiah Colley, the Registrar, had searched his records from John and Elizabeth Flowers' wedding date until the present time. He had found no more children born to the family but had discovered John Flowers' death certificate.

'Miss Flowers,' he said into the telephone, 'I have here a death certificate for John Flowers... please accept my condolences.'

Hearing her thanks, he resumed, 'It would appear he died in a carting accident. To the best of my knowledge, there are no more children born with the Flowers name.'

'Thank you Mr Colley for your efforts, I am most grateful.'

Replacing the telephone on the table, Cara returned to the kitchen and sat by the table. She considered how she felt about this news. John Flowers was her father after all, but she couldn't remember him. She felt sad he had been killed and wondered how her life would have turned out had she still been living beneath his roof. Knowing what she had been told by Charlie, she wondered if he might have been cruel to her too. How did she feel about that? She felt extremely sad that he'd been so brutal to her mother and she would have probably felt as Charlie did. What would it have been like growing up with both a mother and father? She had loved her grandmother, there was no disputing that, but she couldn't help but wonder how it would have felt to have had her parents too. Then again, she thought she may have grown up as a child full of anger.

She then realized Mr Colley had not mentioned anything of her mother. Was she still alive? Where was she? Cara knew if she was still living then she could be anywhere. She also knew that she would have to explain all of this to Daisy and Charlie on their return from school. How would they take this news? Would they be upset? Now she had no idea how to search for their mother. Her last line of enquiry in Mr Colley was closed. Where would she go from here?

Colley knew, as did the whole town, that Cara had found her two siblings and they were living with her. Word of her good works had spread far and wide regarding the poor people of Bilston. She was held in high esteem by everyone for her efforts in attempting to close down the workhouse once and for all.

With two siblings found and her father dead, Josiah Colley wondered what had happened to Cara's mother. Was she dead also? She was not listed in his records, but then she could have perished in another town. If she was still living, where was she? How had she survived? Why had she not returned to her own mother after John's death? Had she remarried? If that was the case she would have a new surname. Without knowing that, Josiah didn't have a hope in hell of locating her.

His eyes still on the telephone he shook his head. Colley then returned to his work sad that there was nothing more he could do.

*

Cara was not surprised but was happy to learn that Molly Barton and Sam Yale had become a couple. Over the course of Sam's visits to collect the wages from The Laburnums, she had seen them strike up a close bond. She was pleased for them both, although she did wonder what would happen were they to marry. Molly obviously would leave The Laburnums to be with her new husband, but Cara felt that was a way off yet. They would have to save their money to get married, and that was no mean feat. Of course she would help them in any way she could, but she knew a wedding would not be imminent.

She and Martin had found little time for their own relationship. Martin's law practice had taken off spectacularly and she had been extremely busy with the shop and tenants.

November had arrived and with it came the first snow flurries. A bitter cold wind blew, carrying the little snowflakes to land on the trees which stood deep in their winter slumber. The wind was lazy which seemed to cut through even the thickest of clothes. It threatened to be a long, harsh winter. Cara dressed warmly in her wool suit. The navy blue jacket fitted her narrow waist and the long skirt to match stopped at her leather boots. A fur cape draped her shoulders with hat and muffler accessories. An umbrella completed the ensemble. Molly, Gracie and the children were wrapped warmly too as they all climbed into the waiting cab. It was the day of the Bakery opening and an advertisement in the local newspaper had broadcast the news to the people of the town.

As the cab rolled down Hare Street, Cara gasped, 'Look at all these women!'

'Bloody hell!' Gracie whispered and Daisy giggled.

'Looks like it's going to be a busy day,' Molly added.

The line of people stretched for what seemed like miles. Cara felt like royalty as she alighted the cab and stepped into her shop. Three women in long white aprons over black dresses and caps on heads stood behind the counter ready for action. Cara looked at the long counter which had shelves beneath and a glass front which displayed cakes, pastries and breads, all freshly baked by her new 'chefs'. Eclairs, cream horns, Eccles cakes, jam tarts and mince pies sat temptingly on large china plates. The aroma from the kitchen reached Cara's nose and made her mouth water.

The sound of clapping reaching her ears as she thought the men had taken to baking extremely well. They had learned quickly under Evie Webb's tutelage, even coming up with new ideas of their own.

The twelve men worked the kitchen like professionals and duly trooped out in their chef's whites to add to the applause given their employer.

Smiling shyly, Cara nodded her acceptance of their gratitude and the bakers strode back to their kitchen. Turning back, Cara threw open the door and stepped to the side as women pushed their way into the shop eager to be the first to try the new treats. Time would see this shop one of the most popular in Bilston. Of course there were those who preferred to shop in the market, so the women's co-operative stall was still going strong.

All morning Cara chatted with the constant stream of customers, some of whom, she learned, were the cooks of the wealthy. Some were the wealthy ladies themselves, dressed in expensive outfits and sporting beautiful hats. She was thrilled her advertisement in the newspaper had brought in this valued custom. She was even more thrilled that the till was working overtime. Cara watched as the bakers constantly refilled the shelves with custard tarts, macaroons, fairy cakes, gingerbread men and small Christmas puddings. By lunchtime she decided it was time for home. Praising the staff, she squeezed past waiting women to leave the building. It was evident the shop would be busy for the rest of the day.

*

The great expanse of heath leading to the Birmingham Canal was covered with old coal shafts or 'gin pits' as the colloquial term had it. Bilston Quarries was situated across the railway line from the station and Millfields Colliery, no longer working, lay further west. The old cottages dotted around these areas housed the poorest of the poor.

On the heath at the further side of the huge canal was another massive area of scrubland. The Bradley Row, Fiery Holes and Bradley Lodge Collieries all lay silent. No longer making a profit they had been shut down, the miners finding themselves out of work. Here, too, the poor scratched out a living as best they could. These small communities were visited often by the Relieving Officer of the Parish, offering 'tickets' into the workhouse. The last few months, however, had seen no one take up the offer. The people were starving yet still they refused him. Unsure of what to do, he eventually decided to report back to the Board of Guardians.

The poor watched from behind torn and dirty curtains as the man walked away, a ticket to their next meal clutched in his hand. Even stuck out here they had heard of Cara Flowers and her good work. Bilston people were fiercely proud and they would hold out as long as possible in the hope the young woman would hear of their plight and offer them assistance.

On the other side of town, Cara was unaware of the folk awaiting a visit from the 'guardian angel'. Her mind was on the men who had finished their work on the cottages. The money coming in from the women taking in washing or selling their baking would help see them over the winter, but the men were now standing idle. Then there were the allotments, there would be no yield from them for some months, so again the men needed something to fill their days.

Cara's mind swirled as did the snowflakes on the wind outside her window. Had she given these people hope only to see it vanish again? She prayed for inspiration, never imagining it to come in the form of the doctor.

*

Joseph Purcell heard again the words of the Relieving Officer after the man left his office at the court building. *'They ain't taking up the tickets, sir. It's my view they'm waiting on salvation from Cara Flowers'*.

That woman again! He would *not* be undermined by this girl! He was Chairman of the Board of Guardians for God's sake! He was a Magistrate!

Contemplating the predicament, he mused the girl was not breaking any laws, so how could he put a stop to her? Despite putting a stop to her entering the workhouse, the numbers were still dwindling. He frowned as he thought she was doing as much damage outside the walls as in. Could he discredit her in some way? He felt it most unlikely – the folk of Bilston saw her as their saviour. How had all this come about? And so quickly? One minute no one had ever heard of her, the next she was a celebrity! Maybe Fred Tulley would have some ideas; he was a sly old bugger! Joseph determined to have words with the man on his next visit to the Spike.

*

Fred and Ada Tulley had problems of their own to deal with. They had no cook, doctor or schoolmaster, which meant they were breaking the workhouse rulings. The advertisement had been placed in the newspaper regarding these empty posts, but no one had come forth to take them up, and Fred knew why. Nobody wanted to work at or for the workhouse. He sat in his office and considered, having the Magistrate onside helped… for the moment, but for how much longer? With only around fifty in the workhouse now and no more coming in due to the tickets not being taken up, he continued to fear for his job. If the place were to close, he would be out of work and a home, with a harridan of a wife to support. Whatever would he do then? The thought made him shiver.

With the inmates settled for the night, Fred returned to his quarters. The rooms were in darkness and there was no smell of supper cooking. Lighting the oil lamp, he carried it through the living room and into the bedroom. The wardrobe door stood open, showing it to be empty. Going to the kitchen, he saw his wife was not in there either. He checked the mustard powder tin where they kept their savings. It was also empty. Ada had left! She had gathered her things and gone!

'Ada Tulley, you dirty rotten bitch!' Fred shouted at the top of his lungs as he threw the mustard tin across the room. Then plonking himself down in his chair, he muttered, 'Damn my eyes, if that don't take the bloody biscuit!'

At nine o'clock the porter arrived with the gate keys as he did every night.

'Have you seen the Matron today?' Fred asked.

'Ar, her went off this afternoon,' the porter answered.

'Where to?' Fred asked as he rubbed his whiskers.

'Ain't got a clue, she don't tell me nothing,' the porter replied with a wry grin.

'She don't tell me much more,' Fred scowled back.

'I don't think she'll be back.' The porter watched for Tulley's reaction.

'Why not?'

'Cos, her had a carpet bag with her. Smacks of leaving home, if you ask me.' The porter shook his head.

'Oh she's left al lright, and she's taken all my money with her!' Fred's rage was mounting again.

The porter pursed his lips and sucked in a noisy breath.

Fred dismissed him with a wave of his hand.

As the porter left, Fred dropped into a chair, unable to believe his wife had slipped away without a word. On one hand he was glad to be rid of her, but on the other he was furious with her. He knew, without a Matron, the Master would be dismissed! Added to that he now had no savings to get by on. Cursing, he banged around in the kitchen like a spoilt child.

Leaning his head back, he screamed at the top of his lungs, 'Ada Tulley... I'll get you for this, you bitch!'

Twenty-Four

The snow fell steadily and silently, forming white piles on windowsills and rooftops. The trees had long since lost their leaves and lay in lazy slumber for the duration; the ground beneath winter's white cloak was granite hard. There was no birdsong to be heard and the town took on a very different look.

A knock on the front door of The Laburnums revealed a near frozen Bertha Jenkins. Invited in by Molly, she warmed herself by the parlour fire. Bertha had come to give Cara her thanks. She was now the cook at the school in Bow Street.

'They told me as how you had telephoned them and recommended me to be their cook. They called me in for a... well, to see me and I was taken on there and then! I ain't half grateful. Thanks, from the bottom of my heart, thanks,' Bertha gushed.

Gracie and Molly and the children joined them for tea and cake, and gossip was exchanged before Bertha said quietly, 'Cara...'

Cara's heart dropped like a stone... Bertha had more to say. Then the cook's tone changed to one of joy, 'It would seem Mrs Tulley, the Matron, has left the workhouse! The word is all over the town!'

'Bloody hell!' Gracie spluttered, droplets of tea flying everywhere. Young Daisy giggled and Charlie drew his lips together tightly in an effort not to laugh.

'Are you sure?' Cara couldn't believe it.

'Ar,' Bertha resumed, 'that means the Master will be chucked out an' all!'

Cara closed her eyes sending up a silent 'thank you' to the Almighty.

'But Cara... there's something you need to see.'

'What?' Molly interjected, unable to contain herself.

'You'll have to come with me to the other side of the town, then you can see for yourselves.' Bertha would not be drawn into saying more.

Wrapping themselves in warm clothes, Gracie and Cara joined Bertha to walk down Proud's Lane. Molly elected to stay home with the children. Cara wondered what could be so important as to drag them out into such cold weather.

At the end of the lane, Cara hailed the waiting cab and the women climbed aboard, Bertha giving the cabbie the address they needed to visit. Gracie and Cara overheard Bertha's words but had no idea about the area they were to visit as they had not been there before. The horse walked on, occasionally slipping on the icy ground, unable to find purchase with his horse shoes. The cabbie kept the horse to a steady walk along the streets and out onto the heath, having crossed the railroad on Millfields Road. Stopping the carriage by a small row of dilapidated buildings, he parked in the lea side out of the bitter wind; wrapped in a blanket, he settled down to wait.

The women climbed from the cab and looked over the

cottages. These dwellings belonged to the occupants, bought when their men were in work in the colliery and earning a fair wage. Money had been scrimped and saved for years on end to achieve their goal of owning their own homes, even if they were only two up, two down and in a sorry state. Cara saw dirty net curtains twitch as Bertha led them towards the door of the first building in the row. Rapping the door soundly, she called out, 'It's only me!'

Cara frowned, wondering if those inside would know who 'me' was. The door opened and Bertha marched in, with Cara and Gracie close behind.

'This lady here is Cara Flowers,' she said, proudly pushing Cara forward.

The thin woman Bertha spoke to dropped onto an old kitchen chair and burst into tears. She sobbed like her heart would break and Cara was mortified at the reaction. Looking at Bertha, questions written all over her face about why the woman was crying, Cara saw Bertha raise a hand, asking they wait for the woman to regain control.

Cara's eyes took in the very small living room with a tiny fireplace. There were no ornaments or keepsakes lining the shelf above the grate. There were no pictures on the walls and the plaster was crumbling away. Glancing back to the woman sat crying, Cara saw her dress was torn and shabby, she wondered how much longer it would last. The woman's hair was lank, and her dirty hands held fingernails chewed down to the quick.

After a few moments the woman, Gladys Percival, wiped her nose on the hem of her cotton dress and said, 'Oh thank the Lord! My husband is out standing in the bread line. He couldn't face it after the colliery he worked at closed down, but seeing the state we're in, he finally managed to stir his stumps and get his arse out there. Oh, begging your pardon, Miss Flowers.' The woman apologized for her turn of phrase before continuing. 'My two boys are coal picking on the slag heaps of that dross which was cleared from the earth by the miners!'

Cara glanced again at the dead fire in the hearth. The room was as cold as the wind that whipped outside and she shivered. She noted there was one chair, the one the woman now sat on. No other furniture was in evidence in the small living room. At Bertha's nod, the woman stood and hooked her finger for them to follow her into the kitchen. Cara saw the cupboards, with no doors, were empty.

Gladys said, 'We had to use the cupboard doors for firewood in an effort to beat off the cold.'

Following her up the dark bare staircase, Cara was led into each of the two bedrooms. She gasped when she saw two straw mattresses on the floor of each room. These were the only things in there. No cupboards – no clothes! Cara was horrified.

Back in the living room once more, Gladys explained, 'We prayed you would find us. The Relieving Officer has come time after time and we refused him, but we was fast reaching the point of accepting a ticket to that workhouse. The market folk have been good to my boys who have had to scavenge often, but they can only help so much.' Cara saw the woman's pride wither before her very eyes.

It was the same story as Cara and Gracie were taken to each cottage in the row, twelve on one side and five on the other side of a dirt track that divided them. All were empty of food and furniture. There was no offer of tea, for there was none; nor any coal to light fires to boil kettles.

After visiting the last cottage, Cara climbed silently back into the carriage with Bertha and Gracie.

The cottagers watched her go from their dirty windows. Would she help them? She had not actually said she would. She had merely thanked them for their time and left. Would this 'guardian angel' forsake them and leave them to their fate? Refusing to believe this of the kind young woman, they settled down to wait.

Cara Flowers cried the whole way home. She knew about the poor but had never seen such poverty as she had that day. Once her tears had dried she formulated her plan.

Back in the parlour at The Laburnums once more, Cara said, 'Sam, I want you to hire six men with the largest carts and meet me at the Atlas Bedstead works off Bradley Street. Also I want the allotment workers and their tools over to the cottages on Millfields Road sharpish. Gracie and Molly, I need you to go to town for food – buy as much as will fit into and onto two cabs and take it to Gladys and her neighbours.'

As everyone rushed out to accomplish their tasks, Cara bundled Charlie and Daisy into the cab that was still waiting in the driveway of her house before getting in herself.

The cabbie set off for Chapel Street first where Cara requested the help of her male tenants.

Then the cabbie moved on to the Atlas works.

Cara asked to see the manager, and seated in his office, she said, 'I need your help.'

The manager eyed the pretty young woman. At last he was meeting the famous Miss Flowers.

'I need beds and mattresses, lots of them, to be delivered to the cottages in Millfields Road – today!' Handing over a slip of paper containing the house numbers and how many beds were needed for each, Cara watched the man scan her writing.

Walking to the door, he whistled loudly across the factory floor, before retaking his seat. In but a moment the foreman dashed into the office. Seeing Cara, he tipped his cap and nodded.

Giving the paper to the foreman, the manager asked, 'Today?'

'Ar, we can manage this,' the foreman said, then turning to Cara he added, 'Nice to meet you, Miss Flowers.' He was out the door before she could speak.

Looking at the manager, she said, 'Thank you so very much. Would you be kind enough to invoice me at The Laburnums?'

'I'll do that,' the manager said, 'I can telephone the mattress factory with your order too if it will help.'

Cara beamed, 'It will help enormously! Thank you.'

By the time Cara's carriage and the six carters arrived in Millfields Road, work was well underway on the old buildings. Windows were being mended, draughts were stopped by doors being fitted properly, and chimneys were swept. The husbands had returned from standing the bread line and were happily helping out. The beds were manoeuvred into their resting places and fires were lit from a few bags of coal brought by the workers. The one standpipe that served all the families was lagged tightly and was working overtime as water was pumped into kettles and then hung on brackets over the fires now burning brightly in the hearths.

Cara requested the carters, with their vehicles now free of the beds from the Atlas works, to fetch enough coal to last the winter and invoices were to be sent to her at her home address.

As the carters moved off, two carriages arrived, full to overflowing with food, bedding and warm clothes. Cara helped the women unload the goods, their happy faces glowing in the cold air. It warmed her heart to see such joy at what she considered simple things. She had always taken for granted there would be food in the pantry and clothes in the cupboards, but now she realized just how lucky she was. She watched children wait patiently as mothers sorted through the clothes to find some that would fit. They took them though whether they fit properly or not, they weren't going to fuss over details, they could work with whatever they had.

Bertha Jenkins appeared shortly afterwards with one of the women from Cara's Cakes loaded down with baskets of freshly baked bread, pastries and cakes.

One little boy about Daisy's age came up to her and said shyly, 'Thank you Miss Flowers.' Cara gave him a hug and as she looked up she saw his mother beaming proudly, a tear glinting in her eye.

Millfields Road was a flurry of activity; men hammering and banging, women sobbing as they brewed tea and children squealing with delight as they dug through the snow for any kindling sticks they could find. As the light began to fade, Cara prepared to leave. Suddenly she was surrounded by people who were sobbing, clapping and cheering. Gracie, Molly and the children climbed into the waiting cab and Cara joined them, waving goodbye to the grateful people who stood in the snow and waved her off.

Alighting the cab at home, Cara made to pay the cabbie who she'd hired for the day.

'Don't want your money, Miss Flowers,' the cabbie said,

'what you did for those folk today... well, buy the kiddies some "suck" instead.' The big burly cabbie wiped away a tear as he turned the horse around and set off down the drive.

*

Martin sat thinking about his sweetheart and how far she'd come in such a short time. Her grandmother, Henrietta Selby, would have been very proud of her granddaughter's achievements. Cara Flowers was revered all over Bilston.

And now she had made herself an appointment with Isaac Ballard, at the Local Government Board office. She was going over the heads of the Board of Guardians... she was about to speak with the organ grinder – not the monkey!

Taking a little box from his pocket, he lifted its lid. Wedged on a tiny red velvet cushion sat a gold ring with a sparkling diamond set atop golden shoulders. Brushing a finger over the ring, he smiled. Would she accept if he asked her? Would Cara Flowers marry him? Drawing in a deep breath, he held it for a moment praying she would. Snapping the box shut, he held it tight in his hand, then brought it to his lips and kissed it tenderly. *Please God, let her say yes!*

Replacing the box in his pocket, Martin thought about their upcoming appointment. Dr Cooper and Bertha Jenkins were to accompany them to add weight to what Cara had to tell the Board. He wondered what the outcome of their meeting would be. There was nothing he wanted more than to see Cara achieve her ultimate goal, but what then? If she succeeded in closing down the workhouse, where would she go from there? He sincerely doubted she would want to just be a housewife. What he was sure of was whatever she chose to do... she would succeed. He needed to support her, too, as she strove to support him.

Martin was aware of Cara's father's death some years before and there was no record of any other Flowers children born in this parish other than Charlie and Daisy. Also Mrs Selby was clearly unaware of their existence when she made the will as the huge inheritance had been left to Cara alone. Charlie and Daisy could at some point contest this, and he would help all he could if that situation arose. Martin smiled. So that just left Cara's mother... if she were still alive. Certainly no death certificate for Elizabeth Flowers had come to light.

Staring through the window, he watched the snow fall silently and he wondered, not for the first time, why Cara had been raised by her grandmother. Whatever had happened to have caused the situation to arise, Martin felt it must have been traumatic for all involved. Then Elizabeth Flowers had given birth to Charlie and Daisy – but she had abandoned them. Why? Had she been forced into that decision somehow? Or had she, herself, chosen to leave her children behind?

Martin knew the only way to answer these questions was to discover the whereabouts of Elizabeth Flowers.

*

The work on the cottages in Millfields Road stopped for the night as the temperature dropped dramatically.

Each cottage had a fire in the hearth and the aroma of cooking, the first in a very long time, filled the kitchens. Some of the children had beds to sleep in for the first time in their lives and couldn't wait to try them out. Parents talked quietly, almost reverently, about the young woman who had arrived to save their lives. The men had been promised work as soon as Cara was able to provide it. Their prayers had been answered. Thanking the Lord for their good fortune, they also silently thanked Bertha Jenkins for her intervention on their behalf.

One thing they knew for sure now was the Relieving Officer would certainly have a shock the next time he called! He wouldn't be able to believe his eyes when he saw the work done on the properties, the new curtains hung, the windows cleaned and sparkling, and the children in better clothing. Spotting all this, he would have to turn and walk away, shoving the tickets in his pocket as he went.

Twenty-Five

Fred Tulley squirmed under the disbelieving gaze of the Board of Guardians as they sat in the boardroom. He had explained that his wife had left him and the workhouse.

'Christ, Tulley!' Joseph Purcell gasped after a long silence. 'The place is falling apart! What happened to cause this?' Raising a hand to ward off the excuse Fred would inevitably come up with, Joseph went on, 'Don't bother...'

Fred nodded as he awaited his fate, his gaze sweeping the faces before him.

Purcell glanced at his colleagues and then back to the Master. 'Well, this puts a whole new light on things. You know, of course, that we are unable to keep you on as Master of this institution.' It was not a question.

Fred Tulley spluttered his reply, 'But, sir, I have nowhere else to go! I only know this work... what will I do?'

Purcell snapped, 'You should have thought of that before! I have no doubt you have money hidden away that will prevent you from becoming an inmate here yourself!'

Tulley sighed loudly as he shook his head. 'Ada took all my money. I don't have two halfpennies to rub together.'

The lie slipped easily from his lips. He said nothing of the household funds which he kept securely locked away in his desk, something to fall back on should the need arise.

'Hellfire and damnation!' Purcell yelled. 'I suggest you get out there and find that thieving drunkard of a wife! You will have to sort yourself out, man! We will give you until the end of January… then you're out!'

The Board members stood as one and filed out of the room. They would have to place an advertisement in the local newspaper for a new Master and Matron, not to mention a cook, doctor and schoolmaster, none of which having yet been filled… more expense. Purcell doubted very much that anyone would be interested in taking up the posts. His plan to marry Cara and inherit her fortune was being pushed back at every turn, and this was a setback he could have done without. He muttered as he left the building, 'Cara Flowers will love this when she finds out!'

*

Joseph decided it was time to meet with Isaac Ballard, Chairman of the Local Government Board, the man who had appointed him and the other members of the Board of Guardians. He telephoned for an appointment and was told he could attend immediately.

Isaac rubbed his whiskers as he listened to the man sat at the other side of his desk.

'The cook of the workhouse was the first to go,' Joseph explained. 'Then the doctor quit. Soon after, the schoolmaster and now the Matron has walked out!'

'I see,' Isaac said, 'then we must place advertisements in the newspapers for replacements.'

'No one will take up those posts, Isaac, you know as well as I that folk fear and hate the place. Besides, there's been no one forthcoming up until now.'

'Quite so,' Ballard nodded.

'It's all that woman's fault!' Purcell's temper was rising yet again.

'Which woman would that be?' Isaac felt he should ask, although he knew precisely who Joseph was referring to. He could see the other man becoming more and more agitated, and he was enjoying the discomfort. Truth be told, he had never much liked Joseph Purcell.

'Cara bloody Flowers! She's intent on emptying the workhouse of its inmates! She is providing work and homes for those signing out. She's buying up all available properties for just that reason. Isaac, she must be stopped!'

'Well now, I don't see how.' Ballard watched calmly as Purcell fumed.

'If she continues and *does* manage to empty the place, I'll be out of the job of Chairman of the Board!' Joseph's voice rose in angst.

'Agreed. But you are still the Magistrate of Bilston, Joseph, quite a prestigious position, I'm sure you'll agree.' Seeing the other man nod, Isaac went on, 'So the loss of your post as Chairman would not be unduly distressing, should it come to the put-to.' Joseph waggled his head from side to side as if undecided. 'Therefore, my advice is to sit by and wait. It may be that we *can* find new staff. As for myself, I have no real need to work. As you know, I am a very wealthy man and look forward to the day when I can relinquish my role here. However, people will always be in the situation where they might well accept a ticket from the Relieving Officer. For myself, the loss of the workhouse will not be unduly distressing, although I do understand that should it close down, the poor of the town will have nowhere to go.'

'But what if they're not in that situation? What if they keep refusing a ticket? What if she succeeds in emptying the workhouse?' Purcell railed.

'Then, my dear Joseph, you will indeed find yourself out of the position of Chairman of the Board of Guardians!'

Isaac Ballard smiled as Purcell left his office, slamming the door behind him.

*

Sitting by his fire in the parlour of Brueton House, Purcell sipped his whisky and brooded. Cara's pretty face loomed in his mind's eye and he felt his pulse rate quicken in anger. What he wouldn't give to have an hour with her… just the two of them! He would show her where a woman's place should be. Women should be at home, not annoying men who go out to work for a living!

As he thought on the matter he realized his real grievance was now personal. It seemed petty, but his reputation as Chairman was on the line here, and he *would not* allow this young woman to better him. Cara was playing him like a fiddle, whether she knew it or not.

As he gazed into the dancing flames of the fire, thinking about Cara Flowers, his mind slipped back to his formative years. His father had died when he was a young boy. Joseph had grown up in a house full of women. His mother had been extremely strict and his five sisters had bullied him at every opportunity. His young life had been miserable, and he had thought, as his sisters had been married off, that things would improve for him. However, as time passed, his mother had turned brutal in her strictness; he suffered constant beatings. Working hard at school, he determined one day he would make something of himself. He would be a man who would be shown respect; he would have a high social standing. Once he attained that, he would be a man of means. He remembered the death of his mother and his misery had been lifted. But the damage had already been done. Joseph Purcell had no time for women, unless of course, they could be used to further his career or add to his finances.

Twenty-Six

The day of her appointment with the Chairman of the Local Government Board had arrived and Cara looked into the twinkling blue eyes of the man sat behind his desk. An older man with a kindly face covered with white whiskers. Isaac Ballard.

Martin Lander, in his role of solicitor, sat to Cara's left and Bertha Jenkins and Dr Joshua Cooper sat to her right.

After introductions, Mr Ballard asked, 'What is it you think I can help you with, Miss Flowers?' He was fully conversant with this young woman's good works with the poor of the town, as well as her dealings with the workhouse after his meeting with Joseph Purcell.

'Mr Ballard,' Cara began, 'not only have these good people resigned their posts at the workhouse…' her arm swept to the doctor and Bertha, 'but it has now come to my attention that the Matron has deserted her post also.'

Isaac Ballard's eyebrows lifted involuntarily. How had she found that out? He only knew himself a matter of days ago.

Cara continued confidently, 'I am sure you have heard

of my dealings with the Master, Fred Tulley, and also that I have relieved the institution of a good many of its residents.' Isaac nodded in confirmation. 'Now, Mr Ballard, Mr Lander informs me that as the Matron has left, the Master must be dismissed should a replacement Matron not be found.' Cara waited for her words to sink in.

'That is correct, Miss Flowers.' Ballard's eyes smiled. He was impressed by this young woman.

'I believe there are very few inmates left in the Spike...' She deliberately used the derogatory term, leaving the man in no doubt what she thought of the place. '...and I'm under no illusion that you do not know of my intentions regarding those inmates.'

'Indeed, Miss Flowers, there is not a person in the town who is not aware of your intentions. However, what is it that you want from me?' Ballard pursed his lips as he awaited her answer.

Cara gave the man a disarming smile. 'May I ask what you intend to do with an empty workhouse?'

'It is not empty, Miss Flowers.' Ballard laughed, surprised at her question.

'But it will be, Mr Ballard... and very soon!' Cara smiled again.

Isaac Ballard drew in a deep breath, weighing up the girl in front of him. She meant what she said – she was going to empty the workhouse of its last inmates. In his heart he hoped she would succeed, but in his mind loomed the destitute people of the town.

'Well now,' he said, 'should that prove to be the case, and providing no others are admitted, we would have to make a decision regarding the building. I am drawn to conclude from your question that you have something in mind? I have to add, I'm very curious what that might be.'

'I do indeed, Mr Ballard,' Cara said. She had decided not to divulge the details, having learned her lesson the hard way from Purcell. 'Be assured the men left in that awful place are awaiting my word. Once received, they will sign themselves out and your building will be a relic.'

Isaac Ballard cast a glance at the doctor then at Bertha. 'May I ask why you resigned from your posts – I have been given an explanation but would prefer to hear it from yourselves.'

Bertha Jenkins tearfully related the cuts in food rations, the sickness of the children and finished with the death of Liza Townsend's little girl. Dr Cooper confirmed Bertha's words, adding that neither of their posts had yet been filled, nor that of the schoolmaster.

Cara then explained her visit from Joseph Purcell. Ballard listened without interruption. It was proving the workhouse problems involved far more than Ballard had been led to believe.

'You are aware, Miss Flowers, I'm sure, that the workhouse building is owned by the council, and until it is actually completely empty of its inmates... with no possibility of more being admitted... there is nothing I can do for you.' Isaac watched Cara's face closely for a response. Yet again he was surprised at her reaction. He had expected her to either shout and bawl about how unfair it all was, or to burst into floods of tears. She did neither.

'Could you tell me then, what exactly you would do with the workhouse building if that scenario proved to be the case?' She pressed. Cara was giving no quarter and maintained her calm demeanour throughout the discussions.

'Well… erm… I suppose… we'd have to sell it off, otherwise it would be standing empty and going to waste.' Ballard knew she had him.

'Thank you for meeting with us, Mr Ballard, it has been very informative.' Cara calmly rose from her seat and extended her hand. After a firm handshake the little group walked from the office, leaving a baffled Isaac Ballard stroking his whiskers.

He wondered what she would do now; whatever it was, he aimed to keep a keen eye on the situation, as well as the delightful young woman he had just spoken with. Smiling to himself, he secretly wished her every success in her endeavours.

In the cab back to The Laburnums, Cara said, 'My friends, get your thinking caps on, we need to get the rest of those men out of the workhouse and into a home and work as soon as possible!'

*

In the meantime, Fred Tulley looked out onto the snow-laden exercise yard. He had until the end of January to find a Matron and to ensure more people entered the workhouse. Why were people not taking up the tickets offered by the Relieving Officer? It was Tulley's guess the man wasn't trying hard enough; in fact, looking at the weather, Fred wondered if the man was even leaving his fireside.

Rubbing his aching arm where Ada had stabbed him, he wondered where his wife was now. Not only had she physically wounded him but she'd run off with his money. Regardless, he had to think about himself and what he would do now.

Turning to look through another window, he watched the men crushing bone and stone in the yard. Shivering, he moved to pile more coal on the fire. Without doing so, he finally made his decision and strode from the room. Marching down the cold dark corridor, he opened the door leading to the bone crushing yard and whistled loudly. As the men looked up, Tulley hooked a finger and the men trooped inside shivering, their thin clothes no match for the cold that seeped to the bone.

'Come with me,' Tulley said.

They followed the Master to the warm kitchen. Much to the men's surprise, Tulley gave a key to one of the men and motioned to the large pantry.

'I'm off out of this bloody place!' Spinning on his heel, he walked out, leaving men with open mouths behind him.

'What the hell is going on?' one said.

'I don't care,' said another, 'let's get warm and have something to eat, I'm bloody starving!'

Returning to his fireside, Fred realized his time here was definitely up now. He would do as Ada had done and flit. Let the bloody Board of Guardians find out on their next visit, for he had no intention of informing them he was leaving.

Throwing clothes into a carpet bag, Tulley pocketed the household funds kept locked away in his desk. He was very glad now that he had not told Ada about where he'd kept them hidden. Then he stepped quietly out into the snow. The porter opened the gate and Tulley nodded as he passed through. He walked away without a backward glance. The Porter stared after him; he knew the workhouse had had its day, its closure was not far off which would see him out of a job. He shook his head and walked back to the warmth of his tiny lodge, concern for his future etching his face.

*

Bertha Jenkins rushed through the front door of Cara's house, shaking snow from her woollen shawl. 'Where's Cara?' She asked a surprised Molly, who indicated the direction of the kitchen.

'Cara... Cara... Oh you'll never guess... Tulley's left the workhouse!' Bertha gasped.

'What? Bertha, how do you know? Are you sure?' Cara was aghast.

'Ar, the gate porter told Mrs Johnson, who told...' Bertha puffed.

Cara looked at Gracie and let out a whoop of delight. 'Bertha, that's marvellous, but what about the men left there?'

Bertha related what she knew and Cara remembered the words spoken by Isaac Ballard at their meeting.

'...until it is actually completely empty of its inmates..., with no possibility of more being admitted...'

The place was not empty, there were still men in there! Until they were moved out, her hands were tied.

'Ladies, we need to get the men out and quickly, otherwise our plan could fail! If we intend to close down the workhouse, then it must be empty, with the certainty that no more people will enter!' Cara began to pace the kitchen.

'Where could they go, though?' Gracie asked.

'I know if I asked they would vacate that building, but the very fact they were in there in the first place proves they have nowhere else *to* go!' The worry showed on her face as she continued to pace.

Excitement that her plan of closing the Spike was almost at an end and worry it may be thwarted at the last turn fused in her brain. She *had* to think clearly now... and fast.

Twenty-Seven

The workhouse porter had watched both the Matron and the Master leave and then had made his own decision. Stepping through the gate, he locked it securely behind him and trudged away over the snow. Coming to an old house in Cemetery Row, he banged on the door. Being shown into the living room, he and the Relieving Officer sat before the fire to discuss their futures.

'Old Tulley left the Spike this afternoon,' the porter said.

The other man nodded, 'I guessed he would. So what do we do now then, Frank?'

The porter answered with a shrug of his shoulders, 'Well, our jobs are on the line, and I don't know about you, but I don't feel the need to be out in the bitter cold all day with no thanks for my effort.'

'Me neither, but… there's no work out there if we quit.' The Relieving Officer looked worried.

However, after an hour's discussion they came to a mutual decision – they *would* quit then they would seek out Cara Flowers and request employment from her. Surely she would help them; she always found an answer to a problem.

Unlocking the gate once more, he strode inside the building. Hearing the men's voices, he followed the sound. The chatter stopped and all eyes turned to him when he walked into the dormitory. He silently laid the keys on an empty bed. Muttering 'good luck', he turned and walked out. He vowed to himself to never return to the place as long as he lived.

The men let out a whoop as they watched the man leave and they jumped up and, throwing their arms around each other, danced a quick waltz around the room. Then, just as quickly, their discussions turned to what would happen now. There were no staff now, they knew, and with the gate unlocked, they could come and go as they pleased. If they left, where would they go? There was no work in the town, and none of them had homes to go to. Whilst they were still in this building, they had coal and food supplies, but how much longer would that last? They had to get a message to Cara Flowers. Each man then wrapped himself in as many blankets as he could and they all walked free from the place that had held them prisoner for so long.

*

Molly answered the knock to the door and led the two men into the parlour. Explaining they had quit the workhouse, the porter and Relieving Officer watched the shocked expression on Cara's face.

'So, what you're telling me is that there are no staff in there at present, is that right?'

Both men nodded in unison.

Frank, the porter, said, 'Miss Flowers we need some work now that we've quit the Spike. Are you able to help? Please, we'll take on anything.'

'Gentlemen,' Cara answered, 'I'm afraid I have nothing for you as yet, but if you can bear with me, I will do my best for you.' She saw the men slump in their chairs. She went on, 'It is my plan to get the remaining men out of the workhouse and into work. Once I have achieved that goal I then intend to buy the building and turn it into living accommodation. So, if you don't mind doing some labouring, there will be work there for you.'

'Anything, we'll do anything!' The Relieving Officer replied with determination. Both men breathed a great sigh of relief. At least with labouring they would work with others and not alone as they previously had. The men leaned back in their chairs, grateful for the help about to be given from this young woman.

'Good, but the problem I have to deal with first is getting those men into housing elsewhere.'

Just then Molly burst through the parlour door, 'Cara... you have to come and see this!'

Cara excused herself, leaving the two men by the fireside wondering what had happened now.

Molly held the front door open and Cara looked out. Plodding up her driveway were what she assumed were the blanket-wrapped inmates from the workhouse!

Over fifty men were welcomed into the parlour, living room and kitchen amid the stares of the porter and Relieving Officer. With everyone crammed in, Charlie built up the fires.

Some of the men, along with Gracie and Molly, helped with making tea and sorting out something to eat. Gracie fussed there would not possibly be enough food for everyone, so a handful of the others were sent to the market with a grocery list provided by Gracie and some money provided by Cara.

Cara listened as yet others explained the events of the past few hours, which reiterated precisely what Frank had told her. Then she asked, 'You are absolutely certain no one remains in the workhouse?' Everyone began to speak at once. Cara's hand went up and silence descended. She was assured the building stood empty, and with the Relieving Officer now sitting by her fireside, she knew there would be no more tickets handed out. Excitement rose in her that she may have finally achieved what she set out to do, but it was tinged with anxiety. She had to make the most of the situation while she had the chance.

Leaving Molly and Gracie to administer to the men, Cara rushed to the telephone in the hall.

'Martin, I need you... now!' She said into the handset.

*

Later that same day, Isaac Ballard looked into the blue eyes of the young woman sat opposite him once more. 'Miss Flowers, it's nice to see you again... and so soon!' The Chairman of the Local Government Board nodded across to Martin Lander, which was returned with a knowing smile.

Cara cut to the chase. 'Mr Ballard, your workhouse, as we speak, is having a closure notice hung on its gate.'

Ballard's mouth dropped open at the shock of her words. Even he had not yet received this news, being cloistered away in his Council office.

A very excited Cara nodded, she was unable to prevent the wide grin spreading across her face as she went on, 'Your porter and Relieving Officer are at this moment sat in my parlour having relinquished their posts, so there will be no more tickets issued to the poor of Bilston.'

'How...? When...?' Ballard spluttered. Shock resonated in him at how quickly Cara had succeeded in her quest.

'The remaining *inmates* have left and are also now at my house. Therefore Mr Ballard, the workhouse is now officially closed!' Cara's smile was triumphant.

'You don't waste any time do you, Miss Flowers?' Ballard finally located his tongue. 'However, I must warn you, the council may well decide to reopen the place should it prove necessary. After all, you can't take care of everyone, now can you?'

'I do not let the grass grow under my feet, sir, and I agree with you, I can't look after everybody who is homeless or jobless, much as I'd like to. However, the council will not be able to reopen the workhouse because... that building now belongs to me!' Cara grinned widely.

'You've bought the building?' Ballard couldn't believe his ears.

'I have!' Cara was ecstatic.

'How on earth did you manage that?!' Isaac Ballard was dumbfounded.

Cara kept her cards close to her chest. It would not do to reveal how she had come by the acquisition of the old workhouse building. After all, she didn't want it to become common knowledge that she had bribed Mr Simmons, the Chairman of the council. She had requested a meeting and after a lot of discussion the Chairman had acquiesced. The bribe had cost her almost as much as the building, but at least now it was hers to do with as she wished.

Seeing Cara was not about to answer his previous question, he asked, 'What, may I ask, do you intend to do with it now you have it?'

'I was thinking I might renovate it and once complete

it can be divided into apartments for anyone wishing to reside there. I felt it right to inform you myself, as you will now need, in turn, to inform Joseph Purcell and the other members of the Board of Guardians that they have been disbanded… unless of course you would like me to tell them?' Cara's eyes twinkled mischievously.

Isaac Ballard laughed loudly, then said, 'I'm sure you'd take great delight in that, Miss Flowers, however as it is my duty…'

'Good luck with that, Mr Ballard,' Cara laughed.

Cara and Martin left a bewildered Isaac Ballard to his task. He would have to suffer the inevitable railings of a disgruntled one-time Chairman of the Board of Guardians, a man he had never really liked. Deep down he knew he was going to enjoy it.

*

It was Christmas Eve and Daisy and Charlie trundled off to bed as they did every night. Father Christmas had always forgotten them, they said, so why would this year be any different? Daisy had told Charlie that Cara was sure to buy them something for Christmas. The boy was not so sure. He tried to explain that their sister had spent an awful lot of money housing and feeding the poor people of Bilston. Daisy was adamant that they would both have a little something, so Charlie left her to enjoy the excitement of it all. He, on the other hand, went to bed as though it was just another night.

Cara, Molly and Gracie excitedly wrapped sweets and toys in the warm kitchen. It was Cara's first Christmas with her brother and sister, and she fully intended to make it a memorable one. A pretty rag doll for Daisy along with a doll's house and a wooden fort and toy soldiers for Charlie. Sweets, nuts and fruit-filled woollen socks hung from the mantelpiece.

The conversation turned to the men who had walked out of the workhouse.

'At least they went back when you explained your plan to them,' Gracie said.

'Yes. I hated having to ask them, but once Christmas is over, the work can begin,' Cara answered.

Molly piped up, 'There's food and coal enough to see them over the holiday they said.'

Nodding, Cara smiled as she remembered how they had sung carols as they trudged away from The Laburnums.

Word had spread like wildfire around the town that Cara Flowers had beaten the system and closed the workhouse and many people considered it the town's own Christmas miracle.

Christmas morning dawned and Cara, Molly and Gracie delighted in the children's excitement of not being forgotten by Santa Claus. Daisy was ecstatic at receiving a doll's house. Charlie had thanked Cara quietly for his gifts. He whispered they really didn't believe in Santa now as they were growing up, but they loved the gifts anyway. Cara hugged him for his kindness, saying she quite understood. She smiled inwardly at his eagerness to become a man.

Martin Lander joined them for lunch and wine was poured.

'A toast! To Cara's incredible success over the last year!' As glasses were replaced on the table, Martin slipped his hand into his pocket and he moved to face Cara. Bending on one knee, he lifted the lid of the tiny box in his hand. 'Cara Flowers, would you do me the honour of becoming my wife?'

Gasps sounded around the dining room and eyes watched as everyone waited for Cara's answer.

*

On the other side of town, Joseph Purcell ate his Christmas lunch alone as he usually did, his staff enjoying theirs in the kitchen. He had little appetite – the meeting a few days ago with the Local Government Board having seen to that.

Cara Flowers had won. She had managed to close the workhouse and his position as Chairman was gone; just before Christmas too. The Board had been disbanded and the building sold, and guess who had bought it? Cara bloody Flowers!

Pushing his plate away, Joseph retired to the parlour, taking his wine with him.

Staring into the fire, he saw Cara's face in his mind's eye; her blue eyes, her golden hair, her beautiful smile. Regardless of the workhouse debacle, he could not get her out of his head. Her gentle voice, her confidence, the passion of taking on the challenges she set herself. She had been a thorn in his side, but somehow the pain was bittersweet. She roused a desire in him… a desire to dominate a woman, which he had not felt in many years, but she also raised his frustration level to boiling point. His mixed emotions conflicted, leaving him exhausted but excited. He would love the challenge of bringing her to heel, to crush her and see her begging for mercy.

Changing the course of his thoughts, he saw there was nothing more to be done regarding the Spike, but Joseph would be interested to see how the transformation would unfold. Ballard had informed him of Cara's plans for the place. Once the renovations were complete, what then? How would Cara find work for those in residence? There were an awful lot of former inmates who would suddenly find themselves with nothing to fill their time. There was also the bread line, which grew steadily longer each day as more collieries closed, and now there was nowhere for the poor and homeless to go. Cara Flowers couldn't feed and house them all.

*

'Martin,' Cara said quietly as she looked at the man on bent knee before her, 'I am surprised to say the least... I had not thought...'

Everyone waited with bated breath, all eyes on her. Martin's heart hammered in his chest. Was she about to refuse him? Did she not love him enough to accept his proposal? In his mind he saw her disappear from his life like a puff of smoke if she said no. He waited as she looked at the others.

Looking back to the man shuffling his weight, she smiled and said, 'My answer is yes!'

Held breath escaped, bursting lungs in cheers as Martin placed the diamond ring on the third finger of her left hand.

'Thank God for that!' Martin said as he struggled to his feet. 'My knees are killing me!' Howls of laughter filled the room as they shared a chaste kiss.

The laughter stopped abruptly as Daisy asked, 'What will happen to us when you'm married then, Cara?'

It was Martin who answered, 'We'll all live together, Daisy; it will be as it was before only I'll be with you too. Now, how about we play with the toys Father Christmas brought you two rascals?'

Charlie leapt forward and before long Martin and the

children were rolling around the floor laughing and squealing out their pure joy.

Martin's words had not escaped Cara, it appeared he had their life together already mapped out. As she watched him playing with her brother and sister, an unease settled over her. Would it be like this when they were married? Would Martin be making the decisions for them both? If so, she would lose her independence. She wasn't at all sure how she would cope with that.

A great weight settled on her chest threatening to suffocate her. She had the most awful feeling she was making a dreadful mistake, but she had committed herself. She began to worry that Martin might intervene with her work with the poor of Bilston and try to put a stop to it. He might insist she stay home and have a family of their own. As she sat, she pondered these things. She did not wish to give up her work, and although one day she might like to have children of her own, that was something to consider in the future.

Trying to put a brave face on for the sake of Daisy and Charlie, Cara found it very difficult to shake off the feeling of foreboding. So, she determined the best she could do for now was wait and see how things progressed.

Twenty-Eight

Everyone Cara had taken under her wing had a good Christmas for the first time in many years. There were roaring fires in repaired homes and hot meal on tables. Carols were sung and gifts were exchanged. Every family toasted Cara Flowers with whatever drink they had in hand.

Once the holiday period was over, Gracie Cox accompanied Cara on her trip to the old workhouse where there were still men in residence; at least they were free to come and go at their leisure now. Armed with pen and paper, Cara was going to make plans for the building's new usage. The cabbie she had used before was sat waiting in the street for a fare and he whistled across to the two women trudging through the snow. Cara beckoned him and with a smiled greeting they climbed aboard.

The horse walked gingerly along the frozen streets, pulling the cab behind it. On reaching the dirt track, the residents of Cara's Cottages spilled out to pass the time of day with the women as the cab stopped. Excited children showed Cara what Santa had brought for them and the mothers thanked her for enabling them to have a wonderful Christmas outside of the workhouse. Eventually they moved on once more. The cabbie drove through the wrought-iron gates of the old Spike, which had been left wide open, and halted the horse just inside.

Cara turned to Gracie and said, 'First thing, the gate and wall will need to come down and... the place will need a new name!'

Gracie frowned when she answered. 'Cara, folk will always think of this place as the workhouse, I don't think a new name will change that.'

Standing looking at the old building, Cara knew Gracie *was* right. Cara determined to get rid of its old connotations and she now realized a new name would not be enough.

Walking in through the front door, they were met by the men still in residence. Over tea in the warm kitchen, the chatter was bright and full of hope.

'I need to have a good look around,' Cara said at last, 'so that I can decide how best to proceed.'

One man stood up and volunteered to show her around the building. Gracie stood also; she wanted to see the other parts of the place.

The women had already seen the office and the stone and bone crushing yards as well as the oakum shed, but they were shocked at the dormitories.

'This where the kiddies slept?' Gracie asked in horror. The man nodded, sadness clouding his eyes. 'Good God!' She snapped.

The men's and women's dormitories were no better.

Moving on to the Master's living room, Cara registered the stark contrast between this relative luxury and the bareness of the dormitories.

Cara looked out of windows which graced all four walls,

each peering out across an arm of the building and its accompanying exercise yard. The layout of the building bore testament to the total segregation suffered by the inmates. The whole place could be viewed from this one room. The more she saw, the more she hated it. The medical ward was clean at least and Cara suspected that to be the doctor's doing.

Once more in the kitchen, Cara said, 'I have made my decision. This place is to be pulled down! I intend to have houses built on the land.' Applause sounded. The question facing her now was what to do with the men chatting happily around her. Cara listened but registered nothing of what was being said. Her mind was in turmoil. The men could remain in part of the building when the work of demolition began, but she felt that to be an unsatisfactory solution. She had to find them alternative accommodation – and soon.

*

Sam Yale was in the kitchen with Molly and the children when Cara and Gracie arrived home. He had brought the rent from the cottagers across town and an update on their welfare. Wally Webb soon arrived from Cara's Cottages for the same reasons.

Gathered in the warmth of her kitchen, Cara explained her predicament. 'I have to move those men out but there's nowhere for them to go.'

Wally said quietly, 'Beggin' your pardon, Cara, but if everyone at Sam's end and everyone at my end took in one, maybe two, for the duration of the work... would that help?'

'Wally! That would be the perfect solution, but would there be enough room? And... what will the women say about it?'

'Our women will say bugger all if they know it's helping you out!' Wally laughed.

'Then would you ask them on my behalf? After all, the worst that can be said is no.' Cara gave a cheeky grin. Her excitement mounted as she allowed herself to believe her plan could now actually work. With the men in alternative accommodation, she hoped the work to be undertaken would be done as swiftly as possible. The sooner that workhouse was demolished, the better.

Wally and Sam set off with the request and Cara telephoned her fiancé, with another favour to ask. 'Martin, do you know anyone who can draw up housing plans?' She asked. Noting down the name and telephone number he gave her, Cara thanked him. They chatted for a couple of minutes then Cara telephoned the man Martin had recommended.

Bill Rowley was an architect held in high esteem in the town.

'Mr Rowley, Cara Flowers here,' she said, 'I wonder if I may have a moment of your time.' Cara explained her plan to demolish the old workhouse and build housing in its place, and finished with, 'I would be most grateful for your assistance, thank you.'

Cara was delighted Bill agreed to look over the area as soon as possible and draw up some plans for her approval. She had stressed the need for haste and Bill assured her he was on the way out of the door the moment their conversation ended. Cara danced her way back to the kitchen deliriously happy.

Bill Rowley wanted the work. He wanted to be instrumental in seeing the old Spike disappear, and he knew Cara Flowers would not let the grass grow under her feet regarding this particular project. Grabbing his coat, he left the house to look over the old Spike.

Within the week the men from the workhouse were taken in by the cottagers and some welcomed into the living area of Cara's Cakes. It was a squeeze, with some sleeping in the living rooms, but knowing the plan for the new housing site, everyone made do. Cara couldn't believe how quickly things were moving.

Bill Rowley gathered the men and explained the best way to dismantle the wall that had surrounded the workhouse and pile up the bricks to be reused. Cara had given Bill Rowley carte blanche to get the project underway after he had agreed to her proposals. The great wrought-iron gate was taken down, leaving the building in full view. Although not many people of the town ventured that way as a rule, curiosity won out and it was not long before they stood around in groups to watch the work going on. They wanted to see with their own eyes if what they'd heard was true; that the old workhouse was being taken down. Newspaper reporters were busy writing articles on the new venture Cara Flowers had undertaken. Yet another challenge taken on, yet another to be accomplished.

*

Fred Tulley had landed on his feet. Finally arriving in Wolverhampton, he strode into the nearest public house. Ordering a beer, he picked up the newspaper which lay on the bar counter. He flicked the pages over as the barkeeper watched and asked, 'You looking for work?'

Tulley nodded. The barman placed a glass of ale on the counter and pointed to an advertisement. Giving his thanks, he paid for his beer and asked if he could keep the newspaper.

With a nod from the other man, Tulley found a seat by the window and began to read.

An hour later and striding purposefully down the street, Tulley made his way to the address given in the advertisement.

Wolverhampton was much like Bilston but much bigger. Spread over a vast area it was a coal mining town, the dirty buildings bearing testament to that. Disused mine shafts dotted the scrubland that divided parts of the town and the poor roamed its streets in search of work or a handout from any that would give it. Carts rumbled on the cobbled streets going to and from the canal basins. Carriages trundled past small shops with filthy windows. Steam train whistles blew as the engines drew into and out of the railway station. Rich and poor alike trudged through the snow, the difference in their clothing the only thing telling them apart.

Walking into the office, Fred said he'd come about the job. The secretary led him through to another office, where he met with the Chairman of the Local Government Board for Wolverhampton Union Workhouse. Shaking hands, Tulley introduced himself.

'So, Mr Tulley, you're here about the position of Union Master?' Tulley nodded, watching the man sat opposite him. 'Do you have any experience in this field of work, may I ask?'

'I was workhouse Master over in Bilston for many years,' Fred answered as he saw the man's eyebrows lift.

'Why did you leave that position?'

Fred was prepared for the question. 'I'm not sure if you know, but Bilston Spike is a small place and after being in charge for so long I had it running like clockwork. I felt in need of a change. I need a challenge.' Fred smiled inwardly as his thoughts turned to Cara Flowers at his use of his final word.

'I see. Well, Mr Tulley, I won't lie to you, we are desperate for a new Master. I do, however, find it strange that you left your last position without having first secured another one. Can you tell me why that is?'

This was a question Tulley was not prepared for. 'Well,' he drew the word out, playing for time. 'Truth be told, I had an altercation with the Matron. She actually tried to murder me!' Fred felt his temper rising at the memory.

'I see, and what did you do about that? Did you report it to the police?'

Fred began to sweat as he thought, *this man wants to know the ins and outs of Peg's arse!* 'Erm… no,' he said, 'I thought it best to just… move away from the area.'

'Hmmm. Can you provide any references, Mr Tulley?'

Fred's mind whirled. *Bloody hell, he wants references now!*

'I'm afraid not, sir, as I left in rather a hurry, you see. After all, the Matron had injured me quite badly and I didn't want to give her a second chance, if you understand me.' Giving the impression he was running his hand through his hair, Fred swiped away the beads of sweat that gathered on his brow.

'Very well, I can understand that.' The man shuffled the papers on his desk then said, 'All right, Mr Tulley, I am willing to offer you the position.' Tulley grinned. 'Your predecessor and his wife died of the influenza some months ago. It swept the town, taking young and old to the grave. The doctors were run ragged and the undertakers were on overtime in an effort to keep up with burial demands.' Shaking his head, he added, 'So you see my predicament.'

Tulley nodded again, saying, 'I'm afraid I have no Matron to accompany me though.'

'Oh don't worry about that, we'll sort something out. Firstly we need to get you ensconced in the Union.' Fred watched as the other man made a telephone call before he said, 'Right, Mr Dower the Chairman of the Board of Guardians will meet you at the gate of the workhouse and get you settled in.'

Shaking hands again, Tulley left the office a happy man. He was the Master of the workhouse once more, and this time without his wife to deal with. He couldn't believe his luck!

The tall thin man waiting by the gate of the Union introduced himself. 'Dower by name, dour by nature,' the man said with a sickly smile. Fred frowned at his strange sense of humour. 'Pleased to meet you, Mr Tulley.'

'Likewise,' Fred answered, giving the man a shifty gaze.

Mr Dower showed Tulley to his private quarters before taking him on a tour of the building. Strolling around the huge building, he was introduced to the staff, each showing deference to his status.

He noticed the gas lamps high up on the corridor walls which were whitewashed and clean. The oakum sheds were equipped with wooden benches and the workers supplied with thick gloves. The kitchen was spotlessly clean and large; the aroma of cooking food very appetizing. The laundry had large double doors at one end for washing trolleys to be pushed out into the garden where the clothes and bedlinen was pegged on clothes lines strung out in a criss cross fashion. Everything here was bigger and better than the poky little workhouse in Bilston.

Fred Tulley was a happy man to have been so fortunate, especially as the wages here were higher than he had previously earned. He was going to like it here.

As he familiarized himself with his new home, he thought this was one place Cara Flowers would not endeavour to shut down; it was far too big. With close on a thousand residents, Fred Tulley knew he had his work cut out. He needed to stamp his mark on the place and those within its walls immediately; they needed to be under no illusion he was their new boss. Thanking God for his luck, Tulley could hardly believe he had been made Master of the workhouse once more. Nothing was going to stop him this time.

*

As work on dismantling the Spike in Bilston proceeded, Cara had employed men from the bread line to assist, along with those from Millfields Road cottages. She met again with Bill Rowley. The architect had brought his plans for her to see.

'This is the basic idea, Cara, I hope it meets with your approval.' Spreading the drawings on the table in the kitchen, he began to explain them to her.

Cara's enthusiasm was contagious and he was effusive as he noted Charlie taking a keen interest.

There were to be many blocks of four houses back to back, a small communal garden between each block. With a kitchen, living room and two bedrooms, they would house four men; sharing a bedroom with another was preferable to sharing with fifty others. The standpipe network was to be extended, ensuring each block had access to fresh water, and a double lavatory building would be built at the back of each block. A trackway, the width of a cart, would run all around the perimeter of the land, which would later be cobbled. Each house would have a front and back door and a fireplace. The two bedrooms were to be reached by stairs leading off the living room.

Basic accommodation, but Cara knew the residents would be happy enough when they eventually moved in.

Cara met with her two foremen, Sam Yale and Wally Webb in the parlour of The Laburnums.

'Gentlemen,' she began, 'I am looking ahead to when our new houses are built…' Holding up a hand, she said quickly, 'I know they are only in the planning stage at present, but once completed the men will be standing idle again.'

Nods confirmed her words as the foremen looked at each other, hoping she had a solution to the problem. Their eyes returned to her as she continued.

'So I need ideas to help these men build a future for themselves and their families.'

Sam said, 'Most can turn their hands to anything, but I know there are blacksmiths, cabinet makers, and plumbers.'

Wally added, 'There are also tailors and shoe repairers.'

Sam intervened with, 'I think there's a couple of painters and carpenters too.'

Wally spoke again as he nodded, 'Their women are fine bakers and cooks – dressmakers an' all, I believe, and… they all know their numbers and letters.'

Cara and her foremen discussed at great length the setting up of small businesses that could be worked from home.

*

The new year of 1902 had come and gone and the winter was reluctant to release its firm grip. The snow had melted away leaving dirty puddles everywhere, but the freezing wind cut to the bones of the men working on the site of the old workhouse, despite their warm clothing.

Alone in the parlour, Cara's mind drifted to her grandmother. Henrietta Selby would never believe how much had been accomplished in such a short time. Cara smiled inwardly, albeit still feeling the pangs of her loss. She thought of her father, killed in a carting accident and of her mother who she knew nothing about. Maybe now would be a good time to attempt to discover more.

Staring into the heart of the fire, Cara wondered how she could find her mother. Who would know? Josiah Colley, the Registrar, had come up empty regarding further information, and Cara had no idea where to look next. Why had her grandmother not told her more about the woman who had brought her into the world? What had Henrietta been hiding all those years Cara was growing up? Why had she become so upset when Cara asked about her parents?

Feeling again the sting of the loss of her grandmother, Cara walked from the room, up the stairs and entered Henrietta's bedroom which had remained untouched since her death. Sitting on the end of the bed, Cara suddenly felt very lonely and tears welled in her eyes. Looking around her, she knew it was time to clear out her grandmother's things. The clothes could be bundled up and passed to anyone who could make use of them. Jewellery and trinkets would be sold. Cara didn't feel the need to keep anything but the letter left for her.

Opening a drawer in the cabinet by the side of the bed, Cara drew in a breath. Nestled inside sat a diary. It had Henrietta Selby's name in gold lettering on the front. Cara gasped in disbelief as she looked at it then chided herself for leaving it so long before sorting the room out. Just looking at the name brought the tears tumbling and she allowed herself a good cry.

Twenty-Nine

Cara picked up the diary and held it reverently, looking down at its leather cover. Maybe there were other diaries, maybe her grandmother had always kept a journal. Searching the drawers and wardrobe frantically, Cara found nothing, then lifting the lid of an ottoman, she saw them. Diaries piled one on another, years of experiences written down.

Carefully Cara lifted them out of their hiding place and laid them on the bed. Twenty leather bound journals waiting to be read. Staring down at them, Cara wondered if they would contain information regarding her mother. Would they provide the answers she was seeking? Did she really want to know? Yes, whatever was contained on those pages would provide, at the very least, an insight into her grandmother's thoughts. Gathering them up, she carried them to her own bedroom. Setting them in date order, she settled herself on the bed to read, the clearing of her grandmother's bedroom quite forgotten.

The first entry was dated twenty years previous and Cara looked over the beautiful copperplate writing.

Elizabeth has decided she wishes to marry…

Cara read on.

She has met a man by the name of John Flowers. I have my doubts about the man. He is a carter by trade and I had such high hopes for Elizabeth to marry well. She is besotted with the man, but for the life of me I can't see why. It would have pleased me immensely had she chosen a doctor or a lawyer, but love is fickle. How I wish her father was still with us, he would have advised her. Elizabeth always did listen more to her father than to me.

A knock to her bedroom door disturbed Cara's reading and she looked up when Molly walked in to tell her dinner was ready. She walked down to the kitchen with the maid.

Once seated, Cara told the others about her discovery. 'I never knew Grandma kept a diary,' she said, 'and I've only read the beginning so far.'

'Well, good or bad, at least you might learn something,' Gracie said.

Cara nodded and turned her attention to the children who were bickering light-heartedly. Once her brother and sister were settled in bed she would return to the diaries.

No matter what she discovered she knew she would be glad she'd read them. She was a little apprehensive, but maybe they would fill the gaps in her life she knew nothing about. There had obviously been a rift between her mother and grandmother; would the diaries explain how and why this occurred? She certainly hoped so. There was so much she wanted to know.

Cara read long into the night and the story of her mother

began to unfold. Elizabeth Selby had met and begun a relationship with John Flowers. This was no dalliance, they planned to marry. However, some months before the wedding, Elizabeth realized she was pregnant. Much to everyone's surprise, John stood by his obligations and the ceremony was brought forward. They had moved into an old cottage on the heath as John refused to move into The Laburnums with his 'interfering' mother-in-law. Elizabeth had refused any financial help from her mother, saying John would provide for his family himself… thank you very much! If Henrietta couldn't support her choice of husband, then Elizabeth didn't want the support of her mother's money. The couple would manage to scratch out a living for themselves.

As Cara read, her emotions swung every which way. She felt sorrow that her mother had found herself pregnant outside of marriage; the stigma attached to that must have been unbearable. She felt happy that her father had owned his responsibility and married her mother. Cara was proud that John wished to be independent and provide for his own, but hurt that her grandmother had been seen as interfering. She read on.

The day Elizabeth's pains had started she had staggered home to her mother and Cara was born with the help of Henrietta. John had arrived some time later very drunk. He took his wife and newborn child home immediately. Elizabeth could have her 'laying in' time at home he had said.

Henrietta Selby had been distraught at her daughter and granddaughter being moved so quickly after the birth. She despaired at them living in the hovel John called home.

As time passed, Elizabeth had struggled to manage on John's carter's wage, or what hadn't been spent on beer, and Cara was suffering. Constantly ill, the child was not thriving and Henrietta had helped as much as she could unbeknown to John and much to Elizabeth's not wanting help from her mother. When Cara turned two years old, she contracted influenza and Henrietta sent the doctor to the cottage to administer to the sick child. John Flowers had thrown the man out, saying the little girl had nothing more than a sniffling cold. Cara's health deteriorated and Henrietta arrived to take on the temper of John. She told him his young daughter would die if she remained in that filthy hovel. Henrietta wanted to take Cara and Elizabeth home to The Laburnums in order to care for them both. John refused to allow his wife to leave but said if Henrietta took Cara now, she could keep her. Henrietta didn't think twice, she bundled up the little girl and took her home, despite Elizabeth's wailing. She hoped Elizabeth would soon follow; Elizabeth didn't. Henrietta suspected John refused to allow Elizabeth to visit her, but she had no proof of this. His way of keeping Elizabeth close must have been to have her travel with him on his cart everywhere he went, for whenever Henrietta visited the cottage there was no sign of husband or wife.

Cara closed the diary with tears streaming down her face. Dousing the lamp, she lay in the darkness reflecting on what she'd read. So it seemed Cara had been the catalyst in the breakdown of the family. Her heart ached as she thought about the misery her mother and grandmother must have felt. John's need for independence, his jealousy of the relationship his wife shared with her mother had caused him to abandon his child. How could a man be so heartless? Why had Elizabeth allowed it? However her mother had not abandoned her willingly it seemed. The thought gave her some comfort as she drifted off to sleep, the tears still wet on her cheeks.

*

Fred Tulley answered the telephone in his new office and was informed by Mr Dower, the Chairman of the Board, that a Matron had been appointed and he was to expect her arrival within the hour. He knew a Matron had to be appointed sooner or later as laid down in the workhouse rulings. Replacing the earpiece on its cradle on the side of the telephone, he leaned back, wondering about the new employee. Would she be young and pretty? Would she be susceptible to his charms? Where would she sleep? Certainly not in his quarters with her not being his wife or sister. Closing his eyes, his mind wove pictures of a voluptuous young woman... with good teeth!

As Fred dreamed on about who would be joining him in his task in the Union Workhouse, he considered the circumstances. He knew jobs for matrons were few and far between and he wondered why the new one was alone. Had her husband or brother died? If he was honest with himself, he didn't really care. He had his position secured and that was all that mattered.

Fred's eyes shot open as the office door flew open, and Ada Tulley strode into the room.

'What the bloody hell...?' Tulley gasped as he stared at his wife.

'Hello to you an' all,' Ada grinned, showing her blackened teeth. 'I'm the new Matron. Well now, aint this just grand!'

'I ain't having this!' Fred snarled.

'You ain't got a choice!' Ada laughed.

'Christ! I don't believe this!' Tulley ran his hands through his hair.

'Well you'd better because I'm here. Now then, once I'm settled in you can show me around.' Ada puckered her lips and sent her husband air kisses.

Fred scowled and shuddered at the thought of having to share his life and bed with this woman again. As he stomped from the office, he thought, *I should have killed her when I had the chance!*

Ada Tulley followed behind her husband, cackling like an old witch.

*

The whole of Bilston was buzzing about the demolition of the old workhouse. The wealthier residents were reading about it in the newspapers over their breakfast tables; the poorer people were gossiping in the market and over garden fences. Whatever their social standing, the people of the town were delighted to be rid of the building once and for all; the horror of the place had never been far from people's thoughts.

The freezing winds had dropped and the inclement weather had warmed a little as Cara travelled by her usual cab to visit her tenants. It seemed the cabbie had deemed himself responsible for transporting her to and from her appointments and visits, and was always on hand at the end of her driveway.

With everything in order and going well with the people she visited, the cab travelled on to Green Lanes. A group of onlookers whispered to each other as Cara alighted the cab. Smiling broadly at the gawkers, she walked gingerly across the muddy ground to the men piling up bricks. Pleased to see her, they updated her on the progress, which she could see for herself was well underway. At the rate it was going, she mused, the building would be reduced to rubble in no time. Then they could clear the land in readiness for the blocks of houses to be built.

Work ceased for a short period while Cara was given tea in a tin cup and chatted with the workers.

Happy with the work being undertaken, Cara climbed into the cab once more and set off for home. To her surprise Martin was waiting for her as she arrived.

Cara told him about her grandmother's diaries over tea in the kitchen and shared the story of her mother and father.

Sitting around the fire later that evening, Daisy perched herself between Gracie and Molly on the sofa and Charlie occupied an easy chair. Cara sat in the other easy chair and Martin sat on the floor, leaning his back against her seat.

'Won't you read the diaries to us?' Daisy asked with the innocence of youth.

'Maybe one day, Daisy, but not now.'

'Awww,' Daisy moaned.

'Why don't you and Charlie play a game? Maybe if you ask nicely he'll let you play with his soldiers.' Cara was trying her best to distract Daisy's attention from the diaries.

Later when Cara retired to bed, she began to read once more.

Cara is doing so well in school, I'm so proud of her. She was awarded a book as first prize in a writing competition. Christmas is looming and she is excited about Santa calling at the house.

Cara turned the pages carefully as she continued to read.

As school began after the holiday, Cara came down with a cold. Poor little mite, she is feeling thoroughly miserable. Still I have received no word from Elizabeth; I can only hope she is well.

In another diary.

It is devastating to have no word of or from my only daughter. How I miss her. God willing she will contact me one day. I visited her cottage again this afternoon, but there was no sign of life. I will continue my search for Elizabeth, but as time passes I am beginning to lose all hope.

On yet another page;

Yet another fruitless search, it is my contention Elizabeth must have moved away from the area altogether.

Written on the last page of the diary she was reading Cara drew in a breath as her eyes scanned the words.

I heard on the market grapevine today that John Flowers has died in a carting accident. I'm unsure when this occurred or even if it is true. I visited the cottage again – to no avail. It was empty. I'm thinking it's time to give up my search and concentrate my energy on Cara. I have to give her my all now to ensure she grows into a fine young lady. It grieves me to abandon the search for Elizabeth, but I see no other choice. I'm so afraid she may have died in the accident too! My heart is broken!

Cara choked on those last words and felt the tears begin to rise.

As she closed the diary, the questions began to form in her mind. What had happened to Elizabeth after John's death? Had she died too? If not, where had she gone? Where was she now? If she managed to find her mother, would she welcome Cara contacting her? Or would she be shunned? Did her grandma know about Charlie and Daisy, Cara suspected not as there'd been no mention of them.

Exhausted by it all, she lay back on her pillows and whispered, 'I don't know where to look for you, Elizabeth Flowers, but I will do my best. I won't give up trying to find you.'

Thirty

Dr Cooper had been called out by the superintendent to visit the lunatic asylum. She had telephoned to request his attendance to administer to a woman who had been attacked by another, resulting in what she thought might be a head trauma.

The building was situated on the edge of the town, as the workhouse had been, and was surrounded by a high wall with a huge locked wrought-iron gate. Every window had bars on the outside to prevent anyone from escaping, and each 'cell' door was locked.

The men were segregated from the women and all were only allowed out of their rooms, at separate times, at meal times and the hours set aside for exercise and activities. The more severely affected were kept locked up night and day.

Dr Cooper was given admittance by an attendant.

'There's been an altercation in the dining room,' the attendant said over her shoulder as she led the doctor down the corridors, 'although no one is sure why. We think it may have occurred over one woman stealing the food of another.'

The wails of some of the patients bounced off the walls

as they heard the footsteps pass by their rooms. It sent a shiver down the doctor's spine. Stopping outside a door, the attendant unhooked a metal plate at eye level and as it dropped it revealed a slit. The doctor peered in and saw a rail-thin woman sitting on the bed, with her knees pulled up to her chest. Her hands were holding either side of her head as she rocked from side to side. Wide eyes stared at the doctor as the attendant unlocked the door, and he entered the room warily and introduced himself to the bedraggled woman.

The woman on the bed did not answer Dr Cooper as he talked quietly. 'I'm not here to hurt you, I just need to see to your injury.' Her wild eyes constantly flitted from him to the attendant standing in the doorway. She hissed as he moved towards her and the attendant stepped forward, a wooden baton in her hand. The woman shrank back, trying to push herself further into the corner.

Dr Cooper approached the terrified woman, who had become meek at the sight of the baton. Checking her head, the doctor announced, 'There are no obvious cuts or bleeding, but you will have quite a headache for a while.' As he turned to leave, the woman leapt on his back, the momentum taking them both to the floor. In an instant the attendant swung the baton, catching the woman sharply across her back. A scream sounded and the woman was lifted off the prostrate doctor and thrown back on the bed by the attendant.

'We will have none of that Josie Perkins!' Snapped the attendant.

Dr Cooper scrambled to his feet and shot from the room. He turned as the attendant marched out after him, slamming and locking the door behind her. The attendant merely pulled her mouth up at one side then led him once more down the corridor to give his report to the superintendent in charge.

The incident had shaken Dr Cooper badly and the superintendent poured him a cup of tea to calm his nerves as he sat down in her office.

'I must apologize, Joshua,' the superintendent said, 'I realize you are not used to dealing with patients such as ours very often.'

The doctor and superintendent had known each other for many years, and he had on a few occasions visited the asylum. However, he had never been attacked by one of the residents before. His hands still shook, rattling the cup on its saucer.

'Are they all like that?' he asked, his voice still a little shaky.

'No,' she answered. 'Most, but not all. When you've had your tea, I'll show you around and you can see for yourself.'

Dr Cooper nodded, not at all sure he was up to it, but agreed nevertheless.

As he was taken on a tour of the building, he noticed each door had a gap at eye level for attendants to see into the room to check on the patients. Some doors had a larger gap at the bottom for tin plates of food to be pushed through. Screams, wails and crying echoed as he walked down the corridors and peered into each room. Some patients were seen silently rocking to and fro on their beds, ignoring the eyes that watched them through the door slits. It was more like a prison than a caring institute, but after being attacked, the doctor could understand the necessity for such security.

The very last door stopped Dr Cooper in his tracks. The woman inside sat calmly on her bed reading a book. Her head swivelled and as her eyes met his she smiled.

'Hello,' the woman said. The doctor returned her greeting and watched her return to her reading.

Looking at the superintendent, the doctor furrowed his eyebrows. As they walked away, the superintendent said, 'Very sad, she doesn't belong in here. She's not insane, Joshua, she is still grieving the loss of her little girl.'

'It's the woman from the workhouse,' Dr Cooper said quietly.

'Yes, she's not dangerous, in fact she helps out in the kitchen. It seems she's quite an accomplished baker!'

'If she's not deemed dangerous or insane, why is she still in here?'

'There's nowhere else for her to go,' the superintendent said simply.

*

Liza Townsend still held her book but she was no longer reading the words. Other than the attendants, superintendent and cook, she had just spoken to the only other sane person in the building – the doctor. She had recognized him from the workhouse. He had been the kind one; the one who had washed and dressed her little girl. He had explained gently what had caused the child's death. He had laid her out ready for the final visit from her mother and had given Liza time alone with her dead daughter in order to say her goodbye in private.

Liza sniffed as she felt again the weight of her deceased child in her arms. Her broken heart would never mend she knew, and the sadness that constantly surrounded her threatened never to allow her to laugh ever again. Being kept in this hellhole of an institution might, in the end, prove to be her saving grace. It would give her time to help her come to terms with her loss, but she knew she would forever be in mourning.

Liza felt the warm tears running down her face but made no move to wipe them away for that would staunch them. Her intermittent bouts of crying were all part of the healing process. She needed to heal – but not forget. Her eyes moved back to the eye slit in the metal door and she nodded.

The doctor was a good man and if she ever got out of the asylum she would give him her thanks for the kindness he had shown to her.

Liza had learned to shut out the noises and screaming of those in the asylum. At night the patients could be heard yowling their woes into the darkness, which at first had frightened her witless. Would she become like them? Fear that she might had gripped her tightly as she had listened to the echoing screams. However, as time went on she no longer heard the shouting and swearing of the others who were incarcerated there.

The superintendent and attendants were good to her, allowing her to have books to further her reading skills. She worked in the kitchen during the day alongside the cook as she was not considered to be a danger to anyone.

Liza smiled, the only person on the earth she was a danger to was Ada Tulley; the woman who had sanctioned the use of bad meat in the workhouse, which had caused the death of her little girl. Liza prayed every night that she would be released from the dreadful place she found herself in, because when that day came… Ada Tulley would be the first to know.

As Liza recalled a picture of her young daughter to mind, more silent tears rolled down her cheeks. 'I'm so sorry,' she whispered, 'I'm sorry I couldn't save you, my little wench. I promise you this, though, I will avenge you. If it's the last thing I do, I will avenge you!'

*

The following day Joshua Cooper sat in his doctor's office and contemplated his visit to the asylum. It truly was an awful place, but unlike the workhouse, it was needed, for there was nowhere else for the mentally ill to go. They certainly were in no position to care for themselves, and their families very often couldn't control them.

His thoughts turned to Liza Townsend and her plight. The superintendent was correct in what she'd said: Liza didn't belong in there. The question was how to get her released? This question led to others; if she were to be released, where would she go? What would she do? How would she take care of herself? Could she find work and somewhere to live? She could end up being one more homeless person on the streets of Bilston, and now there was no workhouse to take her in. Weighing the options, Dr Cooper reached a decision. He would go to visit Cara Flowers to ask for her advice and help.

*

'As much as it pains me to say this, Dr Cooper, I am unable to help at the moment.' Cara eyed the man sat opposite her in the parlour. 'You see,' she went on, 'there will be accommodation for Liza Townsend eventually, but I have a responsibility to house those in lodgings with other workers first.' Dr Cooper nodded his understanding. Cara picked up, 'With the number of houses Bill Rowley has allowed for on the old workhouse site, there will be more than enough tenancies available... but they have to be built first and it's a slow process.'

'I understand that, Cara, I really do, but the thought of that poor woman stuck in the asylum when she should never have been put there in the first place makes my blood boil!' Joshua Cooper's temper flared.

'I understand. Look...' Cara said soothingly, 'I will ask if any of the tenants have room for another lodger, but I warn you, it's very unlikely. Besides, knowing where Liza Townsend has come from, namely the asylum, won't help our cause.'

The doctor knew Cara was right. Who would want a patient from the lunatic asylum living in their house, even if she wasn't deemed insane?

Cara spoke again. 'Are you able to visit Mrs Townsend again?' At his nod, she said, 'Then please explain to her we are doing all we can to get her released.' The doctor brightened at this and smiled. 'We *will* help her, Dr Cooper although it may take a little while.'

The doctor left in a far better mood than when he'd arrived.

Cara sighed. How was it that as soon as she solved one problem, another would arise? Would the time ever come when she had no more difficulties to deal with? She very much doubted it.

She thought about Liza Townsend and what Dr Cooper had told her. She couldn't imagine what it must be like to lose a child. Turning her thoughts to Charlie and Daisy, she instantly realized how it would feel if she lost either of them. The heartbreak would destroy her. Determination filled her as she tried desperately to think of ways to help Mrs Townsend be freed from the asylum.

Thirty-One

Cara had made the same request to each of her tenants on her visits and they had all given the same answer. They were very grateful for what she was doing for them, but no one wanted to take in 'Mad' Liza. Even after being told Mrs Townsend was not insane, they refused. Some of the women had taken care of her whilst in the workhouse, but they said they weren't sure the woman could be trusted and didn't want her around their children. Cara understood their concern and thanked them for their honesty.

'What you gonna do then?' Molly asked.

'I'm not sure,' Cara replied, 'but I have to find a way of helping Mrs Townsend.'

Gracie passed over a cup of tea, saying, 'You just be careful with this... you never know.'

'I will,' Cara said, 'I think my next step is to visit Mrs Townsend with Dr Cooper.'

'You must be mad wanting to go to that place!' Molly spluttered. Gracie gave a scowl at the maid's choice of words. Realizing her faux pas, Molly apologized.

Cara replied, 'I know you're worried, but it will be fine.

Dr Cooper is going to see Mrs Townsend tomorrow, so I will arrange to go with him. I will be quite safe.'

Over the telephone Joshua Cooper vehemently advised Cara to stay home rather than visit the asylum with him. He emphasized how horrified she would be at the sight and sounds of the place and that, much as she would want to, there was nothing she could do for those living within its walls and bars.

'But Joshua...' She began.

'No, Cara!' Dr Cooper replied. 'It will break your heart to see those poor patients. All that can be done for them is being done. This is medical, Cara, far outside your remit. Please understand I say this for your own good.'

Cara acquiesced albeit not happily.

On his second visit to the asylum in as many days, Dr Cooper carried with him a pile of books, and on entering Mrs Townsend's room with the superintendent he saw the woman's eyes light up. Handing the books over, he watched as Liza stroked each one lovingly.

'Shakespeare... wonderful. Oh and a Penny-dreadful,' Liza smiled. 'Thank you, I will enjoy reading these. It was most thoughtful of you. Please, won't you take a seat?'

Joshua parked himself on the end of the bed; the superintendent remained in the doorway.

'Mrs Townsend,' the doctor said quietly, 'the superintendent and I both agree you should not be in this place, and I want you to know I'm doing my utmost to get you released.'

Liza answered in the same quiet tone. 'Thank you again, Dr Cooper.' Seeing his surprise, she went on, 'I remember your kindness at the workhouse regarding my daughter and I extend my gratitude for that also.'

Joshua smiled and nodded. Poor she may be, but Liza Townsend appeared to be a well-educated woman. Her use of language and her interest in reading attested to the fact. This only emphasized the fact that Liza didn't belong here.

Liza continued, 'We all have to die, doctor, it eventually comes to us all. However my young daughter, Phoebe, was an innocent and didn't deserve to slip off her mortal coil in such a manner.'

This was the first time he had learned the child's name; the little one he had so carefully laid out ready for burial. He looked over at the superintendent and her nod said it all – *I told you she shouldn't be in here!*

'Mrs Townsend...' the doctor began.

'Liza, please call me Liza, if anyone has deserved the right, you have.'

'Liza,' he began again, 'I am at the moment seeking accommodation for you outside of this place and hopefully employment also. Then the superintendent has agreed that you can be released into my custody.'

Liza nodded her thanks to them both before she said, 'Be assured, doctor, I will not end up back in here or the Spike.'

'The workhouse has been demolished, Liza!' The doctor gave her a wry grin. 'A friend of mine managed to empty it of its residents and, after buying the building, had it pulled down. Houses are to be built on the site; the work is underway as we speak.'

'What of the staff?' Liza asked, maintaining her calm demeanour.

'All left, the porter and Relieving Officer are now in other employment. The cook quit shortly after... you left; and the Tulleys walked out! No one knows where they went.' The doctor watched for any change in Liza at his words. There was none.

'Well now,' Liza said quietly, 'it's a blessing the place is gone for good and I'm sure the whole town is grateful to your friend.'

Joshua gave her a wry grin. He thought, *this woman is not insane, she is wily, but she's certainly not mad*. She was fishing for more information rather than asking outright who his friend was.

'Liza, I need to know what sort of work you are willing to undertake on your release, it will help me search on your behalf.'

Liza looked at the pile of books in her lap, saying, 'I think I always wanted to be a school teacher. I had an accident before Phoebe and I entered the workhouse which caused me to suffer some memory loss. I'm afraid, I remember little of my life prior to that time.'

Joshua and the superintendent exchanged a quick look of surprise at the woman's answer. 'Right then, we'll have to see what we can do, but for now, I'm afraid, you are stuck in here. I am sorry, Liza, and be assured I'll be along again soon with more books. As soon as I find you a home... you'll be out.'

'Thank you, Dr Cooper, I am grateful for your efforts on my behalf.' Liza smiled, her blue eyes twinkling.

Liza looked over her new books as her two visitors left her cell. She didn't hear the key turn in the lock so intent was she at having new reading material. Then looking again at the closed door Liza's mind revisited the doctor's words. *'As soon as I find you a home... you'll be out.'* Liza's eyes travelled to the ceiling as she said a silent thank you to the Almighty. In her mind she added, *'I could have done with your help sooner, you know, but this will do nicely thank you.'* Picking up a book, Liza began to read.

Returning to his surgery, Dr Joshua Cooper thought about the woman he had just left. How had she ended up in the workhouse in the first place? Where was her husband? Had he abandoned his wife and child? Was he dead? Questions followed one after another as he prepared his medical bag for his visits to the sick. He knew eventually he would discover the answers, but for now there was one thought that pushed all others aside: Liza Townsend reminded him of someone, but who it was eluded him.

*

Bertha Jenkins sat in Cara's kitchen enjoying tea and the company of Gracie and Molly as well as Cara and the children.

'Bertha, I'm not sure whether you've heard, but I'm looking for a place for Liza Townsend to live. We can't get her released from the lunatic asylum until she has somewhere to go. I wondered if you knew of anywhere.' Cara broached the subject carefully and kept her fingers crossed that Bertha could provide a solution.

'Cara, I ain't sure if you know, but I live over in Pinfold Street at the back of the marketplace. It's only a two-up, two-down but it's clean and I live on my own... been widowed a long time. But I ain't sure I want a lodger if that's what you're thinking... I've lived alone for so many years I don't think it would work out.'

'Surely, if you have a spare room...' Cara persisted. 'The poor woman is locked up in that place, Bertha. She shouldn't be in there, but there's nowhere else for her to go!'

'Cara... look, I'm really grateful for all you've done for me and the rest of the folk in the town, but...'

'How would you feel if it were you in that place? Locked up night and day, hardly allowed out, with all the other patients who are suffering...' Cara was not about to give up that easily. 'However, if you are adamant I could always find room for Liza here with us.'

'Oh no you can't!' Bertha huffed. 'Not with those two kiddies living here, it ain't right.'

'The poor woman has to go somewhere Bertha...' Cara sighed.

'Oh bloody hell! All right, all right. Let her come and we'll see how we get on,' Bertha conceded.

'Oh Bertha! That's wonderful!' Cara gasped. 'No one else would entertain the idea, they all think she might be dangerous.'

'She ain't dangerous!' Bertha snapped. 'She's bloody grieving and lonely! Besides, it was me who was the cook and...'

Cara held up her hand, glancing at the children who were munching their way through a plate of jam tarts. 'What about when Mrs Townsend sees you?'

Bertha eyed Cara over the table and lowered her voice to almost a whisper. 'The one Liza holds responsible for young Phoebe's death is Ada Tulley, and I'm sure she will understand my job was on the line. So, the room is there if she's a mind to take it.'

'Thank you, Bertha, thank you.' Cara smiled, snatching another quick look at Daisy and Charlie. They appeared to be oblivious to the conversation, but Cara knew they were taking it all in. She knew what they had seen and witnessed during their time in the workhouse, and it was far worse than what they were hearing now.

'Least I can do in thanks for your helping me. 'Sides, Liza shouldn't be in there. You get her out and I'll see to the rest.' Bertha plumped up her ample chest, her chin lowering to meet it.

The women chatted for the rest of the afternoon about how well the old workhouse site was coming on now the better weather had arrived. It wouldn't be long before the first block of houses would be ready for its occupants.

It was pure coincidence that Joshua Cooper arrived just as Bertha left and he settled himself in the kitchen with the tea and cake Gracie provided.

'I took some books in for Liza Townsend,' Dr Cooper explained, 'she was delighted. She's a learned woman, Cara, she mentioned she always wanted to be a teacher.'

Surprise showed on Cara's face before she said excitedly, 'Bertha has offered to house Mrs Townsend!'

It was the doctor's turn to be surprised. 'Wonderful! Now we just have to find her some work,' he said.

'I think it most unlikely any of the schools will take her on though,' Cara added, shaking her head, 'I'm afraid the stigma of her being in the asylum will stick like glue.'

Dr Cooper nodded thoughtfully. 'I think you're right, but no matter, the first thing to do is get her released. Now she has a home to go to the superintendent will release her into my custody. Then we can worry about finding her some work. I will collect her tomorrow and escort her to Bertha's house.'

'Thank you, Dr Cooper, another job well done!' Cara's smile radiated at her pleasure of another soul saved and given freedom.

*

Liza closed her book when she heard footsteps in the corridor. She listened hard, wondering where they would lead, then sucked in a breath as she heard the keys jangle outside her cell. Nerves gripped her until she saw Dr Cooper enter.

'Dr Cooper, how lovely to see you again. More books?'

'Not this time, Liza, I've come to take you away from this place.' The doctor grinned.

Liza could not hide her surprise, and getting to her feet she smoothed her hands down her long skirt. 'Thank you, I'm ready,' she said.

The doctor saw that even after all she'd been through her dignity was still intact. He didn't miss her wiping away a silent tear which rolled down her cheek in pure relief at being released.

Holding her head high, Liza followed the doctor and attendant along the corridor to the superintendent's office. She watched as the release paperwork was completed and she was given a copy. The doctor and superintendent exchanged a glance as Liza carefully read the document. Nodding once, she folded it neatly and placed it in her skirt pocket.

'Thank you, ma'am,' she said, extending her hand across the desk.

The superintendent stood to shake Liza's hand, saying, 'You're welcome, Liza, good luck.'

Liza nodded and turned to the doctor, 'Shall we go?'

Smiling, Dr Cooper led Liza Townsend out of the lunatic asylum and into the waiting cab.

'Bertha Jenkins has offered you a room in her house, Liza.' Then added hesitantly, 'She… she was the cook… at the Spike.'

'I remember her, she's a kind lady.' Looking at the man who sat next to her in the cab, she went on. 'I know what you're thinking, Dr Cooper, and no, I don't hold Bertha responsible for my daughter's death. I will assure her of that. Once that is out of the way, I'm sure Bertha and I will reach an accord. It's good of her to open her home to me, Dr Cooper, as I'm sure no one else would,' Liza said in a matter-of-fact voice.

'Well, Liza, I can't lie to you. It was difficult trying to persuade people,' the doctor returned.

'I'm sure,' Liza raised her eyebrows. 'No one wants a madwoman living in their house...' she raised her hands as the doctor made to speak. 'Oh... I know I'm not mad, but these people don't. I can understand how they feel. Putting myself in their shoes, I expect I would feel the same.'

Dr Cooper merely nodded.

Arriving at their destination, Bertha welcomed Liza into her house. Dr Cooper left them to it. Returning from seeing the doctor out, Bertha drew in a deep breath and walked into the living room. She was almost knocked off her feet as Liza rushed up to her and threw her arms around her benefactor. As Bertha hugged back she heard Liza's sobs. The woman was so relieved to be free from the asylum and also to have been given a home.

Bertha's voice cracked as she said, 'Sit you down and have a nice cup of hot tea.'

'Thank you, Bertha, for this kind gesture, it is much appreciated,' Liza said on a dry sob. 'You have no idea what is was like in that place.' All at once the floodgates opened and Liza's shoulders heaved as she cried out her anguish in the quiet of the kitchen.

Bertha rushed to her and wrapped her arms around the sobbing woman. 'Let it go, Liza, let it go. It ain't no use hanging on to it, it don't do you no good.'

Liza cried until there were no more tears to come, but the dry sobs continued as she explained about her time in the asylum. 'I thought I'd be in there forever. I never dreamed a kind soul like yourself would save me. I will never be able to thank you enough.'

'Don't you think nothing of it, wench,' Bertha said. 'You just get yourself by the fire while I mash fresh tea and then we can have a good chinwag.'

The two women settled one each side of the fire and talked for hours, looking back on their past in the workhouse. After lots of tears from both women, Bertha's words to Cara were proved right: Liza did indeed hold Ada Tulley responsible for the death of Phoebe.

It was the following morning while Bertha made breakfast that Liza pored over the old newspapers her new friend kept for lighting the fire. The cook thought Liza was catching up on news she'd missed whilst incarcerated in the asylum, but Liza was looking for anything she could find on the whereabouts of Ada and Fred Tulley. She had a score to settle.

Thirty-Two

Joseph Purcell, one-time Chairman of the Board of Guardians, was fed up of reading about Cara Flowers in the newspaper. First there had been the news of her closing down the workhouse, which he knew about first hand anyway and didn't appreciate having his humiliation publicized for all to read about, then there had been the news at Christmas of her engagement to Martin Lander. Now details of the new development that was taking place on the former workhouse site, yet another reminder of how she had thwarted him. The young woman had become a sensation virtually overnight and he again wondered how this had happened? She had duped him out of his position of Chairman and it still stung. He was a Magistrate, a man of learning, highly regarded in Bilston, yet this *girl* had emptied the workhouse – bought the building – then demolished it! It really galled that he, Magistrate Purcell, had been unable to do anything to prevent it! Now he had lost his prestige and his position of Chairman of the Board of Guardians. He had also lost the monies and perks that accompanied that position.

Isaac Ballard at the Local Government Board had informed him of the Tulleys taking up their new appointments as Master and Matron of Wolverhampton Union Workhouse. Joseph's grin was feral as he thought about this, he doubted even Cara bloody Flowers would take on the might of that institution! His grin changed to a scowl when he thought of how he had been made to look like a fool in the eyes of the town. He fully intended to pay her back for that, someday... somehow.

In a foul temper, Joseph stomped from Brueton House and out onto the street where he hailed a cab. Snapping out instructions to the cabbie to take him to the workhouse site, he settled himself inside. The carriage rumbled up Mount Pleasant and along Wellington Street then branched off onto the dirt track leading to Green Lanes. Joseph stepped down expecting to be alone save for the workmen on site, but he was astonished to see a crowd of people standing gawking.

Nodding to the few who spoke to him, he made his way over to the man who looked to be in charge. He introduced himself and Bill Rowley did the same.

'So, Mr Rowley, I understand this land is being built on?' Joseph asked.

'Indeed, Miss Flowers instructed me to draw up the plans for the whole site,' the architect answered.

Bill and the Magistrate walked around the first block which was almost finished. Two-up, two-down; back to back, front and back doors, lavatory at the rear; all the blocks would be the same and would make strong and sturdy dwellings that would probably outlive them all.

'This is one hell of an undertaking!' he said at last.

'It most certainly is,' Rowley acknowledged, 'but then Cara Flowers is not one for refusing a challenge, as everyone knows.' Bill's tongue pushed the side of his cheek out as he stifled a grin. He silently chastised himself for making fun of the other man.

Purcell thanked Rowley and returned to the cab. His mood was blacker than ever now he'd witnessed the massive construction going on.

*

Many miles away, Ada Tulley had settled herself into her new position as Matron. She knew it stuck in Fred's craw that she had acquired this post and the thought tickled her. Allowing herself an evil grin, she thought she was now in a perfect position to exact her revenge on the man who had stabbed her. She had laid down her terms on arrival; she was going to have a day off work every week, and if he didn't like it – tough!

Ada grinned as she ambled along the streets to the market. She had the lie of the land, having arrived in Wolverhampton at Monmore Green railway station. Following the street that ran between the railway line and the canal, she had arrived at the workhouse. She had stood in awe at the size of it. Built in a six-pointed star with a porter's lodge at the entrance, it had many outbuildings surrounding the main building. There was a fountain near the lodge and even a small fish pond at the back! She was very glad she had seen the advertisement in the newspaper for the post of Matron.

Passing the tramway depot and the cattle market now, Ada walked into the outdoor market, with row after row of stalls selling everything from fruit and vegetables to old clothes and boots. It was not Ada's day off, but she had gone out anyway. She and the porter had already formed a good friendship, so Ada was able to come and go as she pleased; an occasional coin in the porter's hand securing their alliance.

Ada shoved her nose in the air and strolled between the rows of stalls. The market women saw her coming, and although they hated what she stood for, they nevertheless traded their goods for her money. They had to make a living after all.

The noise of stallholders calling out to prospective buyers assaulted Ada's ears as she passed by. The smell of fresh vegetables floated on the warm air and the aroma of freshly baked pies reached her nose. She heard the clatter of empty wooden crates being piled on carts ready to be hauled away for refilling. In the distance came the shrill sound of the steam train's whistle on its approach to the station.

Moving to Wolverhampton had been a smart move on her part, she thought, she was going to enjoy living here. The only thing marring it was she had to live with her swine of a husband, Fred Tulley, once more! Never mind, nothing lasts forever.

*

'You looking for anything in particular?' Bertha Jenkins asked as she watched her new lodger scan the newspapers.

'I'm searching for work, Bertha,' Liza said, without taking her eyes from the newsprint.

'Any work in them old papers will be gone by now, I would think,' Bertha nodded at the stack piled on the table.

'Probably, but it's worth looking, besides I'm learning what's gone on in the town while I was... indisposed,' Liza said, exchanging a smile with her benefactor.

Returning to her reading once more, Liza's eyes suddenly found what she was looking for. Avidly reading the tiny article near the back of the newspaper, she learned where the Tulleys had relocated themselves. For many, the news reporters were seen as vultures picking over other people's misfortunes, but for Liza Townsend they had come up trumps.

Moving the stack of newspapers as Bertha placed her meal on the table, Liza smiled her thanks. Thick broth steamed in front of her and she savoured the aroma as Bertha cut large chunks of soft fresh bread.

'Get it down yer, girl, it'll do you good,' Bertha grinned as Liza tucked in.

Over tea by the fire later, the women discussed the prospect of Liza finding work, both aware it was unlikely anyone would take her on. Retiring to her bed, Liza set her mind to finding a way to get *to* Wolverhampton and get *at* Ada Tulley.

*

'Where the bloody hell have you been?' Fred was waiting for his wife on the steps of the workhouse. Ada ignored him and strode through the open door going straight to their personal quarters. Her burly husband trotted along behind her. 'I asked you...'

'I heard you, I ain't deaf!' Ada interrupted.

'Well, where...?' Fred tried again.

Ada turned to face him her hands on her bony hips. 'Now you listen to me, Fred Tulley, and you listen good. I don't have to explain myself to you. You can ask all you like, but I ain't telling you nothing!'

'You don't talk to me like that! I am the Master here!' Fred yelled.

Ada grinned. 'You may be the Master here… but you ain't the master of me!'

Tulley glared at the woman he called wife. So that's how it was going to be. Bloody women! As he stormed out of the living room, he thought, *it's to be hoped they're never given the vote!*

Ada cackled as she poured herself a glass of beer. She had no intentions of working herself to death in this place. She would do the bare minimum and no more. Let the Master do his share of hard work for a change. Sitting on a chair, she propped her booted feet on the table, taking a swig of her beer. Wiping her mouth with the back of her hand, she cackled again. Yes, she was going to enjoy this job.

Fred stomped down the corridor, his mind on the change in Ada. She had always had a fiery temper but this quiet confidence unnerved him. He wasn't sure how to deal with it. Maybe if they got into another fight he could finish her off, then he'd be rid of her for good.

His rounds of the workhouse completed and everyone in their beds, Fred returned to his quarters where he found Ada asleep with her mouth open, her feet on the table. Her snores resonated around the living room. Watching her a moment, he wondered why he had married her? Was she ever young? Was she ever pretty? He couldn't remember. Stepping forward, he pushed her feet off the table. Ada was awake in an instant, fury plastering her face.

'Where's my damned supper?' Tulley boomed.

'Same place as mine!' Ada said sharply as she poured herself another drink.

'Ada…' Fred said.

'Don't you "Ada" me, Fred Tulley! I ain't cooking for you no more. I ain't doing your washing and don't you even think about sharing my bed. From now on you will be sleeping on there!' Ada pointed to the sofa.

Fred shook his head in despair as he walked into the kitchen to find something for his supper. Slicing bread and cheese, he determined the sooner he was free of Ada, the better.

*

Joseph Purcell boarded the train at Bilston station and sat in the first-class carriage. He was on his way to see someone who might have some ideas about defaming Cara Flowers. He could not prevent her from building her houses or buying up old properties, but maybe he could slur her name somehow.

He saw nothing even though he sat by the window in the train, his mind was on the blue-eyed blonde who had ridiculed him. He had heard the titters of women and overheard the men's conversations in the local taverns.

Fancy, who would have thought a woman could close down the workhouse?
The Board of Guardians had been outwitted and ousted!
Cara Flowers had given housing and work to the inmates.
She had reduced the bread line. She was a Saint!

Joseph fumed quietly as the train chugged along, even the steady sound of the wheels on the track unable to calm him. He snarled at a child staring at him then turned to look out of the window. He smiled inwardly as he wondered what dirty tricks could be played to besmirch the good name of Cara Flowers.

Thirty-Three

Certain that Bertha Jenkins had left the house to go to her work down at the local school, Liza dressed herself in her oldest clothes and set off for the heath. For her plan to work it was important to look destitute. She needed to get to Wolverhampton and she'd reasoned her best bet was to hope for a lift with a carter going that way. Sure enough, no sooner had she set foot on the scrubland than a kind carter said for her to climb aboard. Telling him she was visiting family in Wolverhampton, the two chatted amiably during the journey.

Arriving in the huge town, she left the carter at the market by the side of St. George's Church and with a cheery wave she walked down Cleveland Road. Not entirely sure she was going in the right direction, Liza trudged on nevertheless. She marvelled at the massive building which was the general hospital as she passed by.

Stopping at the blacksmith's yard, she asked directions to the workhouse. Pointing further down the street, the smithy shook his head sadly as he watched her move on.

Liza stood before the lodge gate and called out in a weak voice.

The porter came over to her. 'What you want?' he asked gruffly.

'I want to get in,' Liza said quietly.

'You got a ticket?' Liza shook her head. 'Then you can't get in. Bugger off!'

Leaning against the gate, Liza forced tears until they ran down her face.

'Please, sir, I ain't got any money,' she sobbed, 'I got nowhere to live and I ain't had anything to eat for days.' She saw him cast a glance over her. Knowing she was thin beneath her ragged clothes and her hair was still short from being in Bilston workhouse, she added, 'I've been in the Spike in Birmingham, but I came here looking for work.' Still her tears flowed.

The porter laughed saying, 'You'd have been better off staying there, wench!'

Liza could see he was a tough nut to crack and her tears were having no effect on him. But she knew if she was to take her revenge on Ada Tulley, she *had* to get herself a place here in the Union Workhouse. Time for a new strategy, she thought. Liza crumpled to the ground and lay with her eyes closed.

Seeing her fall, the porter muttered, 'Oh Christ!' Opening the gate quickly, he moved to the prone woman. Pushing his arms beneath hers, he helped her to stand, saying, 'Come on, you poor bugger.'

'What happened? Where am I?' Liza asked as if in a daze.

'You'm at the workhouse, wench,' the porter said as he struggled to relock the gate and hold Liza upright. 'Come on, let's get you inside.'

'Oh,' Liza swooned again against the man helping her to walk. 'You am a kind man.'

As they entered the large front door, Liza silently congratulated herself on her consummate acting skills. *Liza Townsend, you should have been on the stage,* she thought.

Liza had rubbed ash from the fire into her fair hair before she left Bertha's house in an effort to disguise herself, and keeping her eyes down during her interview with the Master she was relieved when Tulley didn't recognize her. She had secured a place in the Union Workhouse. As she was led to the bath house, Liza wondered why the Matron had not been in evidence. No matter, their paths would cross soon enough, she was sure.

Having been given the workhouse uniform after bathing and being checked for lice, Liza was taken down a long corridor to the kitchen. She was presented with a bowl of soup and chunk of bread. Then she was told to peel and chop a great mound of vegetables. Even from the little she had seen so far, it seemed this place was far better than the one in Bilston.

In her bed that night, along with many other women in the dormitory, Liza prayed Bertha Jenkins would forgive her for just taking off without a word. Liza knew she would be in this place for a while. She had to await the perfect opportunity to execute her plan. Ignoring the sobs of the other women, she settled down to sleep. She had done with feeling sorry for herself... now it was time for action.

*

Bertha did not immediately worry on her return from the school, seeing Liza Townsend was not at home. She may have gone to the market; she may even have gone to see the site of the old Spike and the new building taking place there.

However, by the next morning Bertha became concerned – Liza had not returned.

Going to her work, Bertha decided to wait and see if Liza was home when she got back before taking matters further. Fretting all day, wondering what she could do about the absconding Liza, she went home. After a quick search she realized the house was still empty. She immediately walked out again and trudged across to Dr Cooper's surgery. Liza was in his custody after all, and she felt he should know his charge had done a flit.

The doctor listened as Bertha explained that Liza had gone missing. She answered his questions patiently. No, Liza had not seemed upset about anything. Yes, she had eaten well. No, she had given no indication of her intentions. Bertha said, 'Liza did pore over the old newspapers looking for work though.'

Dr Cooper made a request. 'Would you check every word of the last newspaper Liza read please? It might provide a clue as to where she has gone.' Bertha assured him she would do that straight away.

Dr Cooper had an inkling about where Liza may be, but he needed to wait and see what, if anything, Bertha uncovered in the newspaper. If his thinking proved correct, the doctor knew they might never see Liza Townsend again.

*

Ada Tulley was heard before she was seen and Liza pulled her cotton bonnet further down to shield her face. The Matron strode into the kitchen screaming out her orders. Liza kept her back to Ada. She knew the woman was newly appointed to the position of Matron and couldn't possibly know all the inmates as yet. Be that as it may, Liza was taking no chances of being recognized; keeping her head down, she continued to chop the vegetables.

An argument broke out between Ada and the head cook and the inmates ceased their work to watch. Only Liza ignored it. She'd heard it all before. The cook insisted on peeling vegetables, Ada said it was wasteful. The screeching stopped as the cook slammed a lid down on a pot of broth. Suddenly the kitchen was silent, then pushing her nose forward, the cook spoke quietly.

'I know you are new here, Matron, but this is my kitchen! You can always do the cooking yourself if you think you can do better!'

Ada snorted and moved around to inspect the bins. Dipping her hand into the first bin, she pulled out what looked like a package. Unwrapping the paper revealed a chunk of meat. Ada hit the roof. 'Why is this being discarded? It is still good enough to use!'

Liza's shoulders tensed as she struggled to keep her temper as well as her anonymity. Ada Tulley was up to her old tricks again. Liza smiled at the cook's next words.

'All right Matron, I'll use it... hand it over and I'll cook it up for your supper!' The cook held out her hand. Titters sounded as Ada harrumphed, then the cook refolding her arms continued, 'I ain't using bad food and that's final! If you ain't happy with that – let's me and you take it to the Board of Guardians!'

Returning the meat to the bin, Ada strode from the kitchen in a foul temper.

Back in her living room Ada knew it was unlikely she would get the better of this cook. Bugger it! Pouring herself a beer, she flopped into a chair. She decided to stay put and get drunk. She had telephoned the brewery for a regular order of beer to be delivered every week which she kept in a cupboard in the living room. She didn't care whether Fred liked it or not, she did and that was all that mattered.

Liza continued her work in a far better mood as she listened to the cook chuntering about 'that bloody woman', 'I ain't never heard the like', 'fancy expecting me to use meat that's on the turn!'. Chatter amongst the women in the kitchen continued about the new Matron and her mean ways. The cook assured everyone there would be no using bad food in her kitchen. 'After my shift I intend to have a word in the Master's ear concerning his interfering wife.'

Turning to Liza, the cook asked, 'Wench, can you bake?' Liza nodded. 'Right, let's get baking, the inmates are going to have a cake pudding tonight!' More applause rang out as the baking began. Puddings of any sort were unheard of in the workhouse; bread and gruel being the staple diet. The cook shouted above the noise of the kitchen. 'The cakes are to be set out in the centre of the tables before the dinner is served so everyone knows they have a pudding! If Ada Tulley don't like it... refer her to me!' Cheers and applause sounded again and Liza Townsend thought, *Ada Tulley won't like it but then, with luck, she won't live long enough to complain!*

*

Joseph Purcell sat in the Master's office in the Wolverhampton Union Workhouse. Tulley was uncomfortable under the man's gaze as he knew he had contributed to the fall of the Spike in Bilston by just walking out.

'What can I do for you?' Tulley asked eventually.

'As you know, Tulley, the workhouse in Bilston has gone!

There are houses being built on the land by Cara Flowers.' Purcell paused dramatically as he flicked imaginary lint from his trousers.

Tulley nodded and muttered, 'Bloody woman!'

'Quite so.' Purcell said. 'Now, we both know we cannot prevent her from doing that, we cannot stop her buying up old premises and housing the inmates either, so we need to find another way to exact our revenge. We need to besmirch her name. We have to convince the people of the town that Cara is not quite the angel they take her for.'

'How?' Tulley asked.

Joseph Purcell leaned back in his chair and outlined his plan.

'What?!' Tulley shouted. 'You have to be joking!' The look on Purcell's face left him in no doubt this was not a joke. 'What about if Ada finds out... she might think... my life would be hell!'

'Your life is hell with her as it is!' Purcell smirked.

Pulling out his wallet, Joseph withdrew one hundred pounds, laying it in a fan on the desk in front of Tulley. The Master's wide eyes roamed greedily over the money. 'There's more where that came from.' Replacing his wallet in his pocket, he smiled.

Fred Tulley rubbed his chin and considered his options, his eyes switching from the money to the man and back again. He could take the money, and more besides, and hope his wife remained ignorant of his part in Purcell's plan or... he could refuse the offer and remain poor. In his mind there was no contest, Fred Tulley had no intentions of being a poor man forever. This plan would see him wealthy in no time and he could then remove himself from this pitiful place, leaving Ada behind once and for all. He would have enough money to retire from work altogether and live the rest of his life in luxury.

Leaning forward, Fred shook the hand of Joseph Purcell sealing the bargain before he swiftly pocketed the money.

Joseph congratulated himself on a good day's work.

On the train journey home Purcell ironed out the details of his plan. Stepping from the train carriage onto the platform at Bilston station, he walked to the street and hailed a cab to take him back to Brueton House.

Arriving home, he ran up the steps into his house. He would have his dinner then he had a telephone call to make.

'Lander old boy, how are you?' Purcell spoke into the handset of the telephone. 'I wonder if I might call on you tomorrow morning. No, no, it's a personal matter. Yes, nine o'clock would be perfect. Thanks, see you in the morning.' Hanging the earpiece on the side of the telephone stand, he replaced the whole on the table.

Snipping the end of his cigar with a cutter, he struck a match and held it to the end, rolling the cigar in his fingers until it caught light. Puffing on the cigar, he threw the match into a heavy glass ashtray. Lifting a cut-glass whisky glass, he sipped its contents.

Glass in one hand, cigar in the other, Purcell smiled into the dancing flames of the fire. He had started the ball rolling regarding his plan to destroy Cara Flowers' reputation. Quaffing his whisky, Purcell laughed out loud.

Thirty-Four

The following morning Martin Lander found himself shocked to the core as Joseph Purcell finished speaking. 'I can't believe it!' he said at last. 'Do you have proof of what you've told me?'

'Of course, Martin, I'm the Magistrate – I know the law!' Purcell had anticipated the question. 'I'm sorry I had to be the one to tell you, but I felt you should know. After all, this does affect you directly.'

Martin nodded before he raked his hands through his hair and sighed audibly. 'Thank you, Joseph, I appreciate how difficult this must have been for you.'

'What will you do now?' Purcell asked, feigning concern.

Shaking his head, Martin answered, 'I don't know... I'm not sure as yet.'

Apologizing again for being the bearer of such bad news, Purcell left Martin Lander's office. Riding back to the courthouse, he chuckled to himself. How long would it take for the town to learn what he had just divulged to Lander? Would the people believe it? How would they react? All

Joseph had to do now was sit back and wait. It would be interesting to see how events unfolded.

Martin Lander sat in his office, his mind endeavouring to make sense of what he'd been told. Surely it was untrue? How had he not known? He'd heard no gossip. There was only one way to find out – he would ask Cara – now!

Dashing out of his office, he hailed a cab and told the cabbie to hurry.

The journey to The Laburnums seemed interminably slow but eventually the cab pulled into the driveway. Pushing coins into the cabbie's hand, Martin launched himself up the steps and banged on the front door. Shoving past Molly in the doorway, Martin yelled, 'Cara!'

'She's in the parlour with…' Molly's sentence faltered as Martin ran for the room she indicated.

'Martin! How lovely…' Cara's words were cut off.

'Is it true?' Martin demanded.

'Is what true?' Cara asked, wrinkling her brow.

'*Is it true?*' Martin yelled. 'Have you been having an affair?'

'What?!' Cara was astounded. 'No! Most definitely not!'

'I have been told you have had a relationship with another man!' Martin was beside himself.

'I have not, Martin! How could you believe it of me? Besides, when would I have the time?' Cara looked from him to Gracie and Molly.

'I… I…' Martin stuttered.

'Who told you this?' Now it was Cara's turn to demand.

'Joseph Purcell has just been to see me and…' Martin attempted, his glance moving from one shocked face to another.

'And…?' Cara urged.

'He said you have been seeing another man behind my back.' Martin was already beginning to feel like a fool.

'Seeing who? Who, Martin? Who am I supposed to have been seeing?' Cara was furious.

'I don't know,' Martin said quietly. He hung his head in shame, suddenly realizing the stupidity of the whole thing.

'I see!' Cara's voice rose an octave. 'For God's sake, Martin!'

Dropping into a chair, Martin Lander's emotions spilled over and he looked close to tears. He pushed his hands through his hair and sighed loudly. Then he gave a sob.

Cara rushed to him, wrapping him in her arms. Gracie raised her eyebrows towards Molly and they made a swift exit to the kitchen. Gracie put the kettle to boil; Molly rushed to the pantry to fetch the cake. This would take some discussing and tea would smooth the way.

Eventually Martin gained control of his emotions.

'I ask you again, Martin, how could you believe it of me?' She was shaking with rage as he shook his head. 'Do you really think so little of me to believe I would do such a thing?' Not giving him time to answer, she raged on, 'Honestly, Martin! You surprise me, you really do! This certainly has cast a shadow over our relationship, you do realize that, don't you?'

'Cara... I...' Martin began.

'Don't, Martin! Don't you dare apologize! You should have challenged him. You should have defended me; fought for my honour! I am to be your wife and if that wedding is to go ahead you will have to grow a backbone!'

'I know, I'm...' Martin's words halted for fear of Cara yelling at him again.

Cara resumed, 'Why would he say such a thing?'

Martin shook his head. 'I have no idea,' he said wearily.

They both knew this was going to take a lot of thrashing out.

*

The gossip regarding Cara Flowers having had an affair with another man needed to be passed around the town and Purcell debated where it should begin. Sitting with tea in his living room, he eyed his cook who was informing him dinner was ready.

'Have you heard the news about Cara Flowers?' he asked.

The cook shook her head. 'Well, it would seem she has been having an affair with a man behind Lander's back!'

The cook was shocked and her hand flew to her mouth. 'I don't believe it!' She muttered.

'I thought the same at first,' Joseph went on, 'but I was reliably informed that it's true.'

As the cook left the room, Joseph knew word would be passed the following day in the market. Gossip would be rife in no time and he knew that tittle-tattle such as this had ruined lives in the past.

Purcell would wait and watch. The people of the town would draw their own conclusions and once they did – Cara Flowers would be finished. Her reputation would be in tatters. He would enjoy watching the young woman's downfall from her high and mighty status in the town. He would crow when she was shunned by everyone. All he had to do now was be patient. Sipping his tea he smiled his satisfaction. All was going to plan.

*

The discussion in the parlour raged on. Why had Purcell tried to blacken her character? Whatever could he gain from it?

'The workhouse is dead and gone now!' Cara snapped.

'And so is Purcell's job of Chairman of the Board of Guardians,' Martin added, suddenly aware of the reason for the malicious intent.

A discussion in the kitchen was also going on about what had been overheard.

'Bastard!' Molly muttered under her breath as a knock came to the back door and Sam Yale, her sweetheart, walked in. Molly flushed at being overheard cursing by Sam.

It was then that Cara and Martin joined the little group in the kitchen.

Given tea, Sam was drawn into the conversation. 'Nobody will believe it,' he said.

Cara thanked her foreman for his support, 'Gossip is a very strong weapon. It can ruin relationships and destroy lives. I will have to find a way to fight it!' Cara was becoming upset and wrung her hands in her lap.

'Well,' Sam said, 'why don't you pre-empt it? We could let folk know before they hear this gossip that it's not true.' Seeing Cara's puzzled face, he went on, 'Molly and I could go to visit all your tenants and tell them, they would then tell others, and... before you know it, it will be all over the town.'

'Also,' Martin cut in now fully restored to solicitor mode, 'this gossip is defamation of character. It's up to whoever started the rumour to prove its authenticity, it's not up to Cara to disprove it!'

'Why didn't you say that to Purcell at the time then?' Cara asked pointedly.

'I was upset, Cara.' Martin answered.

'*You* were upset! What about me? Did you stop to think how I might feel?' Cara's anger rose once more.

In an effort to diffuse the argument she felt was surely to come, Molly grabbed her coat and then, tugging on Sam's arm, she said, 'Right, let's get to it! We'll decide where to start when we get out there.' She tilted her head towards the back door.

Cara watched them go. Although quietly confident their plan would work, she sent up a silent prayer anyway – it wouldn't hurt to have God on her side.

*

After her shift in the kitchen, and staying true to her word, the cook in the Union Workhouse strode down the corridor and hammered on the Master's office door. Hearing him yell for her to enter, she walked in and banged the door shut behind her.

Fred sighed inwardly. Judging by the look on the cook's face, he was about to get an ear-bashing.

'Mr Tulley!' Hands crossed and resting on her stomach, the cook addressed the man slouching in his chair. 'I would be grateful if you would tell the Matron to kindly keep her nose out of *my* kitchen!'

Sighing through his nose, Tulley asked, 'What's she done now?'

'She waltzes into my kitchen, Mr Tulley, and proceeds to try and tell me how to prepare the food! I have been working here for many years and I will *not* be told how to do my job by one who is not qualified to do so! It wouldn't be so bad but she's only been here two minutes!'

Tulley held up his hands in an effort to quieten the cook's temper. 'I understand, I really do!' he said. 'Please be assured I *will* be having words.'

'Good! I'm glad to hear it. That woman is an interfering menace!' The cook nodded sharply.

You have no idea! Fred thought but said instead, 'You are doing an excellent job and I'm grateful for your hard work. I will instruct Mrs Tulley to kindly keep her nose out of *your* kitchen.'

The cook nodded again before she turned and left the office.

Leaning back in his chair, Fred closed his eyes and rubbed his temples. 'Bloody hell Ada!' he muttered. 'Don't you even think to bugger things up for me in here!'

Fred Tulley had no notion of the upset taking place in Bilston as he closed up the workhouse later that night. It was nine o'clock and the whole building was in darkness, the only light coming from the moon. He found Ada sprawled on the floor of the living room, drunk out of her mind. Stepping over her, he retired to bed, leaving her where she lay to sleep off the beer. He knew this couldn't go on and thought again about the money he had hidden away. Purcell had promised more and Ada was ignorant of the deal the two men had struck regarding Fred being Purcell's witness to seeing Cara Flowers stepping out with another man.

Fred had hidden the money he'd received from Purcell. His worry now was Ada finding out about the deal, the payment made and wanting her share of it.

Ada had attacked him once before and who was to say she wouldn't do it again? Fred fell asleep determined to keep a close eye on his wife.

Thirty-Five

The coronation day of King Edward VII had arrived and preparations were underway in streets all over the country. Bunting was strung from house to house and shop to shop, crisscrossing the cobbled thoroughfares. The tiny pieces of rag flapped in the gentle breeze as the sun beamed down. Laughter and jocularity was in evidence almost everywhere. Tables, stools and chairs were dragged out into the streets and loaded with edible contributions from the residents. Those lucky enough to own a piano saw it hauled outside for the festivities and children waved small flags glued to sticks. The pomp of the coronation ceremony would not be viewed by the majority of the country, but the occasion was one to be celebrated nevertheless. The revelling began early in the morning and would not see people in their beds until very late that night.

There would be no coronation celebrations in Wolverhampton Union Workhouse however, life and work was to go on as usual. Ada woke with a headache from hell and a temper to match. She ached from having slept on the floor and the thought of breakfast turned her stomach. Hair of the dog was what she needed and she was pouring herself a beer as Fred stepped into the living room. Her husband shook his head in disgust as he walked past her, out of the door and onto the landing. Going down the stairs he entered the workhouse proper.

Downing the ale, Ada decided she would not bother working but go into town instead. She needed fresh air... as fresh as could be found in the industrial town of Wolverhampton.

Changing her creased clothes, she donned a dark brown skirt which fell to her leather ankle boots. A high-neck cream blouse with sleeves to the wrist complemented the full skirt, and with a cheap straw hat sporting a feather, she was ready.

At the gate she dropped a coin into the porter's hand and walked away from the Spike.

Ada made her way to the market and strolled between the stalls. With nothing much to interest her, she strode away again.

As she walked back towards the workhouse, she heard her name being called. Turning, she saw a carter wave to her. Stopping his horse, he jumped from the cart.

'So this is where you went,' he said.

'Ar,' Ada replied, 'we'm up at the Union Workhouse now. So what's new in Bilston then?'

'Well, gossip has it that your Fred saw young Cara Flowers out with another man!' the carter said.

Wondering why her husband hadn't shared this information with her, she asked, 'Ain't she engaged to that Lander fella?'

The carter nodded. 'Word is, Fred saw her and another bloke out and about in Wolverhampton and he told Mr Purcell, the Magistrate, who then told Lander!' Seeing her surprised look, he went on, 'Right, I'd best be on my way, nice to see you, Ada.' The carter climbed into the driving seat and waved again as Ada walked away.

Ada thought hard about what the carter had told her as she made her way back to the workhouse. Fred never gave anything away, not even gossip. So, if he'd told the Magistrate then there must have been something in it for him. It was her guess he'd been paid for that snippet of gossip he'd passed on.

Ada's temper flared. Not only had he not told her the gossip, but he hadn't told her of the money she suspected he had hidden away! Striding out, her anger building, she determined to have this out with Fred and ensure she got her hands on half that money.

Once through the front door, Ada slammed it behind her. Walking through the corridor, she drew in a deep breath and yelled, 'Fred! Fred Tulley, where are you?' Hearing no reply, she muttered, 'Bloody hell, Fred, that's typical, never there when you want him!'

Ada Tulley could not keep her counsel regarding the rumour about her husband's gossip about Cara Flowers. Marching down the corridor, she strode into the bone crushing area.

'Tulley!' she yelled. Fred rolled his eyes and sighed heavily. 'I want a word with you!'

Strolling towards his wife, he thought, *Now what?*

Ada's voice carried across the yard, halting the work the men were undertaking. 'What's this I hear about you passing gossip about that strumpet in Bilston?'

Fred paled visibly and heard the mutterings of the men behind him. How had she found out? He knew the gossip would travel, but he had not thought it would be so swift.

'Keep your voice down woman!' he rasped.

'I will not keep my voice down!' Ada snapped back. 'Did you think I wouldn't find out about you taking a back-hander, you swine? Well let me tell you, I want half of that money, and don't you even think to deny you have it!'

The workers tittered and sat down to enjoy the show.

Deny everything, Fred's mind was telling him as Ada railed on.

'I bloody knew you was up to something. Well, now I know!'

Fred raised his hands in a manner of surrender, but Ada misread the action and screamed out, 'Don't you dare think to strike me again, Fred Tulley! You did that once before and don't you dare think to try it again!'

The men sitting on the ground looked at each other and raised their eyebrows.

Fred finally retaliated with, 'We will discuss this matter later, Ada, now go about your business… NOW!' As he turned away from her, the men jumped up and returned to their work.

The Matron spun on her heel and fled to her living room and the solace of her ale.

Later in the afternoon with yet another beer-befuddled brain, Ada made her rounds of the laundry and exercise yards before entering the kitchen. Throwing the cook a malicious glare, she inspected the work being undertaken. The cook crossed her arms over her white pinafore which covered her long dark dress, and her cap wobbled in time with her tapping foot. Ada was in no mood for confrontation with the woman and nodding once, she left the room.

Liza Townsend had watched this silent stand-off between the women from the corner of her eye and a minute later she too quietly left the confines of the busy kitchen. The time had come and she knew where the Matron would be headed. Liza slipped off her boots and tying them together by their laces, she hung them around her neck. Walking along the corridor in her stockinged feet, Liza followed where the Matron led. Keeping out of sight and hardly daring to breathe, Liza tiptoed up the stairs to the private quarters of the Master and Matron. Pinning her ear to the door, she heard no voices; Ada was alone. Looking around her, Liza's thoughts came together and if all went according to plan, Ada Tulley would breathe her last very shortly.

*

The family at The Laburnums had been invited to share in the festivities at Cara's Cottages. By the time they arrived, the celebrations were in full swing. Gracie and Molly were loaded down with bread and pastries; Charlie and Daisy had bags of sweets for the other children and Martin arrived in a cab with a barrel of beer; Cara provided homemade lemonade.

Given a chair placed in the shade, Cara watched the children running around enjoying each other's company while Gracie and Molly were gossiping with the wives. Cara's thoughts were interrupted by Wally Webb, her foreman for the area.

'Nobody believes the rumour, you know,' he said as he sat on the ground next to her chair.

'I hope not, Wally,' Cara answered quietly. 'I am worried though. No one has actually said anything, but I fear it may only be a matter of time.'

'Look, everyone knows what you've done for this town and they know you're a good woman. All that hard work you've put in with the poor folk. All that money you've spent! You're all set to marry a solicitor for God's sake! You would never jeopardize that for a fling with another man!' Seeing her about to speak, he rushed on, 'You wouldn't and everyone knows that. You did Purcell out of a job as Chairman; you made him look a fool in front of the whole town and now he's out to blacken your name in retaliation.'

'But I never meant to!' Cara's distress was evident.

'We all know that, wench,' Wally said, 'you caused one man some embarrassment, but look how many lives you saved! Look how many refused the ticket into the workhouse because of you and your good work! People all over the town see you as their guardian angel, Cara; you are their saviour!'

Cara blushed at Wally's words. 'Thank you Wally.'

Taking her hand, he kissed the back before scrambling to his feet to rejoin the party.

'He's right,' Martin said, moving towards her. He had stood a little way off but had heard every word. 'Now Mrs Lander-to-be, come and join in the festivities!'

Cara laughed as he lifted her from the chair and set her on her feet.

Leaning down, he kissed her gently and Cara flushed to the roots of her hair at the applause from the people watching them. He was glad things were back to normal between them.

*

Liza could hear Ada Tulley muttering to herself as she listened at the door. She heard the woman's 'Ahhh...' before the smacking of lips. Ada was having a drink, and it was Liza's guess it wasn't tea.

Reaching into her apron pocket, Liza's hand closed on

a cold object that nestled there. She had swiped the paring knife from the kitchen before she had slipped unnoticed from the room. One of many it would not be missed.

Liza cast another quick glance around her… she was alone. She knocked on the door. Hearing footsteps approaching the door, Liza pulled the knife from her pocket and held it behind her back.

The door opened and Liza lowered her head.

'What? What you want?' Ada said, none too happy at having her drinking time disturbed. She didn't notice the boots hanging around Liza's neck.

'Accident in the laundry, Mrs,' Liza mumbled.

'Oh Christ!' Ada sighed. 'What's happened now?' Liza shook her head, keeping her chin on her chest. 'Right! Let's go and sort it out!' Ada snapped as she walked forward, closing the door behind her.

Liza fell in behind her as Ada strode toward the stairs. Just as Ada made to descend, Liza stepped to the side and swung the knife round, burying it hilt-deep in the woman's neck.

'That's for Phoebe Townsend!' Liza rasped in Ada's ear. Ada's hands moved to remove the knife, but Liza held on to it. Shocked eyes stared into Liza's and recognition dawned. Ada's mouth opened to try to speak but she could only manage to emit a gurgling as Liza twisted the knife before pulling it free, making sure to step back quickly as she did so. 'Say hello to the devil for me, Ada… I told you God sees all!' Liza said quietly before pushing the woman down the stairs.

As Ada fell, Liza heard the grunts coming from the woman who bounced off the steps and then lay sprawled at the bottom, unmoving.

Rushing into Ada's living room, Liza threw the blood-covered knife on the table and returned to the top of the stairs.

Descending the stairs, Liza could see the woman was dead; the open eyes unseeing. Stepping over the prone woman, she dashed along the corridor to the kitchen. Putting her boots on once more, Liza slipped quietly through the door and went straight to the sink. Pouring water into a bowl, she washed the blood from her hands and checked her clothes for tell-tale signs. Seeing spatters of blood on her apron, Liza grabbed the nearest knife and stabbed her hand. Yelling out, she waved her hand about. The cook rushed over with a cloth, pressing it to the wound. No one realized the blood on Liza's apron and boots was not her own.

*

In Bilston, the coronation celebrations came to an end in the early hours of the morning and everyone drifted back to their respective homes to sleep off the ale and tiredness. The street would be tidied later in the day.

The newspapers the following day were full of the pomp and circumstance of the ceremony at Westminster Abbey. The country now formally had a new King. The gossip around Cara's supposed affair was virtually forgotten, having moved quickly on to whether this new king, Edward VII, would rule as long as Victoria had before him, and if life for his subjects would improve in any way.

Sitting in his study, Joseph Purcell was furious with himself. He realized in his haste that he had chosen entirely the wrong time to start the rumour about Cara Flowers. He was an idiot; he should have known the timing would coincide with the new king's coronation day. The money he'd paid to Fred Tulley for his part in the plan had been wasted, but worse was the fact no one had believed the gossip anyway!

Purcell sipped his tea, believing Cara led a charmed life. No matter what, Miss Flowers came out on top. With the amount of luck she had she must have been born with a horseshoe on her belly! He reflected on her achievements of the past couple of years. She had emptied and closed the Spike, moving the people into work and housing. She had opened a cake shop, which was doing a roaring trade. She was engaged to a brilliant young lawyer and she had reduced the bread line by half. Not bad going for a woman who was only just in her twentieth year.

Donning his knee-length black coat, Joseph grabbed his hat and cane and set out for the courthouse. He had work to do and anyone brought before him today would suffer his wrath no matter what the crime committed.

*

Cara strolled around the gardens of her home in the sunshine before sitting beneath one of the large trees. She had promised Martin she would begin planning their wedding, but so far she just hadn't found the time. There was more work to be done in the town and she had a missing mother to find.

Her brother, Charlie, was now fourteen years old and was working alongside the men, erecting the houses on the site of the old 'Spike'. No sooner a house was finished than it was occupied by the former inmates lodging with her other tenants. As many as possible needed to be habitable before the winter months set in. The allotments were providing fresh fruit and vegetables and being sold on and Cara was now receiving rent from them too. Cara's Cakes was doing a brisk trade and profits soared.

Her sister, Daisy, at twelve was fast becoming an accomplished baker under the tutelage of Gracie, and Molly and Sam Yale were making plans for their own wedding.

Everything in her garden was rosy, but Cara could not shake the unsettled feeling that wrapped around her most of the time. This past year had been a flurry of constant activity and worry, but her achievements had seen success. Now Cara Flowers felt... redundant.

Thirty-Six

The scream that reverberated around the workhouse had the women come running to see what the commotion was all about. Fred Tulley wasn't far behind them.

'What's all the bloody noise about?' Fred yelled as he approached the group of women gathered at the bottom of the stairs. Pushing his way through, he saw his wife lying on the floor.

'Ada?' His voice was hoarse with shock as realization dawned. Ada Tulley was lying dead in a pool of blood. 'Christ Almighty! Ada…?' Fred looked around at the women, then he shouted, 'You… get to my office and telephone for the police!' The frail woman he pointed to took to her heels. 'Right you lot, get back to work, I'll deal with this.'

The muttering women slowly moved away from the grisly scene, Liza Townsend among them.

Fred stared down at his deceased wife hardly able to believe his eyes.

This was how the police found him half an hour later; still standing by his wife's body with a blank look on his face.

The police sergeant was told by the Inspector to escort

Mr Tulley to his office where they should stay. The two constables were instructed to round up the women in the dining hall and take statements from each. The Inspector himself would call in the coroner and get the body removed.

It was evident the woman had been murdered by the amount of blood pooled around her upper body. On closer inspection the knife wound to the neck could be seen clearly, confirming his suspicions. The position the body lay in supported the Inspector's conclusion she had fallen or had been pushed down the stone stairs. His eyes moved up the steps to the small landing. Pound to a penny there would be more blood splatter in that area.

Picking his way carefully to the landing, he saw the blood spots on the floor and wall. Looking around, he saw nothing more. No sign of the murder weapon here.

The door to Tulley's quarters stood ajar and the Inspector pushed it open with his elbow. Stepping inside, his eyes immediately found what he was looking for. The knife used to kill Ada Tulley was lying on the table, dried blood coating the blade. Leaving the knife untouched, he strode to the office and informed Tulley of his findings.

'This is looking bad for you, Mr Tulley,' he said.

Fred gasped, 'I didn't do it! It wasn't me!'

Shaking his head, the Inspector left the room, nodding to the Sergeant as he went.

The dining hall was in an uproar, the two constables struggling to keep order and take statements. The women were yelling that a murderer was on the loose in the workhouse; they could be the next victims; they could be murdered in their beds. The yelling and chaos stopped in a heartbeat as a shrill whistle sounded across the room. All eyes went to the Inspector who stood in the doorway, his fingers still in his mouth.

'Right,' he said as he strode forward towards the constables, 'let's have some order here! Ladies...' he addressed the distressed women, 'please answer the constables' questions quickly and quietly. Once you've given your statement you can then go about your business.' A nod to the constables and the Inspector walked smartly from the room.

Making his way to the bone crushing yard, the Inspector had the men sit on the floor before explaining his reason for being there. Taking out his notebook and pencil, he made detailed notes of what he was told about the altercation between the Tulleys. He learned quickly that Fred had struck and stabbed Ada on a previous occasion. One man who had also been in the workhouse in Bilston told of hearing Fred shouting, *'Ada, tonight you die!'*

Meanwhile, Fred Tulley sat at his desk, with the sergeant standing guard by the door.

Fred said, 'I need to telephone my friend, he's a magistrate.'

The sergeant nodded once.

Tulley's shaking hands held the telephone, 'Joseph... you have to help me! Ada has been murdered and the police think I did it!' He explained the situation then listened to Purcell's answer. 'But Joseph, we had an agreement. The police are going to put me in jail for something I ain't done!'

The telephone line went dead and Tulley looked at the earpiece held in his hand with total disbelief. Slamming it on the side of the stand, he looked at the sergeant standing in front of the door, hands clasped behind his back. The sergeant smirked and then resumed looking out of the window over Tulley's head.

'Bastard!' Fred muttered, then sweeping his arm across the desk sent everything crashing to the floor.

The sergeant smirked again.

After many hours of questioning and taking of statements the Inspector was adamant he had found the perpetrator of the crime. Fred Tulley was the only person not to have an alibi. Not one inmate could – or would – attest to the man's whereabouts at the time the crime was committed. As far as the Inspector was concerned the case was cut and dried: Fred Tulley was guilty of murdering his wife.

Ada's body was taken away by the coroner's wagon and women set themselves to cleaning up the blood at the top and bottom of the stairs.

Liza Townsend had watched all the activity from the sidelines. She had given her statement to the constable and the kitchen workers and cook had sworn Liza had been in the kitchen the whole time. They had explained about Liza's accident and how the cook had tended to her injured hand. The bandages proving their words. She had been cleared of all suspicion.

Knocking on the office door, Liza faced the sergeant who opened it.

'I want to sign myself out,' she said with a worried expression plastered across her face, 'I don't feel safe in here anymore!'

The sergeant looked at Tulley who nodded. Liza was signed out under the assumed name she entered with and was told to leave immediately. Liza was relieved Fred Tulley had not recognized her. She was aware he had other things on his mind.

Just as Liza stepped through the front door, she saw the black Mariah, the police carriage, arrive at the workhouse drawn by two black horses. She watched as the only door – at the back with bars on the window – was opened and Fred Tulley was bundled inside still yelling his innocence. The carriage set off to rattle across the town to the police station situated in Lower Walsall Street. Tulley would be held in the cells until such time as he was to appear in court, and then he would be going to jail... for a very long time.

Liza smiled and followed the Mariah out of the workhouse gate.

Liza strode towards the basin at Waterloo Wharf. With luck she could hitch a ride on a boat headed for Bilston. The canal towing path was dotted with basins and wharfs, so it was likely someone would be going her way. Strolling along the towpath in the sunshine, Liza stopped often to ask if anyone was going to Bilston.

The narrowboats moored up were painted in bright colours, their nameplates sitting proudly on the sides. Buckets and kettles, also painted with bright flowers, sat on top for sale to any who would buy. The barges were being loaded and unloaded, their cargo piled onto carts bound for factories, shops and the market. The noise of the canal people, 'cut-rats' as they were locally known, filled Liza's ears and she revelled in it. It was the sound of freedom. The smell of the canal water reached her nose and she breathed it in, along with the aroma of fish coming from one of the barges close by.

She heard the chatter and banter of the folk working the canal and a deep serenity settled over her. She had avenged her daughter and whatever happened now, Liza felt she could die in peace.

Seeing an older woman struggling with a large crate on the towpath, Liza rushed to lend a hand. Dragging it to the waiting cart, her good deed was rewarded with the offer of a ride… to Bilston. Accepting gratefully, Liza dragged the last few crates to the cart and hitching up her long skirt, climbed aboard the boat.

*

Liza Townsend had left Bertha Jenkins' house more than a week ago, leaving no word as to where she was going, and now Bertha was dishing up her supper of faggots, made from pork shoulder and pig's liver, with onion gravy, when there was a knock on her back door. Tutting loudly, Bertha opened the door and there on the doorstep stood Liza Townsend.

'Hellfire and damnation! Wherever have you been, wench? I've been worried sick…' Bertha ushered Liza indoors and immediately divided up her supper between two plates.

Over supper Bertha wanted to know all, but Liza refused to divulge where she'd been or what she'd been up to. 'Bertha, ask no questions – get no lies. I'm very grateful to you for taking me in, you were the only one in the whole town that would. But… please don't ask me where I was. I had something very important to do.'

'All right wench, I understand.' Bertha said. 'Just answer me this – did you do that important thing?'

Liza nodded and so did Bertha. They had reached an understanding.

Bertha explained, 'I had to tell Dr Cooper of your sudden disappearance but I will let him know you're back tomorrow. He will be fine with it – he is a good man.'

Liza smiled her agreement.

The two women sat before the fire after supper and Bertha chatted on about the coronation of the King and how, if at all, his reign would affect them.

Liza's mind was elsewhere. She heard the drone of the other woman's voice, but nothing registered. Her thoughts swirled around what she'd done. The initial relief had passed and now the realization hit her. She had killed someone! She had committed murder! Her mind told her Ada had deserved all she got, but on the other hand should she have died for it? The woman was evil and had caused the death of Liza's child, she had taken a life, albeit by proxy. An eye for an eye, Liza thought, desperately trying to justify her actions.

Liza yawned, she was exhausted. The whole debacle had robbed her of her strength and she knew her dreams would be full of the images which still now played behind her drooping eyelids.

Bertha Jenkins kept her word and informed Dr Cooper of Liza's return before going to work the following morning.

Joshua Cooper decided to go and check on Liza himself and set off in his trap. The wooden wheels rumbled over the cobblestones of the streets and the doctor tipped his hat to those who shouted a greeting. Pulling into Pinfold Street, he halted the horse and jumped from the driving seat. Settling the horse with a nosebag, he rapped on the door to Bertha's house.

No words were spoken as Liza served tea and cake. She eyed the man sat at the table in the small kitchen. Liza then repeated what she had said to Bertha the previous night: ask no questions – get no lies. Dr Cooper nodded. Pulling a newspaper from his pocket, he slapped it on the table, pushing it towards Liza. He waited patiently while she read the article he pointed out. When she looked up at him, he tipped his head to the newspaper. Liza merely raised her eyebrows and said nothing.

The headline read, '*Workhouse Master, Fred Tulley, arrested for murdering his wife!*'

*

Joseph Purcell saw the cab coming up the driveway of Brueton House. He watched as the cabbie helped the woman alight before the cab moved away. Opening the door, he said, 'Miss Flowers! What a delightful surprise, please do come in.' His anger at her dissipated as he was once again confronted by her beauty. He did not notice the cabbie pull his vehicle to the side of the house to wait.

Leading Cara into the living room, he offered tea, saying he would be happy to make it as his staff were on their day off. Cara refused the offer.

'My visit to you, Mr Purcell, is for the sole reason of asking why you felt it necessary to pass on gossip to Martin Lander? Gossip, I might add, which is completely untrue!' Cara watched him carefully as she awaited his answer.

Purcell was confidently calm as he said, 'I have to say I'm surprised it took you this long to confront me, I thought you might have come before this. However Miss Flowers, I was told in the strictest confidence from a reliable source and assured of its validity. Simply put, I felt Martin had a right to know.'

Cara's anger rose as she glared at the pompous man. 'To be perfectly honest Mr Purcell, I was unsure whether to come at all, but in the end curiosity got the better of me. Besides a man in your position, a magistrate no less, should have known better than to pass on such gossip!'

Maintaining his calm demeanour, Purcell said, 'I reiterate, Martin had a right to know, gossip or not.'

Cara was horrified at the gall of the man and told him so.

Purcell said, 'My dear Cara, consider, who would not wish

to have an affair with you? You are the most beautiful thing I have ever seen!'

Cara blushed at his words and shifted in her seat as he stood and joined her on the couch. Taking her hand, he went on, 'Cara, I would give my eyeteeth for one kiss from you.'

Snatching her hand away, Cara jumped to her feet in pure anger. In her haste, her shoe tangled in the hem of her skirt. Losing her balance, she fell against him and he wrapped his arms around her, pulling her close. Cara struggled against him as he whispered, 'Don't fight me, Cara, this is one time you will not win!'

Grabbing the bodice of her blouse, he yanked it apart, sending tiny cloth-covered buttons flying across the room. Cara hit out at him, trying to beat him off her. Purcell laughed before pushing her back roughly onto the couch. Pinning her with his weight, he slapped her cheek hard and the shock of the blow halted Cara's efforts to free herself. Pressing his lips to hers and holding her head in place, he kissed her fiercely before saying, 'I've wanted that and more for a long time now.'

'Get away from me!' Cara rasped into his face.

'No, my dear, not yet. First I will have my fill of you, then you can go back to your *fiancé*!'

'Noooo!' Cara yelled as her struggles began once more.

Purcell slapped her hard, catching her cheek with his ring and the scratch instantly began to bleed. Ignoring it, Cara's adrenaline fuelled her efforts to push him off her, but he was too heavy. He laughed as he tore at her blouse and grabbed her breast roughly, kneading it as he kissed her forcefully. Lifting his body slightly to feast his eyes on her, he winced as Cara's piercing scream almost burst his eardrum.

Joseph gave her yet another slap, but Cara continued to scream for all she was worth.

'Get off me! Leave me alone!'

Suddenly Purcell was flying through the air and landed with a thud on the thick carpet.

The cabbie was standing over him, legs astride, with a look of pure fury etching his features. 'Get up, you dirty swine! Get up, so I can knock you down again!'

Joseph scrambled away from the burly man, muttering, 'She wanted it! She instigated it!'

Taking a step forward, the cabbie yelled, 'You're a liar, Purcell! I came running at the first scream and had you not been so intent on abusing Miss Flowers, you would have heard me!'

Turning, he held out his hand to Cara whose shaking hands were clutching her torn blouse. Leading her out of the door and settling her in the cab, he climbed into the driving seat and led the horse down the driveway.

The cabbie now sat in the kitchen of The Laburnums telling Gracie and Molly what he'd seen and heard. Cara had changed her clothes and given the torn blouse to Gracie to be burnt. She didn't want to be reminded of the incident by seeing the garment again.

'Shouldn't you telephone Martin, and let him know what's happened?' Gracie asked tentatively.

'No,' Cara said firmly. Her tone indicated she would brook no argument. 'I just want to forget all about it. I'm just grateful this kind man intervened on my behalf.' Cara pointed to the cabbie.

After chatting for a while and a hot cup of tea, Gracie saw the cabbie out, giving him her thanks also for his speedy intervention in saving Cara.

It was a while later when Martin came calling, and he was led into the kitchen by Molly. Discussions were still taking place about the incident, but Cara had begun to feel a little better. Her shaking hands had stilled and she sipped her hot tea as she listened to the conversation.

When Martin entered the room, her heart sank a little. Now he would find out what had happened. How would he react? she wondered. She didn't have to wait too long to find out.

She explained the whole thing and Martin was furious! He stamped around the kitchen, his hands dragging his hair back.

'He overstepped the mark, Cara! He assaulted you!' Martin said when Cara refused to pursue the matter. 'You have a witness… the cabbie! Purcell needs to be brought to justice!'

'No, Martin! I just want to put it behind me.' Cara's temper began to rise.

Martin slumped into a chair and sighed his frustration at her words.

'I wouldn't worry, Martin, things like this have a way of sorting themselves out.' Gracie winked surreptitiously at him, who smiled his understanding in return.

The unspoken pact between them would ensure the truth of Purcell's disgraceful behaviour towards Cara would spread across the town like wildfire via the cabbie.

Thirty-Seven

Word of Joseph Purcell's assault of Cara Flowers had reached every pair of ears in the town within a week. It was ironic that this gossip had more purchase than his own manufactured story about Cara's affair ever did. The man who had tried to shame the young woman now found himself shamed once more. He was shunned by all. The humiliated Magistrate returned home from his office to an empty house, the cook and maid having left a note on his desk in the study saying they had quit his employ. The man once held in such high esteem was now holed up at Brueton House without a friend in the world. He smouldered with hatred at Cara Flowers, the woman he once thought to marry.

Cara was dismayed that everyone knew what had happened but had guessed in her heart that the incident would never have remained a secret. Cara was satisfied. Her dark red jacket nipped into her tiny waist flaring out slightly at the hips. The reveres were open to the waist, revealing a pink lace blouse with a high neck. The skirt fell from the waist into an inverted 'V' to below the knee from which a deep frill hung. The jacket piping was black and the lower half held black embroidery. Red shoes peeped from beneath the skirt frill and a large pink hat sported pink and red feathers. A parasol completed the ensemble.

Waiting with the others in the living room, all dressed in their finery, the door finally opened and in walked Molly. Gasps sounded as she entered in her wedding gown. A white silk dress lay over a corset which pulled in her waist to an impossibly small size. From the high neck to the waist were layers of white chiffon ruffles which also edged the hem and short train. The back of the skirt was split almost to the waist and was inset with fine white lace over a silk lining. A lace veil to match trailed down over her shoulders, held in place by a circlet of white roses. Long silk sleeves ended in a small chiffon ruffle. She carried a simple prayer book. The applause answered Molly's unasked question. She looked beautiful.

Molly and Cara led the small entourage down Proud's Lane into Fletcher Street. It was still customary for the bride to walk to the church in the summer months accepting the good wishes of people who stood to watch her pass. Women came to their gates to wish Molly well as the group proceeded into Walsall Street and eventually reached St. Leonard's Church.

Sam Yale in his smart trousers, shirt, cravat, waistcoat and tail coat was waiting at the altar.

Having no family of her own, Molly had asked Cara to escort her down the aisle. As the wedding ceremony began, Martin held tight to Cara's hand and she read his look of longing. He wanted to be the next to marry his sweetheart.

*

Cara watched Molly and Sam board the last train to Birmingham that evening. Their first night as a married couple was to be spent in a fancy big hotel before they took another train the following day. They were to have a week's honeymoon at the seaside, courtesy of Cara. They had all enjoyed a meal at The Laburnums after the wedding and now they were waving to the young couple setting out on the rocky path of marriage.

Cara smiled as Molly hung out of the pulled down window of the door of the train. The girl was looking deliriously happy as Sam's laughing face joined hers.

'See you all in a week!' Molly yelled.

Cara nodded.

Martin slipped his arm around her waist and she stiffened. 'That will be us soon,' he laughed.

Cara smiled as she took a step closer to the train to blow a kiss to the happy couple.

The train whistle blew and the engine puffed out clouds of steam before chugging its way along the tracks. Everyone waved until the train was out of sight before turning to make their way home.

The moon lit the way as the group walked along the deserted streets talking quietly about the lovely wedding and how happy the couple looked.

Houses and shops which showed a layer of grime in the daytime all stood in darkness now, and the black silhouettes looked almost majestic against the moonlit sky. Other than the odd sound of a working factory and their quiet chatter, the town held an eerie silence. Horses were stabled and carts stored away, but Cara knew it would only be a matter of a few hours before the streets came to life once more.

Martin parted company with the others and headed home to Alice Street. Cara walked home with Gracie, Charlie and Daisy with a heaviness hanging over her.

The children went happily to bed and Gracie and Cara sat in the kitchen with tea.

'What's up, wench?' Gracie asked.

Releasing a long sigh, Cara replied. 'I know Martin wants us to be married soon, but...'

'You ain't ready yet,' Gracie finished the girl's sentence.

Shaking her head, Cara said, 'There are so many things I want to do first, Gracie!'

'I know, but you can't do everything, and Martin won't wait forever.' The cook smiled to lessen the impact of her words.

Cara nodded. 'I can't even think about marriage until I've found my mother and... the bread line grows ever longer. I have to find those men some work!'

'I understand how you feel, but you have to slow down or else you'll kill yourself!'

Cara retired to bed with her friend's words ringing in her ears.

*

Cara's next challenge came when she received a visit from Wally Webb.

'I'd thought you'd like to know that all the lodgers with your other tenants are now in their own properties.' Wally said with a grin.

'That's marvellous!' Cara was elated.

'It is, and it won't be too much longer before the rest of the houses on the old workhouse site are complete.'

'Oh Wally! How wonderful, I'm so pleased!' Cara's hands clasped together as if in prayer.

'The thing is...' Wally said tentatively, 'once they are, the men will be out of work again.' Cara laid her hands in her lap with a huge sigh. 'Sorry to spoil the mood,' Wally added.

'You haven't, Wally, it's not as though we weren't expecting it. Leave it with me, I'll give it some thought.'

Nodding, he slipped from the room quietly, leaving her to do her thinking.

Cara decided to go for a walk and strolling across Proud's Lane and into the allotments she returned the waves of the men working their plots. These plots would not see much work over the winter months, she knew, and other work would be needed for those workers then too. Cara sighed as she passed the small shops in Fletcher Street.

Walking on into Walsall Street, she stopped to gaze at St. Leonard's Church where Molly had been married. A slight breeze tugged at the hem of her long white dress and her hand moved to hold onto her straw boater. Following along Church Street, she glanced at the buildings lining each side of the roadway. They were tall and dirty and each looked the same as the next. Walking down a side street, Cara was then in the marketplace and waves and calls greeted her warmly from the stallholders. At least these women had work even if their men didn't. Cara's heart weighed heavy at the thought. Strolling between the stalls she pasted a smile on her face, she didn't want anyone seeing how down-hearted she was feeling.

Deciding on a different route home, she left the market by way of Broad Street. Halfway along she came upon a massive building which looked to be empty. She was intrigued. Walking down the entry to the side, she realized just how big it was, and she wondered how she'd not noticed it before. Enclosed by four streets, the 'L' shaped structure was two storeys high. It almost filled the enclosure in which it stood and it was indeed empty. Peering through a dirty window,

Cara saw nothing but space. She walked the entire perimeter, looking in each window. Her mood lightened as she returned home at a brisk pace. If she could acquire the property it could be the answer to her problems.

Later in the day, Gracie joined Cara and Daisy on her journey to the building once more, the key, given over by the ever obliging Mr Harris, the estate agent, firmly in her hand.

As Cara flung the door open, she gasped. The room stretched so far back she could barely see the end. All along the one wall were windows, tall and arched. The other wall held a door and, further along, more arched windows. Walking through the door on the right revealed another 'L' shaped room with windows. Moving back into the main area, they walked its length. Dust flew up from the stone floor as they went and a musty smell hung in the air. At the end stood another door, through which was yet another massive open space. To the left was a staircase to the upper floor which was identical to the ground floor. To the right was a corridor which led into half a dozen smaller rooms. Outside was a brick building which was partitioned off into four separate lavatories. A huge yard had a large water standpipe at its centre. At the end of the main structure which backed onto Princess Street stood two high and wide doors – the loading gates. Another half a dozen small buildings were dotted around the yard.

'This property is up for sale, Gracie,' she said, 'but it won't come cheap.'

'No, wench, it will cost you more than a bob or two,' Gracie nodded.

As Cara's eyes roamed, her mind whirled as to how it could be used in the most efficient way. Gracie smiled as they watched Daisy skip around the large room.

Relocking the door at Broad Street, they set off to return the key and try to strike a bargain with the estate agent.

*

Cara had refused to pay the extortionate price asked for the enormous building in Broad Street after Mr Harris had said, 'I can't lower the price without first consulting with its owner.'

'Of course, I understand,' she answered. 'May I ask the name of the owner?'

She almost fainted when she learned the owner was none other than Joseph Purcell!

'Mr Harris, I would prefer Mr Purcell not to know the identity of the party interested in his building due to... personal reasons.' Cara erred on the side of diplomacy.

'Certainly, Cara, be assured I will maintain your anonymity.' Harris smiled. He had heard the gossip concerning Purcell's inappropriate behaviour towards the young woman and was inclined to believe it.

'Besides,' Cara continued, 'the property is doing the man no good standing empty. Even at a reduced selling price he would benefit from its sale.'

'I can't argue with that,' Harris agreed. 'Give me a moment and I'll telephone him and see what we can do.' Giving her a wink, he pulled the telephone towards him.

And so, after much toing and froing and Mr Harris assuring Purcell it was the best price he would get for the building, Purcell capitulated and the title deed was eventually signed over to Cara Flowers. Joseph Purcell remained ignorant of the new owner's identity... at least for now.

Thirty-Eight

'Now you've bought it, what the bloody hell you gonna do with it?' Gracie asked.

'Well...' Cara began. 'Well...'

'You ain't got a clue have you? I knew it!' Gracie went about her business in the kitchen still muttering. 'You get these mad ideas and act on them before you think it through to the end! That damn great hulking building...'

Just then Sam and Molly walked into the room. Molly had been adamant she did not want to leave The Laburnums after her wedding and so Cara had obliged by offering the newlyweds her grandmother's bedroom. It was the largest in the house and the couple had accepted gladly.

Gracie continued, 'Sam, you tell her. She's got a massive monstrosity of a property and doesn't know what the hell to do with it!'

All eyes went to Sam and he smiled uncertainly. 'Are you thinking about work for the men when Flowers' Fields is finished?'

'When what is finished?' Cara asked.

'Sorry, but the old workhouse site appears to have acquired a new name. It is now known as 'Flowers' Fields', like the old cottages became 'Cara's Cottages'. You have to admit it has a nicer ring to it than the Spike,' Sam explained.

'Oh that's a bloody lovely name, that is!' Gracie wiped a tear on her apron as titters sounded.

'Well, when the work is finished the men will be out of work, am I right?' He saw Cara's nod. 'All those men have one trade or another, builders, carpenters, cobblers... there's even a couple of tailors too who've been doing the labouring.'

Cara saw where Sam was heading and said, 'So some could train others in different professions... if we divided the building up into small workshops...!'

Sam nodded and said, 'They could rent them from you.'

Applause sounded at the idea and chatter began around how to get started.

*

Bill Rowley, the architect for Flowers' Fields was on site at the new housing development and although he didn't *need* to be there, he always wanted to see his drawings come to life. He had put down on paper what now stood before him in the form of housing for the poor, and even after many years in his chosen profession, he marvelled at the finished constructions. It still excited him that what he drew on blank paper could be viewed, interpreted and constructed by competent builders. He had seen men move into the properties no sooner than they were finished. He had watched as friends and neighbours as well as Cara had contributed to fixtures and fittings. He was amazed at how the men who once had nothing, not even a hope of a better life, rallied together and erected the buildings that now stood on the old workhouse site. The name of the development had been burnt into a huge plank of wood, and the sign – 'Flowers' Fields' now stood proudly at the beginning of the cart track which ran around the perimeter of the houses.

It was the whistles and calls that drew his attention to the young woman who stepped from the cab that had come to a standstill close by. Cara waved to the men who had shouted their greetings as she walked over to Bill. All eyes watched as she handed the architect a large rolled up paper. Unrolling it, Bill looked it over and nodded, a huge grin on his face. Whatever Cara Flowers was up to now, it seemed Bill Rowley was in agreement.

Cara waved a goodbye and climbed into the cab once more. As it rolled away, everyone was wondering what challenge she had set herself this time. Everyone except Bill Rowley. The rolled paper tucked under his arm he walked towards his horse and, climbing into the saddle, he set off for home. He had another job to do for the enchanting Miss Flowers.

As the cab rumbled along, Cara's thoughts drifted to Liza Townsend. She had not been to see the woman since her release from the asylum. Cara felt bad that she'd been too busy and only now had thought about it. She made a mental reminder to pay a visit to Bertha soon, and hopefully then she would be able to meet Liza.

*

Bertha Jenkins and Liza Townsend were getting on like a house on fire, and with the former working at the school, the latter took over the cooking and cleaning in the house they shared.

Bertha was readying herself for work one morning when Liza said, 'I believe there's a property vacant over on Flowers' Fields.'

Liza Townsend's eyes held a sadness as they met Bertha's. 'I suppose I should investigate the possibility.'

Bertha felt the words pull at her heartstrings. Sitting at the table where Liza was reading the newspaper, she said, 'Let me put this plainly… and I don't mean to hurt your feelings, wench, but… you ain't got any work, so paying rent will be a problem. Also, you don't know any of the folk there, and it's my thinking you'll find it lonely. So, here's what I thought. Why don't you stay here with me?'

'Bertha, you've been so very kind to me allowing me to share your house and not asking bed and board. I can't impose on you further…'

Liza's words were cut short by a blustering Bertha. 'Impose, my arse! You ain't imposing on me! We get on well together, and God knows I need the company as much as you do. As for rent… you cook and clean, and I appreciate that more than money. So what do you say, will you stay?'

Liza nodded. Both standing, they gave each other a hug, the first either had enjoyed in a very long time. It sealed their friendship tight.

Bertha left for work and Liza resumed her reading of the newspaper. She was keeping her eye out for any work to be had, but there was something else she was looking for.

Finding the article, Liza smiled as she began to read avidly. Fred Tulley's trial.

With no evidence or witnesses to prove his innocence, Mr Frederick Tulley was jailed for the murder of his wife, Ada Tulley.

Liza lifted her eyes from the newsprint and stared into the flames of the fire.

Liza still harboured doubts about what she'd done knowing it would be jail time for her if anyone discovered the truth. A picture of her little girl sprang up in her mind. These two people had robbed her of a life with her daughter. Knowing it was terribly wrong what she did, she still felt justified in her actions. The woman responsible for her child's death was now six feet under, and the man who had not prevented it was rotting in a jail cell and would be there for the remainder of his life. Revenge was sweet, and Liza was going to enjoy its flavour.

Now that justice had been done, Liza felt she could finally move on to what mattered to her most: her daughter. Putting aside the paper, she made her way out of the house. Walking into the Funeral Director's office, Liza made her request. Could he tell her where her daughter had been buried?

Jack Grindall said, 'I can do more than that, Mrs Townsend, I can show you.' Grabbing his hat and coat, he led her from the office.

As they walked down the street to the little churchyard, Liza said, 'Mr Grindall, I appreciate what you did for my Phoebe.'

'Mrs Townsend, you are very welcome. It fair broke my heart that day in the Spike seeing you in that state.'

Liza nodded as she recalled the last time she saw her little girl, and she felt the ache in her heart once more.

Grindall went on, 'I did the best I could for her, you know, she had a pauper's grave.' He saw Liza nod in acceptance as they continued to walk. 'Well, there were no mourners and as I knew you couldn't be there either, I said a little prayer over her.'

'Thank you, Mr Grindall, that was a very kind thing to do. Phoebe would have appreciated that, as I do.'

Coming to the paupers' area of the burial ground, Grindall led Liza to a small grass mound, the place he had laid the child to rest. As they both stared down at the spot, he heard again in his mind the screams of the woman now standing beside him. A chill ran down his spine as he thought then of his own five daughters and how he would feel if he lost any one of them.

Placing a hand on her shoulder, he whispered, 'Stay as long as you want, wench, and come back any time.'

Turning, he walked away with a heavy heart.

Clutching a handful of wild flowers from nearby, Liza knelt by the grassy mound. Laying the flowers on the grass, she stared with unseeing eyes. Silent tears rolled down her face as she lay down by the grave with no marker. Phoebe's gaunt little face appeared in her mind as she relived the memory of their entrance into the workhouse.

Liza had tried desperately to feed herself and her child. They had wandered the streets with no money and no home until eventually she had accepted the ticket from the Relieving Officer. She saw again Phoebe's calm acceptance of being separated from her mother, no kicking and screaming like other children in the same situation. It was this calm acceptance that had chilled Liza to the bone. Phoebe had known her mother could no longer care for or protect her. In that moment, the last look they shared, Liza saw her six-year-old turn into a young woman way before her time.

Silent tears became heart-rending sobs as Liza lay by the daughter she would never see again. The sobs racked her body and her shoulders heaved as she grasped hands full of grass. Drawing in a lungful of air, the wail that came from her soul seemed to last forever. Liza lay by her daughter's grave all day and only moved when her tears slowly subsided and darkness crept around her.

Kissing the grassy mound, Liza stood and stretched the stiffness from her body. Blowing a last kiss to the flowers on the grass, Liza turned and walked away. She had said her last goodbye.

*

Bill Rowley had visited Cara's new acquisition in Broad Street, and now at home with the original drawings spread out on his dining table he scanned them carefully. Cara had told him of her plans for the building and it was his job to turn the massive old structure into light airy units. Each unit would house a different trade and once he had a list of these trades he would have a better idea of where each could be placed.

The dividing up of the structure would prove more challenging to him than drawing up plans from scratch and he relished the task set before him. Dragging a blank sheet of paper over the originals, he began to plan section by section, constantly referring to the original for measurements. He noted the situation of doors and windows, and before long his ideas began to take shape. He envisioned dividing walls in place with doorways leading from one room to the next. Archways rather than doors to the inner rooms where they could steal daylight from the outer rooms. Large mirrors strategically placed would bounce the light to reach into corners. For trades that might need plenty of air, doors that could open top or bottom… similar to stable doors.

As the plans took shape in his mind they were transferred to his drawings. Removing his small round spectacles, Bill rubbed the bridge of his nose. He was tired and his eyes ached but his ideas had him firmly in their grip. Replacing his spectacles, Bill grabbed his pencil and with renewed vigour returned to his sketches.

*

Sam Yale and Wally Webb, Cara's foremen, were tasked with taking the names and original trades of each man in Cara's employ. The young woman was astonished when told how many men she had working for her. Sitting in the parlour with the foremen, Gracie, Molly, Charlie and Daisy, she scanned the lists given to her. Gardeners, roofers, plumbers, painters and decorators, builders, boot makers, tailors, carpenters, cabinet makers, locksmiths, tilers... the list seemed endless.

'Bill Rowley is drawing up new plans for the building in Broad Street,' Cara said, 'so he will know where to place each set of tradesmen. What we have to decide upon now is how to get these men set up in their respective trades.'

'You can't be thinking of spending more money, Cara, surely to God!' Gracie was horrified.

Shaking her head and with a smile, Cara answered, 'What I propose to do is this... and I'd like your opinions, I thought to loan each trade a capital sum to outfit their workshop. It would then be up to them to draw in custom so they are able to pay rent for their premises. Naturally, there is nowhere near enough room for each man to have his own workshop, so they will have to form co-operatives, as the women did with the baking stall in the market. Once the workshops are set to trade, I will give them one month rent-free. After that I will expect rent to be paid at the end of each month and on time. Sam and Wally as my foremen will collect the rent and keep a careful tally… that is, of course, if you are both willing?'

Both men nodded.

Gracie spoke again, 'What if they can't pay? What if they don't get the custom?'

'It will be up to them, Gracie, to ensure they do. Once the… building… is up and running I will ask the newspaper to write an article regarding the men's achievements. I will place an advertisement outlining what is on offer there. Hopefully that will bring in some custom at the outset.'

With everyone's agreement, Cara said they would meet again with Bill Rowley when his drawings were complete.

When everyone left to go about their business, Charlie remained behind with Cara.

'What is it, Charlie?' She asked.

'I'm fifteen now, Cara, and I…' Cara nodded, urging him to continue, but Charlie faltered.

'You want a proper job? Not just labouring with the men?' She asked. His nod gave her the answer. 'All right, brother, have a think about what you'd like to do and we'll see if we can make it happen.' Cara smiled at the young man.

'I want to be an architect like Bill Rowley,' Charlie said simply.

'I will ask him if he will take you on as an apprentice, how would that be for you?' Cara asked.

'Yes please!' Charlie was overjoyed at the prospect. 'I promise to learn all I can and show you how good I can be!'

Daisy jumped up at his enthusiasm saying, 'I want to be a baker. Gracie shows me all the time what to do so I can have my own bakery one day.'

'That would be marvellous Daisy,' Cara encouraged. 'What will you sell?'

'Cakes, bread…cakes,' Daisy was thinking hard.

'You said that already,' Charlie interrupted.

Daisy harrumphed and cast him a frown.

Cara said quickly to dispel any forthcoming argument, 'What about muffins and pikelets? Will you bake and sell those too?'

'Yes!' Daisy said as if she'd thought of it herself. 'See Charlie Flowers, you don't know everything!'

Cara wrapped an arm around Charlie's shoulder and beckoned to her younger sister to join them. Wrapping her other arm around Daisy she whispered to them both. 'I love you two very much, and I know you will both be very successful.'

Thirty-Nine

As the finishing touches were made to the last block of houses on Flowers' Fields, the men moved to turning the perimeter track into a cobbled street. The first chill winds of the approaching winter blew and the men worked fast before the ground froze hard.

Daisy was helping Gracie to pickle onions bought from the allotment workers and Cara and Charlie were in the parlour with Bill Rowley and Martin Lander.

'Bill,' Cara said, 'I have the greatest of favours to ask of you.' Seeing his nod, she continued, 'I wondered if you would take Charlie under your wing and teach him about architecture.'

Rowley was not at all surprised by this request as the boy had been his constant companion on the old workhouse site.

Spreading his drawings on the table, he called for Charlie to take a look and tell him what he saw.

Charlie pored over the diagrams before saying, 'Mr Rowley, if it were me I would move this window...' he tapped a finger on the paper, 'and put it on this corner wall, then another could abut it here,' he tapped again, 'letting in far more light.'

Bill Rowley smiled as he nodded, 'You're right, Charlie!' Taking his pencil, he amended the plan. Turning to Cara, he said, 'Seems I have myself an apprentice... a good one too by the looks of it!'

Charlie was beside himself with joy and sat down to scrutinize the drawings. He wanted to know where every wall, door and window was to be placed; he wanted to be on site when it all began; he was desperate to learn all he could.

Whilst the two of them were deep in discussion, Martin took Cara's hand and whispered, 'My love, isn't it time we made plans for our wedding?'

Looking into his brown eyes, seeing the longing within, she said, 'How does a summer wedding sound?'

Martin's grin lit up his face as he said, 'It sounds wonderful to me!'

Cara had committed herself at last and as she heard Bill and Charlie muttering together she tried to come to terms with the promise she'd made. Maybe by next summer she would feel more at ease about becoming Mrs Lander.

*

Before they knew it the autumn chill gave way to the driving bitter winds of winter. People of Bilston ventured out only when absolutely necessary; the coronation parties of the summer now a forgotten memory. Fancy straw boaters were replaced by thick woollen shawls draped over heads and pulled tight about the ears before being crossed at the chest and wrapped and tied at the back. Side-button boots replaced shoes and long thick skirts shielded legs from rain threatening to freeze. For men lucky enough to own one, overcoats were donned and cravats were exchanged for mufflers. Everywhere, chimneys smoked as fires were built up in the hearths, adding to the pall hanging over the town. Cab drivers draped blankets over their outdoor clothing in an effort to stay warm. Winter had come early and it was going to be a long and harsh one.

The construction of dividing walls had begun on the new building under the watchful eye of Bill Rowley and his new apprentice Charlie Flowers. The cold wind whistled through the building as bricks were removed in readiness for windows to be installed. Steel lintels were put in place to take the strain of the roof over new doorways being marked out. Each area of the new building had been allocated to a different trade and each was clearly shown on the plans.

Cara was thrilled when told everything would be finished before too long and the men could take possession of their units. Having already decided who would work with whom in their small co-operatives, all that was needed now was to get the place up and running as soon as possible.

The newspaper office had sent a reporter to the site and he was writing an article on the work being undertaken. The reporter had interviewed Bill Rowley to glean as much information as he could knowing the populace would be very interested to know about Cara Flowers' latest challenge.

The reporter now sat in the parlour at The Laburnums. 'So, Miss Flowers, tell me more about this new venture.'

Cara raised her eyebrows and said, 'I discovered the building some time ago. It was lying empty so I bought it.'

'Just like that?' The reporter was amazed.

'Yes, I'm lucky enough to have a little money. Knowing the men would be standing idle again once Flowers' Fields was finished, I needed to ensure they had further work to go to.'

'I see. Mr Rowley tells me the units will be up and running

very soon.' The reporter scribbled in a notebook as he spoke.

'Indeed. Exciting, isn't it?' Cara laughed.

Looking up, the reporter smiled at her exuberance. 'This will be a rolling article...' He saw her frown. 'It means each week I will inform the reader of the progress made and of the businesses *in situ*. We can then have a grand finale article inviting the people of the town to visit, and hopefully spend their hard-earned money there.'

'That sounds wonderful! Thank you on the men's behalf.'

'I will pop down every week to see how things are going and then I'll be in touch about that grand finale. Maybe we can get a photograph of you on site and I can persuade the editor to put it in the newspaper with the article.'

'Oh goodness me!' Cara said all of a fluster. 'I will be famous!' She added with a laugh.

'Miss Flowers, you are already famous,' the reporter said as he waved goodbye.

*

Other than visiting her tenants occasionally to check on their welfare, Cara found herself again with little to do, so wrapping up warmly she took her usual cab to the wedding shop in the town. Now was as good a time as any to choose her gown. The cabbie pulled the carriage out of the wind in the lea side of the building and settled down to wait.

Cara entered the shop, which doubled as the owner's front parlour, not at all enthusiastic about her shopping trip. Gown after gown was brought out for her inspection, none of which caught her eye. Eventually Cara explained to the shop owner what she was looking for and after having her measurements taken, and being shown a quick sketch of the finished dress,

Cara left. The woman would make the gown and Cara would return for fitting sessions at a later date.

Climbing into the cab, Cara thanked the cabbie for his patience and the carriage rolled back to The Laburnums. Once more by a roaring fire, Cara reflected on her achievements.

The workhouse had closed and the houses on the site were all but filled. The cake shop was doing a brisk trade; her tenants were doing well and now the new building units were under renovation. Her brother and sister were living with her and she was at last planning her wedding. What was left to fill her time? With rents coming in from tenants, the allotments and soon the units, she could always buy up more property. She could get it renovated and sell it on to wealthy people. It was certainly something to consider. Then again, would she be expected to settle down and become a wife and mother? Cara sat by the fire to ponder the idea.

Her thoughts turned again to ever increasing numbers standing in the bread line and she sighed loudly. Never mind the wealthy, it was the poor who still needed her help. She would find a way to aid them somehow.

Her mind drifted to her mother and how the search for her had stalled. Cara didn't know which way to turn regarding this. Mr Colley's search of his records was fruitless so where could she look next? Cara had no idea.

*

Having prepared an evening meal for herself and her friend Bertha, Liza Townsend sat at the kitchen table reading the newspaper. So this was the young woman who had taken on the workhouse and won. Cara Flowers. In the depths of her mind the name rang a bell. Where did she know the name from? Maybe Bertha or Dr Cooper had mentioned it. Reading on, she spotted the names Charlie and Daisy Flowers, all siblings it seemed. Again the feeling came to her that she recognized these names, but she could not recall from where or why. Folding the newspaper, she sat with her tea and dredged her mind for clues.

The doctor had told her of his friend, the one who had demolished the Spike – that was it. Cara Flowers had been the 'friend' he had spoken of. Had he mentioned her by name? Liza didn't think so, he had just called her his friend. So how was it Liza knew the name of the young woman she'd never met? Perhaps she'd read it in the papers when news was reported of the workhouse closure. That must be it. She had scanned piles of newsprint in her efforts to locate the Tulleys so she must have come across it then. Liza settled with the notion, but not completely. Something still niggled in her brain, something she couldn't quite put her finger on. Maybe Bertha could shed some light on the conundrum.

*

Bertha Jenkins had answered Liza's questions about the closure of the workhouse and the girl who had brought it about. She told about her finding her brother and sister and how she looked after them at the behest of her grandmother. She explained how Cara had set out to aid the poor of the town and succeeded with every challenge she took on. She ended with news that the Flowers girl was soon to marry Martin Lander.

'Why are you so interested?' Bertha asked.

Liza answered, 'The names seem familiar to me, but I don't know how or why.'

Bertha frowned and then asked, 'You don't seem to know much about the folk around here, and I was wondering why that is?'

Liza sighed heavily then began to relate the last thing she could remember.

'I woke up on the heath with my young daughter by my side. Phoebe was only five years old and she was crying her little heart out. She grabbed my hand and led me back to our small cottage, but we'd found it occupied by another family. So with Phoebe at my side I had to beg in the streets, it was the only way I could get money to feed us.' Liza's tears formed along her lashes. 'Eventually I was forced to enter the workhouse; I was destitute. I couldn't feed my little girl, Bertha! I felt a failure. The poor little thing was starving. She cried all the time with bellyache and it tore me apart to watch it. I had to do something!' Liza's tears rolled unchecked down her cheeks and then she sobbed. 'We had been in there for a year when I learned of the death of my little girl. It broke my heart, Bertha. I'm not sure I'll ever get over it.'

Bertha felt sick at the reminder and shuddered, but Liza appeared not to notice. Instead she said, 'Ada Tulley paid for her mistake though, I made sure of it.'

Bertha's gasp was audible. 'You mean... you...?' Bertha spluttered. Liza merely nodded. 'Christ!' Bertha stammered. Realization dawned that she was now living with a murderer. Tentatively she asked, 'Have you...? I mean, you ain't...?'

'No. I've never done it before, and I'll never do it again.' Liza's sad eyes watched Bertha relax a little.

Bolstering herself, Bertha then asked, 'So how come you were on the heath in the first place?'

'I don't know, Bertha. Every now and then something

comes to mind. For instance, I know I always wanted to be a school teacher, but I don't know if that dream ever came to fruition. I recall waking up on the heath that day and I had a gash on my head. I've no idea how I came by it though. Phoebe told me we were on our way to see her daddy but… I have no memory of who or where he was. Phoebe was scared witless. Whatever had occurred had my little girl terrified and she would say no more. No amount of questioning or coaxing would make Phoebe tell me what had happened to frighten her so badly.'

'Poor little bugger!' Bertha said with a tear in her eye.

Liza went on, 'Phoebe told me my name, but I have no recollection of a life before that day on the heath.'

'Christ wench! You ain't half been through the mill an' no mistake!' Bertha sympathized as she poured more tea for them both.

'The memories I do have are muddled, disjointed you might say.' Liza resumed as Bertha sat once more. 'There must be more to it, but I just can't remember. That's the worst of it, Bertha, the not knowing. It's almost as if I didn't exist before that fateful day. The questions I ask myself are never answered. Who am I? Liza Townsend, I know that now. Why was I on the heath with Phoebe? I don't know. Do, or did, I have any other children? If so, where are they? Where were we going? Who was my husband? Where is he? Why do I feel I know the name Cara Flowers? I have no answers Bertha, I have no information about my life and it drives me mad at times!' They shared a grim smile at her choice of words.

'I can imagine,' Bertha said quietly, 'you must have had a right old bang to the head out there on the heath if it caused you to lose your memory.'

'Indeed, but how? What happened to cause such an injury?'

Bertha shook her head and they sipped their tea in silence.

*

When Molly and Sam had moved into her grandmother's bedroom after their wedding, Cara had had the ottomans moved into her own room. Other than retrieving Henrietta's diaries, she had done nothing more with the large chests. Cara decided now was a good time to empty the chests of her grandmother's things.

Lifting the lid of one of the huge ottomans, Cara began to remove its contents. Retrieving a thick book, she opened it. Inside were photographs, pictures of her grandmother and grandfather, of herself as a baby and her later years. Cara smiled at the pictures and traced a finger over the figure of her grandmother. The hurt of her loss still burned deep within her.

Another book revealed photographs of someone she didn't recognize – was it her mother? There was a picture of the woman in a wedding outfit standing next to a tall dark-haired man. Her father? Cara stared but she had no memory of the people in the picture.

Placing the books aside, she continued with her task. A large bundle wrapped in paper revealed a wedding dress, the same one as in the picture of the woman she didn't know. Laying the dress on her bed, she went back to the chest. She pulled out boxes of costume jewellery, a squashed hat, and a box of papers pertaining to the house.

Going to the other chest, she began the same procedure. Another wedding dress, presumably her grandmother's, was laid on the bed also. Books, papers and more jewellery were unearthed. Lifting out a box at the bottom, Cara peeped inside. Letters. She set them aside to read later.

Running down the stairs to the kitchen, Cara asked Gracie, 'Would you and Molly help me to clear out Grandma's belongings? All I want to keep are the papers and photographs. You can have the jewellery if you want it and I think the wedding gowns should be disposed of. Someone will be grateful for them I am sure.'

Brushing out her hair and plaiting it for the night, Cara's eyes fell on the letters she had removed from the ottoman earlier. Unfolding the first one, she began to read by the light of the oil lamp on the dresser. Little did she know that these letters would turn her world upside down, and lay a burden on her shoulders she never thought she would be able to carry.

*

Spring came in like a lion and howling winds threatened to take the legs from beneath people walking in the streets. Chimney pots were wrenched loose and sent crashing to the ground below. Trees bent, breaking in the ferocity of the gales that swept the country. Eventually the winds dropped and an eerie silence fell over the battered town as the clean-up began. Debris was scattered everywhere and people swept their houses clear of dust, as well as clearing the streets of detritus carried on the wind.

Over their evening meal, Cara explained, 'I have ordered my wedding dress and I wondered if you, Charlie, would give me away at the ceremony?'

Charlie said he would be honoured then Daisy piped up, 'What about me, our Cara?'

'Well, I wondered if you would consider being my bridesmaid.'

'Ooooh yes!' Daisy beamed. 'Can I... can I have a new frock?'

Cara assured her she could, with hat and shoes to match. Daisy was ecstatic already discussing colours and designs. Everyone laughed at her enthusiasm... everyone but Cara. A weight settled on her chest, threatening to suffocate her. This should be the happiest time of her life, planning her wedding, but she could not shake the feeling of foreboding that still gripped her. Watching Daisy laugh, Cara thought, *At least someone is happy about this wedding.*

*

Arriving at the wedding shop, Cara was shown into the fitting room, which was also the shopowner's living room. There she slipped on her wedding dress. The high-neck bodice of lace ended just above her bosom where a chiffon ruffle trailed over her shoulders. Below the ruffle lay silk, embroidered with flowers of the same shade of cream. Just below the nipped-in waist which appeared to be a jacket, was where the flowers finished. Below the 'jacket' hem the rest of the silk dress fell to the floor with a large chiffon ruffle around its hem. Long chiffon sleeves puffed out slightly and were held at the wrists with silk-covered buttons set on a deep cuff. Cara had decided against a train, and instead of a veil, she donned a cartwheel hat made completely of cream feathers. A silk embroidered parasol with matching ruffle round the edge completed her look.

Gazing into the long mirror, Cara checked her image; the dress fitted perfectly. Turning this way and that, she noted how well the dress hung at the back with no bustle. Although it was to be her wedding dress it was made in such a way as could be worn after the ceremony.

Cara was pleased with her purchase and the woman gushed her thanks as she boxed the dress, wrapped the parasol and found a large box for the hat. Paying the woman for her services, Cara climbed into the cab and piled the boxes on the seat next to her.

Once home she hung the dress in the wardrobe covered by a linen bag and the hat box and parasol were pushed on top of said piece of furniture. Daisy had wanted a dress of pale blue, like the sky, with shoes to match. Her sketch had been given to the dressmaker who said it would ready in plenty of time.

The following week when it was collected, the young girl was beside herself. Pale blue gauze with a ruffled round neck, it fell to her shoes ending with a matching chiffon ruffled hem. A wide blue ribbon tied at the waist plus some ribbons for her hair and a small parasol finished the outfit. Her dress complimented Cara's beautifully. St. Leonard's Church had been booked by Martin for August and everything was organized. All Cara had to do now was wait.

Forty

In the dining room at The Laburnums, Martin listened to the conversation and he reflected on his own life.

Joseph Purcell had upped and moved from Bilston, unable to stand being shunned by the town's society any longer, and he, Martin, had been lucky enough to fill the vacant position as Magistrate. He had also maintained his office in Earle Street; having let it to two solicitors looking for business premises to share.

Martin, also, had been measured for his wedding garb and was eagerly awaiting the day he would marry Cara Flowers. The summer had seemed an eternity away as the winter months had dragged on, but now with the springtime bloom not far away he felt more at ease. He was kept up to date with the renovations at the new building and he surmised the workmen would be in their units and trading by Easter.

Martin watched his bride-to-be as voices buzzed around the dinner table. Something was wrong. Cara had suddenly withdrawn into herself, her moods becoming sombre.

'Are you all right, sweetheart?' he asked.

Cara turned her glance to him, saying, 'Yes Martin, I think this cold weather is getting me down.'

'If you're sure,' he said.

Cara nodded and turned her face away from him.

She had brushed his concern aside but he thought there was something more on her mind than the weather. Could it be she had changed her mind about marrying him and was afraid to say? No, Cara was afraid of nothing. He determined to say nothing more; she would explain when she felt the time was right, he was sure. He dismissed these thoughts as he was drawn into the conversation.

Gracie Cox had seen the change in Cara too and had wondered what had happened to bring about this sudden alteration. Was it the forthcoming marriage that was eating away at the girl? It was possible, for Gracie knew Cara wanted to accomplish more to help the poor folk of Bilston before settling down to housewifely duties. It was after Martin had left and everyone else was in bed that Gracie broached the subject.

With just the two of them now sat in the kitchen, Gracie said, 'You want to tell me about it?'

Cara's blue eyes flashed to her friend before once more returning to her teacup. 'There's nothing to tell.'

'Right, and I'm the Queen Mother! Come on wench, something is on your mind, we've all noticed it.' Gracie watched the girl sitting opposite her.

Suddenly the flood gates opened and tears streamed down Cara's face.

'Bloody hell girl! Whatever is the matter?' Gracie rushed round the table and threw her arms around a sobbing Cara.

At last Cara gained control of her emotions and began to speak.

Deciding to go for a walk, Cara had ambled down Proud's Lane and as she neared St. Leonard's Church she stopped abruptly. Was that Martin walking briskly through the churchyard? Why was he here and not at his work? Maybe he was organizing their wedding service with the vicar. Surely that was something they should do together? But then that would be typical of Martin... taking control.

Stepping through the lychgate, Cara had followed the small paved path dividing the church from the gravestones. She called out but Martin didn't hear her. Coming to the corner wall of the imposing building, she stopped. She could hear Martin's voice then laughter. Peeping around the corner, Cara couldn't believe her eyes. It was indeed Martin Lander, her fiancé, and he was passionately kissing someone else!

Cara had watched as Martin embraced the dark-haired young woman. Then she had pulled back quickly behind the wall as the two scanned the area, assuring themselves they were alone.

After a moment, she had peered round the corner once more. Swallowing her shock, she saw them move off to the trees that shielded the gravestones from the street. Skirting around the church, she approached from the other side, her footfalls muffled by the grass.

Following the sound of the girl's giggles, Cara had moved stealthily to a point where she hid behind a large oak. Listening to Martin's coaxing, her anger had mounted. Should she step forward and confront them? She knew what was about to occur. She had tasted bile in her mouth and her stomach rolled. How could he do this to her? Especially after he had accused her of doing the same thing! Breathing heavily, she stood stock-still and watched.

She saw Martin lower the girl to the ground. With a hand covering her mouth, Cara had watched with mounting disgust as her fiancé made frantic love to another woman. She heard their groans as their passion increased, until at last their lust was sated and they lay together laughing.

Dressing quickly, the pair had walked back the way they had come, totally unaware that they had been observed throughout their liaison.

Cara had leant her back to the tree's trunk and gazed up into the sky. Anger rose swiftly and she began to shake from head to foot. Her fiancé was having an affair with another woman! Judging by what she had just witnessed, this was definitely not the first occasion they had made love! Cara had dredged her mind, focusing on the times she and Martin had not been together. Had he been with this other woman during those times?

'You bastard!' she had muttered. Never in her life had she sworn, apart from the occasional 'damn', but there was a first time for everything and she had felt it totally appropriate right then.

Cara had stood by the tree a long time trying to quell the anger in her. She felt utterly betrayed by the man who had asked for her hand in marriage.

Finally retracing her steps still feeling full of rage, Cara debated how to confront Martin Lander about his tryst with the dark-haired young beauty.

When she had finished, Gracie gasped, 'Christ A'mighty!'

*

Everyone ate a huge lunch before retiring to the parlour. Molly called for quiet.

'I have a toast to make,' she said as all raised their glasses, 'to Cara and her accomplishments.' The toast was made and Molly spoke again as she turned to her husband Sam. 'Sam, you are going to be a daddy!'

'Thank God for that!' he gasped. 'I thought you were just getting fat!'

'The baby is due in late summer so you may have to rearrange your wedding date Cara, so I can attend.' Molly laughed.

Cara smiled indulgently.

Applause sounded and hugs given.

Sam cleared his throat and all eyes turned to him. 'We'd best be finding a home of our own, Mrs Yale. I can't rightly turn the tenants out of my cottage, so we'll have to find somewhere else.'

Molly grinned, 'Blimey, you're right! Maybe Mr Harris at the estate agents can help?' They agreed to start looking for a house not too far away.

Cara watched the joy in Molly's eyes and thought she would order a new spring built perambulator for Molly's baby. This could not be delivered until her say-so. Carriage before baby was deemed back luck.

As talk centred on Molly and the baby, Cara's thoughts led her to how she might feel about having a family with Martin Lander. As her eyes rested on him laughing with Sam, her stomach rolled. No, most definitely not. She could not envisage herself being a wife to this man, never mind having his babies! Watching him now, the seed of a plan began to take shape in her mind. Could she do it? Could she be that cruel? Time would tell.

*

Nothing more had been said about the discussion between Cara and Gracie on that night Cara bawled her eyes out, other than the girl needed to decide what to do in her own time and in her own way. Cara now felt she had made that decision.

Sitting on her bed, Cara picked up the letters she had found in the ottoman and began to read once more. Then laying them aside she closed her eyes and digested the information contained in them.

Why had her grandmother not told her of these? Why had Henrietta Selby denied hearing anything more about her daughter, Cara's mother? She had said that she'd *heard* John Flowers had died in a carting accident, which was true. What she hadn't said was *how* she'd heard. Her daughter had informed her by letter. One of the letters now lying on Cara's bed. John, apparently, had been knocked down by a fully laden cart which had then rolled over him, crushing his chest. He had not survived long. Now widowed, Elizabeth Flowers had written to her mother begging forgiveness and leave to return home to The Laburnums. Whether Henrietta had replied, Cara didn't know.

One letter after another all held similar requests. Could Elizabeth Flowers come home to her mother? Could she bring her other two children with her? Could she resume caring for her own daughter Cara? Begging Henrietta to forgive her, she promised to take care of them all and never again disobey her mother. Cara remembered from the diaries her grandmother had made no mention of Charlie and Daisy. Cara had assumed she hadn't been aware of their existence. These letters proved that to be false. Why had her grandma not searched for the children?

Whether by fault or design, Elizabeth Flowers had stayed

away. Could this be what Henrietta alluded to in the personal letter left for Cara? *'Also, if you find my daughter, please tell her I rue the day I ignored her plea.'*

Elizabeth had begged to come home, but her grandmother had ignored it. Why? Was she still upset and angry that Elizabeth had married John against her wishes?

Cara packed away the letters, she could not bear to read any more. She knew what was contained in them and it was heart-breaking. This was something she would have to deal with at a later date, for now her forthcoming wedding was occupying her every thought. Cara shut the letters from her mind.

Forty-One

Time passed quickly and then before anyone realized, the summer had arrived. The units at the new building were up and running and the tradesmen were in their rent-free month. The newspaper article had helped enormously and work was pouring in. The new sign proclaimed it to be 'Flowers' Arcade' and people were able to stroll from room to room watching tradesmen at their work, besides buying any products set out for sale.

Mr Harris, the estate agent, came up trumps finding a beautiful cottage at the other end of the allotment gardens in Mountford Lane for Molly and Sam. It was only a hop, skip and jump from The Laburnums and the couple moved in within the week. A gentle rain began to fall as their belongings were carted to their new residence but no one seemed to mind.

Then day after day the sun scorched the earth and the heat became unbearable. Just as a few short months ago people thought they would freeze to death if they stood still, now the pall hanging over the town trapped the heat beneath it.

These same people were tired and lethargic, irritable beyond belief.

Molly sat in Cara's kitchen fanning herself; even with all the doors and windows open there was no relief. With a sudden intake of breath, Molly muttered, 'Oh God! My waters have just broken! Oh Cara, it's too early!'

Gracie took charge immediately. 'Daisy wench, get yourself outside and tell the cabbie to fetch the doctor.'

Daisy dashed off happy to be of use.

'Right, Molly, let's get you upstairs and out of that frock.' Gracie slipped an arm round Molly and helped her to her feet.

'Take her into my room,' Cara said as she dashed upstairs to find a nightgown.

Gracie undressed the panicking Molly and a voluminous white cotton nightgown was slipped over her head. A faint breeze wafted through the open window as Molly's pains began.

'Ooooh…' Molly moaned as she held her stomach, 'Oooh Gracie…'

'I know, wench,' her friend said, 'but it will all be over soon and then you'll have your little 'un in your arms and not your belly.'

Molly smiled but as another pain racked her body she yelled out, 'I can't do this, Gracie, make the pain go away! Please make it go away!'

'You stop that row this minute!' Gracie snapped. 'You ain't the first and you won't be the last. Now then, let's have you on your feet and walking round the room until the doctor gets here!'

With Gracie holding one arm and Cara the other, Molly was walked back and forth, sweat trickling down her face.

Each time a pain gripped her, she stopped. Wide eyes looked at Gracie, who nodded, and a miserable whimper escaped Molly's lips. Then on again they paced.

Molly whispered, 'I ain't never doing this again!'

Cara winced as another pain rolled over her friend.

Just then Daisy banged on the bedroom door, 'Dr Cooper's here, Cara!'

Laying Molly down on the bed, Cara gave the doctor admittance. Thanking Daisy, she asked if tea could be prepared. Molly would certainly be wanting a cup very soon. The young girl said she would get right to it and thundered down the stairs.

Rolling up his shirtsleeves, Dr Cooper felt all around Molly's abdomen. His eyebrows shot up when Gracie told him they had called for him immediately. 'Well, Molly, my girl,' he said smiling, 'it looks like this is going to be a quick birth!' The doctor, however, would be proved wrong.

Cara held Molly's hand as the young woman screeched and cried. No longer able to contain her emotions, Molly screamed her pain as contractions threatened to split her body. Pains rolled over her time after time, and Molly was becoming exhausted. She gasped for air, holding it tightly as the pains once again took hold of her. Sweat rolled down the sides of her face and Cara mopped it away with a cold damp cloth.

'Ooooh dear God!' Molly gasped. 'I can't do this! Why isn't it coming?'

'You have to do it, wench, now get a grip of yourself and do what the doctor tells you!' Gracie snapped. She knew it was the best way to try to divert Molly's attention away from the pain and focus on the doctor's words.

Molly yelled again as yet another pain came, she grabbed the iron bedstead and held on tight.

The hours passed and Molly was so exhausted the doctor feared for her health as well as that of the baby. Seeing her tense at the rise of yet more agony, he shouted, 'Right Molly! This time, this is it. Push, girl! Push!'

With one ear-splitting scream from her mother, Tansy Yale came into the world yelling her tiny lungs out.

Molly collapsed back onto the bed completely and utterly exhausted. The doctor cut the cord and handed the baby to Gracie to be swaddled. Gracie had found a single bed sheet which she had folded into a swaddling cloth. The doctor finished his ministrations with Molly before laying her daughter in her arms.

'A little early... but healthy. Well done, Molly! What a beautiful daughter you have,' he said with a smile.

Cara heaved a great sigh of relief and only then realized both she and Gracie were crying their eyes out.

The cabbie had taken it upon himself to fetch Sam from his work who now sat at his wife's bedside, his baby daughter in his arms. Cara left to pay the cabbie for his forethought and only now realized she didn't even know his name. She felt thoroughly ashamed; all the times he had been on hand to help her and she hadn't even bothered to learn the man's given name.

Apologizing profusely for her oversight, the man laughed and said, 'George, Miss Flowers, and don't you worry about it. Just glad I could help is all.'

Cara insisted Molly, Sam and baby Tansy stay where they were until the new mother felt well enough to return home. Cara would sleep in Molly's old room in the interim.

Within the fortnight, the family had moved back to their own house and Cara returned to her own bedroom, the one she thought she'd be sharing with Martin in a matter of weeks. Tired from being disturbed in the night by Tansy's lusty cries, Cara lay on her bed and before long she was sound asleep.

Gracie woke her with a cup of tea as night fell and they sat together on the bed talking about the new baby. Unable to hold her tongue any longer, Gracie asked Cara what she would do about what they'd discussed the night Cara burst into tears.

Drawing in a deep breath, Cara nodded. 'I can't forgive Martin, Gracie, no matter how hard I try. He betrayed me!'

'I guessed as much, wench. I've seen the way you look at him now. I watched you while Molly was having young Tansy too. Not something you'd want to go through with him?' Gracie patted Cara's hand.

'Oh Gracie! The very thought of... well you know... with Martin – I couldn't!' Cara screwed up her face in disgust.

'So what's your plan? I mean to say, everything is organized and you have your dress an' all.' A shake of Gracie's head said she couldn't fathom what was to be done about it.

Cara whispered what she planned to do and then waited for Gracie's reaction. It was not what she expected. The older woman nodded and said simply, 'Good plan. No more than he deserves.'

*

The sun rose full and strong on that day in August, Cara's wedding day. Gracie was exasperated with Daisy who was flouncing around the kitchen in her blue bridesmaid's dress.

'If you get that frock dirty you won't be going to no wedding, my girl!' she said sternly.

Daisy sat down suddenly, aware Gracie was right. Sam, Molly and baby Tansy had arrived dressed in their finery and Gracie went up to Cara's bedroom.

'Come on, wench, you ready?' Gracie urged.

Cara looked up at the woman who she loved like a mother and said, 'Oh Gracie, Charlie will be so disappointed, and Daisy will be heartbroken!'

'Ar well, they'll get over it,' Bertha said in a typical West Midland response.

'Am I doing the right thing? Should I rethink because of the children? They will hold me responsible for their disappointment, Gracie. Oh, now I'm not so sure this is a good idea!' Cara was becoming agitated at the thought of her brother and sister's reaction to what they would very soon find out.

'Bloody hell, girl, make up yer mind!' Gracie was exasperated as she paced the room.

'Right, I'll have to deal with the children's disappointment later. I have to do this.' Walking to the door, she yelled out for her brother Charlie. The boy was very concerned at the urgency in her voice but before he could speak, Cara said, 'Charlie, would you go to the church and bring Martin back here please? Also, I'd like you to give this letter to the vicar. It's very important, Charlie.'

Nodding, Charlie ran from the house wondering what was going on.

'Does he know you know?' Gracie asked as they walked downstairs to the parlour.

Cara shook her head, 'I never found the right time to confront him with it,' she said, 'and I've been so busy…'

'Ar well... so that time will be now then?' Gracie was full of thunder that anyone would treat Cara so badly.

'Yes. I will confront him now,' Cara said simply. 'Would you be kind enough to tell the others there will be no marriage taking place today between Martin and myself? They will want to know why, of course, and I will explain when I have dealt with Martin.'

'Are you sure about all this?' Gracie's concern filtered through her words.

'I've never been more sure of anything in my life.' Cara nodded.

*

Martin Lander stared open-mouthed at the girl he thought was to be his wife. Cara Flowers had just told him the wedding was off. She had said she didn't love him in the way a woman should love her husband – she only loved him as a friend.

Cara watched him as they sat in the parlour, the shock of her words written all over his face.

'Cara, I beg you, please don't do this to me! Please...!' Martin was beside himself.

Holding up her hand, Cara said, 'Martin, I'm truly sorry but I cannot marry you, it would end in disaster. It wouldn't be fair on either of us. Please try to understand.'

'Understand!' Martin shot back. 'Understand what? That you allowed me to believe you loved me all this time? That not once did you give me any cause to think otherwise? We planned this Cara, for months we planned this together, and now you tell me just like that...' he clicked his fingers, 'that it's all off? I *don't* understand! I will never understand!'

Cara's next words stopped Martin in his tracks. 'I saw

you... that day in the churchyard... I saw you kissing and... with another woman!'

Once more the sting of betrayal stung her and her anger rose.

'What?' Playing for time, Martin thought quickly. How could he get out of this one? How could he placate Cara and ensure they were married? Closing his eyes, he saw her money, which would become his on the occasion of their marriage, disappear. No wedding – no money. 'You don't understand...' he began.

'Martin!' Cara yelled. 'What is it you think I don't understand? That I saw you kissing someone else? That I saw you on the ground beneath the trees? I saw you, Martin!' She knew her voice would carry and thought at least her explanation to the others would be unnecessary now.

'It was a friend, Cara...' Lander was clearly in a panic.

'Do you always kiss your friends so passionately?' Cara boomed out the words. 'Do you always make love with friends? Martin, don't treat me like an idiot, I *saw* you! I watched you make love to her! Now, understand this, Martin Lander, the wedding is off and I'll thank you to leave this house... right now!' Cara pointed to the door. 'Go! Get out, and don't ever come back!'

Knowing he was beaten, Martin jumped to his feet and rushed from the room, from the house, and from her life.

Cara sighed heavily before walking to the kitchen where everyone was quietly gathered. They knew the wedding had been called off, Gracie had explained already, now after hearing Cara's yelling, they knew why. It was Charlie who gathered Cara in his arms; Daisy joined them and the three hugged with no words spoken. None were needed, they were family.

Daisy broke the hush with, 'At least it don't matter if I get my frock dirty now!'

Unable to contain herself, Cara burst out laughing. A great weight had lifted from her shoulders and she felt free of the burden she had carried for so long.

*

The vicar had been given the letter by Charlie immediately after Martin Lander had rushed from the church. His eyes scanned the words as the congregation mutterings began. Something was up, they said. Asking questions of each other, heads shook. No one knew what was amiss.

Clearing his throat the vicar said, 'I have here a letter... from Cara Flowers.' The people who sat in the pews leaned forward in their eagerness to hear what was coming next.

Drawing in a breath through his nose, the vicar continued as he shook his head. 'Miss Flowers has requested I read this letter to you, but...'

More mutters rumbled in the pews and a man shouted out, 'Well go on then, read it!' He received a dig to the ribs from his wife for the untimely outburst.

'I... ahem... I... This is most unusual, to say the least. Right, let's get this over with!' With a quick glance at the people sat in front of him, the vicar returned to the letter and began.

'I have requested the vicar to kindly inform you that my wedding to Martin Lander will not take place today – or any other day.' The vicar paused as the rumblings began again. *'The man I thought to be my husband is a liar and a cheat!'* The vicar drew in another breath before continuing. *'I have discovered he has been having a liaison with another woman!'*

The crowd in the pews drew in a collective breath and

the vicar looked up with sad eyes. Holding up his hand for silence, he went on. *'I am unaware of this woman's name, but I know her to be a raven-haired beauty. I saw them together beneath the trees in the churchyard and... they were making passionate love on that consecrated ground!'*

Another pause from the vicar as he shook his head. His eyes travelled to the ceiling and he made a silent apology to the Almighty on Martin's behalf, for the indiscretion committed on Holy ground. The noise from the wedding guests became a cacophony as men laughed out loud and their wives berated them for being so indiscreet.

The vicar called for order and lowered his eyes to the letter once more. Silence descended as he resumed reading.

'So this is my reason for calling off the wedding. Some of you will be disgusted at my actions today and to those I say... put yourself in my shoes. Ladies, would you feel betrayed as I do? I'm sure you would. Gentlemen, it is one thing to be "Jack the lad", but quite another to betray your betrothed. It is my contention Mr Lander only wanted to marry me for my money.

'However, on a lighter note, the reception booked at the Red Lion is all paid for so please go and eat and drink your fill courtesy of the Flowers family. Kindest regards, Cara Flowers.'

Rapturous applause and chatter erupted as the vicar finished speaking. The pews emptied rapidly as people fought to leave the church and get to the Red Lion as quickly as possible. There was free food and drink to be had.

The vicar was standing with an open mouth when a man came up to him and grabbed the sleeve of his cassock. 'Come on vicar,' he said, 'you look like you could do with a drink!'

The man laughed as the clergyman merely nodded and walked out of the church in a daze.

*

Gossip in the town was rife, with some saying what Cara Flowers had done was a terrible thing; leaving Martin at the altar. Others said in no uncertain terms that she'd done the right thing calling off the wedding before she'd made the biggest mistake of her life. Everyone was wise now as to the real reason Cara elected to stay a single woman – Martin Lander was a lying, cheating philanderer.

Cara ignored the gossip and went about her business much as she had before. She knew soon enough the folk of Bilston would find something else to gossip about. What had surprised her though was that Martin Lander was not quite as heartbroken as he'd led her to believe. In a very short time he was seen out and about with yet another woman, the daughter of a wealthy merchant. The dark-haired beauty he had had a tryst in the churchyard with had dropped Lander like a hot potato, the news of the letter read to the people in the church by the vicar having reached her ears swiftly. The newspaper she was reading reported Martin's imminent wedding to the merchant's daughter! So Lander had been playing both ends against the middle in an effort to ensure he would become a rich man.

The town buzzed with the news of the letter read out in church and a furious Martin, unable to cope with the gossip, upped and left within the week.

The whole household had kept a wary eye on Cara after the debacle of the wedding cancellation. However, she appeared to have vigour once more and a lightness in her step they had not seen in a while. Cara Flowers was back to her old self again.

*

As the leaves fluttered gently on the wind to land quietly on the ground, Cara realized that autumn had rolled round yet again. She sat on a bench in the allotment gardens and gazed at the beauty that surrounded her. Russet and golden leaves fluttered lazily in the zephyr that carried them from the branches to land in her lap. Birds sang and in the distance the train's steam whistle blew. She considered life was good, not only for her but also for the people she had helped over the years. Her only regret was… her mother.

Striding from the gardens, Cara made her way home. In her bedroom once more she lifted out the letters she'd found in the old ottoman. Sitting on her bed, she began to read them in order once more.

Cara's challenge now was one she wasn't sure she could complete. She looked at the last letter and the newspaper clippings attached to it. Finding a screwed up clipping attached to the back of the letter she realized it was one she had not seen before. It announced the wedding of the widow Elizabeth Flowers to a wealthy banker, Arthur Townsend, based in Birmingham. A later one reported the birth of a daughter to the happy couple. Surely this had to be her mother! It could not possibly be a coincidence! Cara's heart soared as she re-read the clipping. She had found their mother!

Refolding the letter, Cara shook her head, she had yet one more thing to do. How could she complete this last task? How could she tell Charlie and Daisy she thought she had found their mother? How could Cara explain to 'Mad' Liza Townsend that she suspected they were mother and daughter?

Forty-Two

Daisy was spending the day with Molly and baby Tansy who she doted on, and Charlie was off with Bill Rowley somewhere or other, thoroughly enjoying his role as apprentice, which Bill had informed her was going extremely well.

Cara and Gracie sat in the parlour, toasting their toes before the blazing fire. Suddenly Cara asked, 'Gracie, will you come with me to see Liza Townsend?'

'Of course I will wench…' she said, 'can I ask why you want to see her?'

Nodding, Cara said, 'Gracie, I believe Liza is our mother.' Cara saw Gracie splutter tea everywhere then wipe her mouth on her apron.

'God's teeth! You sure? How do you know?' Gracie asked.

Cara explained as she passed the letters to her friend, a nod giving permission for Gracie to read them.

'Bloody hell!' Gracie said as she finished.

Climbing into the cab at the end of the driveway, Cara gave George the cabbie the address they wished to visit. The chill that reached Cara's bones was more to do with her final challenge than the autumn breeze.

During the journey no words were spoken and Cara shivered with a nervous anticipation.

Knocking lightly, on Bertha Jenkins' front door, Cara and Gracie waited patiently. Cara's nerves jangled as she considered what was to come. The door was opened by Bertha herself who had just returned from her work.

'Cara! What a lovely surprise! Come in, come in. Gracie, nice to see you, wench.' Bertha ushered them into her living room.

Liza Townsend sat in a chair pulled up to the fireside. She eyed the young woman being introduced to her. So this was Cara Flowers, the one she'd heard so much about. As she stared Liza could have sworn she'd seen those eyes before.

Cara couldn't help staring with an open mouth at the woman she recognized from the wedding photograph. It *was* her mother! She felt an overwhelming desire to rush to Liza and throw her arms around her, for all she couldn't remember having seen her before. She felt ashamed she had not found time to visit earlier, especially as she'd promised herself she would.

Bertha set about brewing tea and cutting cake for them all as the visitors sat on the sofa.

There was an uncomfortable silence as Liza stared openly at the young woman. She was trawling her mind for memories. None came.

Cara's nerves jangled and her eyes darted from Liza to Gracie and back again.

Drawing in a breath, she said, 'Forgive us just arriving with no warning.'

Bertha waved away the apology with, 'You're welcome here any time… you know that, both of you.'

Grasping her courage in both hands, Cara went on, 'To

be truthful Bertha, it's Liza I've come to see.' All eyes turned to the named woman before returning to Cara. 'I have something I think you should see, Liza.' Passing the letters and photographs over, she waited.

'These letters are addressed to Henrietta Selby; why would you think I should see them?' Liza asked, full of suspicion.

'Liza, please read them, they pertain to you.'

Bertha directed a frown to Gracie who gave an imperceptible shake of her head. *Just wait, you won't believe what's coming next*, the head shake said.

In the quiet of the small living room, Liza read each letter then came to the photographs. 'Oh my God!' She gasped as she looked at Cara then back to the photograph. 'That's me, there in the picture, that's me and... John!' She caught her breath at the sudden memory and felt the tears begin to sting her eyes. Tracing a finger over the picture, she then went on to read the newspaper clippings.

Liza replaced the clippings in the envelope saying, 'It would appear from this that after John's death, I married again to an Arthur Townsend.' Liza shook her head. 'I don't remember him, but that would explain my name being different to yours.' She looked again at Cara who nodded.

'It would seem, Mrs Townsend, that you and I are mother and daughter!'

Bertha's gasp resounded as she looked at Gracie who nodded in confirmation. 'Hellfire, damnation and buckets of blood!' Bertha's cursing broke the spell.

Then Liza drew in a deep breath, letting it out slowly as she digested Cara's words. Sitting silently for a while, Liza tried desperately to recall memories, but still they eluded her.

'Cara Flowers,' Liza said at last, 'I know the name, from somewhere deep in here.' She laid a hand on her heart.

'What about Charlie and Daisy Flowers, do you know those too?' Cara urged.

Liza screwed up her face as she thought hard. 'I'm not sure, but I think so.'

'They are your children too, Liza, yours and John's,' Cara said gently.

'Oh God! I wish I could remember!' Rubbing her tired eyes, she dragged her hands down her face then Liza began to cry.

'Oh please don't distress yourself! I'm sorry, I didn't mean to upset you!' Cara felt a rush of love for the woman sat by the fire sobbing quietly, her head now held in her hands.

Bertha muttered, 'Gracie and I will be in the kitchen if you need anything. We'll get a bit of dinner on the go.' Gracie frowned as Bertha tilted her head and shoved her into the kitchen.

Liza looked into the eyes of the daughter she couldn't remember. 'We have the same eyes you and me,' she whispered, 'and hair, at least until mine started turning grey.'

'Daisy and Charlie have the same eyes and hair too, Liza.' Cara smiled.

'Tell me about them… please?' Liza asked.

'Oh Liza, they are an absolute delight!' Cara began. 'Your son is a young man now and training to become an architect. He took care of himself and Daisy after you and your husband, John Flowers, disappeared.' Cara saw the sadness creep across Liza's face as her tears fell once more. 'I'm just telling you as it is, Liza, I'm not saying these things to hurt you, please understand that.' Liza wiped away her tears and nodded. Cara went on. 'Charlie tried his best to take care of them both, but they were eventually sent to the workhouse.'

Liza gasped her distress at the thought, knowing that

although very recently they had all probably been in the 'Spike' at the same time, it would have made no difference. After all, segregation was in effect; besides which she wouldn't have known who they were anyway.

'Henrietta Selby…' Cara said then nodded as Liza held up the letters, 'yes, she was your mother, my grandmother. She tasked me with a challenge to find and care for any blood relative. I found Charlie in the workhouse and got him out. Daisy had been sold on by Tulley.'

'That swine!' Liza rasped through gritted teeth.

Cara went on quickly, 'Well, we found Daisy and brought her home. It appeared John died in a carting accident. I've been searching for you for a long time.'

At that moment Gracie bustled in with fresh tea. 'How's it going, ladies?' She asked as she placed the tray on the table. Curiosity was written all over her.

'We're getting there,' Cara said.

Gracie bustled back into the kitchen, wishing she could stay and listen.

Cara spoke again. 'Charlie is a talented young man; caring, considerate and passionate about the things he loves.'

She saw Liza give the tiniest of smiles at her words.

'Daisy… Oh my goodness! Daisy has a dry sense of humour, she's full of energy and chatters constantly. She has the prettiest face. Blue eyes, blonde hair – a real picture. She still prefers to eat with her fingers…'

'Fingers came before cutlery,' Liza whispered almost to herself.

'That's exactly what Daisy says!' Cara beamed excitedly.

Everything she was told made sense to Liza, but the frustration of being unable to remember was driving her mad. She had remembered John from the photograph so that was a start. The children's names were strangely familiar to her too, but she could remember nothing else.

Holding her head once more she thought, *they* must *be my children, the newspaper clippings and letters prove it.*

'Liza, how did you come to lose your memory? Do you have any idea?' Cara asked tentatively.

Rubbing her temples as if to provide inspiration or provoke memories, Liza shook her head. 'I only remember waking on the heath with Phoebe beside me, anything before that is lost to me.'

'Phoebe Townsend?' Cara whispered.

'Yes. She died in the workhouse.' Liza's eyes closed but the tears squeezed between her lashes.

'I'm so sorry. I heard about it,' Cara said quietly. 'Then Phoebe must have been the baby mentioned in the newspaper.'

Opening her eyes again, Liza said, 'It would seem so.' Holding up the letters, Liza added, 'If these are correct, Phoebe was your step-sister.' Watching Cara, she saw the realization dawn.

Cara's eyes began to well with tears as she thought about the little girl who had died long before her time.

'Where Mr Townsend is, I have no idea. All I know is we ended up in the Spike and my Phoebe died in there.' The threatened tears began to roll down Liza's face and Cara's heart went out to her. 'They threw me in the asylum when I attacked Ada Tulley. She made them use the bad meat and my little girl died because of it!' Liza's temper began to rise as she thought again of that woman. Her mind then formed a picture of Ada lying dead at the bottom of the stairs and her anger quelled. 'It was Bertha and Dr Cooper who saved me from that awful place.'

'Dr Cooper kept me abreast of it,' Cara said, much to Liza's surprise. 'He told me about you and we worked together to get you released.'

Liza tried her best to smile. 'I thank you for that.'

A silence descended which was broken by Gracie and Bertha trundling in with steaming bowls of thick broth and a large fresh loaf which Bertha hacked into chunks.

'Time to eat,' Gracie said. Everyone gathered around the table and began their meal.

As they ate, Cara thought the women had more than likely heard some of the discussion; probably with their ears pinned to the door. They ate in silence, each enjoying the food given. Bertha made more fresh tea and while they drank it, Cara spoke again.

'Liza, are you up to a meeting... with Daisy and Charlie?'

'Oh... I'm not sure it's a good idea,' she shook her head, 'they most likely think I abandoned them – they'll hate me!' Liza felt fear grip her.

'No they don't!' Cara said quickly. 'I promise you, they don't hate you – they miss you dreadfully!'

Bertha added, 'Be brave, wench, take that first step.'

Cara said, 'Look at what you've already faced, Liza, and you overcame all that. This is a walk in the Allotment Gardens in comparison.'

Liza's eyes moved to each of the women in turn before returning to Cara. 'Do you think it will be all right? Oh God, I'm so afraid!'

'Yes!' Cara answered enthusiastically. 'I think it will be more than all right! You don't have to be afraid, Daisy and Charlie will be thrilled to see you again!' Turning to Bertha, she said, 'Thank you for our meal and the use of your living room. Why don't you come along with us? Would that help, Liza?'

'Oh yes it would,' Liza said, giving Bertha a nod of thanks.

'You bet your life! I ain't missing this!' Bertha threw over her shoulder as she rushed off to grab a coat for Liza and herself.

The four women climbed into the cab and George clucked to the horse to walk on. Apprehension hung heavy in the air on their journey back to The Laburnums. Liza's eyes constantly darted from one face to another; she looked like a frightened bird.

Cara was excited at the prospect of Daisy and Charlie seeing their mother again.

Liza on the other hand, was terrified. Maybe the children would not like her, what if they blamed her for leaving them? Yet again she dredged her mind for anything that could shed light on why she had been separated from them. Breathing heavily, Liza shook her head in sheer frustration. She felt the feeling that had been stirred however, and she longed to see the children she couldn't remember.

Climbing from the cab, Liza looked up at the house and gasped. 'I remember this house!'

Cara beamed as she took Liza's arm. 'Yes, you grew up here, Liza.' Liza began to shake and Cara wrapped an arm around her. 'It will be fine, you'll see.'

Leading them all inside, Cara heard her brother and sister in the parlour laughing together. Turning to Liza, she said, 'It might be best to forewarn them…'

'I'll wait here in the hall with Bertha and Gracie,' Liza said quietly. Her throat was dry and sweat lined her brow. She wiped her damp hands down her skirt.

Leaving the door ajar so her words could be overheard, Cara said, 'Hey you two, I have a surprise for you.'

'Oooh what is it?' Daisy asked.

'We have visitors and I'd be pleased if you would make them feel welcome.' Cara smiled.

'Don't we always?' Daisy said full of mischief.

'Ah, but one of them is a very special visitor. Shall I invite them in?'

Daisy plonked herself into a chair and nodded.

Cara pushed open the door and the three women entered the room.

'Mum?' Charlie said in disbelief. 'Mum? Is that really you? Oh my God! Mum, mum!' He jumped up and ran to Liza, throwing his arms around her. For all he was a young man now, he did nothing to stem the flow of tears.

Daisy fled to her mother's side, floods of tears coursing down her face. 'Our mum's home! Oh mum, we ain't half missed you!'

Liza folded her arms around the two youngsters who were hugging her so tightly and looked up at Cara who could see by her eyes that Liza had finally remembered her children.

'Oh my babies, my dear sweet babies! Oh thank God!' Liza burst into tears. As she held her children tightly, she smothered them in kisses. 'Oh, I can't believe it! My God, oh my darlings, I love you so much!'

Bertha and Gracie wept openly as they saw Liza beckon Cara to her. 'Cara my darling, come… oh sweetheart, I love you. I love you all so very much!'

Tears flowed freely as Cara joined the family hug. Liza whispered quietly, 'Cara, I can't recall everything, but now I've seen them, I do remember my beautiful children. Thank you so much, my beloved daughter.'

Once everyone had settled, Cara watched as Daisy and Charlie chattered incessantly, Liza listening attentively.

Bertha and Gracie, still sobbing, were wiping away tears on damp handkerchiefs.

Wiping her eyes, Cara leaned back in her chair. She realized she had, at last, completed her final challenge.

Over the following days, Liza had been a constant visitor to The Laburnums to see her three children. Then one evening Cara asked, 'Why don't you come and live with us here mother?'

Charlie and Daisy watched as Liza considered the idea. 'It would be nice I have to admit but, please don't get upset when I say this, but I'm not sure I'm ready yet. I need to get you all again. At the moment I'm settled in nicely with Bertha and we enjoy a good gossip. Besides, we're company for each other. I love you all very much and it gives me something to look forward to each time I visit.'

Daisy wrapped her arms around her mother's neck and gave her a peck on the cheek. Charlie said, 'We love you as well mum, and I'm sure if you change your mind we'll all be over the moon, won't we Cara?'

'We most certainly will,' Cara answered. 'Hey, tomorrow is Sunday so how about we all have a picnic in the Allotment Gardens?' It was agreed and chatter surrounded what should be packed into a couple of picnic baskets. 'You will ask Bertha to join us won't you mother?'

Liza nodded as Daisy ran down to the kitchen to invite Gracie too.

Bertha and Liza arrived at twelve o'clock on the dot. Cara, Charlie and Daisy were ready and waiting. An excited Daisy shot off to the kitchen shouting, 'Come on Gracie, we're ready for the off!'

Charlie carried the two picnic baskets and they began their

stroll down Proud's Lane, deciding to walk the long way round rather than cut through the working allotment site.

It was as they reached the intersection with Dover Street that a loud clatter of hooves and the rumble of cart wheels could be heard. They all stood to the side and gasped as the horse and cart thundered towards them from Fletcher Street. It was travelling fast – too fast for this small road.

Suddenly the driver yanked on the horse's reins in order to turn it around the sharp bend into Dover Street. It was travelling so fast the cart slid across the cobbles. As the driver glanced over his shoulder to see if the cart had overturned, he didn't see the woman standing on the corner. Turning his eyes forward again he watched, as if in slow motion, the horse's flank catch the standing woman as it tried to avoid trampling her down.

The woman was knocked off her feet and landed with a thud on the hard cobbles. The driver pulled with all his might on the reins and the horse skidded to a halt, its eyes wild and nostrils flaring. Jumping down he ran to the woman who was now trying to get to her feet and was rubbing her sore back.

Cara and the others watched as the woman eventually drew back her arm and swung her heavy bag hitting the man on the shoulder. The woman was tearing him off a strip about going far too fast on a narrow road. She yelled she should rightly tell the coppers and he'd be dragged off to jail.

The little group watching could see she wasn't hurt thankfully, and as they turned to resume their walk, Cara saw Liza standing holding her head.

'Mother, are you alright?' Cara asked rushing to Liza whose face was ashen.

'Oh my God!' Liza gasped. 'I remember!' She glanced at each of them. 'I remember it all now!' Then Liza began to sob.

'Come on, let's get you home,' Cara said then turning to Daisy added, 'I'm sorry sweetheart, we'll have to have a picnic another day.'

Daisy nodded as she wrapped her arms around her mother.

Charlie's eyes brimmed with tears as memories also flooded back to him. Passing the baskets to Bertha and Gracie, he rushed forward and swept Liza into his arms. He carried her home as the others followed quietly behind.

Gracie and Bertha made tea and carried it to the parlour, then they returned to the kitchen to wonder just what it was Liza had remembered.

Liza sat on the sofa with Daisy on one side of her and Charlie on the other, she was shaking and the cup rattled on its saucer as Cara handed her the tea. Sipping the hot liquid Liza finally brought her emotions under control.

Finally Cara asked gently, 'Are you able to tell us what you remember?'

Liza nodded. Drawing in a deep breath she said in a low voice, 'It was the accident in the street that triggered it and then it all came flooding back.'

Daisy leaned against Liza and Charlie laid his arm across her shoulder protectively.

Liza looked at Cara. 'I was so pig-headed when you were little. I wouldn't listen to your grandmother. She hated John and when you were about two years old you were really poorly. She brought you back here to take care of you; she asked me to come too but John wouldn't let me.' Liza gave a sob then continued. 'I was forbidden to see you or my own mother – John wouldn't allow it, he was such a bully!'

'We remember mum,' Charlie said as his heart went out to her.

'I'm so sorry,' Liza nodded. Daisy moved to sit on her knee. 'My but you're getting big now,' Liza added as she laced her arms around her young daughter who laid her head on her mother's chest.

'Well, I had to go with John on the cart until you were born Charlie, then I stayed at home. I took you with me when I went scavenging and coal picking… we never had any money – John was a drinker. That became a bit more difficult when our Daisy came long, but I managed.'

Daisy lifted her head and kissed her mother's cheek before nestling down again. Liza gave a tiny smile at the gesture.

'Why didn't you come back here to Grandma?' Cara asked quietly.

'Oh I wanted to, believe me, but I knew John would find me. God knows what he might have done then.' Liza shook her head. 'I remember the last time I saw you two,' she said giving Daisy a squeeze and looking at Charlie.

'Don't mum…' Charlie began.

'You need to know son,' she said with sadness in her voice.

'John came home drunk, he beat me badly. Then he sent you two scavenging. While you were out he forced me onto the cart and drove away.' Liza's tears flowed as she spoke.

Cara saw Daisy was quietly sobbing and tears filled her own eyes. Dragging a cushion from the chair she plopped it down on the floor in front of her mother and sat on it. Taking Liza's hand she held it and stroked the back with her thumb.

'John and I stayed in a derelict cottage in Birmingham while he was carting there. The roof leaked and it was draughty. I was so poorly all the time with coughs and colds. Well, one day a man came to tell me John had died in a carting accident. The loaded cart knocked him down and crushed his chest as it rolled over him. So, then I was on my own.'

'Why d'aint you come back for us then mum?' Daisy asked, her tears having subsided as she listened to Liza's story.

'I wrote to your Grandma and asked if I could come back but she never replied. She ignored my pleas.'

Cara remembered the words in her grandmother's letter, *Also if you find my daughter, tell her I rue the day I ignored her plea.*

Cara told Liza what had been said in the letter.

'Oh my God!' Liza cried out. 'If only I had tried harder, so much misery could have been avoided!'

'I'm sure you did all you could,' Cara tried to comfort her mother.

'I thought so at the time...' Liza began, then taking another deep breath went on. 'I came back to Bilston and searched for you both. Our old cottage was always empty so I thought it was abandoned. I wanted to find you and bring you here to this house with me, so we could all be together again.'

'We would have probably been in the workhouse by then mum,' Charlie said quietly as he thought about Liza's words.

Liza gasped, 'Oh my poor children, I'm so very sorry!'

'Mum, don't get upset, we're all together now and that's what is important.' Charlie comforted her with a hug.

Liza nodded sadly then resumed. 'When I couldn't find you, I came back here but there was never anyone at home. I wondered if your Grandma had sold up and moved on. Eventually I went into service for Mr Townsend.'

'Phoebe's father?' Cara asked softly.

'Yes. As time went on we married and had Phoebe. I

thought my son and daughter must have died... possibly of starvation, when I couldn't find you. I was distraught and constantly asked Arthur – Mr Townsend – if we could keep looking for you.'

'What did he say?' Daisy asked

'He said sweetheart, that you had most likely died and were lost to me forever. It broke my heart.'

'So how did you come to be on the heath that day?' Cara asked.

'I found out Arthur had been having an affair with another woman, I found a letter in his pocket. He was going to leave me and move in with her, so Phoebe and I set off to confront him at the bank where he worked.'

'Oh mum, you don't have much luck with men do you?' Charlie asked in an attempt to dispel a little of his mother's gloom.

Shaking her head Liza went on. 'There was a horse galloping over the heath – it must have broken loose from somewhere – and as it raced past it knocked me flying. I must have hit my head on a stone or something because the next thing I remembered was waking up with Phoebe crying her eyes out.'

'What happened to the horse?' Daisy asked.

'I expect when it calmed down it went home,' Liza answered.

'That would account for no one looking for it and finding you injured on the heath,' Cara added. Then she said, 'Why didn't Arthur search for you when he discovered you and Phoebe were missing?'

'I'd left the letter on the table and he probably thought I'd left him taking Phoebe with me. I suppose that would have left him free to move in with his mistress.' Liza snorted her disgust.

'Bastard!' Charlie rasped.

'Language young man!' Liza said as she tapped his knee.

'Sorry mum,' Charlie looked suitably berated.

'What happened next?' Daisy asked frowning her annoyance at Charlie's interruption.

'I tried to scavenge but I couldn't feed Phoebe and myself and eventually we ended up in the workhouse. It was in there that Phoebe died of food poisoning.' Liza's tears flowed freely once more.

'So, Phoebe Townsend was our half-sister?' Charlie asked.

'Yes son, she was.' Liza sighed as silence descended. Everyone was wrapped up in their own thoughts about what Liza had told them.

Liza however, had no intention of divulging the events that had taken place in Wolverhampton Union Workhouse concerning the Tulleys. That was a secret that only she and Bertha shared and she knew they would both take it to their graves, so certain was she of the bond of friendship.

Cara broke the silence with, 'I still wish you would come and live with us here.'

'I'll talk to Bertha about it,' Liza said, 'you never know, she might be glad to have her house to herself again. Then again, she might want me to stay. Either way, I promise I'm going to see a lot more of the Flowers family in the future now we have all found each other. I swear nothing will part us ever again.' Then she kissed each of her children in turn. Gazing down at her daughter she whispered, 'Thank you Cara for bringing my workhouse children safely back to me.'

Acknowledgements

The Llanfyllin Workhouse Restorers